D1252190

OBSESSED

Also by T.R. Ragan

Abducted (Lizzy Gardner Series #1)
Dead Weight (Lizzy Gardner Series #2)
A Dark Mind (Lizzy Gardner Series #3)

Also by Theresa Ragan

Return of the Rose
A Knight in Central Park
Finding Kate Huntley
Taming Mad Max
Having My Baby
An Offer He Can't Refuse
Here Comes the Bride

OBSESSED

T.R. RAGAN

THOMAS & MERCER

Text copyright © 2014 T.R. Ragan
All rights reserved.

Published by Thomas & Mercer, Seattle

www.apub.com

Amazon, the Amazon logo, and Thomas & Mercer are trademarks of Amazon.com, Inc., or its affiliates.

ISBN-13: 9781477824153
ISBN-10: 1477824154

Cover design by Scott Barrie

Library of Congress Control Number: 2014902718

Printed in the United States of America

DEDICATION

In memory of my dad, Jim Cunningham, and Mary Regan, better known as Aunt Mary. I miss you both.

CHAPTER 1

Sitting in his Honda Civic, his gaze focused on the two-story house across the street, he listened to Dr. Blair's voice come over the airwaves, soft and soothing as she wrapped up the night's show. A tremendous urge to call her swept over him. He wanted to let her know all was clear—nobody was creeping around her house tonight. But he refrained—perhaps another time, when he wasn't so darn cold.

Whistling winds made the tree branches dance as rain splattered against his windshield. Seth had been parked in the quiet Sacramento neighborhood for over two hours. The back window wouldn't roll all the way up, so the cold flowed directly through the window and into his bones. He turned the key and put on the heat, which came out in bursts of frosty air. His joints were stiff, his knuckles puffy and swollen. He would be forty-two next week, but he might as well be sixty-two.

Seth adjusted his glasses on the bridge of his nose and tried to get comfortable. He scanned the neighborhood, then settled once again on Dr. Blair's house.

He'd been listening to her radio show for months now. After his wife confessed to having an affair with a coworker and then promptly begged his forgiveness, his first inclination was to put a bullet through his head. But he'd refrained. Days later, while flipping through radio stations on his way to work, he'd heard the voice of an angel. Dr. Madeline Blair was talking to another shattered man. Their situations weren't identical—this man was struggling to make it through the anniversary of his wife's death—but it was still as if Dr. Blair were speaking directly to Seth. The connection was instantaneous. She understood him. She knew what he was going through.

As far as he was concerned, Dr. Blair had saved his life.

And now it was his turn to repay the favor. Ever since Dr. Blair had told her listeners that a madman was stalking her, he'd been keeping a close eye on her property, looking for his chance to put an end to the craziness. Someone, she told her listeners, was leaving "gifts" at her house while she was at work. He wasn't sure what sorts of things were being left, but the fear he'd heard in Madeline's voice left him shaky and tense. Clearly, the items being left behind were not truffles and flowers.

Last week, the man assumed to be the stalker had called in to the show. His voice was deep and throaty, with lots of exaggerated breaths between each sentence.

A shadow drew Seth's attention to the house—nothing but wind blowing through the trees.

The first time he watched Madeline's house, he'd worried about his intentions, but after some reflection, he'd realized he only wanted to protect her and keep her safe. She had rescued him and now he would do the same for her.

Did he love her? He had no idea. Wouldn't trust himself to say. He thought he'd loved his wife, and what had that gotten him? A kick in the gut when Janelle came clean about her affair. Seth all but doubled over behind the wheel now, just thinking of it.

They had been married for fourteen years. They'd met in college. Her passion was nursing and his was medicine. His dream was to become a doctor. Together, they'd studied physiology and anatomy, biology and biochemistry. They'd spent long nights studying and making love. But it was all for naught. Despite Janelle's help, he'd failed to pass the med school entrance exams.

If not for a frontal-lobe injury caused by a skiing accident when he was a young boy, he was certain his life would have turned out very differently. After the accident, he'd become irritable and frustrated easily, unable to concentrate due to the constant flashing of lights inside his head. The doctor told his mother she'd need to take care to monitor the effects of his injury, especially any changes in his decision-making ability. More than likely, Seth wouldn't be a danger to himself or his family, but he might have trouble gauging right from wrong.

The notion that he might not understand right from wrong worried Seth greatly. And there were some incidents that fed that worry. But thankfully the episodes, as his mother used to call them, became less frequent as he grew older.

And besides, people who *did* know right from wrong chose to do wrong all the time. Take Janelle, for instance. It hurt when he thought of Janelle and what they'd once shared. Up until the day she told him about her affair, he had loved her like no other.

The man she'd hooked up with no longer worked at Sutter General, where Janelle was head nurse.

No matter.

Once she'd taken a bite of that forbidden fruit, a part of him died. Nothing would ever be the same. His heart no longer belonged to his wife. It belonged to Madeline Blair, a woman he'd never uttered two words to. Well, that wasn't exactly true. He'd called in to her show a couple of times. On one occasion, the board operator put him through. After untangling his tongue, he'd managed to ask her a question, but that was months ago and he couldn't remember what he'd said.

Dr. Blair's show dealt with everything from insomnia to relationship problems. He quickly learned it wasn't easy being a popular radio host. The job entailed long hours. Most nights her Toyota 4Runner didn't pull into the driveway until after midnight.

A movement in his rearview mirror caught his attention. This was no dancing tree branch in the wind. It was a man on the sidewalk carrying an umbrella and he was coming straight for him.

Straightening in his seat, Seth let out a ponderous breath. It was too late to drive off. The man leaned over and knocked on the passenger window. He was a large fellow with a barrel chest and short, silver-streaked hair.

Seth opened the window a few inches.

"My wife says you've been parked here for some time. Is there something I can help you with?"

The man's gaze swept over the interior of his car, making Seth perspire even though he had done nothing wrong. "I'm sorry," Seth blurted. "My mother passed away recently and that house right there is where we grew up. It's been an emotional time."

The man with the umbrella relaxed; his eyes softened. "Are you one of the Johnson boys?"

Forcing a smile, he continued to lie. "As a matter of fact, I am."

"I'm sorry for your loss. Sit here as long as you need to."

"Thanks, but I should get going. I'm sure my wife is worrying about me by now." He quickly pulled away from the curb. As he drove off, he could see the silver-haired man standing there, watching him.

He probably should have told him the truth—he was there to protect Dr. Blair. The fear in Madeline's voice during her last show had been palpable. Her voice had quivered as she explained to her listeners that she'd called the police but was told there wasn't much they could do. Her property had not been damaged. No locks on her windows or doors had been tampered with. Until her stalker made a move, she said, her voice cracking, he was free to do as he pleased.

And that's why Seth had sat outside her house every night for the past week. He was going to find the bastard and let him know he'd chosen the wrong woman to toy with.

CHAPTER 2

Hayley Hansen drove into the middle of what was known as the Nightclub District and parked her 1973 Chevy Impala at the curb. She climbed out, slammed the door shut, and headed down the pitted road looking for a bar . . . preferably a bar filled with unsavory characters. She knew this shabby end of the district offered several candidates. She'd been feeling a lot of tension lately and needed to release some of it before she did something really stupid—like, say, walk down the middle of a dangerous street after midnight looking for a fight.

Her boots clacked against pavement as she passed by a homeless man. He was sitting on the broken sidewalk, his back against a weather-beaten fence, his head bent forward, his stringy gray hair covering his face.

Without looking up, he extended a thin arm for a handout.

She went to him, bent down on one knee, and placed a five-dollar bill on his filthy, callused palm. "Get something to eat," she said before continuing on, heading for the grungiest establishment in sight.

Today marked two years since her mother's death—two years, and she still hadn't found Brian Rosie, the man who'd killed her. Where the hell had the bastard gone? She'd leveraged every contact she had to help in her search for him, but she had nothing, not one clue as to where he was hiding out. The man was a god-damn ghost, which made no sense, since Brian had never struck her as a clever man.

A couple of assholes whistled the moment she entered the Blue Moon.

She gave them the finger as she walked straight for a stool as if she'd been coming to this shithole for years. She rested an elbow on the well-stained bar and asked the bartender for a shot of whiskey.

He asked for her ID and she showed it to him.

He held it to the light. "By the hair of your chinny-chin-chin," he said.

She said nothing.

He handed back her ID. "I don't know if this is the right place for you, honey."

"Trust me," she said without emotion, her body weightless, her bones hollow. "This is where I'm supposed to be."

He shrugged, grabbed a bottle from the shelf behind him, filled up a shot glass, and placed it on the bar in front of her.

It wasn't long before the bartender was busy with other cus-tomers and forgot all about her. Her focus remained on the con-tents of the glass—the gold liquid swirling about. For the first time in her twenty-one years, she felt the pull, the desire, the crav-ing to let the whiskey burn a fire down her throat and take some of the pain away.

No, not pain. More like hatred and disgust.

For the world? For mankind?

No, just for Brian, the man who had managed to wreak havoc on her life, time after time, before he dissipated like the morning fog.

She heard a scuffle at the back of the room. There was a *slap* and a *crack*. The sounds made when the palm of a hand makes contact with flesh.

Hayley turned and discovered a greaseball of a man with a big mouth and lots of missing teeth in the process of methodically hitting on his woman. She was tough, taking the openhanded blows pretty well, not even rising from her seat beside him. She had streaks of gray in her dark hair—thirty going on sixty. Hayley watched the woman take three slaps to the face without complaint, but when the prick used his knuckles, it was too much for her—she came to her feet so fast she upset the table and the toothless man lost his drink.

"Sit back down, whore," he shouted, "so I can teach you a lesson."

Despite the woman's haggard look and the haunted eyes, Hayley fully expected her to fight back. Instead, she merely stood there. She had already given up.

"Put your hand on the table," the man demanded as he raked his fingers through long, greasy hair.

The woman did as he said and he promptly leaned over and put his cigarette out on her white flesh.

Her cries were muffled beneath the hand she held over her mouth.

Hayley could smell the burned skin from where she sat. Letting her gaze drift around the room, she noticed that most of the people in the place didn't give a rat's ass about what was happening.

"Leave her alone," Hayley said. She should've interceded before now, before the cigarette, but she'd just sat there, dead on her stool. Now, though, she felt a bit of life creep up her hollow spine. She pulled out a ten-dollar bill and slid it next to her drink.

It took him a minute, but Greaseball finally looked at Hayley and grinned a wide, mostly toothless grin.

"Whatchya gonna do about it, girly?"

"Apologize to the lady," she said without moving from her stool.

He stopped grinning and took his sweet time getting his ass off the chair. Then he stepped slowly around the table and grabbed his woman in a choke hold. Why the lady hadn't left while she had the chance, Hayley couldn't imagine.

Hayley looked toward a group of big, beefy men who could easily take Greaseball out with their breath alone. "Is anyone going to help the lady?"

"She ain't my bitch," one of the beefy men said.

"Yeah," another one said with a laugh. "She ain't my bitch either."

Original.

The woman's face had turned a light shade of red, her eyes bulging as the life was choked out of her.

Blood rushed through Hayley's body—exactly what she'd come for. She lit a cigarette of her own, then stood and walked toward the grinning son of a bitch until she could literally count the exact number of rotted teeth he had left. Seven. He had seven teeth left. Not for long. "Let her go, asshole."

He backed up a half step, holding the woman in front of him as a human shield, big hands still gripping her throat. She was turning blue. The woman's eyes met Hayley's and despite the good chance she had of passing out at any moment, she choked out the words, "You don't want to do this."

"Oh, yes, I'm afraid I do." Hayley took another long hit off her cigarette and then jammed the hot tip into the guy's arm and held it there as he squealed like a pig, stepping after him as he tried to pull away without loosening his hold around the woman's neck. When he finally had to release her, his drunken state got the best of him and he fell on his ass.

While the woman stumbled backward out of reach, holding her throat and catching her breath, the idiot scrambled to his feet. He wasn't grinning now. He pulled out a shit-for-nothing switchblade and held it in front of him. "You're gonna pay for that, darlin'."

Hayley had an aversion to being called *darlin'*, so she jammed her right foot into his crotch, crushing his worthless balls so hard and fast he didn't know what hit him. His switchblade slid across the floor and before he could get hold of it, Hayley reached for her ankle and her newly sharpened five-and-a-half-inch Choker fixed blade, a gift from Kitally for her twenty-first birthday. A few more steps and she had the man in a choke hold of her own with her blade to his throat.

His eyes were bulging now.

A drop of sticky blood slid over Hayley's fingers and onto his shirt.

"Say you're sorry."

He grunted.

Hayley pressed the knife deeper. More than a few drops of blood dripped onto his already-stained pants. She glanced around to make sure the man had no friends willing to help him out, but it was as she expected. Everyone in the place was enjoying the show too much.

"I'm sorry," he croaked.

She looked at the woman standing with her back to the wall. "You might want to leave now." When the woman began making her way to the door, Hayley told the idiot, "If you ever touch her again, I promise you I will hear about it. And if I do, you're going to lose every rotted tooth in that mouth of yours—one by one, which would suck because there's nothing I hate worse than watching a grown man cry." She dropped her hold on him, twisted him hard aside from her, and headed across the room toward the exit, her blood pumping rapidly through her veins. *Finally.*

"What about your whiskey?" the bartender called after her.

"It's all yours," she said. "I don't drink."

CHAPTER 3

Seth's ass was sore and half-numb. Once again he'd been sitting in his car watching Madeline's neighborhood for too many hours. It was a Thursday evening, just past eleven.

After the nosy neighbor approached him last week, not only had he invested in a pair of binoculars so he could watch Madeline's house from farther away, but he'd also rented a car with four windows that actually worked. The bad news was the car smelled as if decade-old smoke had seeped into every crack and crevice. He'd paid cash for the month's rental of the Nissan, since he didn't want his wife to know what he was up to. Every night he parked the car somewhere different, somewhere close to home so it was easy to get to.

Eyelids heavy, he was about to call it a night when he caught sight of a dark figure approaching Madeline's house.

A man, on foot, head held down. He wore jeans, sneakers, and a padded coat with a hood.

It was cold outside, but not cold enough to warrant a hood pulled up around the face. The guy was obviously trying to hide his identity.

Seth's pulse raced as he watched the man through his binoculars: crooked nose and unshaven jaw. Was this Madeline's stalker—the man who'd caused her so much grief?

Sure enough, the hooded figure made a right, walking at a brisk pace up Madeline's walkway. The man didn't bother looking around to see if he was being watched. It was as if he'd gone to her door a million times before.

Madeline would be returning home in another hour. Seth needed to think. *Keep your head straight*, he told himself. He leaned over and opened the glove compartment, pulled the hunting knife from its sheath and tucked it inside his jacket pocket. Then he slipped out of the car.

If he was lucky, he would catch the guy in action, maybe see him placing one of his gifts on Madeline's welcome mat. Two nights ago, she'd told her listeners that the gifts were appearing less often, but were much more disturbing.

With quiet steps, he walked toward Dr. Blair's house.

Hidden within a grouping of birch trees across the street, not far from where the neighbor had questioned him, he watched the hooded man curl his fingers around the door handle and try to push the door open. Giving up on the door, he peered through the front window.

Seth's fingers curled around the knife handle. He should call the police.

The streets were empty. Where was the busybody neighbor when he needed him?

The hooded figure disappeared through the side gate to Madeline's backyard, then returned to the front before Seth had the chance to follow him back there.

Although Seth wanted nothing more than to see what gift he'd left for her this time, he didn't want to lose him, so when the man walked away from the house, Seth followed, staying far enough back so the man wouldn't know he was being followed.

Now that he was outside, the man's hooded jacket made more sense. The temperature had dropped considerably. They walked for three blocks before the man took a sudden right between two office buildings down an alleyway a block after the single-family homes stopped and the commercial buildings began.

If Seth didn't hurry, he was going to lose him. He stepped up his pace. Despite the intense cold, sweat covered his forehead. His breathing had grown heavy, his legs already cramping. Clearly, he didn't get enough exercise.

Making the same right into the alleyway, Seth saw that it ended in a loading dock some thirty feet ahead of him and stopped. Nothing stirred. He crept past a Dumpster overflowing with garbage along the brick wall to his right. Boxes and trash littered the ground. Dark shadows threw him off, but he finally noticed the man standing where the Dumpster met the wall.

"Why are you following me?" the man asked.

Seth stepped closer as he peered into the dark. "What are you doing in this neighborhood?"

"That's none of your business. Tell me why you're following me or I'm going to call the police."

"Go ahead," Seth said with a snort, relieved. "That's a great idea." He pulled his cell phone from his pocket so he could make the call himself, but the man batted it away, sending the phone clacking against the rough pavement and sliding out of reach.

The hooded man squinted into the dark in the direction of the phone. "Listen, man, sorry about your phone. I thought you were going for a gun or something. We both need to chill out."

This was the man who had been stalking Madeline. Seth was sure of it.

The man stepped farther down the alley, his head bent down as he searched the ground. "I'll get your phone."

Slowly, Seth reached into his coat pocket and made sure he had a good grip on the handle of his knife.

"My name is Chris Porter," the man said as he peered, still bent over, into the blackness against the next building's wall. "I live around the corner. I was visiting a friend, making sure she was OK. I'll get your phone, and then why don't you tell me why you're here and we can both return to our homes and call it a night?"

Bright lights, a kaleidoscope of colors, flashed inside Seth's head. The man was lying. He knew a liar when he heard one. His wife, Janelle, it turned out, had lied to him many times. So had his mother and every person he'd ever befriended.

While the guy's back was still to him, Seth pulled out the knife and advanced on him with it held straight out in front of him. The sharp blade glinted in the darkness. He didn't want to hurt the guy. He wanted the truth, and then he wanted to see him locked behind bars.

The throbbing in his temples felt like a metal vise pressing against his head. The pain was excruciating. His palms were drenched with sweat, and he tasted something metallic and horribly familiar.

The same thing he tasted during his episodes when he was younger.

Shit. Not now.

"Here it is," the hooded man said as he turned. "I found your phone." Screwing with Seth's mind—the man didn't even look up at him as he came at him, pretending to try to piece the phone back together until he got close enough to strike.

Bright lights zipped and zapped, making the advancing man look as if his arms were flailing about in a roomful of strobe lights. Every movement distorted. Shadows everywhere.

Panicked, Seth thrust the knife forward, hitting the man dead center.

He felt the blade go deep.

Chris Porter, if that was really his name, gasped. He sucked in a breath as the knife went deeper.

Their gazes met, the whites of the stalker's eyes gleaming like a wounded animal's in the darkness.

The phone hit the pavement again. The man wobbled. "Why?" he asked.

Still holding on to the handle, Seth felt the blade slicing through the man's soft innards. In his mind's eye, he could literally see the blade cut through the upper part of the abdominal cavity, piercing through muscle and tendons, hitting the diaphragm and then the pancreas. As he'd always suspected, the human body was complicated, but vulnerable and easily destroyed.

The hooded man put his hands to his stomach where the knife protruded, but it was too late.

Feeling a flash of disgust with what he'd done, Seth pulled the blade out. He felt confused, disoriented.

The man was still standing, struggling to stay on his feet.

Seth thought of Madeline and how relieved she would be when she realized her stalker was no longer bothering her. He was her hero. His groin tightened as he stepped toward the man and thrust the blade into his chest.

A kick of adrenaline registered. He inhaled sharply. What a high. With each thrust and twist of the knife came a series of involuntary contractions as his excitement peaked. He stabbed Madeline's stalker, again and again, enjoying the suctioning as he pulled out. The knife easily cut through flesh and muscle as he guided the blade into the man's left side. He thrust the knife into the man's shoulder next, saving his neck for last.

He froze, shuddered, closed his eyes.

Moments passed before he stood tall. He took a good long look at the body on the ground. Raw emotions flooded through him. The first thrust had been prompted by a burst of confusion replaced with rage. Then had come that wave of disgust, and finally something he could hardly comprehend: something sensual, bordering on erotic. He'd never experienced anything like it before.

He had killed a man for Madeline, and he was glad.

The skies opened up suddenly and heavy rain quickly seeped through his clothes and gave him a much-needed jolt. He needed to get out of there. He needed to be smart. He took off his eyeglasses and rubbed the bridge of his nose as he tried to think. There was lots of debris and trash scattered around. The man's hood no longer covered his face. He was quite young.

Noticing a grate, he bent down, grabbed the man's sweatshirt and dragged him over the grate so that the blood had somewhere to go. Next, he got down on one knee, patted the man down and found a wallet. The name on the ID read Chris Porter.

Had the man given him his real name?

When he slipped the wallet into his pocket he noticed blood covering his hands. He took off the man's sweatshirt and used it to clean himself up. Working quickly, he covered the body with boxes and trash, figuring he'd have to come back and find the strength to lift the body into the trunk of his car. He then went in search of his broken cell phone, relieved to find it close by.

Exiting the alleyway, both hands hidden within the pockets of his bloodied pants, he clicked his tongue as he walked off.

CHAPTER 4

Dr. Madeline Blair had eight minutes before she would be on the air.

Earlier today she'd had a talk with her boss. Ratings had tripled since she'd mentioned having a stalker on air. Although she felt a bit of guilt at deceiving her listeners and her boss, it was all in the name of entertainment. It wasn't like she was doing *real* therapy, after all—though she might have to do just that, go about the daunting business of reestablishing an actual therapeutic practice, if she didn't maintain these ratings.

And if she wanted to keep the momentum going, she needed her stalker to call in one more time.

Drastic times called for drastic measures. She picked up her cell and made the call. Her friend David picked up on the first ring.

"What's up, Jelly Bean?"

She'd been addicted to Jelly Belly jelly beans almost as long as she'd known David. And thus her nickname had been born. "Hey, Stalker," she said.

"No, no." She could hear the smile go out of his voice. "Let's dump that nickname."

"Oh please, David. That's a little dramatic, isn't it?"

"Maybe. Someday we'll look back on this and laugh, maybe. But for now, let's put it behind us, all right?"

"Well . . ." she said. "Maybe not just yet?"

She could hear him breathing.

"I need you to make one more creepy call."

"You can't be serious. You promised me that the last call I made would be the absolute final call."

"Please, David. Just one more time, I promise. My ratings went through the roof. You *sold* it! So many listeners called in to ask about the creepy caller. It was perfect. Do you have any idea what that means for my career?"

He lowered his voice. "Do you have any idea what this could do to *my* career if anyone found out what I did? And what about my wife? Debra would kill me if she knew what we were up to."

"Nobody is going to find out. And besides, Debra would love you more for helping out a friend in need. One more call and I will never ask you to do it again, I swear. I'll watch your kids for an entire week straight so you and Debra can go on a second honeymoon."

No response.

"Please, David. I have to be back on air in a couple of minutes."

A ponderous sigh. "When should I call?" he asked, clearly not happy with her. "And what do you want me to say this time?"

"It will be sometime in the next few days. I'll call you an hour before the show to remind you. Use the same voice you used the first time, but try to keep it going for as long as possible—you know, lots of deep breathing and long pauses, like last time. And if you could ask me a few questions about what I'm wearing, that would be great. Or maybe you should ask me why I refuse to go out on a date with you. Ask me something very personal; make my listeners stop what they're doing and turn up the volume."

"God, Madeline. Listen to yourself." She could hear him swallow thickly. "This is so not right. It's not worth just some temporary spike in ratings."

"I'm begging you. Think about all the people who call in, all the people I'm able to help because of this show."

"I want to go on record saying I don't like it, Madeline. We've been friends for a long time, but for the first time ever I'm questioning why I even like you. It's time for you to get a life. You need to get out there and mingle with real people instead of the voices on your radio show. You're scaring me."

She laughed. "*Now* you're being dramatic. You'll be happy to know I've been spending time with a neighbor of mine."

"A real live person?"

"Yes, David, a real person. A man, in fact."

"I don't believe it. What's his name?"

"Chris Porter. He's a few years younger than me, but he's adorable and a real, honest-to-God gentleman. He's a great guy. You and Debra are going to love him."

"Have you told Chris that you're pretending you have a stalker?"

"No, of course not. I doubt he listens to my show."

"If he's the great guy you think he is and he's interested in you, then believe me, he's listening to your show. And if that's the case, he's probably worried for you."

"Since when have you become such a worrywart?"

"Since I married and had two daughters. Promise me you'll tell this new guy of yours what's going on, and I'll make the call."

"It's a deal."

CHAPTER 5

The café in Roseville had an outside seating area. It was nine in the morning, chilly enough to turn every breath into a tiny cloud of white mist. Jessica Pleiss was the only one sitting in the back area framed by latticed wood walls and a couple of potted plants. She looked over her shoulder when the back door of the café opened, surprised to see that Hayley had actually come.

She didn't come to her feet. Instead, she waited for Hayley to take a seat across from her, which she did. "Thanks for meeting me," Jessica said. "Care for some coffee? Something to eat?"

"No, thanks. Why don't you go ahead and tell me why you asked me to meet you."

Jessica took a breath and processed the moment. After she'd quit working for Lizzy, she really wasn't sure if she'd ever see Hayley again. And now here they were. "It's hard to believe it's been two years since I saw you last. How have you been?"

"The same."

Jessica knew that was a lie. Hayley looked as if she'd lost fifteen pounds she didn't need to lose. With her pale skin and dark circles under her eyes, she looked like death. "I asked you to meet me because I need your help."

No raised eyebrow. No crossing of the arms. Nothing.

"A little girl was shot and killed about two weeks ago," Jessica continued. "Her name was Taylor. It was in the news. A twelve-year-old, minding her own business, just sitting alone at the table doing her homework. Her older brother, it turned out, had pissed off some idiot in a gang, so they did a drive-by and happened to tag his little sister."

"Where's the connection?"

"What do you mean?"

"The connection to you," Hayley said. "Why do you care?"

"The connection is Eloise Hampton, the girl's mother. Back in the day, before my sister disappeared and my family fell apart, Mom paid Eloise to clean the house and help with laundry. Eloise is only ten years older than me. I think of her as family. Eventually she married, moved away, had kids. Then her husband left her and the kids to fend for themselves. We've stayed in touch. Every now and then, I watch her kids for her." Jessica drew in another deep breath and willed her pulse to slow. "I need to know who killed her daughter. I need a name."

"I heard that you were accepted into the academy."

"That's right."

"Good for you."

"Thanks."

"Since you work for the feds—"

"Hardly—"

"—it shouldn't be too hard for *you* to find out which gang is responsible and then go knock on their leader's door."

"I already did. A member of the Franklin gang is responsible. Nobody's talking."

Hayley snorted. "But you think they'll talk to me?"

"Not you. Your friend." She tried to remember the girl's name and came up empty. She'd only met her once or twice. She was younger than Hayley, maybe sixteen when Jessica had met her two years ago.

"Kitally?"

"That's the one."

"So because she was in detention, you figure she would have connections to a gang—"

Jessica gestured toward her own elbow. "She has a tattoo on the back of her left arm, near her elbow. It matches the Franklin gang's tattoo. Looks like a crescent moon with three dots."

"Very observant."

Jessica said nothing, although she wondered if Hayley realized she'd just complimented her. Probably not.

Hayley's eyes narrowed. "You seem different."

"Ditto."

"You're serious about this, aren't you?" Hayley asked.

Jessica nodded. "Two thousand dollars if you get me a name."

"Nobody is going to tell Kitally or me the shooter's name. What you're asking us to do is dangerous. We could get in some serious shit if we choose to get involved, maybe even get killed."

Jessica didn't waver. "There's always that possibility."

Hayley laughed out loud. "Holy shit. What has happened to you?"

"I have no idea what you mean."

"I haven't seen you in months, years, whatever, and you call me out of the blue, not to say hello or ask how I've been, but to do you a favor. The Jessica I knew wouldn't have had the balls to ask her friend to risk her life for a few thousand bucks, let alone a stupid name."

"First of all," Jessica said, leaning over the table, "you and me, we were never friends. You made that clear on numerous occasions. Secondly, at the age of twelve, this little girl"—she held up a picture of Taylor, the girl who was killed—"was smarter than you and me put together. She used to tell me she was going to be the first woman president and I never once doubted it. She died and I can't bring her back, but I can make damn sure the person responsible is locked behind bars and pays for what he did."

"I'll talk to Kitally," Hayley told her.

Jessica slipped the picture of the girl along with a business card across the table, just in case Hayley had deleted her number from her phone. "Let me know what she says, will you?"

"What if she tells you to fuck off?"

"Then I guess I'd have to go to plan B, which would mean making sure a pregnant girl named Kiki stays in jail for a very long time."

"Kiki?"

"Someone who happens to mean a lot to the leader of the Franklin gang." Jessica looked at her cell phone. "I should get going."

Hayley gave her a sloppy two-fingered salute. "See you around, Agent Pleiss."

Jessica climbed in behind the wheel of her car and sat there for a moment, trying to catch her breath. It wasn't easy swallowing the lump in her throat. When she'd first seen Hayley walk through the door, she'd had a difficult time not showing alarm at her appearance. But Hayley didn't respond well to caring, nurturing people, so she'd kept any and all emotions to herself.

She hadn't seen her since Hayley's mother's funeral. After Lizzy had hired Hayley, Jessica had done her best to get along with her. Although they were complete opposites and had constant disagreements, she'd grown to like Hayley. She even came to think of Hayley as a sister. Although it was true that Jessica had kept her distance over the years, that didn't mean she didn't think about Hayley. She cared deeply about her, in fact. But being around her used to make Jessica feel inadequate. Hayley had a way of taking control of every situation. Once she got away from her, Jessica had gained confidence not just in her decision-making abilities, but with being herself.

Jessica considered returning to the café to tell Hayley to forget the whole thing. The last thing she wanted to do was put her or Kitally in danger. It hadn't really occurred to her. While it was undeniably true that the Franklin gang was a bunch of degenerate, law-breaking fools—they carried deadly weapons, and many of them had not only spent time in prison but were proud of it—they also lived in exactly the sketchier areas of Sacramento that Hayley liked to frequent in the dead of night. Jessica had figured it would be just another night out for her.

Clutching the steering wheel tighter, Jessica could still hear the wails of the little girl's mother after Jessica had raced to the house when she'd heard what happened. She pictured the young girl, the first woman president of the United States, studying at the kitchen table one moment and shot dead in the next, all her hopes and dreams obliterated in an instant. Why?

Jessica wiped her eyes, then turned on the ignition and drove off.

She needed a name.

CHAPTER 6

Hands on the steering wheel, Lizzy watched the diamond ring on her left hand sparkle, sending an electric current of tension through her body.

An impending wedding to the man she loved should cause her to feel giddy, not tense. At thirty-four, she wasn't getting any younger. And Jared was one of the good guys, the last of the unicorns. Time after time he'd proved to be her rock, her safety net. And yet here she was again, sweaty palms and dry mouth at the mere thought of walking down the aisle in three months. Her sister had given up trying to pry details about the wedding from her—always calling to ask Lizzy if she'd decided on a color scheme, flowers, music. Had she written her vows? When would they go dress shopping? Cathy had also been badgering her to tell their parents the news, but Lizzy didn't see the point; she rarely talked to either of them. Her mother was busy with work and a new man. Her father wanted nothing to do with her.

Up ahead, Lizzy saw a bolt of brown—a dog?—shoot across the street at the same time a flashy sports car sped around the corner. "No, no, no," she said.

A screech of brakes. *BAM.*

The animal flew through the air like a catapulted rag doll, landing on the hillside in high grass.

The car wasn't stopping. Lizzy caught a glimpse of the driver as he passed: male, broad shouldered, light-colored hair trimmed short around his ears.

Bastard.

Pulling to the side of the road, she shut off the engine and climbed out.

It was eight in the morning. Still early. Freezing cold.

She was on her way to North Laguna to see Hayley. Thought she could save a few minutes by taking a couple of back streets. No such luck. Murphy's Law had struck again.

She crossed the road, taking in the fresh tire marks left on the pavement. She hopped over the ditch and trampled through weeds and stickers.

Hands on her hips, she looked around, the air crisp enough to elicit goose bumps. She held still. Listened. Waited. Thirty seconds passed before she saw movement behind an oak tree.

Maybe it wasn't a dog. It could be a coyote or a giant raccoon. Whichever, it could have rabies, she reminded herself as she headed for the tree.

The first thing she saw was a tail—more like a stump—thumping against the ground.

Although the animal smelled like a skunk, it was actually a dog: a medium-sized, mangy mutt without a collar or tags. Even injured and vulnerable, he wasn't growling. In fact, looked downright friendly.

Extending her arm, she moved closer and let him sniff her hand. His ribs were showing and his wiry hair was matted. Big grayish eyes matched the color of his fur. The dog looked wary, frightened, but his tail thumped against the dirt every time she talked to him.

"Are you hurt?"

Thump, thump.

"Can you walk?"

Thump, thump.

She took a few steps back the way she'd come and said, "Come on, pooch. Come with me."

He pushed himself to his feet and limped toward her.

"That's a good dog. You can do it."

Amazed the dog had survived the impact and ejection onto the hillside at all, much less was well enough to haul itself after her, she continued on. "You look hungry. I have a croissant in the car."

Stopping at the side of the road, she waited for the dog to catch up. The animal was so skinny, his ribs looked as if they might poke through his skin at any moment. He was even more pitiful looking at closer view: small eyes lined with pink; wiry, unmanageable fur; a half of a tail that looked as if it had been chopped off at midpoint. The poor thing was a mess.

He plopped down at her feet. He was definitely hurt. Hoping he wouldn't take a bite out of her, she leaned over and scooped him into her arms, trying not to breathe in the horrible smell as she crossed the street.

It wasn't easy, but she managed to open the door and lay him on the backseat. "Now what am I going to do with you?"

Thump, thump.

She grabbed her coffee cup from the front, dumped it out, and used her water bottle to fill the cup, then offered the dog some water. He slurped up every drop and then ate the croissant in dainty little bites.

"Just so you know, I can't keep you. I'm not good with animals and I really don't have time to take care of a dog. I can hardly keep plants alive."

The dog stared at her, unblinking.

"Oh, no, you don't. Don't give me that look. It won't work. I have enough problems right now. It's nothing personal." The mutt had wise old eyes, the kind of eyes that looked at her in such a way as to make her wonder if he'd run into the street on purpose.

Shaking her head at her wayward thoughts, she climbed in behind the wheel, turned on the ignition, and cracked the windows before continuing on her way. Using the rearview mirror to keep an eye on the dog, Lizzy wondered what the heck she was going to do with the animal.

It was another mile before she spotted a group of kids walking to school. She pulled over and rolled down the window. The tallest boy in the group told the rest of the kids to hang back while he stepped close enough to the car to hear what Lizzy had to say.

"I found this dog running around without a collar or tags," Lizzy told him, pointing to the backseat. "Any of you know whose dog it is?"

"Nope. Never seen him before."

The rest of the kids were already peering through the back window. They all shook their heads while the dog appeared to grin up at them, wagging his stump.

"OK," Lizzy said. "Thanks for your help."

She drove on, figuring she'd deliver the files and groceries as planned and then find a vet to look at the dog. He certainly didn't seem to be in such dire straits.

The street where Hayley lived had seen better days. There were lots of abandoned buildings and foreclosure signs. For over a year now, she'd rented an apartment atop a detached garage. A grim setup, but an improvement. After finding her mother murdered, Hayley had, despite Lizzy's pleas, wandered the streets of Sacramento for months on end. She was still stubborn and refused to talk to a therapist. Her only friends, Tommy and Kitally, didn't seem to mind that Hayley was nothing like the young woman they had once known. She was all darkness with no light.

Lizzy couldn't think of anything to do but hope the passage of time would bring Hayley back to life. Time didn't solve all problems, but she knew firsthand it helped distance a person from their past. Although Hayley had enough money from the sale of her mom's house to keep her living in the small apartment without heat for more than a few years, she'd never stopped working for Lizzy. She showed up at the office when it suited her, and Lizzy brought her extra work, as she was doing today, when she needed more help, which was more often than not since Jessica quit.

Hopefully Hayley would come to the realization that although life wasn't fair and never would be, it was still worth fighting for.

Poor Hayley. She'd been to the bowels of hell more than once and had not come away unscathed.

If anyone could pull through, though, it was Hayley.

Lizzy parked the car, locked the dog inside with the window cracked, and headed out. She climbed the dozen wooden steps leading to Hayley's apartment, seeing no sign of the landlord, the young woman living in the main house, a single mother who'd inherited the tiny house from her grandparents.

With a bag of groceries in one arm, Lizzy used her other hand to knock on the door. As she waited, she took note of the abandoned playground across the street, the kind of deserted wasteland you might see in a movie after a nuclear explosion. Bolted to the ground in the middle of an old sandpit was a metal seesaw, all rust and sharp edges.

The door opened to Hayley's back—she was already on her way back inside, leaving Lizzy to find her own way.

"Hey, there," Lizzy called to her when she spotted her in the bedroom as she headed on for the main room.

"Hey."

The place was dark. With her free hand, Lizzy pushed smoky curtains to the side and opened a window so she could breathe and also let in some light. Hayley came into the main room and took a seat on the small crushed-velvet couch. The skirt at the base of the sofa was torn and stained. An old wooden chest served as the coffee table and was covered with a laptop, an ashtray filled to the brim, and a stack of papers.

Lizzy put the groceries on the kitchen counter and opened the refrigerator. It was empty. She glanced at Hayley again, took in the sunken cheekbones and dark circles under her eyes. With a sigh, she deposited a gallon of milk, a jar of pickles, sliced turkey from the deli, a loaf of wheat bread, and a family-sized package of string cheese inside before shutting the door. She left a box of Honey Nut Cheerios on the counter. She checked the cupboards and saw that most of the cans of soup she'd brought last time had been eaten, at least.

Lizzy turned to the sink that was half-filled with dirty dishes.

"Leave those."

"OK. I don't have much time anyhow. There's an injured dog in my car, and, well, I just wanted to bring by a couple of new cases I was hoping you could help me with. I'm up to my neck in work."

"Injured dog?"

"Yeah, a hit-and-run only a mile from here. A businessman, obviously in a hurry."

"Fucker."

Lizzy nodded in agreement.

"What kind of car?"

"A red sports car," Lizzy said. "Sleek. Fast."

Silence followed. Lizzy didn't mind. She knew the drill. Hayley had already said more this morning than she had in the past few months put together.

Lizzy grabbed a spindly chair and placed it on the other side of the wooden chest so she was facing Hayley after she took a seat.

"Is the dog dying out there?" Hayley asked.

"No. He'll be fine. This will only take a few minutes. After I leave, I'll find an animal hospital where someone can take a look at him and make sure nothing's broken."

Hayley's fingers tapped away at the keyboard and then she peered at the screen. "The closest vet is less than a mile from here. If you're sure the dog isn't in too much pain, you're probably better off taking him to the Animal Station on L Street, close to the office."

Nodding, Lizzy felt hopeful. Not only was Hayley talking about something other than work, she was showing compassion. And that gave her an idea. "After the dog gets checked out, and if I can't find his owner, maybe you would be interested—"

"Nope. Not interested."

Lizzy sighed. A dog—any animal, for that matter—could do Hayley a world of good, but she let it go for now and opened one of the files she'd brought instead. "So, do you think you can handle a few more cases?"

"What do you have?"

"We need to locate a deadbeat dad named Owen Santos. He disappeared three months ago, leaving behind two teenage daughters and a wife of seventeen years whose job hardly pays for groceries and gas. She can't make the mortgage payment and—"

"Another pro bono case, then."

"No. The wife's brother, Andrew Morales, came to me. He's hiring us to find Owen, his brother-in-law. He's offering a five-thousand-dollar bonus if we find Owen Santos within thirty days." Lizzy handed her the file.

Hayley skimmed through it. "What else?"

Lizzy opened another file. "A woman, Kat McBane, design engineer at Intel, is having trouble at home. Every night when she returns home from work, she finds something has been disturbed—sofa cushions shifted around, food items missing. She swears someone even used her shower, but there is no evidence of a break-in. The police were supposedly keeping half an eye on her house for a few weeks, but didn't see anything suspicious."

"What's your plan?" Hayley asked. "There's not much we could do for her that the cops didn't already do, other than move in with the lady."

"You mentioned once that Tommy had used a night-vision camera to catch a car thief in his neighborhood. Maybe the two of you could set up a camera or two. One in the front yard and one in the back."

"I'll talk to him."

"Thanks."

Hayley took that file, too, then plopped it on the table with everything else.

Lizzy's attention slid to the pile of pictures scattered across the wooden chest next to Hayley's laptop. Pictures of Brian Rosie and various thugs he used to hang out with, back when Hayley's mom was still alive. "I thought we agreed to forget about Brian and let the police handle the matter."

"I changed my mind."

"They will find him. Brian won't get away with murder. They always get caught in the end."

"In the *end*," Hayley said, her tone lined with bitterness. "After how many more people are raped, abused, and murdered?"

Lizzy opened her mouth to speak, but Hayley cut her off.

"Don't say another word, Lizzy. I don't want to hear it. Brian's drug business is growing into an empire and yet they can't catch him. The police obviously need a little help."

As Lizzy sucked in a breath, the door came open. A little boy appeared—four years old, maybe five. His clothes were dirty and stained. His brown hair was matted. He hadn't knocked, and he seemed perfectly at home inside the apartment until he saw Lizzy. He set his gaze on Hayley.

"Your mom didn't come home?" Hayley asked the boy.

He shook his head.

"This is Lizzy, my boss. Why don't you go ahead and get something to eat. There's stuff in the fridge." The boy didn't need to be told twice.

Lizzy didn't try to strike up a conversation as he passed her. It was obvious he was not comfortable around strangers. "I should get going," Lizzy said.

Hayley stood.

Lizzy grabbed her purse from the kitchen and followed Hayley outside. "What's the deal?" she asked, referring to the boy.

"Just another kid with a mother who can't get her shit together."

"Maybe you should call child support services."

"Nope," Hayley said, then scratched her arm. "Hudson is a great kid. His mom is trying. She's been better lately, sticking around longer. He'll be fine."

"OK," Lizzy said. "Sounds like you have it under control. I better get the dog to a vet."

"Thanks for the groceries. If I need to talk to the deadbeat dad's wife and daughters, is that a problem?"

Lizzy shook her head. "Talk to anyone you need to."

"I'll get cameras set up at McBane's house, too. Anything else?"

"There is one more thing."

Hayley waited.

"I was wondering if you would do me the honor of being one of my bridesmaids?"

Hayley rubbed her forehead as if she were trying to completely erase the question from her mind. When she dropped her hand, she let out a moan. "You're serious?"

Lizzy nodded.

"Do I look like the bridesmaid type to you?"

Lizzy nodded again.

"You know how I feel about you and Jared, but I don't know the first thing about being a bridesmaid. Would I have to do anything? Do I have to wear one of those god-awful dresses?"

"Not sure about the dress yet, but no, you wouldn't have to do anything, I promise."

"When is this thing happening?"

"December 20, two months from today."

"Who else is going to be in it?"

It was Lizzy's turn to smile. "My sister, Cathy, and Brittany and Jessica."

The hiss that came out of Hayley's mouth sounded like a leaky gasket. "I'll have to think about it."

"No problem," Lizzy said. "Take your time." She headed down the stairs, stopping when she reached the landing. "You'll stop by the office next week to give me an update?"

"Sure." Hayley was about to disappear inside when Lizzy called her name again.

"Sorry, one more thing. Would it be possible for you to come by the office on October 30 at two o'clock to help me interview another assistant?"

"What happened to Lucy?"

"During her last surveillance, a man came out of the house with a camera and took a bunch of pictures of her. It freaked her out and she quit."

"That's three people in less than a year."

"Yeah, I know."

"Sure, I'll come."

"Thanks. I appreciate it." Lizzy turned to walk off and nearly knocked into someone. It took her a minute to recognize Hayley's friend Kitally, from the detention center. Every time Lizzy met the girl, she looked different. The last time she'd seen her, she'd shaved her head bald except for a long, inch-thick dreadlock that hung down her back. Today, her sleek black hair hung an inch past her ears. The dreadlock was still there, but it had been dyed the colors of a rainbow. The girl definitely had her own unique style. She wore a short black sheath dress and ankle-high black boots. A huge leather bag was strapped onto her left shoulder. The three-inch heels put Kitally at about five foot eight.

The two of them stared each other down. With her square jaw and high cheekbones, Kitally was an exotic creature. Her dark brown eyes bore into Lizzy. "Is that your dog barking in the car over there?"

Lips pursed, Lizzy turned and headed for her car without answering. She couldn't pinpoint what it was about the girl that bothered her, but something about her rubbed Lizzy the wrong way. Maybe it was the fact that she'd done time and Lizzy still didn't know why. Maybe it was her high-octane energy, the way she flitted around like a hummingbird, darting this way and that, never holding still.

If she were honest with herself, Lizzy would acknowledge that the reason she didn't like Kitally was quite simple: she didn't think the girl was a good influence on Hayley. But that wasn't fair, and she knew it.

Kitally jogged up the stairs. "Your boss lady is strange."

"She's fine."

"Did you tell her that I've been helping you out? Am I on the payroll yet?"

"That's not how it works," Hayley said as she went back inside her apartment. "There's actually an opening, but you'll have to apply for the job. Interviews will take place on October 30 at the downtown office at two o'clock. Don't be late."

"You're always late."

"Because Lizzy knows she can count on me."

"Not fair. I know how all of this private eye stuff works."

"Lizzy has no idea you've been helping me out. This is all new to her. And no gum chewing when you come in for the interview," Hayley added. "Lizzy hates that."

Kitally blew a bubble, then used one finger to pop it and stuff the pink wad back into her mouth. "I've never understood why people give a shit about stuff like that."

Hayley shrugged.

"Anything new on Brian?"

"No. Every lead has turned to shit. It's as if he never existed."

Kitally waved at the kid who was now sitting at the table eating cereal before she hovered over Hayley to see what she was doing. "So, what are we working on next?"

"Did you bring your laptop with you?"

Kitally plopped into the chair where Lizzy had sat earlier and pulled a sleek silver laptop from her bag.

"Is that new? Another gift from Dad?"

"Yeah, he's still trying to buy my love."

"I thought the gifts and money he gives you were to stop you from telling your mom about his mistress."

"Yeah, that too."

Once Kitally had her computer set up, Hayley handed her the Owen Santos file. "Here, start with this one. I need you to find everything and anything you can about this man. Three months ago, Owen Santos disappeared, leaving behind his wife and two teenage daughters. If we can find him within thirty days, there's a bonus."

"What kind of bonus?"

"Five grand."

Kitally shrugged, unimpressed. She needed five grand about as much as she needed a second asshole.

"Most people in the real world work for money so they can eat and keep a roof over their heads," Hayley informed her.

"God, I don't know how you people do it. Day after day, doing shit you don't want to do. That would suck."

Hayley had no comment.

Kitally went to the kitchen and spit her gum in the plastic trash can under the sink. Seconds later, she returned to the chair and sat down. "I came by yesterday morning, but you weren't here."

"I went to see Jessica."

"The one who's afraid of her own shadow?"

"She's changed since I saw her last. She's pissed off."

"At who?"

"A few weeks ago, a random bullet came through the front window of a home and killed a twelve-year-old girl who happened to be the daughter of a friend of Jessica's. Jessica wants the name of the shooter. Because of the tattoo on your elbow, she thinks you might be able to help."

Kitally rubbed her elbow. "Are you serious? I'm not getting involved in any more gang shit."

"Any more?"

Kitally waved the subject off.

Hayley sighed. "Just tell me where the leader of the Franklin gang lives and I'll do the rest."

Kitally laughed. "They'd kill you just for asking for directions, much less who the shooter was."

Hayley knew that wasn't true, since Jessica had asked them and still had her head intact. She searched through the pile of papers for the photo Jessica had given her and handed it to Kitally. The twelve-year-old girl who had been shot had big green eyes and a sweet smile.

"Nice touch." Kitally dropped the photo on the table in front of Hayley. "You might be interested to know that you're not the only one who wants Brian dead."

"Is that so?"

"Brian Rosie and his foot soldiers have been cutting into Wolf's territory for years. Bad blood between those two."

"Wolf?"

"He's the leader of the Franklin gang."

"Good to know."

"So," Kitally said. "When do you want to go?"

"How about tonight"—she glanced at the kid eating quietly a few feet away—"after I figure out where the kid's mom ran off to."

CHAPTER 7

Seth walked through the emergency room entrance and made a right at the first corridor, just as he had hundreds of times before. And yet this time it felt different. He had killed a man. Nothing would ever be the same. The cornucopia of hospital smells was suddenly overwhelming: antiseptics, blood, and the pungent smell of decaying flesh.

After making the usual rounds, checking on his patients, as he liked to think of them, he entered the break room reserved for staff and used the hot water to make himself a cup of tea. Although he considered himself to be a male nurse, he'd been demoted a few years ago. He'd heard whisperings from his coworkers; he knew some considered him to be nothing more than a volunteer, but Janelle assured him he was much more than that. She needed him. His patients needed him. Hell, the hospital was lucky to have him.

The relentless whirring and beeping of the ancient refrigerator grated on his nerves. He picked up the remote and pointed it at the television set high in the far corner of the room, then switched the channel to the local news. Still no mention of the missing dead man rotting away in the trunk of his rental car. He'd been researching areas where he could dump the body. A wooded area, somewhere he could go and dispose of the body late at night.

He rubbed his head as if that would make all of his problems go away.

At times he felt proud of what he'd done: ridding Madeline of a menace qualified him as a hero of sorts. But then there were moments like this one where he felt the walls closing in and didn't quite understand why he'd killed the man. There were also times when he would jolt upright in bed, in the middle of the night, convinced he hadn't killed Chris Porter at all. He would then hurry into his garage, unlock his toolbox, and see the wallet. That's when he knew it was real. He'd taken a life. He was a killer. There was no going back now.

Overcome with dizziness, he held on to the counter for support. He glanced at the clock on the wall—ten minutes until Madeline's radio show. He was usually home by now. Today had been a very long day.

A clean-cut male nurse in his thirties—Tom or Tim (Seth could never remember his name)—entered the room and proceeded to flip on every light switch, filling the room with a bright fluorescent glow that made Seth's eyes hurt.

"Is everything all right, Seth?"

"I'm fine." He unbuttoned the top button of his shirt, but still couldn't seem to get enough air in his lungs.

"Look at this." The guy bent over and showed him a large knot on his head. "What do you think? Am I going to live?"

"It doesn't look like much. Talk to Janelle if you're really worried. She's around here somewhere." He could feel his lips moving; he knew he was still talking, but the words coming out of his mouth sounded robotic, as if someone else were doing the talking for him—as if he were having an out-of-body experience.

Strange—and yet familiar, too.

It was happening again, he realized. The first time he had experienced this very sensation was in the fourth grade, in Mr. Newman's classroom, not long after his accident. Chaos erupted in the classroom that day while he glided around in his own little world—a giant floating bubble. After the bubble burst, he found himself under his desk and saw that all his classmates were gone. It turned out there had been a fire drill. His teacher was concerned by his failure to respond to the piercing sound of alarms. The episodes, as his mother referred to them after that day, began to occur more frequently after that. His teachers tried to work with his parents, who didn't give a damn, to figure out how to help him concentrate and stay focused in class. His doctors insisted his problems had to do with the injury to his frontal lobe during his skiing accident when he was ten. He was given medication, which helped. Eventually, he outgrew the need for pills altogether.

That was . . . until recently.

He raked his fingers through his hair as he recalled following Chris Porter into the alleyway. No matter how hard he tried, he couldn't remember how the knife came to be in his pocket. And yet, with amazing clarity, he remembered stabbing him again and again.

He had killed a human being.

Perspiration drenched his brow.

Not only had he killed a man, he had enjoyed it.

How could that be?

He was no monster. He didn't belong behind cold steel bars with all those freaks and lunatics. He knew the difference between right and wrong. He was awash in remorse. He'd hardly slept since that night. Always waking soaked in sweat. Twice now, Janelle had asked him about his sleeplessness. She said he was talking in his sleep, too, saying he was sorry for what he'd done. She figured he was apologizing to her for being unable to forgive her for betraying him. Everyone makes mistakes, she often reminded him. He pretended to go along with her theory, since he had no intention of telling her what he'd done. As Janelle had done many times since her affair, she told him she loved him and was worried about him.

He didn't believe her.

He raised a hand to his eyes to shield them from the bright light and that's when he saw a name tag: Tim. That's right. Tim, the resident pervert. Janelle had told him about the guy and how all the nurses complained about him. A few weeks ago, they'd caught him inside the women's bathroom.

Tim was holding a brown paper bag that he hadn't had with him when he first entered the break room. The pervert stopped at the door and turned back toward Seth, his fingers rubbing his jaw as if he wasn't sure whether or not he should say what he was about to say. He raised the bag higher. "Thanks for this. And don't worry about breaking down. I understand. I really do. My ex-wife deceived me, too. Difficult times," he said with a shake of his head. "Things will get better for you, though. I'm certain of it."

And then he was gone.

Don't worry about breaking down? What was he talking about? Did I have an episode without even realizing it? He walked to the mirror hanging above the sink area. His eyes were red and watery, his face pale. Damn. If he could get some sleep, this never would have happened. But it had, and he had zero recollection of having any conversation with Tim. His hands shook as he reached into his pockets. They were empty. He'd given Tim the drugs he'd stolen this morning. How could he be such a fool?

The erratic beep of the ancient refrigerator in the corner of the room screamed like sirens. He covered both ears and rushed out of the room. He went to his wife's office and took a seat in front of her computer, starting to feel better. Janelle's shift would last another hour at least. He pushed a few buttons and turned up the volume.

The sound of Madeline's voice instantly calmed him.

Taking a deep breath, he leaned back in the ergonomic chair with the built-in lumbar support, and exhaled. "Talk to me, Madeline."

He had a burning desire to call her and ask her a question, but he knew he needed to be patient. It was still too soon.

"I wish I had never been born," a caller said. "My mother was right when she said I was better off dead."

"No, she was wrong," Madeline assured her.

"You've never met me, how would you know?"

"This is Kimberly, right?"

Silence.

"I've been hoping you would call back," Madeline told the girl. "I've been worried about you."

Sniffling.

"You are not alone in this. I am here for you."

Seth was certain Madeline was talking to him and no one else. His shoulders relaxed, his breathing calmed.

CHAPTER 8

"You know this is crazy being out here in the middle of the night, right?"

Hayley ignored Kitally and focused on the sound of each footfall against the pavement as she walked. Every once in a while she glanced at the moon. She wasn't used to having someone around on her nighttime walks. She liked her privacy. She liked the darkness, the peacefulness, the quiet . . . especially the quiet.

Kitally was her opposite, seemingly energized by being around large groups of people. She thrived on mindless chatter. As far as Hayley was concerned, people were exhausting.

Hayley wasn't big on questioning her motives for walking the streets at night, but tonight was different and she found herself wondering why she hadn't told Jessica to fuck off. Jessica hadn't called or come by since she quit working for Lizzy two years ago. And that was all fine and good, but for Jessica to call her after all this time because she needed a favor didn't sit well with Hayley.

Jessica was smart enough to know that Hayley wasn't fond of doing anyone any favors. She certainly wasn't doing this for the money. Hell, she knew Jessica didn't have two cents, let alone two thousand dollars to pay her. But how could Jessica possibly know that she would visit the Franklin gang for the sheer sport of it?

"The house will be the third one on the right after we make a left onto Castro," Kitally said. "We've been on Franklin turf for five or six blocks now."

There wasn't a fence, house, or mailbox that hadn't been covered with graffiti marking the gang's territory.

They made a right.

The street was reasonably quiet. A few houses were dark. Some had chain-link fences around their yards. Kitally pointed to a two-story home with a porch and a bench. Two young kids were sitting out front. One was smoking a cigarette. The other was playing around on his phone. Neither looked like he was much older than twelve.

The kid with the smoke elbowed his friend as they came up the walk. Without a word between them, the other kid made his way to the front door. Hayley and Kitally stopped just shy of the porch and watched the kid knock once, wait, and then knock three more times.

Hayley heard the rattle of a lock and chain, and then the door opened. Two giants came outside. One of them whistled like a bird. The kid with the phone went back to the bench and sat down.

The bodyguards or whatever they were wore humongous football jerseys with the numbers twenty-three and eleven.

Another minute passed before a scrawny guy in an unbuttoned plaid shirt appeared. His pale, skinny chest didn't do his badass tattoos justice. His gaze fell on Kitally. "Hey, Kit. Thought I told you never to come around here again."

Kitally chewed her gum; she didn't look too worried, although her shoulders tensed. "Hey, Wolf. My friend here wants to ask you a question."

Wolf didn't look happy about that. A moment passed before he gestured for his two gargantuan subordinates to usher them inside.

"This could get ugly," Kitally warned Hayley as the two guys came forward and led them into the house.

The door clicked shut behind them.

No sooner had the deadbolt slid into place than Hayley recognized the sound of a round being loaded into a firearm behind her. She didn't turn. In another moment, the gun's barrel pressed against her temple. The place hadn't been hopping to begin with, but it was deadly quiet now.

Hayley shrugged. "Go ahead and blow my brains out, moron. I fucking dare you."

Kitally stopped chewing her gum, her eyes wide, her face pale, which was saying a lot considering she looked as if she'd never spent two minutes of her life in the sun.

Wolf doubled over in laughter on the couch where he'd taken a seat.

The rest of his minions, or whatever the hell they were called, looked around, gauging the moment, not sure how to respond.

"So, you have a question, sweetheart?" Wolf turned both palms up. "Go for it. Ask away."

"Tell your gun-happy underling to lower his weapon first."

A nod from Wolf did the trick.

"A twelve-year-old girl was shot and killed," Hayley began. "A kid just doing her homework. One of your guys was the shooter. I need a name."

Wolf wasn't smiling now. He gave his guys the eye, and it wasn't a good eye—it was bad, definitely bad. Two of Wolf's fingers on his left hand began to twitch.

"When a guy walks into this house and starts asking questions," he told Hayley, "he's gotta jump in with a good beating. What do you think about that?"

"Sounds like a dumb-ass ritual. I came here for a name."

He grinned, revealing distinctive gold grills. "Because I believe in equal opportunity around here, you're going to have the opportunity to jump in, too. But it's gonna be a little different for you. The fellas will show you how things work around here."

Wolf took a good look around the room, as if seeing most of the people hanging around for the first time. "Who ya gonna pick to take you in the back room first? Chuckles, the bald Korean standing in the back? Fuck Master, the African-American gentleman sitting on the couch, or my two white gorillas?"

He laughed again. Hayley wasn't sure if he was just plain amused by the idea of anyone screwing the two giants, or if maybe he'd called the wrong guy Chuckles.

"What's it going to be, beautiful? The Asian, the black, or the big creamy whites?"

"I'm color-blind," she said. "Yellow, red, black, white, it doesn't matter to me—they're all assholes. I think I'll let you pick which of these clowns is going to lose his eyeballs first."

Another flash of gold teeth before he said, "I'm starting to like you, girl. You're a mean one, aren't you?"

Hayley wasn't paying any attention to him. She had checked out thirty seconds ago, already working over all the possible scenarios in her head, starting with an inventory of weaponry stored on her body: two small knives strapped to her left leg and a six-inch blade strapped to her right, a small canister of Mace around her neck and tucked into her T-shirt, brass knuckles in her back pocket, and five golden rings, literally, on her right hand. And she never went anywhere without her favorite stick, the one with the extender.

"You're so cocky," Wolf said, "we'll start with a double. My big guys don't get much action," Wolf said. "Take her on back, boys. Show her whatchya got. Don't be shy."

"Wolf," Kitally said, the first word she'd spoken since entering the house—a new record for her. "She just has a question. Don't do this."

"You want some, too, Kit?"

Kitally said nothing.

"Then shut your mouth. You two bitches come around here with a fucking question, a question like *that*, about one of my guys, in the dead of night? Then this is how it's going down."

Hayley felt how she always felt in these types of situations: invincible, like she had just learned to fly and was now soaring over Death Valley—clear blue skies, a wicked breeze, and triple-digit temperatures.

She was pushed from behind as the two big guys in jerseys ushered her down a long narrow hallway. One giant led, the other following close enough to let her know he was excited about the sudden turn of events.

The instant the door locked, the Sasquatch behind her interlocked his flabby arms with her elbows and held her snug against him. His big belly jiggled against her back as he talked to his friend. "I'll hold her while you pat her down, then take her clothes off."

"Man, you look like you're afraid of the bitch."

"She didn't care if Trigger put a bullet through her head. I'm not taking any chances."

"She can't weigh more than eighty pounds. Let her go."

The instant Dumbass let her go, Hayley slammed her right foot into the crotch of the guy in front of her, already gripping the Mace around her neck and spraying as she wheeled, leaving both idiots scratching at their eyes. She stepped away from Dumbass, who was now spinning in place and squealing, while the other guy fell to the floor in a gutless heap. She grabbed the desk chair from the corner of the room and wheeled it to the door, using it as an extra lock to keep anyone else from joining in on the fun.

"What's she doing?" Dumbass asked, his arms now waving blindly through the air, searching for her.

"I think she's locking us in."

"What the fuck?"

She pulled out her longest blade and said, "OK, who's going to volunteer to lose his balls first?"

Dumbass wasn't having any part of it. He started swinging. "You're gonna die, bitch. You're gonna die right now."

Dumbass's twin, still on all fours like the big stupid animal he was, looked at her through one squinty eye. "She's got a big-ass knife and she looks happy. I wouldn't go near her if I were you."

He's not as dumb as he looks, Hayley thought. She had fucking wings. She was soaring on thermals now, excited to reach a higher altitude so she could get to her final destination without using much energy.

Dumbass didn't listen to his buddy's advice, though. He screamed like a banshee as he lunged for her.

When she sliced his arm, blood sprayed across his friend's face.

Somebody pounded on the door.

"I'm not done yet," Hayley shouted to whoever might be trying to get in, her adrenaline pumping.

Dumbass yelled at his twin mongrel to do something.

The other idiot tried to come to his feet, but didn't manage it before she drove all her ninety-five (not eighty) pounds, along with her metal-covered knuckles, into his nose.

He toppled over again, coughing, blood spurting, both chubby hands clutching his face.

It sounded as if a stampede of people were on the other side of the door, pushing and trying to knock it down.

"Calm down, people, I'm coming out." Hayley bent over and reached into the idiot's back pocket for his subcompact Glock 26, a small, versatile gun with a short barrel. She checked the magazine clip to make sure it was loaded, then pulled the slide, put her finger on the trigger and opened the door.

There were six guys lining the hallway, three on each side. "Who's next?"

One brave soul stepped in front of her, blocking her way.

"Let her through," Wolf ordered.

He moved out of her way. In fact, they all did as Wolf said and parted like the Red Sea, making just enough room for Hayley to walk by. Gun raised, she took her sweet time moving down the hallway.

Wolf stood across the room by the door, arms crossed. Despite the gun and what she'd done to his bodyguards, he had full control and they both knew it. Seven to one would be hard to beat. What Hayley had now, though, was respect. She hoped that was enough to get her out of there in one piece. "Where's Kitally?" she asked.

He gestured with his chin outside. "What's your story, bitch?"

"It's simple. I need a name. Until I get one, a pregnant Kiki is going to remain behind bars."

"Is that a threat?"

"Nope. Just stating the facts."

"What are you, a cop?"

"Just a girl looking for a name."

Wolf looked at her for a moment longer, peering into her eyes as if hoping to read her mind, then opened the door and held out his hand, palm up.

She turned over the gun to him and walked outside, knowing she might catch a bullet between her shoulder blades before she reached the end of the street.

Kitally was waiting for her at the bottom of the porch stairs. Neither of them said a word as they walked off.

CHAPTER 9

With a spine-jolting thud, Seth's right front wheel dropped into a pothole, jerking him forward and slamming his chest into the steering wheel. Lucky for him, the front wheel came out as easily as it went in.

Don't panic. Stay calm. Never mind the dead body in the trunk.

It was dark out. With the headlights turned off, he could hardly see two feet in front of him, but he didn't want to risk being seen.

The wheels were out of alignment now and kept pulling to the right.

He stopped for a moment to wipe perspiration from his eyeglasses, then rolled down his window and listened for traffic above him on Highway 50. All he learned was that the frogs in the area were not yet hibernating. There had to be a large body of water nearby, because they were deafening. Since there were fewer trees to his right, he decided it was time to cut off the dirt road and hope he wouldn't get stuck.

With the window down, he drove at a snail's pace through muddy soil covered with thick layers of dead leaves. He wasn't the only one jostled around as the car bounced over rough terrain. Every time he hit a bump, he heard the body clunk and roll.

The stench seeped through the vents, making the drive nearly unbearable. Once he could no longer see the dirt road behind him, he turned off the ignition, jumped out and sucked in a lungful of fresh air.

Without that god-awful smell clogging his brain, Seth could finally think. His first thought was about Madeline. Did she have any inkling that she no longer needed to fear for her life? He looked at his watch. It was after midnight. She would be home soon.

Time to get this over with.

He leaned into the backseat and unzipped the duffel bag he'd brought. He slipped on a pair of thick gloves and put plastic bags over his shoes, using twine to keep the plastic from slipping off his feet.

He grabbed the shovel and for the next thirty minutes he dug, relieved that the earth was fairly soft. Once the hole was deep enough, he walked back to the car and put on a disposable mask to help with the smell. Then he popped the trunk, wincing at the light that snapped on inside.

The exposed flesh was purple, green, and black in some places. The bacteria and enzymes were doing their job, breaking down their host. Even through the mask, he could smell the putrid gases, the same gas that had caused the body to bloat and made the eyes bulge. Death might be inevitable, but it wasn't pretty.

He reached in and took hold of the corpse by its shoulders. Nails and teeth stayed intact, but he could literally feel the skin coming off the bone beneath the sweatshirt. Damn. He let go. This was disgusting.

After a moment, he tried again. This time he slid his hands under the corpse and lifted it out of the trunk, carrying him in the same way a groom might carry his bride over the threshold.

He had no desire to look at the man's face, so he kept his gaze straight ahead, on the hole in the ground, and away from the corpse with its rotting, stinking skin. Standing on the edge of the pit, he thought about tossing the body inside. No. That wouldn't do. Parts of him could fly off in a dozen directions. He needed to be smart. He slid down the side of the small crater and gently laid the body on the bottom of the pit.

Dark clouds had dispersed, making room for the moonlight. Standing tall, he suddenly found it difficult to take his eyes off the dead man. Although the man hardly resembled the person he'd confronted in the darkened alleyway, he knew it was him and he knew what he had done was wrong.

Old emotions that he'd pushed down and kept hidden for so many years began to surface. Instead of releasing tears of remorse, though, he felt the stirrings of amusement rise within, his muscles contracting right before he exploded with laughter. He had no idea what was wrong with him, but he couldn't stop laughing. He had to wipe tears of amusement from his eyes. And then he looked at the corpse again and found himself wishing it were his mother's corpse he was looking at instead. He imagined those were her eyes looking at him. And, of course, she was pleading for his forgiveness.

God, how good would that feel, to look over his mother's rotted corpse? He didn't know if the bitch was still alive. Maybe he would make a few calls and find out.

With renewed energy, he turned and looked around, then grabbed hold of the small boulder he'd moved out of his way earlier. Holding it high in both hands, he twisted back around and slammed the rock into the man's face, crushing his skull.

CHAPTER 10

"Fighters, get into position," the instructor shouted.

Lizzy walked to the middle of the ring. She was at the UFC fighting gym where she, Tommy, and Hayley trained at least twice a month. The floor was covered with thick mats. Sweat dripped from her face after a longer-than-normal warm-up.

As she had been taught, Lizzy staggered her feet—right foot back, left foot forward, about a foot and a half apart. Then she raised both gloved fists to just below her jaw.

The woman she'd been paired with and was now facing did the same.

Although Lizzy continued to teach teenage girls to defend themselves, she also liked to challenge herself and learn new defense techniques. She had been taking UFC fighting lessons for a couple of years. She recognized most of the people in the room, including Rhonda, the woman she was about to fight. Rhonda was stocky and well muscled, with hair cut short around her ears. Rhonda was also pissed off. They both wore headgear, but nothing could hide the scowl on her face. If Lizzy knew Rhonda better, she might have asked her what the problem was, but it was too late now anyhow, since the fight was about to begin.

This was fight night. More people showed up for fight night than any other. There were rules: no knees to the groin or head. No eye gouging or fishhooking. No hair grabbing, no biting. No strikes to the throat or spine.

As instructed, they both jabbed air, first with their left fists, then their right, pointing with their thumbs and aiming with their knuckles. A few shouts from the crowd egged them on, although heckling from the crowd was not something they encouraged there.

The bell rang.

Lizzy moved forward and clipped Rhonda across the chin on the first jab, and then threw another quick combination to her shoulder and middle.

Rhonda literally growled as she lunged forward, hitting Lizzy with an uppercut, two jabs in the ribs, and a jarring right hook to her temple. Despite the padding beneath her shirt and the headgear, it took Lizzy a moment to regain her senses, which gave Rhonda time to put everything she had—her legs, her body, her whole being—into each strike.

Lizzy felt a sting in her face, shoulder, and ribs. She staggered backward until she was pressed against the rubber ropes. She tasted blood. *Where the hell was everyone?* When the referee at last appeared, he made the necessary motions to call off the fight.

But Rhonda wasn't having any part of it. She wanted blood.

Fight nights were supposed to be all in good fun. The refs didn't wear headgear.

Rhonda landed a perfect haymaker on the ref, knocking him to the ground. Before anyone else could get in the ring, Rhonda was coming at her again.

On any other day, Lizzy might have been worried. As it was, though, this chick wasn't the only one who'd had a bad day. Lizzy pretended to wave her off, knowing Rhonda had already committed, then surprised Rhonda with some moves of her own: a fast jab to her chin, two more to the bad left shoulder she always bitched about. Two more strikes to her gut, a knee to her stomach, jab, jab, strike. Bringing her hips around, Lizzy ended with a hard kick to the woman's side, eliciting a loud grunt.

Rhonda spit out every curse word in the book as she came at Lizzy, slamming her head into Lizzy's gut. She was a brawler, pounding her with one blow after another, relentless, using her considerable weight to push Lizzy out of the ring. Lizzy got to her feet, but Rhonda had slipped through the ropes and pushed Lizzy into the wall, taking the breath right out of her. Another left hook and then a right to the side of her face. More blood.

People were yelling now. Somebody tried to get Rhonda off her. It was Tommy, and he took a right hook to his chin and a left to the face that staggered him, allowing Rhonda to turn back to Lizzy again.

Apparently, Rhonda was just getting started.

Lizzy used her legs to block most of the kicks, but Rhonda got in a couple more before a group of trainers managed to pull the crazy woman off her.

Lizzy was on the ground, her back against the wall. She gave herself a couple of minutes to breathe.

Tommy hunkered down next to her. He pulled off her headgear and her gloves. He used a wet cloth somebody handed him to wipe the blood from her chin.

At close view, Lizzy realized Tommy no longer resembled the insecure boy from the past. His jawline was defined, his body bulkier, his eyes bright. He'd grown into a man, and she wondered why she hadn't notice before this moment. Maybe she just needed to have the shit beaten out of her to really see things clearly.

"What the hell got into her?" Lizzy asked him.

"Hayley beat her good a few months ago. You weren't here. They were supposed to have a rematch tonight. I guess you got what was meant for Hayley."

"Wonderful." Lizzy shook her head. "And here I thought I was ready for anything."

"Don't feel bad. You held your own. Rhonda was limping and having a hard time breathing after taking those jabs to the ribs. And unlike Rhonda, you still have one good eye."

Lizzy smiled at him. "I guess that's one way of seeing the glass half full."

He pressed his fingertips to the top of her forehead and tilted her face to the light to assess the damage. "How many months until you walk down the aisle?"

Her smile turned to a grimace. "That bad, huh?"

"You're going to be black and blue for a few weeks."

"At least I didn't lose any teeth." She gestured toward the door where she saw Jared looking around the room. "Looks like my ride is here."

Tommy helped her to her feet. "Want me to put your equipment away for you?"

"No, I need to go to the locker room and clean up a bit. If you could tell Jared I'll just be a minute, I'd appreciate it."

"No problem."

Lizzy put away her equipment before she took a quick shower in the locker room. She was sore and beat-up, but the headgear and body pads had taken the worst of it. She changed into a clean pair of jeans and a T-shirt and then went in search of Jared.

She found him near the front door, looking handsome as always. He tended to grow younger while she grew older. She couldn't remember a time that she looked at him that her heart didn't skip a beat or two.

She planted a kiss on his jaw and pretended she didn't have a bruised face, a swollen lip, and battered rib cage. "Thanks for picking me up. My car is ready, but if you want to buy a girl some dinner first, I won't argue."

"Tommy told me what happened. You look pretty beat-up. Are you sure you're up for it?"

"As Tommy pointed out, I still have one good eye. You should see Rhonda."

"I'd rather not."

By the time they found parking at Zocalo's in Midtown Sac and were served chips and guacamole, Lizzy's head was throbbing. Her swollen lip wasn't helping either.

"Having trouble eating?" Jared asked.

She nodded.

He reached across the table and took her hand in his. "Have you thought more about quitting the PI business?"

It hurt to smile, but she couldn't help it. "Every day and every minute," she said. "And I always come to the same conclusion: I'm not going to give up the business."

"Seriously. Maybe it's time for you to think about doing something less dangerous. You used to make jewelry. Maybe you could open your own shop."

"You're kidding, right?"

"About what?"

"About all of it," she said as she took her hand back and pointed to her eye. "This shiner is the worst that has happened to me in two years. And for the record, the last time I made a pair of earrings was when I was in high school. I'm shocked you even remember."

The waitress brought them their dinner.

"What about Kate and Adonis?" Jared asked when they were alone again.

She wrinkled her nose. "Who?"

"Our kids, the ones we haven't had yet."

"You truly are hopeless," she said.

"A hopeless romantic."

"You're not planning on keeping me barefoot and pregnant, are you?" She pointed a finger his way and feigned a horrified look. "My God, that's it, isn't it?"

He shook his head as if she were a lost cause.

She took a bite of food and chewed carefully.

"Have you given much thought to the wedding?" he asked after a moment. "In case you've forgotten, it's only two months away."

"I finally got the nerve to ask Hayley if she'd be a bridesmaid."

"And what did she say?"

"That she would think about it."

"What about your parents?"

"What about them?"

"Have you told either of them we set a date?"

"I told Mom last week."

"And?"

It was Lizzy's turn to reach over the table and give his hand a loving squeeze. "She's happy for us." Lizzy didn't have the heart to tell him that her mother couldn't care less. She was busy with a new boyfriend and only wanted to talk about the trip the two of them were planning. Chances were they would be gone the entire month of December.

Lizzy's phone buzzed. She read the text. "Damn."

"What is it?"

"I was supposed to pick up the dog today. I completely forgot."

"You got a dog?"

"Oh. I didn't tell you, did I?"

He shook his head.

"On my way to Hayley's the other morning, a flashy sports car hit a dog. The driver didn't slow down for a minute. I took the poor animal to the vet, hoping they would know what to do with the dog after I got him all fixed up. The poor thing had a broken leg and yet he managed to follow me to my car. He's a tough one."

Jared ate as she talked. He looked amused.

"Anyhow," she went on, "the animal hospital told me they would need to keep the dog for a few days. I was supposed to call this morning." She stopped talking. Her eyes watered. "How would I ever take care of our child if I can't even take care of a dog?"

Jared smiled at her. "It's not the same thing, Lizzy. Besides, you've been busy. Don't beat yourself up over it. Where is the dog now?"

"I took him to a place close to Hayley's apartment."

"Why don't you call Hayley and see if she can pick him up? I'm sure she won't mind keeping him at her place for a few days until you find the dog a home."

CHAPTER 11

After driving around the streets of Sacramento for hours, Seth realized he didn't know what to do with himself now that Madeline was safe and no longer needed his protection. More than anything, he wanted to send her flowers, but of course that would be stupid. He needed to lie low for at least a little while.

His mission in life had been removed. He was a wreck and was having a difficult time concentrating. He couldn't remember the last time he got more than a few hours of sleep. When he'd looked in the mirror this morning, he'd hardly recognized himself. His thinning hair hung like wet spaghetti noodles across his forehead and over his ears. He'd lost weight. His eyes had a sunken-in look. He was a mess.

With nowhere else to go, he headed home.

Janelle greeted him at the door. She took his briefcase from him—the one he carried solely because it made him feel like a professional—then helped him remove his jacket. He usually pushed her away, but tonight he was too tired to care.

"Oh, my poor baby," she said. "I made you your favorite meal." After disappearing into the other room to put away his jacket, she promptly returned and patted the worn seat of his favorite chair, insisting he make himself comfortable. He didn't bother trying to help her pull the handle to release the leg extender. Surprisingly, he enjoyed watching her struggle with its weight.

She'd been acting like this for months. If he could've afforded it, he would've moved out the day she'd told him she'd slept with another man. But he didn't have much money of his own, so he'd stayed.

Why, he wondered now, watching her flutter around him, had he been fighting her all this time? It boggled the mind. He should've been taking advantage of the situation! The guilt Janelle felt for sleeping with another man was eating her alive. Until he forgave her, she wasn't going to stop. Whenever she'd tried to wait on him, he'd ignored her and walked away, but now he could see that he'd been a fool. If she wanted to treat him like a king, then so be it.

"Can I get you anything?"

"A tall glass of water. And did you say you cooked my favorite meal?"

Her eyes brightened like a child starved of affection. "Lasagna and garlic bread with lots of butter. We need to fatten you up. You've lost some weight."

"Turn on the television before you see to my dinner," he said, testing his power.

She quickly obliged, happily handing him the remote before hurrying to the kitchen.

He flicked through all the local news stations. Still no mention of Chris Porter. He'd done his best to cover up any signs of blood in the alleyway and air out the smell in the Nissan rental, but he still worried that someone might have seen him that night. What would he do if he was caught? The notion worried him, and yet nothing could override the excitement he felt whenever he thought of what he'd done. Madeline's stalker was dead. Not only had he stopped the man, he'd gotten away with it. He had a sudden desire to celebrate.

As always, he'd listened to Madeline's show every night since he'd killed the man. But Madeline had yet to tell her listeners that the stalker was no longer leaving her gifts. Maybe she wanted to be sure before she told her listeners that she was no longer being stalked. Unable to sit still, he knew he wouldn't rest until he saw Madeline. He needed to see how she was doing. For the first time in months, she'd probably been able to let down her guard a bit as she got from point A to point B every day.

He grabbed his keys and his raincoat from the entry closet and headed out. He didn't bother saying goodbye to Janelle. He wouldn't be gone long. Besides, she would no doubt be happy to warm up his dinner later.

He hopped into his Honda, didn't bother switching to the rental parked a few blocks away. No reason to do that. Madeline would be at work. He wasn't sure what he would say to her when he saw her. Maybe he would explain to her that he was a devoted fan and how concerned he'd been about her recent troubles. Of course, he'd then ask her if there was anything he could do to help.

By the time he merged onto the highway, images of Madeline filled his mind. He often went to her website and stared longingly at her picture. Her thick red curls made a beautiful frame around her heart-shaped face. Those sensuous lips made his pulse race, but those big green eyes were his downfall, the feature that sucked him in and held him hostage. The thought of holding her close, her cheek brushing against his as she thanked him for what he'd done, left him breathless.

The blare of a horn snapped him to and he jerked the steering wheel to the right to get back into his original lane. With his heart lodged in his throat, he ignored the cars around him and forced himself to breathe as he regained control of himself.

Raindrops hit the windshield and it wasn't long before his thoughts were back on Madeline.

He needed to be patient with her. Tonight he would merely introduce himself. Anything else would be considered icing on the cake, so to speak. He couldn't remember the last time he'd felt so ridiculously giddy. Depression had a way of hanging on to a person like an extra thirty pounds around the gut, pulling him down, down, down. Life shouldn't be so difficult.

Although he knew he was being hasty in rushing off to her, he couldn't help himself. He'd been dying to meet her for such a long time. He'd committed the ultimate sacrifice to protect her. He deserved this.

Ten minutes after he exited on Madison, he parked his car in front of a simple brick building. It was seven p.m. The rain pelted his windshield full force now. A flash of lightning sliced through the ominous gray sky.

He climbed out and scurried across the parking lot, surprised to see there was no security around as he pushed through the glass door. There was a waiting area to his left and a receptionist desk to his right, but nobody was there. He tried to open another door, the door he figured would probably take him straight to Madeline, but there was some sort of electronic key device needed for entry. Not certain of what to do next, he noticed the men's room around the corner from the receptionist area. He would dry off, make himself presentable, and then have a seat and wait for someone to show up.

The waiting area consisted of a small couch, a few chairs, and a round glass coffee table littered with magazines. Footfalls sounded moments after he took a seat. The receptionist came around the corner. Before she spotted him, someone entered the building, bringing with him the cold, drizzly air. Seth wouldn't have taken note of the man at all if he hadn't handed the receptionist a package and announced that it was for Madeline Blair.

Of course, that piqued his interest.

The man's appearance, everything from his well-fitted black trench coat to his Rolex, screamed money. He had parked his Mercedes in front of the entrance and left the engine running. The license plate: DLW ESQ. He was a lawyer—a tall, dashing lawyer with a thick head of hair and a deep masculine voice. Had Madeline called in a young, handsome lawyer to help with her stalker problem? No, that wouldn't make sense.

Outside in the distance, he could see his Honda. Looking downward, he noticed his shoes needed polishing and there was a missing button on his coat. He suddenly felt very small and insignificant.

"Can I help you?"

He looked up. It was the receptionist. Out of the corner of his eye, he saw the Mercedes drive off. "I-I'm looking for"—he fumbled around in his pockets, pretending to look for an address—"a school. I'm supposed to pick up my daughter. She's taking a night class."

"Oh, you must mean the Paul Mitchell School across the street."

He came to his feet, forcing a smile and shaking his head as if he'd lost his mind. He approached the young woman's desk, hoping to get a better look at the package. Madeline's name was scribbled on top, but nothing else. "Yes, the Paul Mitchell School." He pointed across the street. "That way?"

The desk plate on the counter told him her name was Cindy St. Louis. Cindy nodded. "Go back out on Madison and make a left at the light. It's right there on the corner. You can't miss it."

He thanked her, stood there awkwardly for a moment, and then said, "Was that George Clooney who just left?"

She giggled. "No, but I wish. That was David Westlake, a friend of one of the radio personalities here at KXFO."

"Ah," he said. "Thanks for your help, Cindy."

As he walked slowly back across the parking lot, oblivious of the rain as it dripped down his face and neck, soaking him to the bone, he cracked his knuckles, one at a time. *Pop. Pop. Pop.*

By the time he was on the road again, he realized he'd been a fool to think Madeline might show interest in a guy like him. He wasn't tall or distinguished. He was out of shape. He had nothing to offer her. But he loved her in a way he'd never loved anyone before. For now, he would have to be content to just watch after her. Some day he might find the courage to meet her face-to-face and say hello. A man could dream.

CHAPTER 12

At the sound of the horn, Lizzy looked out the window and said, "Cathy's here."

Jared frowned as he set his coffee cup on the counter. "It's Saturday. I thought we were going to look at wedding cakes and make a decision about what to feed the guests."

"I thought we were going to keep this simple," Lizzy said as she gathered her things. "You know, barbecue and Rice Krispies treats?"

"You were serious?"

"You weren't?" Another honk. "I'm sorry. Cathy called the other day to ask me to visit Dad with her. He's not doing well."

"How bad is it?"

"I'm not sure, but I'll call you either way to let you know what's going on."

"The cake lady is expecting us at noon. If you don't make it, do you have any preferences as far as flavors go?"

"Just pick anything."

"It's not that easy," Jared said. "According to Heather across the street, they don't make the standard three-tiered cookie-cutter cake any longer."

"Are you talking about Heather Long Legs? The woman who has a new boyfriend every month? What does she know about wedding cakes?"

"Apparently a lot."

Lizzy frowned. "Does this mean no plastic figurine on top of the cake?"

"I believe that's a negative."

"So sad." Lizzy crossed the room so she could give him a kiss. "I'm not very much help lately. I'm sorry."

Jared wrapped his arms around her waist and said, "Go see your dad. I'll take care of the cake."

She smiled at him. "You're too good to me."

"Just remember that when I delicately feed you a bite of carrot cake at our wedding."

"You wouldn't dare."

He laughed. "Say hello to your dad for me."

"I will. Love you."

"Love you, too."

No sooner had Lizzy put on her seatbelt than Cathy began her usual rant about Lizzy's next-door neighbor.

"It could be raining cats and dogs and that woman would be out there in her short shorts, tending to one of those rosebushes out front. It doesn't even have any blooms. Doesn't she have any bushes in the backyard to take care of? I mean, *really*."

Lizzy laughed.

"One of these days, when you come home to see Jared helping her with her plants, you won't be laughing," Cathy huffed. "I bet every man in the neighborhood is looking out their front window right now. It's freezing outside."

"To each his own," Lizzy said.

"I thought Jared was thinking about selling the house."

"It's a buyer's market right now. We've been looking at a few places downtown. Don't worry, sis, it'll happen soon enough. I'm not going to let Heather's skimpy clothes and great body drive me out of town."

Cathy kept her eyes on the road, but couldn't seem to get the neighbor out of her mind. "Jared is a very handsome man."

"I thought you didn't like him."

"Let's just say he's grown on me."

Lizzy smiled, wishing she could say the same about Cathy's ex-husband, who had found a way to convince her sister to let him move back into the house. Her brother-in-law was bad news.

"Are you really that confident in your abilities to keep Jared away from that neighbor of yours?"

"If Jared wanted to be with Heather, he would be with her. And I wouldn't try to stop him."

"He's the man you love, the man you're going to marry."

"Exactly. Can we please talk about Dad? Does he know I'm coming with you today?"

"I decided to surprise him," Cathy said with exaggerated happiness. "It's going to be fine, Lizzy, I promise."

It was a short drive to Sutter General on L Street. By the time Lizzy and Cathy stepped out of the elevator and into the nurses' station, Lizzy's pulse had accelerated. Every muscle tensed as she followed her sister through the long, sterile hallway toward her father's room. He had pancreatic cancer. To prevent certain complications of the intestinal tract, the doctors wanted to perform palliative surgery. Until recently, their father had refused the operation.

"Hey, Dad, it's Cathy. Your doctor called to tell me you might have changed your mind about having surgery. I think that would be a smart move."

"What's she doing here?"

Cathy looked over her shoulder at Lizzy. "Why wouldn't she be here? She's your daughter."

Lizzy paled. He still hadn't forgiven her for lying to him so many years ago. Her father had always been an angry, unhappy man, but his resentment toward her had gone on for too long. Despite the tone of his voice and the anger in his eyes, she stepped closer to his bed. His skin was yellow. He'd lost a lot of weight. "Hi, Dad."

He kept his eyes focused on Cathy. Lizzy hadn't seen him since he'd made it clear he wanted nothing to do with her, but Cathy had convinced her to come see him and try to make amends. The cancer had obviously progressed. His arms looked bony. He appeared much sicker than Cathy had let on.

"I brought you a gift," Lizzy told him. "I remember how much you used to like to read. Cathy told me your vision is blurry right now because of the medication, so I brought you a couple of audiobooks so you can listen to your favorite stories while you're here."

"I never liked to read," he told Cathy. "What is she talking about?"

"Dad, calm down. Lizzy came here because she wants to make things right between the two of you." Cathy maneuvered around wires and tubes so she could take his hand in hers. "It's time to let the past go."

"Dad," Lizzy said, desperate to change the subject, "I have good news. I'm getting married and I want you to come to the wedding. In fact, I was hoping—"

"I'm tired," he cut in. "Please leave."

"Dad," Cathy chimed in, keeping her tone upbeat, "don't be rude. Did you hear what Lizzy said? She and Jared are getting married!"

His nostrils flared and his frail hands began to shake as he reached for the call button, pushing it again and again. "I don't want her here," he said, spittle flying from his mouth. "Why is she here?"

Lizzy hurried from the room, choking on the smell of disinfectant as she walked, unable to get to the elevators soon enough.

It was a few minutes before Cathy caught up to her down in the main lobby. "I'm so sorry. I have no idea what's gotten into him. I've never seen him like that before."

Beyond annoyed, Lizzy turned on her sister and pointed a finger at her chest. "You just couldn't leave it alone. You never leave things alone. You always want to fix everyone, do anything and everything to make this a perfect world. Well, guess what? When are you going to get it? The world is all fucked up and that includes our family."

"I had no idea that Dad would be so hostile."

"Why is that, Cathy? You were there. You saw the way he blamed me for every little problem after I returned from the bowels of hell. He never forgave me for lying to him, but being taken by a madman wasn't punishment enough."

"I always thought he would change."

"I've been telling you for years how he treats me. But you refuse to listen to me. You've always loved being the little mediator, trying to make things better, but always making things worse. I don't need him in my life, do you understand?"

"He's sick, Lizzy. That wasn't Dad in that room. You don't want to leave things unfinished between you two. One day, a year from now, maybe two, you'll wonder if there was something you could have said or done to break through the barrier. I just think it would set you free in a way. You've been holding in so much anger and resentment, it's time to let it all go."

Lizzy took a step back, shocked. "I'm the angry one in the family? Wow, I must say that the past ten minutes have been quite an eye-opener—a fucking revelation. All these years and I had no idea that I was the depressed, angry daughter. I always *wanted* to be abducted by a madman only to come home to unloving parents who blamed me for every shit thing that ever happened in their lives." She raised her hands. "I get it now. I guess I need way more therapy than I first thought."

Lizzy was on the move again, heading for the exit.

"I didn't say I was perfect," Cathy said, staying close on her heels. "Come on, Lizzy. Let's talk about this."

"I'm done talking. I need you to take me home. I have a wedding to plan."

CHAPTER 13

For the first time in a long while, as Seth rummaged through the refrigerator for something to eat, he felt content. He planned to sit in his home office and listen to Madeline's talk show. He would take satisfaction in knowing that she was safe from evil.

Although he had the rental car for another two weeks, he had no plans to use the car again. He'd cleaned out the Nissan, taken care of the blood and the smells as best he could for now. More than likely he'd be better off torching the thing and then reporting it stolen. He had time to think things through. No reason to make any hasty decisions.

He fought the urge to drive by Madeline's house today on his way home from work. She was safe. Beginning next week, he would join 24 Hour Fitness and work out every day, just like he used to when he was in college. He was determined to get into shape before he met the woman he loved. He was going to get rid of his Honda, too. He didn't need a flashy Mercedes, but something decent, something worthy. Next time he ran off to meet Madeline, he would be a new man and he would do things right.

Passing up the leftover lasagna, he grabbed a handful of mini-carrots from the refrigerator instead and walked through the living room and down the hall to his office. He turned up the volume on the radio and got comfortable.

"Please welcome Dr. Madeline Blair, Sacramento's favorite psychotherapist."

"Hello, Sacramento. Today we're going to talk about letting go of childhood trauma. So many of us try, day after day, to push away painful memories, so much so that we begin to disown not only past experiences but parts of ourselves as well."

As always, Madeline Blair's voice soothed Seth, lifted him higher.

"For some," Madeline went on, "pushing away painful memories means forgetting what happened."

He nodded in agreement as he swallowed.

"For others, it means convincing ourselves that whatever happened to us wasn't so bad. If we want to be whole again, we must embrace these painful realities. It's not easy, but once again it comes down to owning the truth. Embracing our past life experiences, no matter how painful, will set us on a path to freedom. It always seems to boil down to this . . . the truth will set you free."

He munched on his carrots and sipped his water, feeling uncomfortable as she went on. Again it was as though Madeline could see deep inside him, driving down to the core of his being. Today he didn't want to go where she was taking him, though. To the day of his accident. The day his life was changed forever.

Seth didn't like to think about his childhood. Although his mother had told the doctors he'd been in a skiing accident, he knew it wasn't true, but somehow over the years the lies had become his truth. That's why he rarely thought about his past. For years after the accident, he'd been confused about everything. Every night he would come awake with a start. The nightmare was always the same: his mother swinging at him, swinging with all her might.

He was certain his accident was no accident at all. In fact, he'd never been skiing in his life, but his mother was always so insistent. His head used to hurt when he thought about it for too long, so he'd gone along with his mother's lies. Tonight, though, as he listened to Madeline tell her listeners they wouldn't be able to let go of the past until they faced the truth head-on, he knew he had to try.

He closed his eyes and allowed himself to return to that day. He imagined himself as a ten-year-old boy skiing on hills at Heavenly, smiling as onlookers envied his natural-born talents on the slopes. The sun was shining and the snow gleamed like a giant snow cone without the syrup.

After a caller relayed her own sad story, which ended on a good note after she was able to face the truth and move on with her life, Madeline sniffled, and then apologized. She was having another rough day, she explained. This morning she'd found a note on her refrigerator that read, "I hear you. I see you. I want you."

How could that be?

He laced his fingers together, turned his palms away from him and bent his fingers back until he heard a *crack, crack, crack* as the bubbles surrounding his joints burst. He did it again and again, his tongue clicking—just another nervous habit his mother detested.

Who left Madeline a note? he wondered.

Impossible. He'd killed her stalker. She should be weeping with joy, not fear.

If her stalker wasn't dead, what did that mean? What had he done?

"I'm listening," she told the next caller.

A deep, masculine voice came over the airwaves. "Hello, Madeline. It's me. I've been dying to know what type of panties you're wearing."

Seth came to his feet so fast his carrots scattered across the floor.

"Who is this?" Madeline said, her voice shot through with fear.

"Cotton or lace?" the voice asked, insistent. "Thongs or bikini? What color? I have to know."

He could hear the man sniffing air. His skin prickled. The bastard was still alive.

"What size bra cup do you wear, Madeline? Do your nipples harden when I call and talk dirty? Are you wet, Madeline?"

Seth's face burned. The silence was deafening. Why the hell hadn't the caller been cut off? His fingers rolled into fists. His thoughts were jumbled. He couldn't think clearly. Had he killed the wrong guy? Perhaps the radio show people had hired feds to tap her phone and were trying to catch the maniac. That was the only explanation.

"I need you to spend one evening with me, Madeline. We'll have dinner followed by a walk beneath the moonlight. We'll go dancing . . . anything you want to do." His breathing grew heavier. "Why won't you go out with me? How many times are you going to make me ask? Don't make me beg." The caller was all bluster one moment and all spineless timidity the next.

It hit Seth in an instant. He recognized the caller's voice: deep and masculine, like Clooney's.

It was David Westlake, DLW ESQ.

Lights flashed, adrenaline soared, knuckles popped and cracked. Apple pie. Homemade crust. His mother in the kitchen making his father's favorite dessert. With absolute clarity, he was ten years old again and reaching into the bowl of delicious sweet apple slices after his mother had told him not to eat any. He popped a thin slice into his mouth, then looked up, a sugary smile on his face. That's when he saw the five-pound maple-wood rolling pin in his mother's right hand, her apron covered with flour. She had told him not to eat the apples and she meant it.

It all happened so fast.

The smile hung on his face as he turned and she swung the heavy cylinder through the air and hit him with incredible force right between his eyes. *BAM. Lights out.*

CHAPTER 14

Kitally jumped into the passenger seat of Hayley's Chevy. "So where are we off to now, Magnum P.I.?"

"We're going to the McBane house, the woman who hired Lizzy to find out who might be sneaking into her house while she's at work. We'll watch the house for a few hours and also decide where the cameras need to be placed."

Hayley drove while Kitally played with the radio. "You seriously need to get satellite radio." Giving up with finding a station she liked, she hit the off button. "I've been thinking about this Brian dilemma of yours, and I have an idea."

Hayley waited.

"Nobody's talking, right?"

Hayley shrugged. "Or nobody knows where Brian is hiding out."

"Someone always knows," Kitally said. "They're just not talking. But there is one thing that will make even the quietest in the bunch speak up, and that one thing is money."

"It would take a *lot* of money for someone to rat on a man like Brian. He has connections. Anyone who knows Brian knows what he's capable of doing."

"Exactly. That's why you need to offer a reward of ten thousand dollars."

"How would I get my hands on ten thousand dollars in cash?"

"I'll put up the money. Dad might not let me touch his fancy-ass car, but ten thousand dollars in cash? Not a problem."

Hayley thought of Tommy and his love for anything with an engine. "Men and their cars."

"These aren't just any cars. Dad's car collection includes a rare Ferrari GTO and a twelve-million-dollar Rolls-Royce convertible. Those aren't even his favorites."

"That's terrific. Can we get back to the part about offering a reward?"

Kitally smiled. "Does this mean you'll give it a try?"

"If you're willing to put up a ten-thousand-dollar reward, I'm not going to stop you."

"How do you suggest we get the word out?"

"We'll hit every dive Brian ever walked into. We'll talk to anyone who will listen, tell them Hayley Hansen, the same girl who cut off Brian's dick, is offering ten thousand big ones as a reward for any tip that leads to his whereabouts."

"If and when Brian hears about this, he's going to come after your ass."

"That's the whole point."

"I wonder why he didn't kill you for what you did."

"He wanted me to suffer. He took away the only person I cared about and he must have figured I wouldn't have the guts to come after him a second time."

"Why didn't you take him out the first time?"

Hayley sighed. "I don't know. I really don't know."

By the time they parked across the street from the McBane house, Hayley was feeling hopeful. Overall, she knew revenge might not be in her best interest. Spending the rest of her life behind bars didn't exactly entice her, but there was no way in hell

Brian was going to get away with killing her mother. He was going to pay, all right. This time with his life.

"So what now?" Kitally asked.

"We do what we always do. We watch and wait."

The McBane house was a small two-story single-family home that looked a lot like the Franklin gang's home, only this house was in a better neighborhood and had a brick patio. According to Lizzy, the owner, Kat McBane, was working late tonight.

Kitally leaned back in the seat, tapped her fingers on the side of the door and then said, "So where do you see yourself in ten years?"

Hayley snorted and left it at that.

"I'm serious. Have you ever thought about your future?"

"I live in the moment," Hayley said, hoping to put an end to Kitally's chatter. "Right here. Right now. This is it."

"Dad wanted me to be an engineer," Kitally said. "Mom had high hopes that I would be a brain surgeon—fifteen years of school, residency, fellowship . . . no problem. Once you get inside someone's head, though—just you, the scalpel, and the brain—the margin of error would be infinitesimal. Think about it. One tiny error could be the difference between life and death. That's the part of neurosurgery that speaks to me. A superstressful occupation with high rewards if you do your job right."

There was a pause and Hayley took the bait. "So why aren't you in med school?"

Kitally kept her attention on the neighborhood. "I would get bored."

For the next thirty minutes, while they both watched the house, Hayley figured Kitally probably had a million questions for her, but she remained silent for the most part. It was a long while before Kitally straightened in her seat, then reached over and grabbed her leather bag from the backseat.

"What are you doing?" Hayley asked.

"I'm going to take a look around and figure out where we want Tommy to place the cameras."

"Maybe I should go instead."

"I've been following you around for months now. I'm a quick learner." Kitally opened the door and slid out of the car. "I'm going to check out the backyard. I'll be right back."

Hayley wasn't going to stop her. Ten minutes after she watched Kitally disappear around the back of the house, though, she began to feel a little antsy. Then, through the front window, she saw someone walking around inside. It took her a moment to recognize Kitally. *What the hell?*

Kitally had broken into the house.

Shit.

They hadn't talked about breaking and entering. Now was not the time or place. What the hell was she doing? Kitally was going to wind up getting them both into serious trouble.

Hayley got out of the car and made her way across the street, thankful that there weren't any barking dogs in the area. Keeping her eyes on the window as she approached, she couldn't believe what she was seeing. There were two people now. A tall, lanky person hovered over Kitally. His hand shot out and he struck her down.

Hayley ran to the back of the house. It took her a moment to unhook the latch on the gate. She growled with frustration and pushed the gate open. Her knee banged against a wrought-iron table as she rushed around the corner and made her way through the sliding glass door.

Two bodies rolled across the floor. Before Hayley could take action, Kitally jumped to her feet. In one swift motion, she pulled a humongous knife from her bag and raised it above her head with both hands.

"No!" The man covered his face with both arms.

"Stop!" Hayley shouted. "What are you doing?"

"What does it look like? This guy popped out of nowhere and hit me. I'm going to have a mark on my face."

"What is that thing in your hands?"

Kitally held the blade inches from the cowering man's head. "It's a machete. Pretty cool, isn't it? This beauty can prune, chop firewood, clear brush, and cut down small trees. If our ancestors had had these types of tools, they—"

"Don't let her slice me in half," the man pleaded.

"Kitally, think about what you're doing. Are you planning on killing him with that thing?"

"It depends." She didn't look away from the guy, but now she looked frustrated. "You use knives. Why can't I?"

"Knives, not machetes. And I've never killed anyone before."

The guy was shaking. He looked to be in his midtwenties, though his long, straggly hair and thick beard made him appear older. He looked as if he might have spent the last month living in the woods. "Can I sit up?"

"Don't move a muscle," Kitally warned.

"I think you should probably do as she says," Hayley told the man.

"If I can't kill him, should I just cut off his family jewels?" Kitally asked.

With a long, ponderous sigh, Hayley pulled out her cell phone and made a call.

Lizzy and Kat McBane both arrived at the house at the same time.

Hayley kept an array of items in her car, which came in handy at times like this: stun guns, handcuffs, pepper spray, Mace, and batons. After handcuffing the man, Kitally detained him with threats of chopping off his body parts with her machete.

Hayley watched Kat, a petite woman in her sixties, hurry up the walkway. "Put away the machete, Kitally, and take a seat on the couch. Let me do the talking."

A gasp escaped Kat the moment she laid eyes on the mountain man.

Lizzy followed close behind. "Do you recognize him?" Lizzy asked.

"I think it's my nephew. Jeffrey, is that you?"

"Afraid so. Could you tell these crazy girls to release me? They threatened me with a machete."

The woman looked from Kitally to Hayley. "Can someone please tell me what's going on here?"

"We work for Lizzy. We were determining where to put the cameras when we saw someone snooping around inside your home. Fortunately, your sliding glass door was open and we were able to get inside," Hayley lied.

"Jeffrey," the woman said, "what are you doing here?"

When he failed to respond, Hayley answered for him. "I took a look around and it looks to me as if Jeffrey has been living in your attic. He used your blankets and clothes to make himself a bed. There's other stuff up there, too, including enough food to last him a few weeks."

"Should I call the police?" Lizzy asked.

Kat McBane looked dazed. "Jeffrey," she said, "how long have you been living in my attic?"

"About a month. Mom and Dad kicked me out of the house. I had nowhere else to go."

"All you had to do was ask."

"Should I unlock the handcuffs?" Hayley asked.

The woman raised a hand to her forehead and began to pace, ignoring Hayley's question. "Why did your parents kick you out of the house, Jeffrey?"

"They caught me smoking weed in the shed."

Kat stopped pacing and shook her head in disbelief. "Your parents have always been too strict. Your mother smoked her share of dope back in the day. A little pot never hurt anyone."

Her nephew was still on the floor, but he managed to sit up.

Kat stood over him. "You can stay here with me—in the guest bedroom, not the attic. But before she removes your handcuffs, you're going to have to promise me you'll cut your hair and get a job."

"I don't have any transportation."

"Well, I guess we'll have to find you a used car. Until then, you can use my old bicycle to get around." Kat gestured for Hayley to undo the cuffs.

"Or take a bus," Kitally told him.

Hayley removed the cuffs.

Jeffrey pushed himself to his feet.

"Do we have a deal?" Kat asked her nephew.

As they shook hands, Hayley noticed that Jeffrey's hands were pale and slender, as if he'd never done a day's work, while his aunt's hands appeared tough and well used. Hayley found herself wondering if this deal of theirs, sealed with a handshake, could actually come to such an easy, uncomplicated end. She seriously doubted it.

"Come on," Lizzy told Kitally and Hayley. "Let's get out of here."

"Thanks," Kat said. "I'll take it from here. You'll bill me?"

"Sure," Lizzy said. Her gaze fell on Jeffrey. Hayley guessed she was having her own doubts about this little reunion. "Are you sure you don't want me to call the police?"

"That won't be necessary. Jeffrey is a good man. He just hasn't had anyone tell him so. We're going to be fine."

"I'm glad. Call me if you need me," Lizzy said before she followed Hayley out the door and down the brick path where Kitally waited.

CHAPTER 15

Seth decided to use his Honda tonight. It was the end of October, the time of year when darkness came early. Gloomy clouds hovered overhead, blocking any sign of stars or moon. Despite the weatherman's report of no rain today, a light drizzle covered his windshield.

David Westlake had worked later than usual tonight.

Seth kept his eyes on the towering building where Westlake's law firm was one of many tenants. The structure had a steel frame and countless windows, but wasn't the tallest building in Sacramento by any means.

And there he was now, the man of the hour. Westlake wore the same coat he had been wearing when he'd delivered a package to Madeline's office. As Seth had practiced, he pulled the Honda ahead to a pinch point Westlake would have to get past to get to the parking lot.

The attorney walked with the confidence of someone who was used to getting what he wanted. Seth pulled past him, stopped and rolled down his window, waiting for Westlake to draw even with him.

"Hey, Mr. Westlake, I need your help."

With both hands deep inside his pockets, Westlake stooped over and looked into the open window, wincing at the rain hitting his face. "Make an appointment."

"I've been calling for days. Your calendar is full for the rest of the month. Hear me out, please. It will only take thirty seconds of your time."

Westlake sighed. "There are plenty of personal injury attorneys in the area."

"I've been told you're the best. My sister deserves the best."

The compliment perked him up. "A car accident?" he asked.

Seth nodded. "Hit by a drunk driver, leaving her with spine and neck injuries, broken bones, and burns."

"I'm sorry."

"Me, too." Time for the kicker. "You might be interested to know that the driver turned out to be a successful businessman worth millions."

Sure enough, the lawyer's eyes lit up like a boy's on Christmas morning.

"Listen," Seth said. "You're up in the lot, right? Let me drive you to your car. That way I can give you the name of the driver and the hospital where my sister is staying and you can decide if you want to take on the case. If your answer is no, I promise you won't hear from me again."

David Westlake straightened, peering into the dark toward his car. The rain was coming down harder now, blowing into his face.

Seth had been watching David Westlake for days. He knew the lawyer parked at the far corner of the lot. Westlake was in good shape. He probably liked the exercise, and he also clearly liked easy cases that paid big. In the end, just as Seth had figured, Westlake was just another greedy asshole. It took the lawyer less than a minute to think about it. He opened the passenger door and climbed in.

Like taking candy from a baby.

He hit the child lock, and then plunged a needle into Westlake's neck before driving off.

The etorphine immobilized him instantly. Westlake slumped back into the seat.

Forty-five minutes later, Seth turned onto the same dirt road off Highway 50 and into the same woods in which he'd buried Chris Porter. It was different tonight, though. The rain was relentless, turning the road into a veritable mudslide. Seth's heart rate soared out of control, making him wonder if he was having a heart attack.

He slowed to a crawl and opened the window. Even through the downpour, he heard traffic in the distance. He closed the window and continued onward, hoping his tires wouldn't get stuck.

David Westlake moaned.

Shit. He should have thought this through a little better. Idiot weatherman had said no further rain until the weekend. Fucking liar. Teeth clenched, Seth kept his eyes on the road. Just a little bit farther.

BAM!

Westlake had throttled him, slamming the left side of his head into his window. The car swerved and crashed into a tree, the force throwing them both violently into the dashboard.

Grunts and moans were the only sounds. He twisted around in his seat, scrambling to release his seatbelt, but Westlake had hold of him. The lawyer was on top of him, both hands on his face, trying to gouge his eyes out.

He bit down on Westlake's finger until he felt bone.

Westlake howled like a wild dog.

Click. With his seatbelt unlatched, he could finally maneuver. Westlake was still half-drugged, which gave him the upper hand. Curled into a ball, he used both feet to push the lawyer off him, then struggled to open the compartment between the seats. He pulled out a .38.

Westlake knocked the gun out of his hand.

Damn it. The thought of losing control of the situation sent him into a frenzy. He jumped on top of the lawyer, could smell the man's cologne as he pummeled him with his fists.

Out of breath, he opened the passenger door and fell out into the muddy earth. Then he twisted around and grabbed hold of Westlake's coat, pulling him outside with him. He was running out of energy, but there was no time to stop and catch his breath. Adrenaline kept him moving. He climbed over Westlake, crawling, really, his clothes wet and heavy as he dragged himself back into the car to find his gun.

Westlake grabbed hold of his leg and twisted. The pain was excruciating. The .38 was just out of reach. Clenching his teeth, he tried to kick and pull his leg out of the man's grasp, and managed to gain a few inches.

His fingers fell around the revolver.

He turned and fired, blasting the man in the shoulder at close range.

Westlake fell backward into the mud. The rain battered them both as he clutched his wound. "Why are you doing this?"

"Madeline."

"Madeline Blair?"

"Yes, Madeline Blair," he said through gritted teeth. "I recognized your voice on the radio. You fucking pervert. I'm her protector. Nobody's going to bother Madeline while I'm around." He raised the gun.

"Don't shoot! Listen! That whole story about Madeline having a stalker is a lie. It was Madeline's idea. I didn't want anything to do with it."

"Crazy talk."

"You have to believe me. I have a wife . . . and kids. I would never hurt Madeline."

"Why would she make up something like that? You're not making sense."

"Her ratings . . . she did it for her ratings." Westlake groaned in pain. "She didn't want to lose her job. It's the truth. I swear."

A sick feeling washed over Seth. "Madeline would never deceive her listeners."

"She was desperate. Her career is everything to her."

It couldn't be true. Madeline would never do something so deceitful.

"She asked me to call in. I didn't want to do it. We've been friends since college. I was only helping a friend."

"Shut up. Just shut up."

Water dripped down Seth's face. Getting to his feet, he circled the area, trying to assess the damage to the car. He needed to think.

If Westlake was telling the truth, it didn't matter. He couldn't let him go now. It would only be a matter of time before Westlake brought the police to the area and they found Chris Porter's grave. He walked back to where the lawyer lay in the mud.

"I'll give you money, anything you want," Westlake said. "Please."

Seth blinked several times, took a breath. "I'm going to let you go."

Westlake took a deep breath of his own, even closed his eyes, so didn't see Seth raise his gun and fire a bullet into his brain.

He wasn't a killer. He didn't want the man to suffer. It was self-defense. He couldn't spend his life in jail for being a hero. He only wanted to save Madeline.

"Madeline."

He squeezed his eyes shut. He wasn't ready to think about Madeline. Not yet. Not now.

A small river had formed in the middle of the dirt road. His plan to drive farther away from the highway was out of the question now. Working fast, he removed his coat and his shirt and tossed them both into the backseat. He grabbed the shovel from the trunk, took it deeper into the woods, and started digging.

Every muscle ached as he dragged the body toward the hole.

Minutes felt like hours as he refilled the hole with dirt. He was glad when he could no longer see the body. With that done, he rinsed off in the rain before putting on his shirt.

Once he was in the car again, he realized getting rid of the body might have been easier than finding a resting place for the car would be. It was slow going, but he headed up the road. His plan was to ditch the car, maybe fill out a police report and say it had been stolen.

He rubbed his forehead.

That wouldn't work. He needed to give this more thought.

The tires whirred, unable to grab hold of the soft terrain. When he'd looked at a map of the area on the Internet, he'd seen a lake. But when he got there, he realized it would never work. There wasn't a steep enough slope to send the car down into the water.

Shit. Shit. Shit.

It wasn't easy, but he managed to turn the car around. For a moment, he merely peered into the darkness. Should he leave the car in the woods and try to cover it with bark and leaves? That was ridiculous. Exhausted, he laid his head against the steering wheel. Westlake's words were like a barrage of shells assaulting his mind. Could it be true? Had Madeline made up the story about having a stalker? *No. No. No.*

He refused to believe it. The man had called in to the show and said disgusting things. Of course Westlake would lie about what he did. He had his reputation to worry about.

Seth's breathing calmed. He would take it one day at a time, listen to her show as he always did. He would give her the benefit of the doubt. But if she talked about any more messages or gifts being left at her house, then he would know she was lying.

Decision made, he took his foot off the brake, headed back down the way he'd come, slow and steady. Time to go home. Tomorrow he would take the car into a body shop and have the front end fixed.

CHAPTER 16

Hayley turned off the engine, looked at Kitally and said, "Leave your bag in the car."

Kitally did as Hayley asked but she didn't look happy about it. Hayley didn't care. After the B&E and machete business at Kat McBane's place, she wasn't taking any chances.

Walking side by side, they approached a beautiful two-story home that belonged to Robin Santos. Her husband hadn't been seen in three months. "I'll do the talking," Hayley said before knocking. "We're here to ask a few questions, then we're leaving."

The short middle-aged woman who answered the door had brown eyes and dark, wavy hair that fell over her shoulders.

Hayley told the woman who they were and asked if she was Robin Santos.

The woman nodded, but didn't invite them in—her expression difficult to read.

"Your brother said today would be a good day for us to visit."

The woman nodded again.

All right, then. Talking to the lady was going to be like pulling teeth. "We need to ask you a few questions. Would it be OK if we came in for a moment? This won't take long."

Reluctantly, Robin Santos stepped back and allowed them inside.

They followed her across a tiled entryway that led to a big, open family room tastefully decorated with leather couches and a stone coffee table. An upright piano sat against one wall, and a mahogany shelf filled with books covered the opposite wall. A large-paned window overlooking the backyard revealed a large pond surrounded by rocks and potted plants.

Robin Santos glanced at the clock before gesturing for them to take a seat on the couch. "My girls will be home soon. I need you to leave before they arrive."

Hayley opened the file she'd brought and got right to it. Robin Santos wasn't the only one who wanted to make this quick. "I read the police report," Hayley said. "You and your brother believe your husband emptied the bank accounts before running off with another woman, is that right?"

"Yes," she said as she paced the room, unable to stop moving. "Can I get you two some water?"

"That would be great," Kitally said, eliciting a sigh from Hayley.

As soon as the woman walked off, Hayley said, "She's not being cooperative and we don't have much time. If she offers you a sandwich, the answer is no, thank you."

"OK, Mom."

For the first time ever, Hayley wished Jessica was still her partner.

Robin brought them water, and then took a seat on the chair across from them. Once again, she looked at the clock.

"Could you give me the name of this other woman?" Hayley asked.

Robin shook her head. "I have no idea who he ran away with. There were so many women, it would be impossible to narrow it down."

"He was an accountant?"

"That's correct."

"Did he have any close friends?"

"If you count hookers and one-night stands, then yes. He was seldom home, so I really don't know."

"What about your neighbor, Helen Smith?"

"What about her? She's a nosy busybody. My husband talked with her every once in a while because he felt sorry for her."

"According to the police records, Helen told police that he worked from eight to five, came straight home every night, and rarely left his house."

"Helen Smith doesn't live here, does she?"

Hayley frowned. The woman seemed dead set on being as unhelpful as possible. She obviously had no interest in finding her husband—that much was clear. "I would like to talk to your daughters."

"Absolutely not. I forbid it." She stood. "That's enough. It's time for you both to go."

"You do realize we're only trying to find your husband so you can collect child support?"

"I understand my brother was trying to help when he hired a private investigator. It's true that I have no idea how I'm going to keep a roof over our heads and food on the table, but the thought of ever seeing that man after what he did to my—to me—it's more than I can handle right now."

Hayley looked over her shoulder as they walked back to the car. Robin Santos peered through the curtains, watching them leave. "That is one strange woman."

"You think?"

Hayley shot Kitally a look. "Yeah. I do. She's hiding something."

"Like what?"

"I'm not sure yet, but she's got something. That was like interviewing a suspect, not a client."

"Maybe she's just bitter," Kitally said. "Her no-good husband slept around and she's pissed off."

Hayley shrugged. Kitally had a point, but still. There was something running under the woman's hatred for her husband. It smelled like fear to Hayley. But of what? There was nothing in the police report about the husband being abusive, so why would Robin Santos be so adamant about not wanting to help them find her husband? "We need to talk to her daughters."

As they drove away, Kitally said, "That will be easy enough."

"How do you figure?"

"Didn't you notice the window on the second floor?"

"Can't say that I did."

"How old are her daughters?"

"Fourteen and sixteen."

"Well, one of them, probably the older one, is sneaking out her window at night. She just opens her window and grabs hold of the tree branch right outside her window. It's got thin, white bark—you can see where she grabs it, and where she shimmies down the trunk. Little game trail through the shrubs, too. She's a regular. All we have to do is come around here after ten o'clock on any given weeknight and wait for her to sneak out."

As she waited for the light to turn green, Hayley looked at Kitally, really looked at her. She had the fashion sense of Heidi Klum and Lady Gaga mixed together. She talked too much. She was unethical and had absolutely no patience for laws and rules. A machete was her weapon of choice.

Kitally also had a knack for this line of work. Lizzy would be unwise not to hire her.

CHAPTER 17

Lizzy found a parking space in the hospital's underground garage and then took the elevator to the third floor. An hour ago, someone from the hospital had called to tell her that her father was out of surgery and had asked for his daughter. Lizzy knew darn well they had called the wrong daughter, but she wanted to talk to him. Alone. She might catch hell later for not telling Cathy, but she didn't care. She'd been thinking about her father a lot lately . . . maybe because of the whole wedding thing, she wasn't sure. But she needed to resolve this strange disconnect between herself and her father. She needed to do it for her sake, and maybe his, too.

After watching her father sleep for forty-five minutes, Lizzy stood to stretch her legs. According to the nurse, he had been wheeled out of the recovery room about thirty minutes before she'd arrived. He was pale, but not as yellow as the last time she'd seen him.

She walked across the room to admire the flowers and cards lined up on a long shelf near the window. They were on the third floor. She could see the parking lot below.

She bent over, stretched until her fingers touched her toes. A pink envelope had fallen under her father's hospital bed. She had to get down on her knees and scoot halfway under the bed so she could reach it. Back on her feet, she took her seat next to her father's bed and examined the envelope. "Grandpa" was scribbled in letters obviously written by a small child. Had he saved an old card from Brittany, his only grandchild? It was hard to imagine her father having such a sentimental side.

Lizzy knew it was wrong to pry, but she didn't care. And besides, it was pretty much her profession. She opened the envelope, then unfolded the piece of paper inside.

Scribbled in the upper right corner was a bright yellow sun. The artist had drawn the picture with pen, then used crayon to bring life to the sun, trees, and grass covering the distant hills. In the center of the picture stood a stick man and a stick child. The man was Grandpa, because the word *Grandpa* was scribbled close by with an arrow pointing to the man with no nose, just a very round head, two eyes, and a big smile. The kid had the identical face, just smaller, with the arrow coming from the name Emma.

Emma. Lizzy had never heard anyone in her family utter the name Emma. She examined the envelope closer. There was an address label in the upper left corner of the envelope: 202 Hickory, Portland, Oregon.

Her father's finger twitched. Moving quickly, Lizzy pulled out her phone and took a picture of the address label and another of the drawing. After she put her phone away, she slipped the picture back into the envelope, slid it under a pile of cards, and plopped back into her chair.

Pulse thumping, looking around for something to do, she shuffled through her purse and found the brochures Jared had left on the kitchen counter. There was one each for Belize, Paris, and Hawaii. The yellow sticky note read, *Where do you want to go for our honeymoon?* Lizzy thought about what Jared had said the other night about quitting her investigation business. Although she liked the idea of having more time for him, something tugged at her insides every time she considered letting the business go.

Was she being selfish?

She looked back at her father. He used to tell her all the time that she was a selfish child. Maybe it was true. If giving up the business would make Jared happy, why wouldn't she do it?

Was she afraid of happiness?

Happiness always lingered right there, just out of reach. She could see it, but she never really got to touch it. If she'd never been kidnapped by a madman at the age of seventeen, what would her life be like now? What sort of person would she be?

Why did she feel as if she were always being tested, over and over again?

What if she sold her business and moved to another country—would the evil in the air disappear then?

Was Jared willing to give up his career with the FBI, his fight for right and justice for all? If so—if they both gave it up—would they still always feel a calling to fight the devil?

All these years, all she'd been through, and she still didn't know herself. Life could be so unsettling, so strange. She'd been a PI for ten years now. The only time she felt truly alive was when she was chasing evil. She tucked the brochures back into her purse and let her gaze drift back to her father. Where did her parents fit into this life of hers? Her father was dying, but everyone died sooner or later. Did this old, feeble man with hatred in his heart deserve her sympathies, her worry, her last thought before drifting off to sleep at night?

In that moment, she somehow knew or at least felt that he did deserve her love. He was family. He was her father. She would keep coming to see him because she wanted to, and not out of some misplaced allegiance. She would come to this room that smelled of antiseptics and decay, and if he didn't want to listen to her tell him stories or talk about her life, that was OK. She would just sit there and make sure he knew that she was there for him if he needed her. She would do it for herself and not for any other reason.

Another selfish act? Perhaps.

She looked at his thinning hair, remembering the thick, dark strands he used to have, and how annoyed he would get when she and Cathy tried to clip bows and ribbons to his hair.

Had her father, she wondered, had a relationship with *his* father before he passed away?

She tried to recall an old memory of her grandparents, any at all, but came up with a big blank. Except maybe of one particular Christmas, when a large box had arrived. The package was for Cathy and Lizzy. Her father had looked angry, bordering on furious, as they ripped open the box. And when he saw them jump with joy at all the presents inside, he went berserk. They never did get to unwrap the gifts. In fact, not only did he return the large box to its sender, but he also took *all* of their gifts away that Christmas.

Why had he done that? Why was he always so angry? Why didn't she know the answer to this? Was it important—did it even matter?

Shit.

She was angry, too. She could feel the resentment in her bones. After all this time, she was still mad as hell. Cathy was right. Lizzy had always known she had a rebellious streak, one of the reasons she'd always understood Hayley so well. But she'd never stopped to put much thought to where the anger came from. She blamed the obvious people and events—Spiderman always at the top of her list. A killer. A madman. But he wasn't the root of her problems, she realized.

For the first time in her life, she understood that her anger flowed from a place much closer to home.

Her dad had been wrong to blame her for having a lapse in judgment. She had told a lie, told him she was saying goodbye to her girlfriends who were going off to college at the time, when she was really meeting Jared. That was the night she'd been taken. The night her life changed. How many times had her therapist— and Jared, for that matter—told her she'd done nothing wrong? Why hadn't she listened to them? Why had it taken her so long to understand that everyone made mistakes and they shouldn't have to suffer their entire lives for those missteps? She was done punishing herself. It was time to lay the blame at the feet of its creator.

Her father strained to open his eyes. Even after he'd succeeded, he appeared to be straining to see her. "Michelle?" he said, his voice a raspy whisper. He looked around the room. "Is Emma here, too? Where's Emma?"

CHAPTER 18

Hayley put her bowl in the sink, sprinkled it with dish soap, scrubbed and then rinsed it.

When she'd placed the bowl on the rack to dry, she stared out the window. She looked across the street, from the crumbling swing set to the broken-down truck with the For Sale sign on the windshield, to the drug dealers standing on the corner. But the only thing she saw in her mind's eye was Brian as he slammed the heavy blade of an axe into her mother's skull, leaving her with a permanent look of bewilderment. Mom must have been wondering why the man she'd stood by for all those years would do such a thing.

Hayley narrowed her eyes. It wasn't the man her mother had been addicted to; it was the drugs. Brian knew how to reel people in and squeeze them for all they had—their money, their hearts, and ultimately their souls. There had been a time when she was just a child that she had trusted Brian, but she no longer allowed her mind to wander that far back in time.

He was the devil and this time the devil was going to see the bowels of hell firsthand.

Hayley took a deep breath. Mom had been one of those women who just didn't get it—who either didn't like to or didn't know how to think for herself. For as long as Hayley could remember, her mother had let Brian make all of the decisions. In her drug-induced stupor, Mom allowed Brian to rape her only child. And yet Hayley had never stopped loving her.

And she refused to let Brian have the last word.

The man had killed her mother. And for the past two years, he'd managed to escape her and the police. But she could feel it in her bones, taste it on the tip of her tongue, sense it as an animal senses the coming rain. His time was up.

Lizzy's dog knocked into Hayley's leg, reminding her she needed to feed the animal. Lizzy owed her big-time for this. The only good thing about the mangy animal was that Hudson liked to play with him. It gave him something to do when his lost cause of a mother left him by himself.

She grabbed the last can of dog food and dumped its disgusting contents into a bowl that she left on the floor.

After making quick work of sharpening her knives, Hayley pulled up her pant leg and strapped on a sheath. With her knives in place and her baton attached to her waistband, she covered herself with a black knee-length coat and walked out the door into the cold night.

Halfway down the steps down the outside of the garage, she saw Hudson sitting outside on the main house's porch step. *Damn it.*

"It's late. What are you doing outside?"

"Mom told me to wait out here until she's done."

"What is she doing?"

"Talking to a man."

Hayley stepped past him and tried the door. It was locked. She knocked, but nobody came.

The kid was locked out of his own fucking house at eleven o'clock at night. Shit like this made her blood boil. "Come with me, Hudson. I want you to do me a big favor and watch the dog for a little while."

"Mom told me to stay right here."

She bent down so she was eye level with the kid. "Look at me, Hudson. You're too little to be outside by yourself. We both know that. Usually—in fact, ninety-nine percent of the time—I would tell you to do what your mom says. But tonight's not one of those times."

"This is in the one percent where I don't listen to her?"

"Who are you, Einstein?"

He smiled and she ruffled his hair. Then he followed her back to her place above the garage.

"Have you named the dog yet?" he asked when they stepped inside her apartment.

"Nope." She poured some chicken noodle soup into a bowl and warmed it up in the microwave. After setting the bowl in front of Hudson, she disappeared inside her bedroom to grab the tools needed to get inside Hudson's house.

Before she left her apartment, she told Hudson not to leave until his mom came to get him.

"Can I name the dog?"

"Go for it, but you might want to give it some thought before you decide, because the dog will be stuck with whatever name you pick for the rest of its life."

"That's a long time."

"Eternity," she said before she walked out the door.

She took the stairs two at a time, crossed to the house and knocked on the front door. "Becca, it's me, Hayley. Open the door!"

She gave her time, knocked a few more times, before she set to work with her tension wrench. Seconds later, she stepped inside. It was a small house. Most of the lights were out. A vanilla-scented candle burned nearby. The house was dirty, but it wasn't a pigsty. She'd seen worse, way worse. Halfway down the hall, she heard grunts and moans. Quietly, Hayley opened the bedroom door and stepped inside.

Nobody noticed her.

Becca lay on the bed with her eyes closed, smoking a cigarette, her head knocking against the headboard while some skinny white boy rode her hard, trying to hit gold.

Hayley pulled out her baton and pushed the button to extend it to its full length. Then she gave the boy a good swat on the ass.

He jumped up, knocking Becca's cigarette out of her hand. Standing on top of the bed, he turned toward Hayley. "What the hell?"

"Get dressed and get out of here. Now!"

He looked at Becca.

She merely sighed as she climbed out of bed to go in search of her cigarette.

"I don't know who you think you are," he said as he slipped his pants on. "I paid good money for tonight."

"You haven't paid me shit yet," Becca said. "You owe me forty bucks."

"I'm not paying for this bullshit." He grabbed the rest of his clothes from the floor and headed off, muttering all the way out the door and down the hallway.

Becca pulled hard on the cigarette she'd found, but couldn't get it to light up again. She crushed it into the ashtray as she glared at Hayley. "What the fuck was that all about? I needed that forty dollars."

"You can't shove Hudson out the door while you make a few bucks fucking the ugliest excuse for a man I've ever seen in my life."

Becca did her best to look offended. "He wasn't *that* bad."

"Get your eyes checked. He was uglier than shit."

"You're a bitch."

"And you're a shitty mother and a whore."

Becca growled and came at her. Hayley had her naked ass pinned to the floor with a knee to her ribs in two seconds flat.

"Who the fuck are you, Lara Croft?"

"I'm the one who pays you rent every month so you can keep food on the table. If you stop spending your money on alcohol and cigarettes, maybe you could feed your kid and buy him a winter coat that fits."

"Where is Hudson? Let me go."

"Not until you agree to never do that again."

"Do what?"

"Shove your kid outside while you whore yourself out to anyone with a dick."

"You're crushing my ribs."

Hayley let up some, but didn't let her go yet.

"I'm not going to stop smoking or drinking because some bitch tells me to. And even if I did, the fucking welfare money doesn't cover shit. I had to borrow five thousand dollars last year to get by and I've been paying five hundred dollars a month in interest ever since. I'm fucked no matter what I do."

Hayley let out a huff as she came to her feet. "That's robbery."

"Tell me about it," Becca said, righting herself.

"I have some money left over from an inheritance. I'll pay off your debt, but only if you swear you'll start setting a good example for Hudson."

"Why would you do that?"

"Because that kid of yours deserves better than this bullshit." Hayley pointed a finger at her. "I want something in writing, though."

Becca laughed.

"What's so funny?"

"That guy was ugly, wasn't he?"

It was past midnight by the time Hayley found Kitally standing in front of dive number one on their list of places where Brian used to hang out. Two men were heckling her, calling her babe and pleading with her to go home with them for a night of lovemaking like she'd never experienced.

Kitally didn't look impressed. Her short, shimmering gold dress and ankle boots made Hayley take a second look. "Aren't you cold?"

"I'm hot. Just ask those two."

"I'll pass."

Ignoring the men's offended looks, the two women headed for the door.

"What took you so long?"

"I had to deal with a problem back home."

The purple and yellow in Kitally's rainbow dread glowed neon under the single fluorescent light shining down on them. Kitally pulled a stack of business cards from her leather bag and divided them up. "I made these cards. We can hand them out and leave some on all of the tables before we go. What do you think?"

$10,000 for any tip that leads to the discovery of Brian Rosie's whereabouts.

"Whose telephone number is on here?"

"I bought one of those throwaway phones. Nobody will be able to figure out where you live, but you'll be able to answer every call." She handed Haley the disposable phone.

Hayley slid the phone into her pocket and they stepped inside.

Smoke filled every crevice of the place. The Barking Dog Bar appeared to be half biker bar and half sports bar. There was a big-screen television in every corner of the room and reruns of earlier games were playing. It smelled like greasy food and beer. Every time some guy tried to start a conversation with Hayley, she told him she was there on business and handed him a card.

Kitally tried a different approach. She flirted with a guy, got him to listen to her entire spiel about how important it was that they find Brian, slipped him a card, and then had to fight her way free of him.

After forty-five minutes of this, Kitally searched Hayley out. "This is exhausting."

"Let's get out of here."

Hayley welcomed the fresh air the minute she stepped outside.

"Maybe we could hire someone to do this for us," Kitally said.

"Give me the cards," Hayley told her. "I'll do the rest."

"Over my dead body," Kitally said. "I'll drive. After we've passed out every one of these cards, I'll bring you back to your car."

CHAPTER 19

Seth had work to do. There were bills to pay. With all the chaos of late, he'd gotten behind. Janelle was working late tonight. He sat in his office and listened to Madeline's show while he worked. She hadn't mentioned a stalker in the past three days.

"My name is Sherri," a caller told Dr. Blair. "That's not my real name. I don't feel comfortable saying my real name over the radio. I just wanted you to know I've been concerned for you ever since you started receiving those crazy calls."

"Thank you, Sherri."

Why was she thanking Sherri? He was the one she should be thanking.

"I wanted to let you know," Sherri went on, "that you're not alone. I had a stalker once. I spent years walking around in fear, always wondering when he was going to show up next. It wasn't easy, but he's behind bars now. I had to call to see how you've been holding up. I've been a huge fan of yours for years."

"I'm glad you called, Sherri. I haven't wanted to burden my listeners with my problems," Madeline began, "but the truth is, things have taken a turn for the worse. The gifts have become much more gruesome, but I want my callers to know I'll be all right. I'm thinking about hiring a bodyguard if things don't improve.

"And if he's listening tonight," Madeline continued, "I want him to know that nothing he does is going to stop me from helping my listeners. I will not be bullied. I refuse to let some maniac ruin my life. We're going to find him."

Seth had stopped what he was doing. What did she mean by "we're"? Was someone helping her look for a stalker he'd already taken care of? He shook his head. The gruesome gifts she talked about must be whatever the creep had left for her prior to his taking care of the problem.

"Just last night a dead rodent was left on my welcome mat. There was a threatening note tied to its tail."

What was she talking about?

He'd taken care of everything. He'd made the ultimate sacrifice and killed for her—twice! He felt a sharp pain in his chest. He could hardly breathe. Heat rose through his body all the way to his face as he leaned against the car and tried to catch his balance.

Madeline sniffled, only this time he could tell it was forced, the same phony noises he'd heard so many times before. She sounded just like his wife.

Madeline was lying.

Why hadn't he noticed it before?

"I've been in touch with an expert in the field," she continued. "I was told that the most frequent type of stalking cases involve a previous romantic relationship between the stalker and the victim. In most cases, the stalker attempts to control every aspect of the victim's life. But I honestly can't imagine that's the case with me. My previous relationships have all ended amicably."

His insides twisted as Madeline talked about how her life would never be the same. He couldn't believe what he was hearing. She'd been playing with her listeners' emotions, all for ratings. She didn't care about anyone but herself.

Were all women liars—his mother, his wife, and now Madeline?

The muscles in his jaw twitched as he made his way into the house. He went to the kitchen and poured himself a glass of water, willing himself to calm down. He twirled around and around like a madman. Dizzy, he grabbed a dishrag, covered his mouth and screamed as loudly as he could. Uncontrollable fury pumped through his veins.

He needed to teach Madeline a lesson. Marching through the house, knocking over decorative items as he went, he looked out the window and noticed it was no longer raining. He went to the backyard, walked toward the shed where he set traps every month. As expected, there was a dead rat, its neck caught between the snap wire. Perfect.

Back in the garage, he found some twine. Then he made a note.

Madeline's lies were about to become very real.

CHAPTER 20

Last week, Lizzy had put an ad on Craigslist to let the world know she was looking for another assistant. Big mistake, since it appeared everyone in Sacramento needed a job. By the time Hayley arrived, Lizzy had already interviewed a dozen people. The first woman she interviewed was passionate about hair. Ever since seeing Lizzy on television, she'd been dying to give her a makeover. The next gentleman she interviewed was seventy-nine. Being a private eye was on his bucket list. The woman who'd just left was in her fifties and would not take no for an answer. She was an albino. With her translucent skin and shock of white hair and light-colored eyes, at first Lizzy thought she might be wearing makeup and a wig. The woman was a little too intense, acting as if she were the only person for the job, her magnitude of energy causing Lizzy to wonder about her sanity. Lizzy assured the woman she would call her in a few days to give her an update, but the woman refused to leave, letting Lizzy know she would be outside, checking out her competition. Every time Lizzy glanced outside her office window, the woman was approaching people walking into or out of the coffee shop down the street or waylaying some random pedestrian.

Hayley entered Lizzy's office and took a seat in the chair facing the desk. "Who's that woman out there?"

Lizzy sighed. "Why, what's she doing now?"

"I overheard her telling someone at the end of the line that the job had been filled and not to bother with the interview."

Lizzy shook her head. "How many people are out there?"

"At least six now. I think the woman might've scared off a few."

Lizzy quickly filled Hayley in on how the morning had gone before they invited the next applicant to join them. The man who took his seat before them had recently graduated from Sac State. He wore oversized eyeglasses and didn't have a hair out of place. He was a manager at McDonald's but was looking for something more exciting.

"Do you have any experience that could be used in the investigative field if you were hired?"

He nodded. "I have a degree in psychology."

Lizzy saw Hayley roll her eyes.

"My dream is to become a profiler," he added.

"Déjà vu," Hayley said under her breath.

Lizzy felt the corners of her mouth tip upward. They were interviewing Jessica's twin. No sooner had the thought popped into her head than Jessica walked through the door and quietly took a seat in the corner of the room.

Hayley visibly stiffened, but said nothing.

After discovering Jessica might have a few months off before she started training at the academy, Lizzy had asked for her help in finding and training an assistant. She was tired of getting people up to speed and then losing them within a few months.

Hours later, after the last interviewee walked out the door, Lizzy leaned back in her chair and wondered if Jared was right. Maybe it was time to give it all up. It wasn't as if she was making a real difference in the world. In her wearied state, her thoughts slid to her father and the way he'd looked at her when he'd called her by the wrong name. What she would have given to have her father call out *her* name. More than anything she wanted to let the past go, but the harder she tried, the more difficult it became. After she'd left the hospital, she'd called her sister and told her the nurses had called her by mistake. She hadn't mentioned that she'd gone to see him. Cathy said she'd go right down, and knew better than to ask her along for the ride. Even if Lizzy had copped to making the visit to their father, she wouldn't have mentioned the mysterious Michelle and Emma. Until she'd gathered more information, her lips were sealed on that subject.

Her gaze fell on Hayley and Jessica, each of them flipping through résumés. In such a short time, these two had become her family. There wasn't anything she wouldn't do for either one of them.

"You have some interesting candidates," Jessica said, breaking the silence. "I know I missed a few, but of the applicants I saw, I think the man you were interviewing when I first walked in had the most potential."

Hayley gave Lizzy a knowing smile.

"What?" Jessica looked back and forth between them. It was all Lizzy could do to keep a poker face. "What did I say?"

"The guy studied psychology at Sac State," Hayley told her. "He wants to be a profiler. Any of that ring a bell?"

Jessica didn't take the bait. She just shrugged and said, "What's not to like?"

In search of distraction, Lizzy glanced outside, surprised to see Kitally talking to the woman outside, the applicant who refused to leave. What was Kitally doing here?

A moment later, Kitally pushed open the interior office door and promptly locked it behind her. She wore skintight purple pants and a sheer red blouse. When she turned toward them, her long, colorful dread swung around with her, falling across her shoulder and dangling over her chest.

Lizzy, Jessica, and Hayley stared at her, unblinking. There was something about Kitally that always demanded a closer look.

"That woman is nuts," Kitally said as she took the only empty seat available and dumped her bag on the ground.

Lizzy looked at Hayley. "Mind telling me what's going on?"

Kitally lifted a perfectly groomed brow. "Hayley didn't tell you I was coming?"

Lizzy leaned back in her chair. "Coming for what?"

"For my interview. Although it seems a little strange I would have to interview for a job we already know I'm well qualified to do. You saw what I was capable of."

"I suppose you're referring to the McBane case?"

"Perfect example," Kitally said. "I had the McBane case solved in fifteen minutes."

"What about the machete you used on an innocent man?"

"Innocent? Not only did he strike me"—Kitally lifted her chin and pointed to flawless skin—"he's been living in his aunt's attic for months. That's not normal. And the guy must have been on drugs because there was no machete."

"Can I take a look inside your bag?"

"Maybe there was a machete involved," Kitally said, "but the truth is, I wasn't going to use it on the guy. I just needed him to stay put."

"I need people I can trust and you're already handing me bullshit."

Silence.

"OK," Lizzy said, "let's talk about normal, since you brought it up. Why would you or anyone else carry a machete, of all things?"

"Are you kidding me? My machete is a workhorse. It cuts through wood as if it was butter. Because of its distinctive curve, the correct term would be parang, not machete." She shrugged. "No reason to get technical, I guess."

"Kitally has a knack for this kind of work," Hayley cut in. "She's resourceful. She notices things most people overlook. Following someone and watching them for hours on end without being noticed isn't easy. Ask Jessica."

Jessica said nothing in response.

Lizzy cocked her head, surprised to see Hayley defend her friend with such conviction.

"Kitally knows this job entails long, tedious hours in the car without breaks," Hayley added. "She can handle it."

"And how do you know this?" Lizzy asked. "How long has she been helping you out?"

"Long enough for me to know she's got what it takes, and not just in the field. She knows her way around databases and knows how assimilate and analyze the data, too."

"It appears your mind is made up."

"It would be foolish of you not to give her serious consideration."

Lizzy looked at Kitally again. "Is it your job to arrest criminals?"

Kitally's eyes widened. "Is this a pop quiz?"

"Yes."

"No, it's not my job to arrest anyone. My job is to gather information."

"She has a record," Lizzy stated.

"So do I," Hayley pointed out.

"She's been locked up more than once."

Kitally sighed. "I'm right here, people."

"OK, Kitally, why don't you tell us why you were in detention?"

"Don't tell her a thing," Hayley cut in. "It's nobody's business why you were there."

"I blew up a car."

Silence.

Kitally shrugged. "It was an experiment. Nobody died."

Lizzy crooked her neck to relieve some tension. "You were experimenting with explosives?"

Kitally nodded. "Did you ever see *License to Kill*? Bond used explosive toothpaste. I was intrigued."

Lizzy gave Hayley a disparaging look. She had no words.

Apparently neither did Hayley.

"Any other hidden talents?" Lizzy asked.

Kitally pursed her lips as she thought about it. "Many. Kali would be number one."

"Kali?"

"Stick and knife fighting, a form of martial art that favors deflection followed by a fast counterattack. Also, computer hacking and engineering would be on the list."

Lizzy figured the girl was toying with her now, pulling her leg. "How old are you?"

"Nineteen."

"High school diploma?"

"I have a master of science in engineering from Princeton."

"Well, who doesn't?"

Kitally just stared flatly at her.

Hayley said, "She's not bullshitting you."

Lizzy looked from Kitally to Hayley and back again. "How is that possible?"

"I graduated from high school at the age of fourteen." Kitally frowned. "I never did make it into the YEGS hall of fame, though."

"YEGS hall of fame?

"Young Exceptionally Gifted Students."

Hayley gave Lizzy a look that said *I told you so.*

"So you went from Princeton to jail, all in the space of five years?"

"It wasn't jail, it was a detention center and I wasn't there for long. Princeton was a breeze and besides, I'm really good at multitasking."

Lizzy closed her eyes and took a breath, then let it out. "Just because you got lucky at McBane's house," Lizzy told her, "that doesn't mean you can enter a house with guns blazing . . . or machetes . . . and get away with it. I have clients to worry about, not to mention my reputation."

"I get it."

"Why this job? From the sounds of it, you could do anything you choose."

Kitally shrugged. "For now, I choose this."

Lizzy wasn't sure she wanted to know the real reason why someone as gifted as Kitally would want to work for minimum wage doing PI work, so she didn't push it. "What do you think, Jessica?"

"If Hayley thinks you should hire her, then she has my vote."

Lizzy felt like she had just entered the twilight zone. Jessica and Hayley never agreed on anything.

Jessica looked at her watch. "I have to go." She placed a torn picture from a magazine on the desk in front of Lizzy. "I thought this would be a perfect bridesmaid dress."

Kitally whistled through her teeth. "I like it."

Lizzy held up the picture for Hayley to see. "What do you think?"

"I wouldn't be caught dead in that thing."

"Everyone can wear their own version of the dress," Jessica explained.

"Cool," Kitally said as if she was already one of the gang. "You would look great in this, Hayley. I could cut the sleeves and fix the décolletage, you know, give it more of a street chic look."

"You sew, too?" Lizzy asked.

Kitally looked bewildered. "Doesn't everyone?"

CHAPTER 21

The first thing Dr. Madeline Blair did when she walked into work the next morning and saw blood dripping down the middle of the receptionist's face was let out a high-pitched squeak. It took Madeline a second to recall that today was Halloween.

Cindy picked up a butcher knife and stabbed it into the air, replaying the scene from *Psycho*, complete with her own rendition of crazy background music.

"Very funny," Madeline said after drawing in a deep breath. "Do I have any calls from David Westlake?" After his last call in to her show, her ratings skyrocketed and she had David to thank for it. She'd left a message on his cell phone at the beginning of the week, but he had yet to call her back. She was dying to let him know what a big difference he made. She owed him big-time.

Cindy's eyes grew round. "You haven't heard?"

"Heard what?"

"I saw it on the news this morning. Mr. Westlake has been missing for a few days now. They found his car parked at his work, but nobody has seen him."

Stunned, Madeline didn't know what to say.

"Dr. Blair," the receptionist called before Madeline could slip her key in the electronic device to get into the main part of the building. She held up an envelope. "I have something for you."

Madeline took the envelope, and then swiped her card to get to her office. She passed the control room where the board operator was preparing for a show, then stepped inside her office and shut the door behind her. David couldn't possibly be missing. Where would he go? She shuffled through her purse, found her cell phone and called his wife.

"Debra, it's Madeline. The receptionist told me she saw something on the news about David missing. What's going on?"

"Listen, Madeline. I'm talking to a detective right now. I'll have to call you back."

"Is there anything I can do to help? Take the girls to school for you?"

"My parents have the girls. I'll call you later."

Madeline disconnected and put her phone to the side. She couldn't believe this was happening. She turned on her computer and read through her contact list for the number of David's good friend John. He was shocked by the news, but he hadn't seen David in over a month. She made a dozen more calls just like that one. Nobody had seen David.

Her gaze settled on the envelope. Wondering if it could be from David, she ripped it open and pulled out a note. Every letter was a different size and color, carefully cut out from a magazine: *I KNOW WHAT YOU DID.*

Her insides tightened. She examined the note and the envelope closely, but there was nothing to clue her in as to who might have made the note. She grabbed her key card and walked back to the receptionist's desk. "Could you tell me who delivered the envelope you gave me?"

"I have no idea. It was here on my desk when I arrived this morning."

"Did you see anyone outside when you drove up?"

The receptionist shook her head. "What's going on, Dr. Blair?"

"Nothing. Never mind. Please let me know right away if anything else comes in for me."

"Yes, of course. Are you sure you're OK?"

Without giving her an answer, Madeline went back to her office. Her phone was ringing. It was Debra. She hit talk and asked, "Did they find him?"

"The police want to talk to you, Madeline."

"Yes, of course. I can come to your house right now."

"No. Not here." Debra's tone was flat, emotionless.

"What's going on?"

"They have a few questions, that's all. Detective Chase is right here and he'd like to talk to you."

Debra handed the phone over before she could protest.

"I can be at your office at two o'clock on Monday afternoon," Detective Chase said in a gruff voice. "Does that work for you?"

Madeline looked at all the papers scattered across her desk. "I would prefer to meet you at my house." After he agreed, she gave him her address and the call ended.

Madeline didn't know what to think. What was going on? She couldn't imagine where David might have gone. Had he and Debra squabbled? If so, where would he go? David used to spend weekends fishing. Maybe things weren't going well at work or at home and he'd decided to pack up and spend some time with his thoughts. But why wouldn't he tell someone where he was going?

Her current line of thinking prompted her to think about her neighbor Chris. She had been so busy lately, so worried about her ratings and her career, that she'd hardly given Chris much thought. A few days ago, she'd stopped by his house on the way home from work. Since he didn't answer the door, she'd assumed he was visiting his daughter. At the time, it hurt her a little to think he wasn't able to take a minute to call her and let her know when he would be back. She looked at her calendar now and realized she hadn't talked to Chris in weeks.

Her heart raced in earnest.

She tried to recall whether Chris had ever talked to her about other family members or friends in the area, but it was no use; she drew a blank.

She gave the cryptic, creepy note one last glance before placing it inside her purse. On her way out, she told the receptionist she would be back in time for her show. She needed to take a ride and calm herself down. David was fine, she told herself. Chris, too.

CHAPTER 22

Hayley rubbed the sleep from her eyes, then looked at the clock on the nightstand: ten o'clock. It took her a minute to figure out that it was Saturday. She hadn't fallen asleep until well past two.

The sheets twisted beneath her as she turned over. Her arm dangled over the side of the bed. She might have fallen back to sleep if Dog hadn't walked over and put his slobbery tongue on her bare arm.

"Knock it off, Dog."

He barked.

"OK, OK." She got up, put on a pair of sneakers and a sweatshirt, then grabbed the dog's leash and headed outside. Before she could clip the leash to his collar, Dog ran down the stairs and disappeared around the corner of the building.

Becca was sitting on her porch step, smoking a cigarette. "What are you doing up so early?" she asked Hayley.

"Dog is messing with my lifestyle."

"Is that his name?"

"I let Hudson name him," Hayley said.

"Great. Ever since you got that mutt, Hudson won't stop badgering me. He wants a dog, too."

"You can have this one."

"No, thanks."

Hayley turned her face toward the sky. "A little sunshine. It's about time."

"I haven't thanked you yet for paying off my debt."

Hayley didn't need or want to be thanked, so she said nothing.

"I got a job downtown. I'm a barista. Pretty fancy, huh?"

"Impressive. Where's Hudson?"

"He's looking around the house for loose change. We need milk."

"Hey, Hudson," Hayley called out. "Walk me and Dog to the store and I'll buy you some milk and a doughnut."

Hudson came running. The screen door slammed shut behind him.

"Can I go with her?"

Becca exhaled a thick stream of smoke. "Sure, yeah, you two have fun."

Dog was already galloping around in the park by the time they caught up to him.

"If Mom says I can have Dog," the kid said, "can he be my dog?"

"Might as well be. I don't want him."

"Mom won't like it."

"As long as I feed Dog and let Dog sleep at my house, I think she'll be fine with it."

Hudson looked hopeful. "Maybe she'll let Dog sleep over sometimes."

"Maybe."

"Mom hasn't been yelling so much lately."

"Have you been doing your chores?"

He wrinkled his nose.

"If you clean your room and help cook dinner sometimes, I bet you she'll let Dog sleep over."

"Did your husband run away, too?" he asked.

"Nope."

"Do you have a boyfriend?"

"Nope."

"Why not?"

"Don't want one."

"Maybe the boys are afraid of your knives."

"Could be."

The kid didn't usually talk much, but today was the exception. He asked another fifty questions by the time they bought groceries and headed back across the park toward home.

Hayley led the dog and carried the groceries while Hudson enjoyed his maple doughnut. When the kid looked up at her, his face was covered with a thin coating of sticky maple glaze. He looked happy and for a moment Hayley forgot about everything rotten in her life.

Dog barked at something or someone behind her. Hudson looked back toward the market, pointed, and said, "Who's that?"

Hayley looked over her shoulder. Her heart dropped to her stomach. A tall guy, big boned, with tree trunks for legs, was coming their way. His gait was steady, his gaze unflinching, both hands hidden within the front pockets of a zippered jacket. His face was unreadable. No expression whatsoever. He looked like a man on a mission.

She and Kitally had spent the past three nights passing out cards, letting every goon in Sacramento know they were offering a cash reward for any tip leading to Brian's whereabouts. She knew it was only a matter of time before Brian got word. She just hadn't thought she'd hear from one of his messengers so soon. She needed to get the kid moving.

"Come on, Hudson. Let's get you home." She handed him the leash. "Let's see if Dog can run faster than you."

Hudson loved to run. And that's all it took to get him going.

She glanced over her shoulder again. The man began to jog.

Hudson was having too much fun. He wasn't taking the game seriously enough. A cold chill ran through her. She gripped the kid's shoulder. "Hudson. If you can make it back to the house in two minutes, I'm going to give you five dollars."

"You swear?"

"I promise. Go! Now! Run!"

He ran so fast, she was afraid he might trip over his own feet. Dog ran after him, barely able to keep up with the kid.

Hayley didn't bother running at all. She turned and waited for the man to catch up to her. She'd left her apartment so fast, she hadn't brought anything with her. No knives, no Taser, no weapon of any kind, not even her stick.

So this would be it. She hadn't planned to go out this way. For two years now, she envisioned being alone in a room with Brian. She'd planned to wait for him to make the first move, and when he did, she'd pull out her sticks, her knives, every weapon she had on her body. After he was dead, his friends would show up and she would claw and fight until her last breath; as long as Brian Rosie was dead, she could deal with that.

Hayley kept her gaze on the man's face with an occasional glance to his hands, which were hidden within deep pockets. If the brute didn't stop and shoot her, if he came up close enough, she might have a chance. She breathed in through her nose and out through her mouth. She was ready.

Six feet away from her, he stopped and stood stock-still.

Hudson and Dog were long gone.

Hayley stood motionless, feet apart, hands at her sides. If he pulled out a gun from where he stood, she would be too far away to do anything about it.

"Kristin Swift," he said in a raspy voice.

"What?"

"Wolf sent me. He said you needed a name. It's Kristin Swift."

She let out a breath. Holy shit. "That's it?"

"You're not easy to find. Next time, you might want to leave a number or some way to reach you. I've been running around this city looking for you for two days."

"Well, you found me."

Leaving her with a grunt, he turned back the other way and walked off.

As Hayley watched him go, she realized she was losing her edge. She never should have walked out of the house unprepared. It wouldn't happen again.

CHAPTER 23

Detective Chase was intimidating as all get-out. Tall and broad shouldered, he came across as ultraconfident and larger than life.

Uncharacteristically, Madeline felt like the complete opposite of confident—timid and apprehensive. No matter how hard she tried, she couldn't relax. Her palms were sweaty and she found it difficult to catch her breath.

For the past twenty minutes, the detective had sat on her leather ottoman, facing her straight on. He kept scribbling in his notebook after asking the same questions over and over, making the past five minutes feel like hours. He worded his questions in a way that tended to put her on the defensive. Simply put, Detective Chase was starting to piss her off. "David was my best friend," she said in answer to his question about why she and David talked on the phone so often.

"You've said that."

"I didn't see you write it in that notebook of yours."

"Debra Westlake told me the same thing—you and David were best friends. It's all in the reports. Nothing for you to get worked up about."

She let out a caustic breath. "If you think that's worked up, you haven't seen anything."

He straightened, like a big, mean grizzly bear being challenged. "Is that right?"

Shit. Talk about putting her foot in her mouth. He was making her feel as if she should call a lawyer. "Listen," she said in a calm voice. "More than anything, I want to help you find David, but I don't understand how asking me the same question over and over is going to assist you in that endeavor."

He ignored her statement and simply asked her another question. "Debra Westlake mentioned that you asked her husband to call in to your radio show recently. Can you tell me more about that?"

Damn. "No problem. David has listened to my shows for years and he sometimes calls in to ask questions to help get things moving along."

"Moving along?"

"Yes, to get listeners involved. For instance, one time he called in to the show to ask about depression—"

"Was he depressed?" The detective scribbled in his notebook.

She gritted her teeth. "No. David was *not* depressed."

"But he called in to your show to talk about depression."

"That's right. He was helping me out by pretending to be a caller and thus getting a conversation going about depression."

"Who decided which subject he would talk about?"

"I really don't remember. It could have been either of us. That really isn't important."

More scribbling in his beloved notebook. She wanted to snatch it from him and rip it to shreds. "Listen, Detective. I've told you everything I know. I do need to get to work soon."

"Your *best* friend is missing, but you're eager to get back to work?"

Son of a bitch. She bit her tongue and remained silent. She had a tremendous urge to bite her nails, a habit she gave up years ago.

"When a person goes missing," he told her, "we often set up a tip line, you know, for people to call in if they know anything."

She waited for him to elaborate.

"We received a tip recently from an anonymous caller claiming to be one of your listeners."

She straightened her spine. "Really? Who?"

"Even if the caller had left his or her name, I wouldn't be at liberty to say. I will tell you, Dr. Blair, this one particular caller seems to know a lot about you and adamantly believes you are up to no good."

Madeline thought about the note still tucked away inside her purse. "Up to no good? What does that mean?"

"I was hoping you could tell me."

"I really don't know what to tell you, Detective. I get strange calls from listeners all of the time. Just ask my board operator."

"I plan to."

"Why do I get the feeling you think I might have something to do with David's disappearance?"

"I don't know why you would feel that way, but now that you've brought it up, is there anything you're not telling me? Anything at all?"

She locked her fingers together, not quite sure if she was doing the right thing. But it was the truth and everything would work to her advantage if she just told the truth. "I do have a concern."

He said nothing, simply waited.

"There's a man in the neighborhood who I've been seeing for the past month. His name is Chris Porter. As soon as I learned that David was missing, it dawned on me that I haven't heard from Chris in weeks."

"Have you gone to his house?"

She nodded. "A week ago I knocked on the door, but there was no answer."

"Did you report this to the police?"

"No, because I vaguely recalled him saying something about visiting his daughter. I guess I just thought he would have returned by now or at least called me to let me know when he would be back."

Judging by the look on Detective Chase's face, the truth wasn't helping her much. Once again, he scribbled in his precious notebook. "Daughter's name?" he asked.

She felt heat rise to her face. "I don't remember."

"Does he have family or friends we can call?"

"Not that I know of." She sighed. This was not going well.

The detective gave her a long, hard look before he came to his feet. "Why don't you show me where Chris Porter lives."

She stood, relieved to be done with the inquisition.

"Before we visit your neighbor, I wanted to ask you about a novel titled *Obsessed*."

She couldn't begin to imagine where he was going with this. "Never heard of it."

"Beau Geste is the author."

Drawing a blank, she shook her head again.

"The caller I talked about referenced the book. He believes you're following the story to a tee."

"I don't understand," she said. "What's the book about?"

"It's gruesome, evidently. Set in a small town. People are disappearing. The killer turns out to be a woman, a radio personality."

Madeline crossed her arms. "This is ridiculous."

The detective pointed to her wall of books in the family room. "Mind if I take a look?"

"Be my guest."

She followed him into the other room. After only a few minutes passed, he pulled a book from the shelf and held it up for her to see.

Obsessed by Beau Geste. Her heart hammered. "This is crazy. I have no idea how that book got there."

He opened the book and read aloud, "'Thanks for being my number-one fan.' Signed, Beau Geste."

CHAPTER 24

At just past noon, Janelle walked in the door and marched over to where Seth was sitting in his favorite chair. She stood in front of him, hands on her hips, blocking his view of the television. He couldn't remember the last time he'd seen her in anything other than those ugly blue scrubs. She disgusted him.

"We need to talk."

He wasn't in the mood. He came to his feet and walked around her to get to the kitchen. She stayed on his heels. He opened the refrigerator and hunted around. "Looks like you need to go shopping again. We're out of beer."

Janelle dumped her purse on the counter. "I can only cover for you at work for so long. Whatever you're doing, it has to stop."

Heat rose to his face. He whipped around with a backhand to her face. He'd never struck his wife before, or any woman, for that matter. The act itself made him feel powerful . . . in control. He brought his hands close to his face and began to examine the deep grooves and fine lines in his palms. These hands had done things that could never be undone.

Eyes wide, nose bleeding, Janelle stared at him. "What is wrong with you? Who do you think you are?"

He answered with a smirk before making his way back to the family room. He felt suddenly restless, like a caged animal.

She followed close behind. "I won't allow you to ignore me forever. You forget who you're dealing with."

That got his attention. His wife, the one who had slept with another man, was making threats. Interesting. He turned about, took a step toward her and stood so close he could feel the beat of her heart. She smelled like bedpans and cheap perfume. "You stupid whore," he said as he wrapped his hands around her throat. "You have no idea who I am or what sort of man I've become." He pressed his thumbs into her larynx and watched her face turn red. "Do you know what I'm capable of? Well, do you?"

She tried to shake her head. Her eyes were wide and fearful, but her gaze never left his.

He let go, watched her struggle to catch her breath, enjoying every minute.

She stepped away, a hand on her throat. But instead of fleeing or threatening to call the police, she croaked, "Why can't you love me like you used to?"

He laughed. "Oh, we're going to discuss our relationship right now?"

"Answer the question. Why don't you love me? You used to."

"Because you're a liar."

"I could never lie to you. I made a horrible mistake, but I told you what I had done. Don't ruin what we still have left. If you would just give me a chance, we could make this work . . . but you must stop obsessing over that woman—"

"Now you're talking gibberish." The notion she might know about Madeline surprised him and intrigued him, too.

"Nobody knows you like I do," she went on. "I see the wistful look you get when you listen to Madeline Blair on the radio. She's not worthy of your time. She could never love you like I do."

Janelle's voice was beginning to sound like an irritating mosquito buzzing around his ear.

"I told the staff at the hospital that you've been sick," she said. "If you don't show up on Monday, what will I tell everyone?"

"It's nobody's concern."

"It is my concern. I care about you."

"So you've said." He grabbed his coat from the hall closet.

"Where are you going?"

"Out."

"I'm not waiting up for you this time."

"Just make sure you have dinner on the table when I get back."

CHAPTER 25

It was one o'clock when Lizzy entered Monty's Bar & Grill on 16th. The smell of garlic bread made her stomach grumble as she made her way to the back of the room where she could see what had to be Dr. Madeline Blair sitting in a booth. The copper-colored hair Dr. Blair had described to her settled over her shoulders in thick curls, making her easy to spot. Their gazes met as Lizzy crossed the room. Madeline gestured for Lizzy to take a seat across from her and said, "Thanks for coming."

Dr. Madeline Blair, psychotherapist and radio personality, sounded even sultrier in person. From what Lizzy had been able to gather since her call, she talked to her listeners about relationships, sex, suicide, bullying in schools, and her listeners treated her as if she were their sister or close friend. Lizzy had her doubts about the whole notion of radio psychology, but couldn't help but admire Madeline's heart-shaped face and sensuous mouth. She imagined the woman must have men lining up for dates.

While they were still exchanging pleasantries, their waitress, a young girl with braids, came over to take their order. When she was done, she looked at Madeline and said, "Are you going to be at the book club next week?"

"I don't think so. I have a lot going on. Tell Megan I'll give her a call."

After the waitress left, Lizzy noticed Madeline's gaze circling the room, her fingers entwined.

"Are you sure you want to do this here?" Lizzy asked. "We could go to my office—"

"No, we're already here." Her gaze swept across the restaurant once more. "I'm sorry. I need to relax."

"You mentioned on the phone that someone is watching you. Any idea at all who it might be?"

"No idea whatsoever." She leaned forward. "You have to help me. I don't know what to do. I'm in a horrible mess."

"Let's start from the beginning," Lizzy told her. "How long has this been going on?"

"Five days ago, somebody left me this note." She pulled an envelope from her purse and slid it across the table.

After Lizzy read it, she looked at Madeline. "What does it mean?"

"I wish I knew."

"You said a detective came to your house to talk about a missing friend, is that right?"

Madeline nodded.

"Did you show this to him?"

"No."

"Why not?"

"Because I believe someone is trying to implicate me."

"I'm not sure what you mean."

Dr. Blair told her everything that had happened since learning her friend David Westlake had gone missing. Apparently there was a man in her neighborhood who was also missing.

"So you think whoever is watching you might have something to do with Chris's *and* David's disappearance?"

She nodded.

"Have you received anything other than that note?"

"Yes, I have." Madeline fiddled with her phone and then passed it to Lizzy. "I took some pictures."

The first photo was of a bouquet of dead flowers. "Where did you find this bouquet?"

"Inside my car on the passenger seat."

"Was your car locked?"

"No, but it was inside my garage, which was locked."

"Did he damage the door?"

"I looked, but I didn't notice anything."

The next picture was of a dead rat with a note tied to its tail. "Disgusting. What did the note say?"

"'I'M WATCHING YOU.' I found the thing on my doorstep two days ago."

"Have you shown any of this to the detective?"

"Yes. The police have the flowers and the"—she wrinkled her nose—"rat in their possession."

Lizzy thought it was odd that she hadn't given the police the note as well, but it was clear she was fearful and probably not thinking straight. The woman was also thin and pale. Dark shadows punctuated her eyes. She looked as if she hadn't slept in a week. "Did you ever talk about your neighbor on your radio show?"

"No. I never once mentioned Chris."

"Can you tell me more about David Westlake?"

"David and I have been friends since kindergarten. He and his wife, Debra, have two daughters. He's a personal-injury lawyer. I called Debra yesterday for an update. Detective Chase interviewed her husband's colleagues and every one of them said it was business as usual the day he went missing." Madeline held up a finger. "But there was one night watchman who says he saw David in the parking lot that night talking to a man in a car."

"Did he get the license number of the car? The make and model?"

Madeline shook her head.

Lizzy sighed. "Crack security operative." She thought for a moment. "Did David know about Chris Porter?"

Madeline nodded. "He was the only one who knew I was seeing Chris. I hadn't even told my own sister."

"I'm confused. Are you hiring me to find your friends or your stalker?"

"Both," Madeline said. "You know what it's like to be followed around day and night? He's watching me, and I have no idea what he wants. If you can find out who this maniac is, I'm hoping it will lead us to Chris and David."

"We'll need to meet again," Lizzy said. "And I'll need you to make a list of everyone you know, especially people who might have reason to cause you harm."

"I've gotten my share of irate callers over the years, but nobody has ever threatened me."

They paused while the waitress served their food and drinks.

"I spend ninety-nine percent of my life at work," Madeline told her. "I have never stepped on anyone to get to the top. I spend my time trying to help people. I have no idea who would want to hurt me. He could be the man sitting over there drinking a beer, for all I know."

"You said earlier that someone was trying to implicate you. How so?"

"According to Detective Chase, an anonymous tipster told police to keep an eye on me. This caller mentioned a book titled *Obsessed* by Beau Geste. It takes place in a small town and lots of people go missing, one at a time. The antagonist is a woman. She's also a psychotherapist and radio personality. The only difference is the setting—*Obsessed* takes place in New Jersey."

"I don't understand how this would implicate you."

"It gets worse," Madeline said. "The detective asked me if I ever heard of the book or the author, which I hadn't. At the end of our conversation, I gave Detective Chase permission to go through my house, and lo and behold he found a copy of *Obsessed* signed by the author to his number-one fan."

"No prints, I suppose."

Madeline shook her head. "Mine either, as far as that goes, but the fact that it was on my shelves seems to have trumped that."

Lizzy exhaled. "It sounds like you may need to hire a lawyer."

"I decided to hire you first. Somebody planted that book. Nobody has a key to my house—not my sister, my brother, or my parents. I need to find out who's doing this to me. I need to find Chris and David."

"Any possibility that Chris was jealous of David?"

She shook her head. "I never once talked to Chris about David. I can't picture it."

"What about the other way around?"

"David jealous of Chris?" Madeline snorted. "Absolutely not."

"I think it would be best if I focused my attention on keeping a twenty-four-hour surveillance on your house," Lizzy said.

"What about Chris?"

"If he has a daughter or family in the area, I'll be able to find them. Maybe they can shed some light on where he's run off to."

Madeline wiped her eyes.

It was the first time she'd shown any emotion. "Are you OK?" Lizzy asked.

"I can't tell you what a relief it is to have someone in my corner. I've never been so scared in my life. I can't open a door without feeling as if someone is waiting to attack me."

Lizzy nodded in understanding.

"The thing that frightens me the most, though, is the thought of never seeing Chris or David again. I have to find them."

Lizzy nodded. "We will find them, but first we need to keep you safe. This guy has found a way into your house. Starting first thing in the morning, I'm going to be your shadow while I get to know your routine. Whenever you can, it would help if you could gather a list of contacts, people close to you or who you might have recently come in contact with. I also need a checklist of your daily routine."

Tears fell freely now. "Thank you."

CHAPTER 26

Seth waited until that time of night when even the insomniacs of the world couldn't fight sleep any longer. The bump key he'd made for Madeline's back door, the one that led into the laundry room, worked perfectly. When he was a teenager, he had lost the key to his house and was forced to find a way in without waking his parents. It was easy—so easy he'd started breaking into his neighbors' homes. Sometimes he would have a snack in the kitchen while they slept, but mostly he left everything just the way it was. Fun and games. He didn't steal anything. No harm, no foul.

He padded quietly across the floor, past the kitchen and dining room before making his way upstairs. At the landing, he stopped to listen for any sound. There were two bedrooms upstairs. Madeline's bedroom was to the right. Her door was open and he could hear her breathing.

Careful not to make the slightest noise, he placed a bag on the floor by his feet and pulled out a syringe. After readying the needle, he pulled the mask over his head. He was finally going to meet Dr. Madeline Blair. Only tonight wouldn't be anything like what he'd originally had in mind.

Two men were dead. She deserved to die for what she'd made him do, but that would be an easy out for the good doctor. She was going to suffer in ways she could never imagine. Madeline needed to be taught a lesson.

Madeline struggled to move, to open her eyes, to scream. It was no use. Tape covered her eyes and mouth. Thick, scratchy rope bound her wrists. She twisted and pulled and screamed beneath the tape.

"Don't struggle, Madeline. You'll only hurt yourself if you do."

He's here.

It had to be him. The same man who had been watching her, leaving her threatening notes, had somehow gotten inside her house. How had he tied her up? She was woozy. He must have drugged her somehow.

Oh, God. No.

He pressed his nose against her neck and sniffed like a dog.

"Stop," she said, her voice muffled behind the tape.

"You smell so good. I have dreamed of this moment for a long time. When I first realized you deceived me, I wanted to kill you, Madeline. Do you understand?" He pushed her hair back from her face and pressed his lips to her forehead.

She twisted and turned, tried to get him away from her, but he held her head to the pillow with one strong hand as he buried his nose in her hair and inhaled deeply, his breath hot against her scalp. "God, I don't know what I feel more. Do I love you or do I hate you? I think there must be a very fine line between the two, don't you think, Madeline?"

She struggled to get loose, squirmed against him, tried to get free.

With his lips pressed against her temple, he wrapped his fingers around her throat and began to squeeze, only slightly, just enough to let her know he could kill her if he wanted to. She pulled at the ropes. The rope around her left wrist felt loose. If she could free one hand, she could gouge his eyes.

The mattress dipped when he pushed himself to his feet. She heard soft footfalls as he walked around the bedroom. She wanted to talk to him, find out why he was doing this and convince him to think about what he was doing, but every word was muffled beneath the tape.

She stopped moving when she felt him hovering over her. He was touching her again, this time with the sharp tip of cold metal. She heard snipping as he began to cut her pajama top from her body. *Oh, God. Please, no. Stop.*

After he removed her top, she felt his breath close to her breasts. He smelled her again. He was a disgusting pig. He sat down on the edge of the mattress and it wasn't long before she felt his bristly jaw against her face and neck.

"You've done this to yourself, Madeline, and soon everyone in Sacramento will know what you did."

She arched upward, wriggled and bucked, anything to get him away from her. The more energy she used, though, the more difficult it was to breathe through her nose.

He pulled away.

She felt nauseous. How would she throw up, though? Her mouth was sealed. She commanded herself to calm down, to breathe evenly through her nose.

"Be still, Madeline." The tips of his fingers brushed slowly over her arm. "I need to teach you a lesson. It wasn't supposed to be this way. When you first told your listeners about some god-awful freak leaving you gifts, I wanted to be your hero. I wanted to help you in the same way you helped me after my wife betrayed me."

She squirmed beneath his touch, relieved when she felt the mattress sag before he stood again.

He walked around the room. Drawers were opened and closed. She heard him leave the room and she prayed he'd left for good. Her heart plummeted when moments later he returned and the mattress sagged beneath his weight once more.

"You never should have lied to your listeners. We trusted you. I trusted you."

She heard a crack in his voice, as if he was trying to stay calm but couldn't hide his anger.

"The first time I heard your voice, I felt things I never felt before. For months now, I've wanted to meet you, talk to you, get to know you. I wanted to be part of your life, Madeline. But you're just like every woman I've ever known. You're all liars."

She pulled at the ropes.

"Don't worry. I'm still going to be a part of your life, Madeline. Just not in the same way I first envisioned."

A few moments passed before he said, "Look at this."

It sounded as if he were flipping through the pages of a book.

"Hmm. Interesting. Hey, Madeline, who's Amber Olinger? How about Lennon Brooks? Does Megan Vos know what a lying sack of shit you are?"

Those were all names from her personal address book. She tried to shout at him, tried to get free, but he climbed on top of her. "Stop moving around so much, Dr. Blair. It's not helping matters. All of your squirming about is only making me angry and I don't think you want to piss me off any more than you already have. Do you?"

His breathing grew ragged as he rubbed against her like a dog in heat. With his full weight stretched out on top of her, she couldn't move, could hardly breathe. She had no idea how much time passed before he climbed off her.

She inhaled deeply through her nose.

His fingers pulled at the corner of the tape across her mouth. "You get one chance, Madeline, to have your say. Scream and you die. Do you understand?"

She nodded, then sucked in a breath when the tape came off. "What have you done with David and Chris?"

"Ten points for Dr. Blair. I didn't think you cared for anyone but yourself."

"Where are they?"

"You act as if Chris Porter was your friend, and yet you didn't report it to the police. If you had, it would have been in the paper or on the news."

"Is he safe?"

"He's at peace, Madeline."

She choked back a sob. "What does that mean? What the hell have you done with him?"

None too gently, he slapped a new piece of tape over her mouth. "Everyone has a beginning and an end, remember? You'll go through a grieving process. Perhaps you'll even be inspired by your own mortality."

He cracked his knuckles before adding, "Coping with loss is a personal journey. Allow yourself to feel pain and sadness. Do not resist these emotions, Madeline. I am here for you."

Oh, God. He was repeating verbatim what she often told callers who were dealing with the death of a close friend or family member. The man was insane.

"I wish I could stay and have a good, long chat with you, but I must say goodbye for now, Sacramento. Until tomorrow."

He began to cut off the rest of her pajamas, his fingertips brushing over the length of her as he removed her clothes. She couldn't see him, but she could feel his gaze roaming over her.

A moment later, he lowered his mouth to her ear. "I want you to listen carefully. I'm telling you this for your own good. Do *not* call the police. If you do, they may decide to lock you behind bars. And I won't be able to help you if you're in prison, Madeline." He pressed his mouth on top of hers and she was suddenly thankful for the tape covering her lips.

"You wanted a stalker and now you've got one."

That was the last thing he said before she felt the prick of a needle in her arm.

CHAPTER 27

Jessica stood at the door to Hayley's apartment and knocked three times. Hayley had left a message on her phone earlier, telling her she had some news about the drive-by shooter.

Hayley opened the door, then spun away and left her standing there like an idiot. She stepped inside and was greeted by a dog. "You have a dog?"

Hayley was in the kitchen. "It's Lizzy's. I'm giving him back to her as a wedding present. Come on, Dog," Hayley called. "Time for dinner."

The dog trotted their way. Leave it to Hayley to name the animal Dog. It was the mangiest-looking mutt Jessica had ever laid eyes on. Judging by the bald spots, facial scars, and limp, the poor thing looked to have been on the wrong end of a fight with a dozen raccoons. Its hair was wiry and coarse, but it looked as if someone had tried to brush it. The animal ran to Hayley, his nub for a tail moving back and forth to the beat of an invisible metronome.

Jessica looked around the apartment, surprised by the shabby-chic décor. An antique suitcase sat in one corner of the main room. Atop it was a glass jar filled with watches and broken timepieces. The round straw rug in the middle of the room was simple and beachy looking. A vintage green refrigerator and a scarred drop-leaf table with two chairs took up most of the small space in the kitchen. "I like your place."

Hayley gave a subtle nod of acknowledgment before she put a bowl of food on the floor for the dog.

"I've been thinking about all the time we used to spend together," Jessica said, hoping to break the tension between them. "I want you to know I'm sorry I didn't call or come by after everything that happened. I should have—"

"There's nothing for you to be sorry about," Hayley interrupted without turning away from the sink. "I didn't call you either."

Fair enough, Jessica thought. She twiddled her thumbs on the couch for a while as she waited for Hayley to finish what she was doing in the kitchen. A laptop and a bunch of papers sat on the wooden chest in front of her. A stack of files and a printer were piled on the floor to her left. A photograph peeked out from beneath the laptop. Curious, she pulled the picture out and held in a gasp. It was Hayley's mother. Dead. Murdered. Her bloodied corpse propped upright, an axe embedded in her skull. Unable to get her next breath, Jessica shoved the picture back under the laptop.

Knowing what had happened was one thing, but seeing it was something else altogether. It was a wonder Hayley managed to keep on going day after day, hour after hour. How often did she look at that photograph?

Jessica started at the sound of Hayley's voice. She was pounding on the window and shouting to someone.

Hayley stalked across the room toward the door. "Fuck. I'll be back in a minute." She was gone before Jessica could ask her what was going on.

Jessica went to the window to see what had freaked Hayley out, but there was nothing but the driveway and an empty park across the street with more weeds than grass. Two minutes later, Hayley was back with a little boy in tow. The boy rushed over to the dog and scratched the animal's back. Jessica found Hayley in her bedroom, fastening sheaths to her legs and snapping her knives into place. "How many of those things do you have?"

Ignoring her, Hayley grabbed her backpack and the Taser next to her bed.

"You keep a Taser next to your bed? Expecting a visitor?"

Once again, there was no response.

"Where are you going?"

Silence.

"You can't leave me with that little boy," Jessica told her. "I'm not good with kids."

"You used to watch that little girl and her brother. Besides, you can't be a worse caretaker than the boy's dumber-than-fuck mother."

Jessica had nothing to say to that.

"I have the name you wanted," Hayley said as she gathered her things.

Jessica couldn't believe what she was hearing. "You actually got a member of the Franklin gang to talk to you?"

"You had any doubt?"

"How?"

"It's not important." Hayley positioned one strap of her backpack over her shoulder and wiggled her fingers. "Where's my two thousand dollars?"

Jessica blew out some hot air and raised her arms. "I don't have it on me. I never thought you'd get a name this quickly."

"Wow, and here I thought you knew me better than most."

"Give me the name," Jessica said. "You know I'll find a way to pay you."

"Keep an eye on the kid until I get back. Then I'll give you a name."

Jessica followed her outside and watched her take the stairs two at a time. Damn her.

Back inside, Jessica realized she didn't know the boy's name, so she asked him.

He sat on the floor, petting the dog. He didn't say a word and didn't make eye contact. Jessica could take a hint.

There was no television in the place. She took a seat on the couch and grabbed the stack of papers next to Hayley's laptop and began sifting through them. There were names and addresses, maps of streets and pictures of homes in at least six different states. There were pictures of men who looked like Brian, sent to Hayley all the way from Florida, Kentucky, and New York. One printed e-mail was from a man who said he and his wife saw Brian in Nepal. Instructions for where Hayley should send money were included if she wanted his exact location.

Stacks of e-mails had been printed. They were dated as early as three months after Hayley's mother was murdered, all the way up to three days ago.

Jessica looked around and tried to picture Hayley sitting in the tiny one-bedroom apartment day after day, trying to find one man. *What was she going to do when she found him?*

There was a knock on the door, but before Jessica could get to her feet, Kitally walked inside. "Where's Hayley?"

"She ran off in a hurry. I have no idea where she went to or when she'll be back."

"She's getting my mom," the boy said, his voice a smidgen above a whisper.

Kitally went to the kitchen. "Hey, Hudson. Do you know exactly where that would be?"

He shook his head.

Kitally didn't bother asking the little boy any more questions. Instead, she walked back into the main room and plopped down on the couch next to Jessica. "Doing a little snooping?"

Jessica looked at the pile of papers in her lap and the picture of Brian in her hand and didn't try to deny it. "Can you watch the boy until Hayley gets back?"

"Nope. Not a chance. So, tell me what it's like working for the feds."

"As soon as I know, I'll give you a call."

"Cool."

Jessica rolled her eyes.

"Do you know if I got the job?"

"I haven't heard, sorry." A business card slipped out of the papers in her lap. Jessica picked it up. "A ten-thousand-dollar reward for information on Brian?"

"Yep. My dad has a few bucks. I figured we might as well put it to good use."

"No wonder Hayley keeps a Taser next to her bed," Jessica said. "Has she been passing these cards out to people?"

"I made those cards myself. We passed out thousands of them."

Not good.

"Hayley's ready for Brian and his thugs. She's been stocking up on gadgets."

"What do you mean by *gadgets*?"

"Weaponry," Kitally said. "You wouldn't believe the equipment and gear people sell on the Internet."

"I can imagine." Jessica gave Kitally the once-over. The girl appeared to have a loose tongue. Jessica decided to see how loose. "Hayley told me she found out the name of the shooter. Assuming you had something to do with that, you would know the name, too. What is it?"

Kitally raised a brow. "I didn't realize she'd gotten a name." She flopped back on the cushions. "After Wolf ordered his two biggest watchdogs to take Hayley to the back room, I didn't think I'd ever see her again. Should've known better." She grinned. "Taught me and everyone there not to underestimate her."

Jessica felt queasy. "They didn't do anything to her, did they?"

"Are you kidding me? Nobody walks through those doors without being properly initiated, but that girl kicked some ass."

"Thank God."

Now it was Kitally's turn to give Jessica a long look. "You're not so bad, are you?"

Jessica had no idea what she was talking about.

"Hayley is always talking about how uptight you were when the two of you worked together. She said you couldn't walk into a strip club without turning all pasty white and looking like you might lose your last meal."

Although Jessica couldn't imagine Kitally and Hayley hanging out together, it was obvious Kitally had gotten more than a few good laughs at Jessica's expense.

"I don't mean to offend you," Kitally went on, "it's just that you don't seem like the pansy-ass she made you out to be."

"No offense taken." Jessica held up Brian's picture. "So what's the plan?"

"What do you mean?"

"What happens when she finds him?"

Kitally raised both arms in front of her, fingers entwined as if she were holding a pistol. And then she pulled an imaginary trigger.

"What a waste."

Kitally frowned. "Why do you say that? You know what he did."

"It won't be long before Brian is caught and put behind bars where he belongs. I'm not saying he deserves to live after what he did, but Hayley would only be hurting herself by killing him. She'd spend the rest of her life behind bars because of him. *That* would be a waste."

Hayley had recognized the car she'd seen Becca climb into. The El Camino belonged to a guy who hung around Becca like a bad smell. He was always getting her high and trying to convince her to join his girls on the street. Hayley had stayed out of it, mostly because Becca did a decent job of holding her own and turning the loser down. But for some reason Becca had climbed into his car tonight.

Hayley drove to the guy's house, but his car wasn't there. Afraid she might have lost them, she kept on driving. Her first stop was his cousin's house a few miles away. Nothing there. No familiar cars. Back on the road, she pulled over to let a car pass, then decided to head for the neighborhood where he often ran his girls.

Ten minutes later, she hit pay dirt. His car was parked at the curb in front of a well-known party house. It was sixty degrees outside and yet people were crowded together on the front lawn, playing beer pong. Music blared.

Hayley double-parked. The front door to the house was open and nobody seemed to care who came and went. She wove a path, squeezing through people to get through the front room. Lots of dancing and making out going on. Two girls ground their bodies against a guy, pushing him to the wall. There were kegs of beer in the kitchen and a long row of empty bottles of booze. The floor was sticky. She looked around the room. No sign of Becca. Not until she made her way to the backyard. There she was, sitting on the loser's lap, taking a hit from a pipe.

Hayley walked over to the cozy little couple, grabbed hold of Becca's arm, and told her it was time to go home.

"I just got here."

Hayley yanked her to her feet and turned to go, only to find two guys blocking her way.

"The girl wants to stay," the taller goofball said before he tugged Becca out of her grip and pulled her to his chest.

Strangely, Hayley wasn't in the mood to fight the goons, so she decided to make up a lie. She looked at Becca and said, "There's been an accident. Hudson managed to get through the fence and into the pool."

Becca's face turned yellow. "I told him to stay in the house."

Hayley shrugged.

"He doesn't know how to swim."

"Someone pulled him out and was giving him mouth-to-mouth when I left. I called 911, but I knew I needed to come find you."

Becca pushed away from the guy who was holding her and marched away. Hayley followed close behind as they made their way through the side yard to the front of the house.

"Where's your car?" Becca shouted over the loud music.

"Right over here."

By the time they drove off, Becca was sobbing uncontrollably.

Hayley didn't tell Becca the truth until they were close to home. "Hudson is fine. He didn't fall in the pool. He stayed in the house like you told him."

It took a moment for that news to register. Becca stopped crying. "What the fuck are you talking about?"

"You have obligations—a little boy to take care of, a new job. You have to work tomorrow."

"You don't own me."

Hayley kept her eyes on the road. "Um, afraid so. I paid off your debt, remember? I own you."

As Hayley made a right, Becca opened the door and rolled out onto the street. Hayley slammed on the brakes, put the car in park, and jumped out. Becca was on her feet, muttering curses as she marched down the middle of the street toward the party.

Hayley caught up to her and grabbed her arm. "Get in the car right now or I'm calling social services."

Becca stabbed a finger at her face. "You wouldn't dare."

"Try me." Hayley turned and walked back to her car. "Go back to your party and have fun." She got behind the wheel and leaned out the window. "When you get home, Hudson won't be there. I just hope they find him a nice family because he deserves to have parents who care more about him than getting a buzz."

Becca came back to the car and climbed in. She sat low in the seat, pissed as all hell. "What are you going to do? Watch my every move?"

"If that's what it takes."

"For how long?"

"Until hell freezes over."

"You're insane."

"So I've been told."

Becca crossed her arms tightly against her chest. "What do you expect me to do?"

"You're coming home right now and you're going to take care of your kid. I'll move in with you if I have to."

"No fucking way." She pointed a finger at Hayley. "Stay out of my house."

"I'm not messing around, Becca. You're better than this. You and Hudson can have a decent life. It's up to you."

CHAPTER 28

Madeline's house sat on a tree-lined street close to Midtown, a popular cultural scene in Sacramento, where bars, clubs, boutiques, and casual dining thrived.

Thirty minutes ago, Lizzy had received a call from a frenzied Madeline Blair pleading with her to come to her house. Lizzy could hardly understand what the woman was saying. She'd managed to piece together enough to figure out that someone had broken into Madeline's home, tied her up, and made it clear he would be back. The police were on their way.

Police vehicles lined the street, forcing Lizzy to park a half a block away. When she arrived at the front door, she showed her credentials to the uniformed policeman. He refused to allow her inside until a crime-scene technician recognized her and told him to let her in. That same technician informed Lizzy that Detective Chase and Dr. Blair were expecting her and she could find them in the upstairs bedroom.

As Lizzy made her way upstairs, she saw two technicians in the living room below dusting for prints. Although she'd never been to Madeline's house before now, nothing looked disturbed. No furniture appeared to be knocked over or out of place. The stairs were wooden and cleaned to a shine. No scuff marks or any signs of any recent turmoil.

Although the bedroom door was open, she knocked to let them know she'd arrived and introduced herself to Detective Chase. He was at least six foot five and built like a tight end—neck like a tree trunk, shoulders so broad he probably had to turn sideways to enter most rooms. He had an intense look about him, as if he could see right through her, the kind of eyes that might make most people shy away.

Sitting on the edge of an upholstered chaise lounge, Madeline thanked Lizzy for coming. She wore a thick white robe, her hair was a tangled mess, and her eyes were red rimmed and bloodshot.

"There was no sign of a break-in," the detective told Lizzy.

Lizzy looked at Madeline. "I'll call a locksmith and have new locks put on every door in the house. The garage, too."

Madeline nodded.

The photographer apologized for interrupting, but he needed to take pictures of Madeline's wrists.

She obliged, holding her arms straight out. Both wrists were red and raw. Lizzy inwardly cringed. She knew what it felt like to be tied with thick rope with no way to get loose. "Where are the ropes?"

The detective shrugged. "Nobody knows."

"He must have taken everything with him when he left," Madeline added, "including my pajamas."

"He tied your wrists to the bedposts?" Detective Chase asked as he moved around the room, checking things out, careful not to touch anything.

"I already told you, I don't know." Madeline looked around. "Maybe he tied the rope to the doorknob or to something inside my closet. Yes," she said, nodding as she pointed toward the closet. "He could've tied the other end to the wooden rod in the closet."

The bedposts were much more likely. Lizzy's heart went out to her. Clearly the woman was in shock.

"How did you get away?"

"I told you I felt a pinch, a sting. He gave me something that caused me to pass out." She closed her eyes. "Before he did, he used scissors to cut off my clothes. He wouldn't stop kissing me and sniffing." She shivered. "When I woke up, he was gone."

"So it's your belief that he untied your hands and your feet, washed all evidence from your body and then took everything with him when he left—syringes, ropes, and the pajamas you were wearing."

"Yes."

"But you don't recall how he came to be in your room?"

She shook her head, then rolled her sleeves back into place after the photographer finished taking pictures.

"Don't you think it's strange he went to all the trouble to unbind you and wash you before he left?"

"Well, yes," she said, beginning to bristle. "I think the whole damn thing is a little strange, don't you?"

Lizzy wasn't a lawyer, so she remained silent, taking notes of her own and wishing there was some way she could make this easier on Madeline. Her wrists had obviously been bound. If the man had drugged her, she could have been raped. But Detective Chase didn't seem to be buying any of it.

A uniformed police officer stuck his head into the room. "Detective. There's something we need to show you downstairs."

Lizzy followed Madeline and the detective out of the bedroom and down the stairs. A crime-scene investigator had found something inside a decorative box on her coffee table. With blue latex-covered fingers, he held up a leather wallet.

"What is that?" Madeline asked.

The investigator looked at the detective, who nodded, letting the investigator know he could tell her what he'd found.

"It's a wallet, ma'am. According to the ID inside, it belongs to Chris Porter."

Madeline paled. Afraid she might faint, Lizzy helped her to the closest chair. Madeline's hands felt clammy. Lizzy went to the kitchen to get her a glass of water. When she returned, Detective Chase had Madeline on her feet. "I'm going to need Dr. Blair to come to the station."

"That wallet was clearly planted," Lizzy said. "She never would have called the police if she'd known Chris Porter's wallet was anywhere inside this house."

"I need to take her in all the same."

After he read Madeline her rights, Lizzy asked Madeline if she had a lawyer.

"Do you know of someone?"

"Of course. I'll give her a call and we'll meet you at the station. Until then, don't say another word." Lizzy turned to face the detective. "Before anything else happens, I must insist she be taken to the hospital for a full examination. If she was drugged, she could have been raped."

He stroked his jaw as if he might deny the request.

"I mean it," Lizzy told him. "If she isn't seen by someone before the hour is up, it'll be your ass on the line, no one else's."

CHAPTER 29

When Jared walked outside to get the mail, their neighbor Heather spotted him and ran across the street to greet him. "Hey there, neighbor. How are the wedding plans going?"

"Not very well. Lizzy has been busy. Without the bride-to-be around to make the decisions, this wedding just might end up being a disaster."

"What's the date?"

"December 20. I have about a month and a half to put this thing together."

"Did you order the cake?"

He shook his head. "I met with the cake lady you told me about, but there were too many flavors to choose from. After an hour of tasting just about everything they had in the bakery, I was high on sugar and I couldn't make a decision."

She laughed. "Go with chocolate devil's food cake and vanilla buttercream. You can't go wrong."

He looked doubtful. "It can't possibly be that easy. I should have taken you with me."

"I used to work for an event planner when I was in college. I've planned a lot of weddings in my day. If you need any help at all, I'm your gal."

He used his key to open the mailbox. "I might just take you up on that offer. I have a long list and nothing is getting done."

"I won't be starting my new job until the end of the month. I'm free as a bird. If you're not busy today," she told him, "we can order the cake."

"I would be forever indebted."

"What else do you have on the list?"

"I need to pick out some food. I've been told people like to eat at weddings."

She laughed. "Easy smeasy. What else?"

"Why don't I run home and grab the list?"

"Perfect. Meet me at my house in fifteen minutes and we'll get started."

His cell phone was ringing when Jared walked into the house. It was Lizzy. He answered his phone and said, "Hello, beautiful."

"Sorry I had to run off so early this morning. My newest client, Dr. Blair, was attacked last night. The detective in charge seems to believe she made the whole thing up."

"No evidence?"

"Not so far. I take that back. Remember what I told you about Dr. Blair's two missing friends?"

"Did they find them?"

"No, but they found one of the men's wallets in Dr. Blair's house."

Jared whistled. "Sounds like she needs a lawyer."

"Yes, indeed. I called Dana Kerns. She's meeting me at the station."

"If it makes you feel any better, I'm going to run out and get some things done so we can cross a few items off our wedding list, starting with ordering the cake."

"I thought you said after your last attempt you'd never taste another piece of cake in your life."

"I ran into Heather Long Legs at the mailbox. She said she would help me out. She used to be an event planner."

Silence.

"Is that a problem?"

"Of course not."

"Good, because I need to overcome my fear of wedding cake before the big day."

Lizzy laughed. "You are a very brave man and I love you."

"I love you, too."

"I should be back in time to have dinner and watch a movie."

"I'll be here."

"Without Heather?"

"Without Heather," he said. "Do I detect a hint of jealousy from my wife-to-be?"

"Maybe just a little."

"You're the only woman for me, you know that."

"Jared?"

"What is it?"

"You sure you're not having second thoughts about being stuck with me for the rest of your life?"

"You wear ugly T-shirts to bed, cry at the end of every movie, and snore in your sleep, but I love you, and I absolutely want to spend the rest of my life with you."

"I do not snore in my sleep."

"Why do you think I have half circles under my eyes every morning?"

She laughed again. "Ridiculous."

"OK," he said, feeling guilty. "Go ahead and list my flaws. I can take it."

"You're perfect just the way you are."

"Not fair," Jared said. He could see Heather coming up the walkway. "Go do what you have to do, but don't make me eat dinner alone. I have to go to Virginia in a few weeks and I miss you already."

CHAPTER 30

Thirty minutes before Dr. Blair was brought to the hospital to be examined, Seth arrived at the hospital for work. His wife was a certified sexual assault nurse examiner. The idea of Janelle being the one to examine Dr. Blair made the blood pump faster through his veins.

He'd known Madeline would call the police, which was why he'd planted the wallet for them to find. He'd selectively placed a few other surprises, too, and he wondered what the investigators found, if anything. Everything was going according to plan. In fact, planting the book in her house last week had been way too easy. Janelle was a big reader. She had a habit of telling him every detail of every book she ever read. When the idea had first come to him to set up Madeline and make her look guilty, he'd remembered Janelle talking about a novel titled *Obsessed*. Hell, she'd even stood in line for hours at the mall just to get the author to sign it. *Obsessed* was a thriller, a story about a female killer, a psychologist, too. It had all been too perfect. His campaign to set Madeline up as the villain was working out well.

The one place examiners and detectives would find absolutely no evidence whatsoever was on Dr. Blair's body. Before he'd untied Madeline, he'd given her enough etorphine to put her out for at least an hour. During that time, he'd searched her house, looking for keepsakes.

He stopped for a moment and took a breath. If he inhaled deeply enough, he could still smell her. Divine.

After using soap and water to thoroughly clean every inch of her creamy flesh, an enjoyable experience in itself, he'd taken a few pictures as keepsakes. He'd made sure her fingerprints were all over Chris Porter's wallet before he gathered his rope and his tape and exited her house.

He stood just outside the examination room. The door was closed, but he could hear Janelle's voice as she explained to Madeline the process, as well as her rights and choices. Madeline was asked to describe the events of the assault, which she did in detail.

He didn't have to be inside the examination room to know what would happen next. Janelle would perform a general health check—blood pressure, heart rate, eyes, ears, nose—and then collect evidence from head to toe, using a bright light to look for semen or saliva before taking samples of her hair and swabbing the inside of her mouth.

And then his wife would examine Dr. Blair's genitalia.

The thought took his breath away. How long would Janelle linger there? Maybe he would put an end to Janelle's sufferings and take her to bed tonight. She'd been slaving over him, covering his shifts, making his meals, washing his clothes. She deserved to be fucked.

As Seth filled out forms at the desk where he sat, another nurse's pager went off. He watched the nurse open a drawer and then take Janelle a camera that he knew would be used to photograph bruises and lacerations. He felt no trepidation, no worries at all. Other than the bruising and scratches on Madeline's wrists, there were no other signs that he'd been inside her room last night.

"I think that woman is a criminal," a nurse named Margery said in a low voice.

"What makes you say that?" he asked.

"Down the hallway. Look. There's a uniformed officer just sitting there. He's carrying a gun and everything. I asked Tim about it and he said the officer escorted the woman into the hospital and all the way up the elevator to that spot right there where he's been sitting this entire time."

He said nothing as excitement rushed through his veins. The police must have found the wallet. Everything was going as planned. Hopefully they wouldn't keep her behind bars for too long. He was already eager to pay her another visit.

"Do you think she murdered someone?"

"I have no idea, Margery. Why don't you go ask the man?"

"Oh, gosh, no. Don't be silly. What if he pulled out his gun and shot me?"

"We have security guards all over the place, Margery. I'm pretty sure they all carry guns and no one has shot you yet."

She laughed. "You're right. I am being silly." She cocked her head as she looked at him. "It's good to see you feeling better. We've all been worrying about you."

"Really?"

She nodded. "Janelle told us everything—well, you know, except the gritty details. Heck, most of us knew what was going on between your wife and Benjamin long before they started meeting every day at lunch."

His insides twisted. Janelle had told him she'd only been with the man on one occasion. More lies? It felt as if a school of tiny fish suddenly darted out of their hiding place and were now swimming around inside his gut.

"Are you all right? Did I say too much?"

"No, it's just that I thought—just assumed, really—that they mostly met after work. I didn't realize they met for lunch."

Margery blushed. "I did say too much. I'm so sorry. My husband always tells me I don't know when to keep my mouth shut."

"Listen, Margery," he said, placing a gentle hand on hers. "Everything's fine. Janelle and I have worked things out. You and I have been friends for a long time. I don't want you to ever feel as if you can't talk to me, OK?"

She smiled, relieved. "Thank you. I appreciate that. She doesn't deserve you. I—oh, my, there I go again." She made a zipping motion over her mouth. "I'm done talking. I think I'll go ask that nice policeman what that woman did, so I'll be able to relax."

He watched her walk away. Janelle was definitely getting laid tonight. When they were first married, she used to talk to him about her fantasy of having kinky hot sex that involved a bit of pain, using whips and hot wax. At the time he'd thought the idea was ludicrous.

Oh, yeah, Janelle was going to get exactly what she asked for, he thought as his knuckles popped, one after the other. He was going to do things to Janelle she'd probably never envisioned, not even in her wildest fucking imagination.

CHAPTER 31

Jessica was surprised to learn that the shooter was female. It wasn't difficult to find information on Kristin Swift. She was sixteen years old and lived with her grandparents in Oak Park, Sacramento. According to the kids in Kristin's neighborhood, she had ongoing problems with depression and substance abuse. Her actions went beyond those of the typical rebellious teenager. Not only did Kristin skip school more days than not, she got into a lot of fights and had had her share of run-ins with the law.

Jessica parked at the curb, climbed out, and walked toward the house. A few of the homes in the area had seen better days, but for the most part the street was quiet and well maintained.

She had yet to tell Eloise Hampton, the dead girl's mother, that she knew who had killed her daughter. Before she called the police, she felt compelled to talk to Kristin Swift to find out why she'd shot the bullet that killed a very special little girl.

In January, only a few short months from now, Jessica would be attending Quantico in Virginia. There would be no room in her future for letting a case get personal.

She knocked on the door and didn't have to wait long before someone answered. The woman stood well under five feet. Her hair was three shades of gray and she had dark blue eyes that peered at Jessica with mistrust. A television blared in the background. The woman held the door close to her chest, making it impossible for Jessica to see inside the house.

"Hello," Jessica said. "I'm here to see Kristin Swift. Is she available?"

"What do you want with Kristin?"

Jessica wasn't fond of using falsehoods to get what she was after. She'd never been good at weaving stories, and besides, the truth worked just as well. "I've been told Kristin might have something to do with a recent incident involving the Franklin gang. I need to talk to her about it before anyone jumps to conclusions based on rumors."

When the woman looked over her shoulder, the door came open just enough for Jessica to catch a glimpse of a young girl about Kristin's age. Eyes wide, the teenager pushed away from the table and ran to the back door. Jessica saw her yank open a sliding door and run.

Instinct catapulted Jessica forward, but the old lady slammed the door in her face, sending Jessica tumbling backward, down two steps and into a thorny rosebush. She cursed as she pushed herself to her feet, ignoring the pain as she ran to the side of the house. She caught sight of Kristin right before the girl jumped the back fence.

Jessica took a faster route through the neighbor's side yard, ran past an aboveground pool and pulled herself over a rotted fence pieced together with plywood. She landed on both feet and ran across the yard before a dog's snarl stopped her from taking another step. One inch at a time, she turned her head until she could see what breed of dog she was dealing with. Not good.

A pit bull. A very angry pit bull, maybe twenty feet from her.

She jumped, her fingers clawing into the top of the wood fence, her feet trying to find traction on the wood.

The dog snarled and snapped and she felt its breath near her leg before she kicked him in the chops. Straining, she yanked herself to the top of the fence and threw herself over. The fence shuddered as the beast plowed into the other side. Every dog in the neighborhood was barking now, sounding like a zillion sirens going off at once.

Not too far ahead, she watched Kristin struggle to climb over another fence.

Already out of breath, Jessica hoped the girl wouldn't make it, but Kristin pushed and pulled, dropped to the other side, and ran toward the main street.

By the time Jessica got to the main street, Kristin was gone. Bent over and trying to catch her breath, she took a good look around the neighborhood. Ready to give up, she heard a commotion and looked to her left just as a man raised his broom to shoo Kristin out of his yard.

Jessica took off again, her left arm stinging after being raked by rose thorns. She darted into an alleyway, close on the girl's heels. She almost had her.

Shit.

Two skinny man-boys stepped into view just ahead of Kristin, stopping her cold. The bigger of the two boys grabbed her arm and held tight. The smirks on their faces told the story. They were up to no good.

Kristin tried to pull away.

Jessica held up a hand and said, "Let her go, boys."

One of them pulled out a switchblade and made sure they could both see the blade. "Or whatchya gonna do?"

Jessica pulled out her gun, then flashed her California driver's license and said, "FBI."

They were too far away and too stupid to take a closer look. Her 20 weeks of training and 850 hours of instruction at Quantico wouldn't start until January, which meant she wouldn't have credentials or a badge until June. They ran off, leaving Kristin to fend for herself. The gun wasn't loaded, but nobody else needed to know that. It certainly had Kristin's attention.

"What do you want me to do?" the girl asked.

"I want you to sit down with your back to this wall here and don't move a muscle."

"You'd really use that thing on me?"

"Don't test me."

Her back against the wall, the girl slid down until she was sitting on the ground.

Jessica tucked the gun into her waistband and slid her wallet back into her pants pocket. Still catching her breath, she rubbed her arm. "God damn, that hurts."

"You shouldn't use God's name in vain."

"You shouldn't run from the FBI."

"How was I supposed to know you were a fed?"

A minute ago, Jessica hadn't thought she could lie her way out of a paper bag; now she was on a roll. "I want to know why you shot a bullet into the house on Fern Street two weeks ago."

"I don't know what you're talking about."

Jessica wasn't the violent type, but she found herself wanting to shake the girl. "You can lie all you want, Kristin, but I already have two witnesses and a gun with your prints that says you're the shooter." Another lie.

The girl looked worried. "What do you mean by witnesses?"

"Two members of the Franklin gang gave me your name to save their own asses. If you want any chance at all of avoiding a life sentence, you need to talk."

Silence.

Jessica bent down on one knee so she could look Kristin in the eye. "Listen, that girl you shot and killed was twelve years old. She worked hard in school and never got in a fight in her life."

Kristin's eyes narrowed. "I bet you she had two parents who loved her. I bet you they made sure she had food to eat. They probably tucked her in bed at night."

Jessica wasn't sure exactly what she wanted to hear from this girl, Taylor's shooter—maybe some remorse, but certainly not this bullshit. "She wasn't that different from you," Jessica said. "She never met her dad."

"I bet if we walked into her room right now, everything would be just right—a brightly painted room with lights that worked so she could read at night," Kristin went on, every word dripping with hatred. "I bet you she has sheets on her bed that smell like soap and flowery perfume."

Jessica stood tall again and crossed her arms.

"I wonder what she had for lunch at school every day," Kristin went on. "Do you think she had to beat other kids up for a quarter? I bet you I could guess what was inside that brown paper bag with her name scribbled on it—peanut-butter sandwich, some pretzels in one of those fancy plastic bags with the zippers and—"

"Listen, you little crybaby," Jessica interrupted. "Her mother worked twelve-hour days and she still couldn't afford to put more than a bowl of beans on the table most nights." Anger caused the blood in Jessica's veins to bubble and pop like hot grease. "That little girl you shot and killed had a name. Her name was Taylor, and in case you forgot, that little girl with the clean-smelling sheets . . . she's dead."

Kristin's gaze fell to the ground, her shoulders quivering.

Jessica wasn't falling for it. "Why did you do it?"

When Kristin looked at Jessica, her eyes were smeared with mascara. "They handed me the gun and told me I had to shoot it if I wanted to be part of the family."

"And so you blindly did as you were told?"

"Why not? I did everything else they told me to do." She wiped her eyes and nose clean against a shirtsleeve. "Thirty minutes before they drove me to Fern Street, they passed me around like a chocolate dessert for everyone to nibble on, so I figured what the hell. What did I have to lose?" Kristin closed her eyes tightly but that didn't stop the tears from leaking out. "I never meant to hurt anyone," she said, whispering now. "I never meant anyone no harm."

CHAPTER 32

Forty-eight hours after Dr. Madeline Blair was attacked and then taken to the police department for questioning, she was released. With a lawyer at her side and no proof of wrongdoing, the police were unable to make an arrest.

In order to get the investigation started, Lizzy needed a list of names—family and friends. She still had a lot of questions for Madeline. Afraid to leave her house, Madeline insisted they meet her at home.

Because Lizzy would need help with the investigation, she'd asked Hayley to join her. Hayley had already arrived, her car parked at the curb. She'd brought Kitally, Lizzy's newest employee, along with her, and the two girls were leaning against the car, waiting.

After Madeline allowed them inside her home, quick introductions were made. Madeline looked much better than the last time Lizzy had seen her. She wore formfitting athletic wear and running shoes. Her hair was tied back, which served to accentuate her high cheekbones.

Once they were seated in Madeline's living area, Kitally and Hayley pulled out their laptops and Lizzy paper and pen for taking notes.

Lizzy spoke first. "As you know, Madeline, I called this meeting together because we can't begin an official investigation until we're familiar with all the facts of your case. I realize the past few days have been tough, but we won't be able to help you until we look at everything."

Madeline nodded.

"About the night you were attacked, do you recall anything unusual—for instance, any strange smells?"

"Moldy, stale," Madeline said. "He smelled like death."

"How about his voice? Can you describe it for us?"

"In my opinion, most men tend to sound monotone," Madeline said. "This guy's voice had much more range. It's hard to explain, but I guess I would say his voice sounded borderline feminine. Quiet for the most part, but then he would get angry and his voice would crack with emotion."

"Did he have an accent?"

Madeline shook her head.

"And you never got a glimpse of him?"

"No. I couldn't see him at all." Madeline's eyes widened. "He did make a strange noise with his tongue and he tended to crack his knuckles every so often."

Lizzy wrote it all down.

"What about the neighborhood?" Kitally cut in. "Did anyone around here see anything? Or what about you, have you seen anything suspicious in the area lately?"

Lizzy sighed. She'd explain the rules to Kitally later when they were alone. There was a pecking order. She asked the questions first, and then if she missed anything, her assistants could speak up.

Madeline held a file on her lap. She flipped it open and handed Lizzy a flyer. "I did find this in my mailbox yesterday. My neighbor Mr. Whitton, a retired MP, passed out flyers to the neighborhood after his wife noticed a Honda Civic parked at the curb for hours."

"If you could give me the Whittons' address, I'll pay them a visit," Lizzy said.

Madeline pointed out the front window. "No need to give you an address. They live in the blue-and-white house right across the street. You can't miss it."

"Thanks," Lizzy said, moving along. "Can you tell us what your daily routine was before you began receiving strange items at your doorstep?" Lizzy had already filled Hayley and Kitally in on the specifics of what Madeline had been through, so there was no need to repeat what she already knew.

"I used to run every morning around seven. I stopped after I realized I was being watched."

"After your run, what did you normally do?"

Madeline gestured toward the file in her lap. "I wrote it all down for you. After my run, I would usually make myself breakfast, take a shower, maybe do some laundry or run a few errands—grocery store, post office, hair salon, et cetera. I like to be at my office on Madison by two o'clock. That's when I determine what I'll be talking about on my show that day. If I have a special guest I want to have on the air, I'll plan weeks in advance."

"Did you say the Honda Civic the neighbor saw was silver?" Hayley cut in.

Madeline nodded.

"This article I found online," Hayley went on, "says that David Westlake was seen talking to a man driving a silver Honda Civic."

"Good work," Lizzy said. "Could you bookmark that page and see if you can find the name of the man who saw David Westlake, or the security company's name?"

"I've got it."

"Great, let's make it a priority to talk to him." Lizzy tapped her pencil against her chin. "How about restaurants? You said Monty's Bar & Grill was one of your favorites. Do you usually eat lunch out?"

Madeline nodded. "I go there a few times a week. Usually Tuesdays and Thursdays. Same table, same waitress . . . Amber, the young girl you met when we had lunch."

It took another twenty minutes to find out which bank Madeline used and also her nail and hair salon, post office, grocery store, et cetera. It was time to move on to her personal life and family members.

Kitally stood.

"What is it?" Lizzy asked.

"I need to use the bathroom?"

"Down the hall to the left," Madeline told her.

"Any sisters or brothers?" Lizzy asked next.

"One of each. Both older. My brother recently moved to San Francisco. My sister lives downtown. Mom and Dad moved to Folsom a few years ago."

"Any ex-boyfriends or old roommates—anyone who might hold a grudge for any reason at all?"

"I have a few ex-boyfriends, but offhand I only know what two of them are up to. One is married, living in Los Angeles, and the other guy is living the good life on the beaches of Thailand." Madeline handed Lizzy a list of names. "Here's a list of everyone I know, family and friends. But I really don't think it could be anyone I know."

"Sibling rivalry?"

"No way. All three of us are proud and supportive of each other's accomplishments."

"If it's all right with you, I'd like to talk to your family members and coworkers."

"That's not a problem."

Kitally returned to the room holding a magazine. Lizzy was about to lecture her about touching other people's things when Kitally opened the magazine and held it up for all to see. The inside pages had been cut up; some pages had one missing letter in the header, others were cut to shreds. "Didn't you say Dr. Blair received a note made out of letters cut from a magazine?" Kitally asked.

Madeline paled.

Lizzy came to her feet. "Set that on the table, will you? Whoever was in this house obviously left more than just a wallet for the police to find. If you're OK with it, Madeline, I think it's time we all take a look around to see what else we can find."

Madeline agreed.

"I have an evidence kit with latex gloves in the trunk of my car." When Lizzy returned, everyone put on a pair of gloves. Without further instruction needed, Hayley focused her search in the dining room/kitchen area, and Kitally made her way upstairs.

Madeline stayed where she was, her face pale.

"We need to search every bit of this house," Lizzy explained, "turn every room upside down. I don't think it would be wise to wait for the police to show up with a warrant and find any more surprises. Every bit of this house, every drawer and closet needs to be—"

"I think this guy is using a bump key," Hayley interrupted.

Lizzy and Madeline followed her through the kitchen and to the back door. Hayley pointed to the doorknob. "If you look close enough, you can see tiny scratches. The window next to the door has been tampered with, too, which tells me that's probably how he got inside the first time. It's easier to make a bump key if you can get the door open. If he got inside, he could have keys to every door in the place."

"How does a bump key work?" Madeline wanted to know.

"It's easy. You just need an old key that fits the lock and a file."

It was hours later when Lizzy and Hayley joined Kitally upstairs. On the bathroom floor, they found a used syringe that Madeline insisted she knew nothing about. A window repairman was fixing all the locks and making sure every window in the house was secure.

"How's it going?" Lizzy asked Kitally.

Kitally was in Madeline's bedroom. "I'm almost done," Kitally informed them. "One more drawer to check—oh, would you look at this?" Kitally held up a vibrator. "It's one of those dual-action rabbit thingy-boppers." She turned it over in her hand. "Huh. I first heard of this thing on a *Sex and the City* episode. I need to get myself one of these."

Lizzy looked at Hayley.

Hayley shrugged and walked away.

It was late afternoon by the time they finished. The locks had been changed and the window repairman had just left. Hayley and Kitally were waiting outside. That's when Lizzy told Madeline it would be a good idea for her to hire all-night security. Lizzy also thought it would be best if she returned to her normal routine. For the next week or so, Lizzy would meet Madeline at seven in the morning for a run in the park.

"I won't be able to keep up with you," Madeline said. "I haven't run in weeks."

"I'm not exactly breaking any records," Lizzy told her, "but either way it won't be a problem since I'll be doing more looking around than running. If we want to find this guy, we need to get you out of this house."

"I guess this means we're going fishing and I'm the bait?"

"Exactly." Lizzy stepped outside and added, "I noticed a gun vault in your closet."

Madeline nodded.

"I suggest you keep a gun loaded and close at hand."

"I will. Thank you for your help. You're the only one who seems to understand what I'm dealing with here. My family thinks it will all just go away if I pretend it's not happening and the police have blinders on. I don't want to give up my life for this maniac."

Lizzy didn't know what to say. Three million people were stalked every year. Too many people wanted control and thrived off of making others miserable. She knew what it was like to feel tightness in her chest every time she heard a creak or quicken her pace if a breeze caused a tree branch to sway. Only recently had she learned to relax within the safety of her own home.

Madeline rubbed her arms as if she were cold. "We need to find David and Chris before it's too late."

Lizzy's heart went out to the woman. At this point, they didn't have much to go by. But sooner or later this man, whoever he was, would start making mistakes . . . Lizzy was counting on it.

CHAPTER 33

Hayley and Kitally left Lizzy at Madeline's house and drove directly to Roseville and the interview they'd arranged with Andrew Morales, the man footing the bill for their search for his missing brother-in-law, Owen Santos.

Andrew's wife left a tray of hot tea and cookies on the dining room table for them before she made herself scarce.

Andrew rested his elbows on the table, hands clasped, and said, "What have you found out so far? Any leads?"

"No leads yet," Hayley said. "In fact, your sister, Robin, doesn't seem too eager to find her husband."

Andrew sighed. "She's angry, that's all. When I first hired you all to find Owen, I had no idea my sister was so bitter."

"Because of the other women in his life?" Kitally asked.

"Apparently," he said. "I can't imagine it, though."

"Why is that?"

"He's not exactly a ladies' man and I never saw him leave the house much. In fact, I never understood what Robin saw in him. When I would visit, Owen was usually on his computer in the den. He's quiet, nerdy, hardly ever says two words to anyone other than his fish."

"His fish?" Kitally asked.

"They have a koi pond in their backyard. If he isn't on his computer, he's outside talking to the fish."

"Talking to them."

He smiled. "That's right. Every fish in that pond of his has a name, too."

Kitally lifted her eyebrows and nodded slowly. "All right then. Only talks to his fish."

Andrew looked over his shoulder as if to make sure nobody was listening in on their conversation. "Anyhow, like I said, I'd have to see it with my own eyes before I could imagine him taking up with another woman."

"But then why else would he leave?"

"I guess to start a new life. Robin showed me their bank account. He withdrew two large sums, cleaning out their savings and retirement account only a few weeks before he disappeared."

"Are you sure he withdrew the money and not his wife?"

He nodded. "Police already checked all of that out. When the bank showed them proof that he was the one who withdrew the money, they dropped the case."

"If Robin doesn't want to find her husband," Hayley said, "maybe we should back off."

"No," Andrew blurted, shaking his head. "I refuse to let that man off the hook. He has two daughters who need looking after. They'll both be in college before long. I love my nieces, but I have my own kids to look after. I don't care how angry Robin becomes; I don't want you to stop looking for him. We need to find him. I'm going to make him pay back every cent he took out of that bank account. Most of that money belongs to Robin and the girls. He needs to come back home and be a man, face his responsibilities."

"We need information," Hayley said, "but your sister refuses to let us talk to her daughters."

"I was afraid of that." He stood. "They're in the back room with my daughter. It's my day to pick the kids up from school and keep them until dinner. That's why I asked you to come today."

Andrew walked to the back of the house and returned a few minutes later. "This is Abbi," he said, "and this is her younger sister, Lara."

He had the girls sit down in the chairs facing Kitally and Hayley.

Abbi, the older girl, aged sixteen, was not happy, while Lara, fourteen, couldn't keep her eyes off Kitally's rainbow dread. Hayley found it difficult to believe they were sisters. Abbi had straight black hair framing dark eyes and a set jaw while her sister, Lara, was all smiles and dimples beneath a wild display of curly brown hair.

After Andrew took a seat at the far end of the table, Abbi said, "What's this about, Uncle Andrew?"

"These women work for the private investigator I told you about. They're here to ask you a few questions, that's all. I know your mom doesn't like to talk about it, but we need to find your father."

"Why?" Abbi asked.

"Because your father has responsibilities. He took your mom's savings, the money she needs to put you girls through college. You want to go to college, don't you?"

Abbi wanted nothing to do with any of this. Definitely her mother's daughter.

"Don't you miss your dad?" Kitally asked.

"No," Abbi said, too quickly.

"I do," Lara said. "Dad used to tuck us in at night and tell us a new knock-knock joke every day."

Abbi glared at her sister. "Mom already told you she'd buy you a whole bunch of knock-knock joke books."

"I miss Dad," Lara shouted. "I don't know why you and Mom hate him so much."

"We don't hate him. You don't know what you're talking about. He left you. He left *us*," Abbi said. "Why don't you get that?"

Lara hit the table with her small fist. "This is why I want Dad to come home. You and Mom haven't been the same since he left. Nothing has been the same. You guys never smile or laugh." Lara looked at Hayley. "We used to do things together. We all used to laugh all the time."

While the younger girl continued on with a list of the good ol' days, Hayley noticed a twitch in Abbi's jaw. The girl obviously didn't feel the same way about her father as her younger sister did. She was a cutter. Abbi wore a long-sleeved shirt and when she saw Hayley looking at the collection of crisscross scars on her wrists, she tugged the sleeves lower until her hands were covered, too.

"Let's all calm down," Andrew said. He looked at Hayley and Kitally. "Any more questions?"

Kitally looked at Abbi. "I was hoping you could tell us about the last time you saw your dad. What was he wearing? What was he doing?"

Abbi's jaw clenched.

"Just answer the question," her uncle prodded, "and then we're done here."

"I don't remember," Abbi said.

"That's not true," Lara cut in. "You told me that the last time you saw Dad he was feeding the fish."

Abbi blushed. "Yes, I forgot. He was feeding the fish." She turned angry eyes on her sister. "Why don't you remind me what he was wearing that day, too? Did I tell you that?"

Lara's eyes narrowed. "I hate you."

"That makes two of us."

Lara shoved her chair back from the table and ran off.

"Girls, girls," their uncle said, trying to get things under control as he went after the younger sister.

For the first time since she entered the room, Abbi looked Hayley straight in the eyes and said, "Mom is not going to be happy to hear about you two coming to speak with us today." She came to her feet. "I think we're done."

CHAPTER 34

It was Wednesday morning. Early.

Seth slunk low in his seat, surprised to see Madeline running in the park. And she was with a woman he didn't recognize. A bodyguard? That made him snicker. Madeline's friend was a tiny thing. Safety in numbers must be what Madeline was thinking. Silly girl. Madeline had stopped running after she lied to her listeners about having a stalker. But now that she really had one, she appeared to be trying to move on with her life as if nothing had changed.

Madeline really knew how to push his buttons.

Without a body, Chris Porter's wallet wasn't enough to keep Madeline behind bars. He needed to up his game, make her see who was boss. Madeline should have lost her job by now. Hell, she should be hiding behind locked doors, afraid for her life, not running around the park, free as a bird.

To make matters worse, ever since discovering that Dr. Blair had been taken downtown for questioning, local media had been hanging out at the radio station. Madeline had also retained one of the best attorneys in the area. The bitch was getting more attention than ever. His jaw twitched at the idea that he might have helped boost her ratings.

"Don't look now," Lizzy told Madeline, "but when we curve around the park again, I want you to glance at the driver and tell me if the man sitting in the Nissan parked along the curb looks familiar."

As they came around the corner, Madeline said, "All I can see is a shadow. What do we do?"

"Just hang tight. Keep a steady pace. Whatever you do, don't let on that you know he's watching us. When we get a little closer, let's try to get a look at the license plate number."

"What if he has a gun? What if he comes after us?"

"If it's our guy, I don't think he'll risk getting out of the car. There are too many people around."

"I don't know if that makes me feel better."

As they drew closer, Lizzy stopped and raised her cell phone as if she'd just received a text. As she tapped out a faux response, she was actually opening the camera app and tapping the screen to zoom in—but instead of a car on the little screen, all she saw was an angry blonde marching toward them.

The Nissan pulled away from the curb and drove off.

Shit.

"That's Debra," Madeline said. "What's she doing here?"

Lizzy frowned, still upset that the car had gotten away before she had a chance to get a good look at the plates. Whoever was inside the vehicle wouldn't make the same mistake twice. Meanwhile, the agitated blonde was still bearing down on them. "Debra?" she asked.

"David Westlake's wife," Madeline said as they waited for the woman to approach.

"David thought you walked on water," Debra said the moment she was within hearing distance. "There wasn't anything he wouldn't do for you." Every word was lined with bitterness. "He fixed your car, loaned you money, spent too many weekends being your handyman, but it was never enough."

Madeline reached out to the woman, as if a friendly hug would make things better, but pulled up short when she saw Debra's expression. "Debra, what are you talking about?"

Debra Westlake stood about an inch taller than Lizzy. Her blonde hair was pulled back into a ponytail. If looks could kill, Madeline would have fallen over dead two minutes ago. Debra's face was all angry lines and flared nostrils.

"It's all over the news," Debra said. "David isn't the only man in your life who has suddenly gone missing. Your neighbor is also missing and they found his wallet in your house." Debra stepped closer and shoved Madeline, making her lose her balance. "You killed my husband. What did you do with his body? Tell me!"

Lizzy stepped forward.

"Stay out of this," Debra growled. "You have no idea what kind of person you're helping, do you?"

Without giving Lizzy a chance to respond, Debra pulled a CD from her purse and handed it to Lizzy. "Go back to your office and listen to that so you can see what kind of monster you're dealing with."

Madeline raked her hands through her hair. "Debra, what is going on?"

Debra tilted her head. "Wide-eyed and innocent until the end, huh?"

This time Madeline didn't take the bait. Instead, she kept her mouth closed and let the woman have her say.

"I have lawyers, too," Debra went on. "Thanks to them, I now have recordings of all your shows, Dr. Blair."

Madeline shook her head.

"Have you told Ms. Gardner here that you asked David to call in and pretend to be your perverted stalker?"

Madeline reached a hand toward the woman as if she wanted to take her in her arms and make the pain go away, but Debra was not having any part of it. She lurched back as if Madeline's hand were a snake ready to strike, then settled her gaze on Lizzy. "Before my husband disappeared, he'd been acting strange . . . withdrawn. I knew something was bothering him, so I asked him about it. He told me that Madeline had asked him for a favor. She wanted him to call in to her radio show in hopes of getting more people to do the same. David told me that if Madeline's ratings continued to fall, she might lose her job.

"The worst part of it all," she continued, "is that I told David he should help her out. What harm could it do him to make a couple of calls?" She wiped her eyes. "He never told me what exactly Madeline was asking of him."

Debra turned back to face Madeline. "The reason I never pressed the issue and asked him to give me details, Madeline, was because I thought I knew you. Who the hell have I been inviting into my house all of these years? What sort of person have I let play with my children? What kind of lunatic would ask her best friend to call in and pretend to be a perverted stalker?"

Madeline said nothing.

"I want an answer." Debra's hands shook wildly. "You killed him, I know it! Tell me where you buried my husband after he refused to make any more crazy calls. Tell me!"

"You can't possibly believe I would ever hurt David."

Lizzy tried to step between them. "Maybe we should take this back to the house and talk there."

"Listen to the calls," the woman told Lizzy, her voice dripping with contempt. "And when you're done, you might want to take a long, hard look at who you think you're trying to help. I wouldn't be surprised if you're the next one to disappear. She's just using you like she's used everyone else in her life."

Lizzy and Madeline watched Debra Westlake walk away. "Is it true?" Lizzy asked.

"I had nothing to do with David's disappearance. How many times do I have to say it?"

"That's not what I'm asking. Is it true that you had David call in to your show and pretend to be a stalker?" Her silence was all the answer Lizzy needed. "Why didn't you tell me?"

"Because I was embarrassed. It was a stupid thing to do."

"Does your boss at the station know what you were up to?"

Madeline shook her head.

Lizzy started walking off.

"Where are you going?"

"I'm done with this."

"What do you mean?"

"I can't work with someone I can't trust."

"I've told you everything but that."

Lizzy was fuming. She thought about the wallet, the note Madeline never handed over to the police, the magazine with the cutout letters . . . and now this. Dr. Blair had asked her friend to call in and pretend to be a stalker. She didn't know what to believe any longer. Debra was right. She didn't know this woman.

Hearing Madeline following her, she turned to face her. "You better think long and hard about what you've done. It was not only an unethical and stupid stunt, it could very well be the reason two people are missing, or worse . . . dead."

"What if he comes back to the house? My life is in danger. Please, I need your help."

Lizzy couldn't recall the last time she'd felt so damn angry. "You said you had a gun," she said as she walked away. "Well, I hope you know how to use it."

CHAPTER 35

At the sound of footsteps coming up the stairs, Brian Rosie reached for his gun. Three knocks sounded before the code word was said aloud. Brian pulled away from the Glock and pushed a button on the remote. The door clicked open.

Merrick, taller than shit, his greasy mustache drooping down to cover his entire mouth, strolled into his office and flicked a card on the table in front of him. "This chick is going to cause you some serious trouble."

Brian didn't like being interrupted. He was doing the books like he did every month but he didn't like the way the numbers looked. "We've got leakage," he said.

"Again?"

"Close to five percent this time. Someone is siphoning cash right off the top. We only have three guys counting the money before they hand it over to me, right?"

Merrick nodded.

"I need you and Frank to figure which of the three it is and then"—he pointed to the chair in front of his desk—"I want him sitting right there by the end of the week." Raking his fingers through his hair in frustration, he noticed the card and picked it up. "Mother*fucker.*" He let out a good long laugh. "That girl doesn't know when to give up, does she?"

Merrick threw himself onto the couch. "Apparently not."

"Where did you get this?"

"I have gotten no less than five calls asking if the reward money was legit."

"What asshole would be stupid enough to call and ask you that?"

"You don't exactly have a bunch of geniuses working for you, but the good news is they have no idea where you've been hiding out for the past two years. Most of 'em think you're soaking up the rays somewhere in the Bahamas."

Exactly why some dickhead thought he could skim off the top and get away with it, Brian thought. He looked at the card again. Where would Hayley Hansen get ten thousand dollars to offer as reward money? It had to be a bluff, a way to flush him out of hiding. "I've got an idea," Brian said.

"What is it?"

"I want you to find someone you can trust, someone who has never heard of my name before, and then I want you to pay them to pretend to be interested in the reward. This guy will call this number and tell whoever answers that he wants proof before he gives her any information about my whereabouts."

"And then what?"

"Let's just take it one step at a time."

Brian had always known that Hayley had a stubborn streak a mile wide. But he'd thought he'd taught her a lesson once and for all when he kept his promise and killed her mother. If that didn't teach a girl to mind her own business, what would?

"I don't know," Merrick said. "From the sound of it, Hayley and her little girlfriend have passed out thousands of those things."

Brian perked up. "What little friend?"

The man shrugged.

"Find out everything you can about this other girl. I want details."

"Not a problem. If they really have the money, it might not be long before someone falls for the bait."

"Anyone who knows me," Brian said, "knows it isn't possible to spend ten thousand dollars from their grave."

CHAPTER 36

As he paced the stained carpet covering the floor in the dingy hotel room, Seth cracked his knuckles and clicked his tongue. The rage he'd felt when he first learned of Madeline's betrayal had continued to build in intensity. Fury threatened to blind him. Madness made it difficult for him to think. The emotions he'd been experiencing went well beyond anything he'd ever felt in his life.

Every time he thought about Madeline and what she'd made him do, all for the sake of her show's ratings, his blood pressure skyrocketed. It happened again now. The flashing strobe lights triggering havoc inside his brain. He raised his hands to both sides of his head and squeezed hard, anything to make it stop.

It didn't help matters that the woman tied to the bed wouldn't stop sobbing.

He marched to the bed, took hold of both her skinny shoulders, and shook her. "You need to . . . stop . . . all that . . . *crying*." He shook her so hard, the back of her head rattled against the headboard and the headboard rattled against the wall. "If you don't *stop* . . . I won't have any choice . . . but to shut you up . . . once and for *all*."

Another minute passed before he realized she'd already stopped crying. He let go of her. "That's better," he said, his voice ragged.

Her body still quivered like the scared little mouse she was, but at least she was quiet now. He sat down on the edge of the bed and ran his fingers through her hair. Madeline's little waitress friend might not be kind on the eyes, but she had nice hair. "I'm going to remove the tape from your mouth so you can blow your nose."

Before he removed the tape, he picked up the box cutter from the table next to the bed and held the sharp tip in front of her face. "Don't make me use this on you, OK?"

Eyes wide, she nodded her head so fast it was almost comical.

He set the knife aside. Her arms and legs were secured. There was no way she could grab the box cutter and use it to defend herself, but he wanted her to know it was right there if he needed to use it. Now that she'd stopped crying, the flickering lights inside his head died down some. He grabbed a tissue from the box on the nightstand and then pulled the tape from her mouth.

He hadn't bothered covering her eyes with anything.

She didn't know it yet, but she wouldn't be leaving the hotel room alive. If she thought she didn't have a chance of surviving, she'd really be making some noise.

He held a tissue to her nose as she blew. The girl probably wouldn't believe it, but he really did feel bad about this. She was just an innocent bystander who happened to have a connection to Madeline Blair.

This was all Madeline's fault, and she'd all but provided him a map to the people best qualified to help him punish her. Madeline's address book contained endless names and addresses, all meticulously organized with titles next to names: waitress, repairman, hairdresser, book club member, and so on.

"So," he said to the girl when she was done blowing her nose like a good girl. "Your name is Amber—isn't that right?"

She nodded.

The room was warm but Amber shivered as if it were thirty degrees in here. She was such a scrawny thing. He glanced at the suitcase he'd brought and realized it was big enough to fit two of her inside. It would be no problem wheeling her out of there. He wasn't worried about security cameras since the hotel was older than dirt and should have been condemned years ago.

It boggled the mind to think of how simple it had been to get Amber to come to the hotel room. Initially, he'd had a difficult time deciding between Madeline's hairdresser and the waitress who served her at Monty's Bar & Grill twice a week. Both women were a part of Madeline's book club. In the end, he'd picked the waitress because Amber made it so damn easy for him. People would do anything for a few bucks. Right there on her Facebook page: not only did she offer massages, but she made house calls.

And as advertised, she'd arrived right on time.

"Why am I here?" she asked, her voice squeaky and irritating.

He opened his wallet, pulled out a one-hundred-dollar bill and set it on the nightstand. "That money is all yours when we're done here. I just need you to do me a couple of favors, that's all."

Her bottom lip trembled. "Are you going to rape me?"

"Oh, God, no." He wanted to gag at the idea of touching her in that way, but instead, he forced a smile. "You have absolutely nothing to worry about, Amber. I'm a married man with responsibilities."

"Then why are you doing this?"

"Because there's a woman," he said, closing his eyes at the thought of Madeline, "who needs to be taught a lesson."

"I don't understand."

"Of course you don't. Do you know who Madeline Blair is?"

Her eyes grew wide. "Yes, of course. She's my good friend. We met at the restaurant where I work. We're even in a book club together."

"You don't say."

"Yes. We meet once a month." Her gaze roamed over him as she tried to relax. "So, did Madeline do something?"

"The sooner you help me out, the sooner I can let you go."

She leaned forward, as far as the ropes would allow. "What do you need to know?" She was chomping at the bit to tell him anything and everything. She was one of those gutless people who would sell their soul to the devil without any negotiating.

"I need you to tell me everything you know about Dr. Blair. When that's done, we're going to make a phone call."

"Is this Madeline?"

"This is she."

"It's Amber . . ."

"What's going on? Is something wrong?"

"There's a man here. He wants you to know that he wishes he could be there with you now. He misses you, and he—"

"What's his name?"

"He hasn't said."

"Amber, I don't know what's going on, but do you know this man you're with?"

"No."

"You're not alone with him, are you?"

"I am, but he just wants—"

"Amber, if this isn't some sort of prank . . . if there really is a man there with you, he could be dangerous and you need to get away."

"He promised to let me go after I told him everything I knew about you. I think he's . . . he's in love with you, Madeline."

"He's obsessed," Madeline said. "He's crazy. You need to get away. Right now."

"I can't. He's tied me up. I—"

"Where are you, Amber?"

Seth slapped a piece of duct tape over Amber's mouth before she could say any more. Then he grabbed the phone from her. "Madeline, Madeline. If she told you where she was, that would ruin all the fun."

"Who is this? What are you doing?"

"I'm your stalker, remember?" His fingers tightened around the phone. "The one who leaves you gifts and keeps you awake at night. I'm teaching you a lesson. How many times do I need to tell you that?"

"Let Amber go. I'm begging you."

He put his face right up next to Amber's so that their foreheads touched. "Hmm, that doesn't sound like begging to me. Does it sound like she's begging to you, Amber?" He pressed the phone to Amber's ear.

"Please," Madeline cried. "I'll do anything. Let her go."

"Anything?" He kept the phone so that both he and Amber could hear. "What does that mean, exactly? If I come to the house right now, will your friend from the park be there?"

"No, she's not here. I'm alone. I'll do anything you want, just let her go."

"Liar. I hate liars."

"I've learned my lesson," Madeline cried. "I will never lie to my listeners again. I was wrong to do what I did. I'm sorry. Please don't hurt her!"

"You have almost convinced me, but not quite. I'm going to put the phone right here next to the bed so that you'll be able to hear everything I do to her."

Amber was thrashing wildly against the bed now. She obviously understood that this was not going to end well.

He pulled out a syringe. "I'm going to give you just enough medicine to take the edge off."

It didn't take long for the fentanyl to take effect. Her eyes were open but her limbs were worthless. He ripped the tape from her mouth. Her screams came out in breathless whimpers.

He grabbed the phone. "Can you hear that, Madeline?" When she couldn't make words, her throat probably frozen in terror, he said, "I know you're there, Madeline. I can hear you breathing. Whatever you do, do not hang up or you'll both pay dearly, I promise you."

He set the phone aside once more, and then used his left hand to squeeze Amber's throat while he used his right hand to wave the box cutter in front of her face. Even drugged, the woman's breathing became frantic, her eyes round as saucers, like a rabid dog taking its last breath. "You should be here to see this, Madeline," he said loud enough so she could hear.

Bubbling with excitement, he used the tip of the blade to poke Amber in the shoulder and collarbone, over and over. The little sounds she made and the terror in her eyes prompted him to ramp it up, slicing her again and again across the chest. He felt like a kid at a circus. "This is Madeline's fault," he told the girl. "She should be here, not you!" He couldn't remember the last time he'd had so much fun.

Out of breath and flushed with excitement, he climbed off the bed and picked up the phone. "OK, Madeline, let's talk. I need to see you again before—"

The line was dead.

The girl was, too.

Madeline would pay dearly for that. He'd told her to stay on the phone and he'd meant it.

CHAPTER 37

By the time Lizzy left her office on J Street, it was cold and dark. She walked for quite a while before she realized she couldn't remember where she had parked. She heard footsteps in the distance. Shivers coursed over her as she stopped to look over her shoulder. A dark, shadowy figure walked beneath a line of trees, out of the streetlights. Someone was following her.

Relieved to see the church a few blocks away, she ran as fast as she could, her breathing ragged by the time she pushed through the double doors.

Everyone was there . . . Cathy, Brittany, Jessica. Even Hayley. They all looked beautiful in the bridesmaid dresses Jessica had picked out. Jared looked better than ever in a perfectly fitted tuxedo. It wasn't his tuxedo or handsome face that made him stand out—it was the way he carried himself, with a dash of cockiness and a barrel of confidence.

Everyone looked her way, everyone except her father, who sat in the front pew and pretended not to notice her.

Raking a hand through tangled hair, she realized she'd been so busy she hadn't had time to fix her hair. Panic set in as her gaze fell to her jeans and T-shirt. And then her head snapped up and this time her attention settled on the woman standing next to

Jared. She wore a beautiful strapless wedding gown with billowing tulle and tiny crystals that twinkled under the lights.

Slowly, the bride turned her way.

What the hell?

It was their neighbor, Heather somebody—she never could remember the woman's name. Everyone's attention had settled on the bride and groom. Something was seriously wrong with this picture.

The church doors blew open. A cold gust of wind rolled over her back, reminding Lizzy that she was being followed. She reached for her gun as she whipped around so fast her hand smacked against something hard.

"Ouch. What's going on? Are you OK?"

She lifted her head from the pillow. It was dark. Her heart hammered against her chest. *Just a dream. Thank God.* "Did I hit you?"

"Right in the chopper."

Blindly, she reached for Jared before she leaned toward him and kissed his jaw. "Sorry I woke you. I was having a bad dream."

He pulled her close. "Want to talk about it?"

"No, it was nothing, stupid, really."

Her phone vibrated on the nightstand.

"It's two in the morning," he said.

She turned over and grabbed it. "Hello?"

It was Madeline. Once again she was hysterical.

"Try to calm down," Lizzy told her. "I can't understand a word you're saying."

"He called me. It was *him*. He has my friend Amber. She's the waitress you met when we were at Monty's Bar & Grill."

"How do you know he's not just telling you he has her?"

"It was her voice. I talked to her. She's the one who was on the phone when I answered. Oh, God, it was awful. She sounded calm in the beginning. I think he convinced her that if she called me, he wouldn't hurt her. Oh, my God, Lizzy. Oh, my God. It was horrible. She was screaming at first. I think he covered her mouth because after that I heard muffled cries for help. I don't know if he was choking her or what the hell he was doing."

Lizzy sat up. "Did she tell you where she was?"

"She couldn't," Madeline said. "He took the phone from her before she could tell me."

"Did you call the police?"

"Yes."

"OK, that's a good start. I'll be there as soon as I can. Stay calm, and if you can, write down what he said so you don't forget. There could be clues that might help us find him."

She shut her phone and turned on the light.

Jared squinted. "What's going on?"

As she slipped into a pair of jeans and a T-shirt, she repeated everything Madeline had just told her. Then, since she and Jared had barely had two minutes to talk over the past few days, she also told him the part about Madeline asking David Westlake to call in to her show and pretend to be a perverted stalker.

"The woman doesn't sound stable."

"It gets worse. Remember the wallet investigators found after Madeline was attacked?"

He nodded.

"When I first met with Madeline, she showed me a note that had been delivered to her work. It was short and sweet, made from letters cut out of a magazine. It said, 'I know what you did.'"

"And?"

"Madeline gave the police everything the stalker had left for her except that note."

"Why would she keep evidence from the police?"

"I didn't understand at first, but now I think it was because she knew exactly what the note meant. Whoever gave it to her must have known she had lied on air about having a stalker. She was embarrassed by what she did and didn't want anyone to know."

"And she was probably afraid of losing her job," Jared added.

"Definitely. Her career is number one."

"Sounds familiar."

"Come on," Lizzy said, "that's not fair."

"You're right. I'm sorry. Anything else?"

Lizzy grabbed her shoes and sat on the edge of the bed to put them on. "During the basic investigation interview, which was done at Madeline's home, Kitally found a magazine with all the cutout letters that were used to make the note I just told you about."

"What did the detective think about that?"

"He doesn't know. Assuming Madeline's attacker planted the magazine when he left the wallet, I figured there had to be more surprises in the house, so Hayley, Kitally, and I performed a search. There was a steel rod in one of the living room windows, which is how Madeline's attacker must have been getting inside. We also found a syringe that I'm sure he planted in hopes that the police would think Madeline was the one who put a needle in her arm, not her so-called attacker."

Jared rubbed his face with both hands. "And what did you do with all of this evidence?"

"I took photographs and I made everyone wear latex gloves. I made sure everything we found was placed inside evidence bags."

"And then?"

"And then I put it all in a box in the trunk of my car."

Jared slid his legs over the side of the bed, and then turned on another light. He looked at Lizzy, his hair mussed, his eyes tired. "What are you doing?"

"I already told you. I'm going to meet Madeline at her house. The police should already be there."

"That's not what I'm talking about. You can't just take evidence away from a crime scene. And no matter how careful you were, you know evidence gathered by anyone but the cops won't be admissible."

"Look," Lizzy said as she came to her feet, "this stuff was obviously planted. Madeline's judgment might be suspect when it comes to furthering her career, but she's not stupid enough to leave wallets on her coffee table and cut-up magazines in her bathroom for everyone to see. If she had anything to do with it, that magazine would have already been burned in the fireplace or shredded."

Jared came to his feet. He stood near the bed, naked in all his glory, and she was running out in the middle of the night to help a woman she wasn't sure she could trust. She grabbed her bag, then walked up to him and gave him a quick kiss on his jaw.

"I guess I'll meet with the photographer and the florist alone," he said.

Her shoulders sagged. "Was that today?"

"Yep."

"I shouldn't be long. What time are we supposed to meet the photographer?"

"Ten o'clock for the photographer and twelve noon for the florist."

"Any chance we can postpone until next week?"

"I'll be gone next week."

She sighed. "That's right. You leave tomorrow, don't you?"

"Just go," Jared said. "Go take care of whatever it is you need to do and I'll figure out the rest."

He ushered her out the bedroom door and when she got to the landing, Lizzy looked back at him, but he'd already disappeared. The bedroom lights went out.

For a moment, she merely stood in the semidark and wondered if she was doing the right thing. Maybe she should tell Madeline to find someone else to help her. And then her cell phone rang and she walked out the door, photographers and wedding plans all but forgotten.

CHAPTER 38

Hayley had been walking the streets for hours. It was cold out, but not cold enough to stop her mind from racing. A dog barked in the distance and she could smell the last remnants of a fire simmering from a chimney or two. She thought about Tommy and wondered what he was doing tonight. Two years ago, before her mother was murdered, she had considered Tommy to be more than a friend. Not a lover, although that had been a possibility, sort of. Now she wasn't sure what exactly he meant to her. She usually saw him at UFC training, but she hadn't been going lately, mostly because she'd felt angrier than usual and she had no desire to hurt someone who might not deserve it. Kitally and Lizzy were the only two people brave enough to step inside her apartment. And now Jessica, too, although Jessica probably had no idea she was playing with fire by coming around. Or maybe Jessica did know . . . she wasn't as easy to read as she used to be.

It was hard to tell what Jessica was thinking these days. There was something about her that boggled the mind. Jessica used to get so emotional and afraid when it came to doing anything outside the law, even outside her own set of unspoken rules. The same maniac who'd abducted Lizzy had taken Jessica's sister. That was their connect, their bond. Jessica's sister had been subjected to some of the cruelest torture possible before she was killed and put out of her misery. And yet despite all the things that man had done to her sister, Jessica was determined to remain on the up-and-up and do things within the law.

What is it that makes the two of us so different?

Hayley knew the answer to the question before she'd finished the thought.

It was all about choices.

People, good or bad, right or wrong, made choices every day.

Hayley's situation with Brian, though, was different. She had no choice when it came to how this would end. She knew what had to be done. She couldn't eat. She couldn't sleep, and she couldn't rest until Brian was dead.

She took a hit off her cigarette, but even the nicotine failed to release enough dopamine to do her much good.

As on many other nights, she found herself across the street from the house she'd once shared with her mother—the house where she'd found her mother propped up with an axe embedded in her skull.

And it was all Hayley's fault.

She'd known exactly what kind of a scumbag Brian was when she'd cut off his dick, but she hadn't had the guts to go on and do what needed to be done. Her mother would be alive today if she'd taken care of business when she'd had the chance.

She hated herself almost as much as she hated Brian.

She couldn't let it go. Never. No way. She would find Brian and this time she would take him out. No last smoke. No last words. She would just point and shoot and be done with it.

CHAPTER 39

Lizzy had been wrong about Detective Chase. She'd thought she was impervious to his intimidation tactics, but that wasn't true. Now that she'd had the opportunity to spend time alone with him, she could see that the man didn't bother with tactics to bully or coerce. He didn't need to. The man was just plain scary. He had a set jaw and dark eyes, not a glimmer of warmth no matter where you looked. She couldn't help but wonder how he could afford the perfectly fitted suit and shiny new watch. She did not trust the man.

The only reason he'd agreed to meet with her at all was because he happened to be pals with Special Agent Jimmy Martin, who'd happened to put in a call for her, asking Chase to meet with her as a favor.

Lizzy turned over the evidence collected at Madeline's house and after the detective had a chance to examine it, he looked across his desk at her and said, "So, what is it you want?"

"Three people are missing now. Dr. Blair's cell needs to be tapped. She needs twenty-four-hour surveillance."

"Who the fuck do you think you are?"

Lizzy straightened in her chair, taken aback by the outburst.

"Do you realize I could bring charges against you for withholding evidence?" he asked.

"I brought the evidence to you as soon as I could," Lizzy said, keeping her voice calm. "Maybe I should talk to my friends at Channel 10 News and let them know that the police failed to do their job in the first place, leaving me to clean up their mess."

His jaw hardened, which couldn't be an easy feat, considering it appeared to be made of granite. She watched as the hand on his desk rolled into a fist. What was he going to do, hit her?

"Under the circumstances," Lizzy went on, "we both know that a missing persons case is not considered a conventional criminal investigation."

"That was before we found one of the missing persons' wallets in Dr. Blair's house."

"Said missing person was reported by Madeline herself. You wouldn't have known anything about her missing neighbor if she hadn't told you."

"Doesn't matter. Dr. Blair is a suspect and there's nothing you can do about that."

"All the more reason for you people to pull your heads out of your—out of the sand and tap her phone, at her home and office. You also need to set up surveillance."

A uniformed officer knocked on the door before he poked his head inside. "I just got off the phone with Amber Olinger's roommate. She said it's common for Amber to be away for days at a time. I also talked to her parents. The last time they heard from her was two months ago when she called to borrow money."

Detective Chase nodded and the officer shut the door.

Chase settled an unflinching gaze on Lizzy and said, "Being that you're sort of like the slug on the bottom of the investigative pond, maybe you don't understand that missing person cases take time. Unless there are obvious signs of foul play, our hands are tied."

She opened her mouth to respond, but he stopped her with a raised hand. "Lizzy Gardner, big Sacramento PI," he said with distaste. "You really think you can just walk in here and get everyone hopping with a snap of your fingers?"

Lizzy kept her voice level. "I was once a missing person, Detective. I know firsthand what it feels like to think everyone's looking for you, but then begin to wonder why nobody's knocking down any doors. Mine wasn't a mere missing person case, and neither are these. Why would David Westlake leave his car at work? And why would Chris Porter's wallet be found in Dr. Blair's home? Do you really think Dr. Blair would lie about being attacked and then go so far as to say a crazy man called to let her know he had another victim? Someone she happened to know?"

"Dr. Blair lied about having a stalker. Why would she stop there?"

Frustration clawed at her insides. Lizzy tried to think, but he was right about one thing. There were too many dead ends. No bodies and no solid leads. "Can you tell me what you're doing around here to find Chris Porter?"

"Seventy percent of reported missing persons are found or return within seventy-two hours. I suggest you practice patience, Ms. Gardner."

"I suggest you read the files again," Lizzy said. "Chris Porter has been missing for weeks. What are you going to do when another one of Madeline's friends disappears?"

"You be sure and come back for a visit and let me know when that happens."

The man's condescending tone brought Lizzy to her feet. "You think you've got everybody cowering under that black-eyed stare of yours, don't you? Well, you don't scare me. You're an asshole, Detective. Plain and simple. If anything has happened to any one of these people, I'm holding you accountable."

"You should watch that mouth of yours. It just might get you into trouble."

"I'll be in touch," she said as she turned toward the door.

"Ms. Gardner," he said, stopping her. "I don't think you want to get on my bad side."

She lifted both brows in surprise. "Are you trying to tell me that this is your good side?"

"That's exactly what I'm telling you."

"Are you threatening me, Detective?"

"Just a warning, Private Eye, just a warning."

CHAPTER 40

"Oh, man, you need to take a look at this."

Hayley had just stepped into her apartment. She hung the dog leash on the nail next to the door before she made her way to the kitchen area, where Kitally was working on her laptop.

"What is it?"

Kitally pointed to a picture of a girl, then zoomed in on the girl's face. "Who does that look like to you?"

"Like a younger Abbi Santos. What site is this?"

"It's not good. It's a porn site, but not just any porn site. Here the parents not only rent their kids out to perverts, they also post nude pictures of their teenage kids. They get paid for every click."

"That is fucked up."

"Earlier today, I ran Owen Santos's name through a database of porn sites and sure enough, it popped up. That was my first clue that Mr. Santos had hobbies other than his fish. The problem with finding the hardcore perverts is that as you get to the more repulsive sites like this one, just about all the men use aliases and they're difficult to track down."

"What made you think to look for him on a porn site?"

"Come on," Kitally said, "the man talks to his fish. He's missing and his daughter is a cutter. We're obviously dealing with a highly dysfunctional family. Anyhow," she went on, "if a pervert wants to do more than just look, if he wants to sell pictures or anything else on any of these sites, the guy needs to give the so-called company a name and a bank account so they know where to send the money. These scumbags treat these sites like a real business, with 1099s and everything."

"Did you sign up with a fake name?"

"No," Kitally said. "I hacked into their system. I found Owen's name within five minutes, which means he's a vendor, not just a viewer. It didn't take me long to find shots of Abbi. No wonder there's no love lost between her and her father."

"I guess you didn't find any pictures of the younger daughter?"

"Nope. But poor Abbi was forced to do some pretty disgusting shit. I'll print a few of the pictures and put them in the file."

A rock hit the window, cracking the glass and making Kitally jump.

Dog barked and Hayley went to the sink and looked out the window. Nobody was there. She ran out of the apartment and downstairs. *Leave Us Alone* was spray-painted in green neon letters across the garage.

Kitally joined her. "Hmm. It's obvious who left this message. She might as well have signed her name."

Hayley sighed. "What are you now, a handwriting expert?"

"Just observant. Didn't you see the green paint on the tips of Lara's fingers the other day?"

"My attention was on Abbi's wrists," Hayley said as she noticed a man sitting in a Chrysler LeBaron parked across the street.

"Well, my guess is Abbi used her little sister's spray paint." Kitally pulled out her cell phone and used it to take some pictures, then looked at Hayley. "What's wrong?"

"Don't look across the street," Hayley said. "Just point to the paint on the garage door and keep talking."

"Fine, but can you at least tell me what's going on while I talk about nothing?"

"There's a car parked across the street by the park. I've seen the driver before. He used to work for Brian."

"What are you going to do?"

"I'm going to go over there and talk to him. While I'm at it, I need you to get his license plate number."

Hayley got halfway across the street before the car took off, tires screeching as it shot right at her. Hayley dove out of the way, rolled a few times, then jumped to her feet and said, "Did you get the number?"

"No. Let's go after him." Kitally jumped on her motorcycle and turned on the ignition. As soon as Hayley threw her leg over the back of the seat, Kitally took off.

After Kitally rounded the first corner, Hayley caught a glimpse of the Chrysler making a left up ahead. Kitally sped up and took the next turn too sharp, just missing a parked car, but managing to hold the lean position and keep the bike upright. The engine growled and screeched when she downshifted in order to swerve around a group of people crossing the street. Hayley had no idea how fast they were going and she didn't want to know.

The Chrysler ran a red light.

Kitally hit the throttle. The front wheel jumped as they sped through the intersection. There were too many cars between them, so Kitally jumped the bike onto the sidewalk. People shouted and shook their fists before she cut back onto the road.

Kitally squeezed down on the throttle as she circled around the car in front of them, then sped up. They were gaining on him as they headed up El Camino.

He took a right. Kitally did the same.

"Which way did he go?"

"I'm not sure," Hayley said. "Pull into the shopping center."

Kitally circled around the area while they both kept a lookout. She stopped and said, "Damn. We almost had him."

"One. Zero. Eight," Hayley said. "Those were the first three letters on his plates. Doesn't do us much good."

They both took a moment to catch their breath.

"I guess you've been driving this thing for a while."

"Since I was a kid."

"Since we're out and about," Hayley said, "let's go say hello to Helen Smith, Robin Santos's neighbor, and see what she can tell us about the mysterious Owen Santos."

Helen Smith resembled a troll. She stood under the five-foot mark. Her rolled back didn't help matters. She had beady little eyes and a mountainous nose. She wore a flowery dress and a lavender sweater with missing buttons. Not only did Helen Smith talk a lot, she talked fast. It was like speed-reading: if you caught the first and last word in every sentence, you could pretty much figure out what the hell she was saying.

"The only normal one in that family is their little girl, Lara. Sweetest thing in the world," Helen said. "Before Owen Santos disappeared, Lara used to come over all the time, mostly after school. We would talk and bake cookies."

"What would Lara talk about?"

"She was always worried about her older sister."

"Did she say why?"

"Well, you see, Lara is a freshman in high school now, which means she still goes to the same school as her sister. Apparently there were—maybe there still are, I don't know—a lot of rumors going around, and Lara was worried about Abbi's reputation. If I were her mother, I would never let Abbi out of the house wearing those skimpy clothes and that crimson lipstick. I mean, come on, ladies, she'd be better off with a colorful braid or tattoos like the two of you."

"It's called a dread," Kitally told her. "Not too many people can rock one."

Hayley scratched her neck and said nothing.

Helen didn't need any prompting to keep talking. Hayley and Kitally sat on stools, watching her talk with her hands as she ran around the kitchen, collecting bowls and a mixer. "So you two work for that Lizzy Gardner woman?"

"Yes, ma'am," Kitally said, which for unknown reasons made Hayley smile.

"Could you grab the flour from the pantry?" Helen asked Kitally.

"You need to put on some weight," Helen told Hayley the minute Kitally disappeared. "That friend of yours is a tiny thing, too, but she looks healthy. Could you grab a couple of eggs from the refrigerator?"

Hayley didn't budge.

"The sooner we get these in the oven," the woman told her, "the sooner you two can try a little bit of heaven."

Kitally ended up getting the eggs and doing the baking while Hayley ushered the woman into the main room and did her best to keep her focused on why they were there in the first place.

"Is Owen a friendly man?" Hayley asked.

"Hmm. I don't know about friendly, but he says hello or thanks me for the cookies I send over with Lara. Overall, I guess I'd have to say he is a strange one. I don't trust people who don't say much." The woman stared at Hayley. "Like you, young lady. You're a tough one to gauge. All of those tattoos on your body are throwing me off. Do they mean something?" She pointed to the snake tattoo on Hayley's neck, the one with the skull for a head and a slithering tongue. Helen winced. "An angel on your collarbone and a snake thing on your neck. I don't get it."

Hayley shrugged. "If I told you it meant something, would it matter?"

Helen wagged a finger at her. "Ah, I get it. This is one of those curiosity-kills-the-cat things, isn't it? If you tell me what it means and I don't like it, I might not like you."

"And why would I care if you liked me or not?" Hayley asked, irritated that the woman was getting to her.

"Everyone wants to be liked. It's human nature."

"She really doesn't care," Kitally told Helen as she stirred the ingredients inside the giant bowl she held in her arms.

"What happened to your finger?" Helen asked next.

Hayley was about to tell the woman to fuck off, that it was none of her business, when Kitally dropped the spoon into the bowl and picked up a framed picture. "Who's this?"

"That's my daughter, my only child." Helen swallowed as if she were trying hard to keep her peppy self in check. "She was killed by a drunk driver."

"I'm sorry," Kitally said. Then she gave Hayley a look that said *give the woman a break* and headed back into the kitchen.

For the first time since they'd entered the house, Helen Smith was quiet.

For some weird reason, Hayley felt the woman's pain ripple right through her.

As Hayley watched the woman sit quietly, she realized that nobody had ever asked her about her tattoos before. Not Lizzy, not Kitally, not even her mom. Hayley unclenched her teeth and said, "This coiled snake tattoo on the back of my neck represents my reality. The serpent holds his ground—fights and never retreats."

Helen lifted her head and her eyes brightened just a little bit. "Is your snake poisonous?"

"No. Its venom provides me with expanded consciousness."

Helen looked doubtful.

"The angel on my collarbone," Hayley went on, "is someone I used to know."

"The other *you* before all the bad," Helen said as if she could read her mind. "She's your guardian just as my daughter is mine. They watch over us and remind us to live in the moment and to dance like nobody's watching."

"Sure, yeah," Hayley said.

The buzzer on the stove began to ding.

"I like your tattoos," Helen said with a gentle pat on Hayley's knee. "Now let's go eat some cookies."

CHAPTER 41

"Dad looks so much better," Cathy said as she and Lizzy headed for the cafeteria to grab some coffee. "I'm proud of you for coming to see him. I do think it's good for both of you."

Lizzy nodded her head as she tried to think about how she was going to tell Cathy what she'd learned about their father.

After they grabbed a coffee and took a seat at the end of a long rectangular table, Cathy looked at her and said, "OK, out with it. You suck at trying to keep things from me, so what's going on?" She pointed a finger at Lizzy. "And please tell me this has nothing to do with you and Jared."

Lizzy frowned. "Why would you say that?"

"Never mind. What is it then? What's going on?"

"It's about Dad."

Cathy frowned.

"Remember the day Dad had gotten out of surgery and I called you to let you know the nurse had called me by mistake?"

Cathy nodded.

"Well, I didn't tell you the whole truth. The fact is I went to see Dad that morning, but he'd just been wheeled out of the recovery room. After watching him sleep for a while, I got up to stretch and found an envelope made out to Grandpa with a handmade note inside." Lizzy pulled up the pictures on her phone and handed Cathy her cell.

Cathy glanced at the drawing. "Emma. Who is Emma?"

"There's more," Lizzy said. "When Dad woke up, he called me by the name of Michelle, then reached out his arms and asked for Emma."

"Well, he was obviously still drugged up . . . you know . . . delirious."

"I was thinking that was the case," Lizzy went on, "but there was a return address on the envelope. I did some investigating—"

"Of course you did," Cathy cut in.

Lizzy sighed. "Michelle and Emma live in Oregon. I found an address and telephone number. I called Michelle, but she wasn't home so I talked to her husband instead. I pretended to be a nurse calling from the hospital and told him that Mr. Gardner had listed Michelle Borell as one of the emergency numbers and that I needed to know if the name and number were correct."

"This is crazy," Cathy said. "What did he say?"

"He said yes, that all of the information was correct. He sounded concerned. He wanted to know how Michelle's father was doing."

Cathy stared at Lizzy as if she had lost her mind. "Are you trying to tell me that Dad has another family hidden away in Oregon?"

"I'm just as confused as you are, but I figured you would want to know about this."

Cathy stood up. "Why would you do this?"

"Why would I do what?"

"You have a wedding to plan but we have yet to try on dresses or celebrate in any way. More importantly, Dad has cancer. He's dying, Lizzy, and yet here you are making phone calls and doing everything you can to find a way to drive a wedge between me and Dad."

Lizzy couldn't believe what she was hearing. "I should have known you would find a way to try to make this my fault." Lizzy shook her head. "Unbelievable."

Without another word between them, Cathy grabbed her coffee cup and tossed it in the garbage by the door as she walked out.

After Lizzy watched Cathy storm off, she decided to let her be for now. Cathy needed time to digest the news and figure things out for herself.

Once again Lizzy's life felt like it was spiraling out of control. Jared was the only stable thing in it. She really did need to take a few weeks off and concentrate on her wedding, now only thirty-two days away. And yet she knew she wouldn't be able to get anything done until she helped Dr. Blair. The woman had made a terrible mistake. But the thing was, Lizzy could sense fear miles away and Madeline was seriously afraid for her life.

Lizzy couldn't just push it all aside. Whether Detective Chase or anyone else wanted to acknowledge it, the truth was that Madeline's friends were disappearing. They needed to find the person responsible before he got ahold of anyone else.

As long as she was here, Lizzy took the elevator to the third floor, where she stopped at the nurses' station to ask about Madeline's clinical toxicology report. There was only one nurse at the desk. According to the tag on her chest, her name was Margery. The odds of getting any information from the nurse were not in her favor, but one thing she'd learned over the years was that it never hurt to ask.

"My client, Dr. Madeline Blair," Lizzy told the nurse, "had some tests done here last week. I called a few days ago, but the results hadn't arrived yet. I was wondering if someone could tell me when we can expect her toxicology report to come in?"

Margery clacked away at the keyboard. "The report is right here. These tests usually take weeks, but it looks like Dr. Blair's tests were expedited. They came in two days ago. When did you call?"

"Yesterday."

"That's odd."

"What?" Lizzy strained to see the report, but the monitor was turned away from her. "I'm a private investigator hired by Dr. Blair. Would it be possible for me to get a copy of the report?"

Margery leaned in and peered at the screen. *Come on, lady, give me the report.* She could always have Madeline stop by for it, but that would be a hassle and would waste precious time.

"Janelle Brown was the nurse in charge that day." Margery looked around. "That's Janelle right there. Wait here. I'll be right back."

Damn. As soon as Margery walked off, Lizzy leaned over the counter and moved the computer screen so that she could scan the report. It was mostly mumbo jumbo, medical jargon she didn't understand, but then she saw the words *etorphine* and *fentanyl* and she knew instantly that's what Madeline's attacker had used to immobilize her. Why both drugs, though? Perhaps there was no method to his madness. Maybe he used whatever he could get his hands on. He must have shot Madeline up in the beginning so he could tie her up and then again before he removed all evidence.

Lizzy had straightened just as Margery pointed her out. Despite the severe expression on her face, Janelle was an attractive woman in her early forties. Her auburn hair was pulled back in a messy bun. A streak of white through her bangs, though, spoke of stress, or maybe she had a pigmentation anomaly. A stethoscope hung down her chest over blue scrubs. Completing the ensemble were black canvas tennis shoes with white polka dots. Interesting.

Janelle walked over to where Lizzy stood. "Margery tells me you want a copy of a report. We have strict rules about these things.

We can't give the report to anyone but the detective in charge of Ms. Blair's case."

"I have his card right here in my bag. Would it be possible to have the information sent over to Detective Chase today?"

She stiffened, obviously not pleased by the request, but she collected herself and agreed to have Margery look into the matter. It would be hard to miss the crackle of bad energy coming off the woman. When Lizzy failed to head off, the nurse's eyes roamed over the length of her, assessing and resentful. "Is there something else I can help you with?" she finally asked.

Despite the woman's wrathful stare, Lizzy held her ground. "I was wondering if you could tell me how many drug diversion cases you and your staff report each month."

"Is that why you're here? Because of a reported drug theft?"

"One of the cases I'm working on involves the theft of syringes of fentanyl, a narcotic painkiller used—"

"I am aware of the drug fentanyl," Janelle said, cutting her off.

"Does your hospital have a password-controlled system for dispensing narcotics in the operating room?"

"Of course."

"And every loss is reported to the DEA within twenty-four hours of the theft?"

The woman's face flushed. Her fingers curled at her sides as if she were getting ready to claw somebody's eyes out, most likely Lizzy's. "Are you trying to tell me how to do my job?"

"Not at all."

"And what was your name?"

"Lizzy Gardner, private investigator. And yours?"

"Janelle Brown, head nurse. It's time for me to get back to work. If you have further questions, I suggest you take the matter up with the hospital administrator."

CHAPTER 42

Kitally spotted Tommy at the kitchen counter, where a minibar of sorts had been set up for his party. She'd only known him for two years, but it was as if he'd transformed from a geek to a real guy within months. With dark curls frolicking around his ears and sparkly blue eyes, Tommy was looking pretty good. The dark jeans and sweater she'd helped him pick out a few weeks ago gave him a whole new look. If he wasn't already taken, Kitally might be interested.

The poor boy didn't even realize Hayley still had a fondness for him that went beyond friendship. Or maybe he did know and they were both good at concealing their feelings. Either way, Kitally didn't get it, didn't understand why people couldn't openly express their dislikes and desires. Lame.

The boy was just lost where women were concerned. Case in point: the three obviously appreciative young women surrounding him in the kitchen of his new one-bedroom Midtown apartment while he yammered on to some pal of his. Kitally thought of Hayley again: you snooze, you lose.

Kitally called him over with one waggle of a finger.

"I think the outfit is a hit," he told her as he joined her near the gas fireplace.

She nodded her agreement. "I'm going to get my coat and take off."

"Already? The party is just getting started."

"I dressed you, I helped you decorate, and I gave a few of your friends a thrill by dancing with them. My work is done here."

He laughed as he looked around his apartment. "I was really hoping Hayley would change her mind and come over."

"Not a chance in hell. For Hayley, coming to a party like this would be synonymous with going back to high school. It's never going to happen."

"How's she doing?"

"About the same."

"Does that mean her every thought is about finding Brian?"

"Pretty much," Kitally said. "Her newest idea involves offering a reward for Brian's whereabouts."

"A reward? How much?"

"Ten thousand dollars."

Tommy let out a low whistle. "The rest of her inheritance?"

"No. Once I realized that Hayley was never going to let this Brian thing go, I put up the cash."

"I don't think that's a good idea. You shouldn't get involved in all of this," Tommy told her.

"Hayley isn't the only one who can pack a lot of wallop in one small fist." Kitally raised her fist and chucked him softly under the chin.

"I'm serious."

"I can tell. You need to lighten up, Tommy boy."

Silence.

"Well, I have to get going. Besides, your girlfriends are getting impatient."

"You know I'm not interested in any of them."

"Yeah," she said as she walked away, "I know."

"Thanks for all your help," he called after her.

Without turning around, she waved a hand in the air, then grabbed her coat from the guestroom and headed out. A chill greeted her as she stepped outside. The clicks of her high-heeled boots echoed off the pavement and into the night. The sky was black. Every night lately there seemed to be fewer stars.

Kitally lived alone in a big empty house in Carmichael that belonged to her parents. She hated the house. It was the same house her dad used to bring his mistress to. After she told her parents she was moving out, her dad told her to pick one of their many properties. She'd picked the house in Carmichael just so her father wouldn't have a convenient place to stay after working long hours at the office. She figured he could take his whore to a hotel instead.

She got off at the Marconi Avenue exit and saw the car that had been right on her ass do the same. She took a right on Marconi as planned, but instead of heading for Palm Drive, she sped up and made a right on Fulton, her tires smooth as she cut through a yellow light.

The car behind her went through the red. So this was serious business, she realized. But she wasn't worried. Her Lamborghini Aventador might only be the fifth-fastest street-legal car on the market, but it was one of her favorites. The beauty had pushrod suspension and a superfast single-clutch gearbox. Whoever was following her was out of his or her league.

She cut down El Camino and took a detour on Morse. Ten minutes later, Kitally waited for the garage door to slide open before she pulled into the garage and turned off the ignition. The chase had her blood pumping in earnest and she considered going to a club and dancing off some of the adrenaline racing through her veins. She couldn't wipe the smile off her face if she tried. She had her father's love of cars. She used to travel with him to Germany and Italy to attend car shows held only for their VIP buyers. They toured the factories and even test-drove a Bugatti Veyron.

Kitally peered into the night, wondering who had been chasing her. She'd danced with a few of Tommy's friends. Some guys thought of dancing as a form of foreplay. Maybe one of them thought he could follow her home and get to know her better.

She brushed her fingertips over the hood of her Lamborghini as if it were her pet. After the garage door slid shut, she fished through her bag for the keys to her house. That's when she noticed the door leading from the garage to the house wasn't quite shut. Slowly, quietly, she reached inside her bag again, this time for her machete, before she remembered leaving it in her bedroom. Her gaze settled on a can of wasp-and-hornet spray.

She grabbed the wasp spray, then peeked through the door. She could see far enough into the kitchen area to determine that the room was empty. Nobody inside as far as she could tell. She stepped slowly inside, then stopped and listened. It was eerily quiet. She didn't have any animals. No roommates. Nobody to greet her. She also didn't have much furniture, which meant there were not a lot of hiding places. Mostly stone floors and marble columns.

Taking careful steps so as not to make any noise, she made her way into the living area. This room was also empty. Her gaze settled on the closet door near the front entrance.

And that's when she felt the presence of someone behind her. With a loud squeal, she came around fast and threw a side kick, hitting the person hard in the stomach.

She then lifted the can of wasp killer and sprayed him in the face.

It was a man, a muscular guy. He was on the ground, groaning and cursing.

She gave him another quick kick to his side. He buckled. She kept at it. A kick to his left, then his right. A high kick to his jaw sent him flying backward.

But it wasn't enough. He was the Hulk. Anger fueled him. He let out an animal howl as he came at her. He lunged. She jumped out of the way. He came at her again and this time she jumped the wrong way. His body felt like a freight train as he slammed into her. She hit the floor hard, the breath nearly knocked out of her, forcing her to fight through the pain. Before he could pin her, she twisted, jabbed an elbow to his face and then shot to her feet.

If she had her rattan sticks or her machete, she could have taken him down already. Instead, she walked backward toward the kitchen. In between backhanded swipes at his own wasp-sprayed eyes, he swung. She ducked. She kept moving, picking up objects and firing at him as she went. The stone vase knocked him in the shoulder.

He grunted.

Get to the kitchen and grab a knife. That was her plan.

He charged forward and got the tip of her boot in his groin for his efforts.

The moment she felt the kitchen tiles beneath her foot, she swiped a knife from the butcher block and wheeled with it, but it was all over.

Someone grabbed her wrist and slammed it to the counter, sending the blade skittering across the floor, and then her arm was wrenched up behind her back almost to the breaking point. Her other arm quickly joined it.

There were two men, and the second was just as strong as the first one, who was now devoted to clawing at his ravaged eyes in earnest. "It took you long enough," he growled at his friend.

"I didn't think you would need my help."

"Yeah, well, neither did I." Squinting at her through weeping, bloodred eyes, he kneed her in the gut, then pulled back and slammed a fist to her cheekbone. When he raised his fist again, she saw blood on his knuckles, tasted it in her mouth.

"Hold on," the man behind her said to his pal. "Let's do what we came to do."

"Let me do what *I'm* gonna—"

"First things first," the man behind her insisted. Then he was talking to Kitally. "Brian wants you to give your friend Hayley a message. Stop or die. Your choice."

"I have a message for Brian. Tell him his time is almost up. We're coming to get him."

The room was spinning now, but that didn't stop her from leaning back into the man behind her and propelling both feet into the groin of the man facing her.

After that, she counted another two blows to the face, maybe three—she wasn't sure, because her legs buckled and everything around her faded to black.

CHAPTER 43

Seth was in the garage, sorting through his toolbox, deciding what he would need for his next kill. He had big plans.

It had all been way too easy. Three bodies so far. He needed to figure out a way to make sure all the evidence could be traced back to Madeline. There was no way he was going to take the blame for any of this. All three of these people would still be alive if it weren't for Madeline's lies.

He heard the front door being opened and closed. He glanced at the clock. Janelle was home early. It wasn't long before he heard the garage door come open. Janelle stood quietly in the open doorway. She looked different tonight, younger somehow. Her hair was pinned up and soft flyaway tendrils touched the side of her face.

"I'm busy," he said. "What is it?"

She stepped inside, looking around as she walked toward him. "I was hoping you would come inside and share a bottle of wine with me." Her silk blouse was half unbuttoned, revealing a lacy bra he'd never seen before.

He went back to sorting through his tools.

She continued walking up close to him, oblivious to the fact that he clearly wanted to be left alone.

"Lizzy Gardner came snooping around the hospital today," she said.

He looked down at her then and wrapped his left hand slowly around her throat. Then he slammed her against the wall. Her feet barely touched the floor. "What did she want?"

"She was asking about drugs missing from the hospital," she squeaked out. "You're hurting me."

He lowered her enough so that her feet touched the ground and pressed his body against hers.

"I know you've been taking syringes from the hospital supply," she rasped. "I've been covering for you, putting the blame elsewhere."

"I didn't take anything. You don't know what you're talking about."

"You don't get it," she said. "I've seen that look in your eyes when you listen to Dr. Blair on the radio. I know she fascinates you."

He released a growl as he grabbed a fistful of silk with his free hand and ripped the blouse halfway off. Buttons flew, rattling over the concrete floor. He took a moment to admire the bite marks on her stomach, the ones he'd given her the other night. "Take your clothes off."

She stepped out of her pants, then pulled off what was left of her blouse and unsnapped her bra. "I think you're doing the right thing. I know what rapes look like and you didn't rape her."

"What exactly do you think you know?" he asked.

"I know how many syringes are missing from the hospital and I know who has access."

"Now touch yourself while you tell me more about Madeline."

She curled her fingers between her thighs. "Madeline's a bitch," she whispered. "She doesn't deserve you. Only I can make you happy."

"This isn't about you. Tell me about Madeline."

"She's a liar. She deserves to be punished."

He stepped close enough so that he could brush his mouth over the soft flesh of her shoulder. And then he bit down, hard.

She cried out and grabbed hold of his crotch.

"You didn't get enough the other night," he said with disgust.

"I could never get enough of you."

"You're pathetic."

"Madeline should have listened to you," she said, desperation lining her voice. "What are you going to do about it?"

He put his hands on both sides of her face and pressed inward as if he were an iron clamp. Rage funneled through him, making his hands shake as he thought about squeezing so hard her head would explode. The idea of getting rid of her tempted him greatly. *Be done with the bitch*, he thought, *once and for all*. But he couldn't lose focus. Madeline was what mattered. He let Janelle go, not wanting to leave any marks that coworkers might see, then turned back to his tools and said, "It's none of your fucking business."

"She's a whore," Janelle cried as she grabbed his arm. "She liked it when I examined her."

"Stay away from her or I'll kill you," he said without looking at her. "Do you understand?"

She picked up her clothes and walked back to the door, then turned. "What about the PI?"

"The PI? You mean Lizzy Gardner?" Seth looked at her now, eyes afire. "Stay away from her, too." The pained expression and the hurt in her eyes not only confused him, it thoroughly pissed him off. "You're not my fucking partner, Janelle. You gave that up when you whored yourself out to your boyfriend at the hospital."

She flinched at that as though he'd slapped her.

"Now go make me dinner. I'm hungry."

CHAPTER 44

When Hayley walked into the hospital, the first thing she saw was Tommy, Lizzy, and Jessica sitting in the waiting room, each looking as if someone had died. Logic told her it was Kitally. She wasn't here, so something had happened to the girl. She didn't like the bitter taste in her mouth. If something happened to Kitally because of her, she was going to lose it for good.

"So what is this?" Hayley asked. "I have six messages on my cell, but nobody knows how to leave a clue about what's actually happening over here."

Lizzy scooted her plastic chair closer to a guy with a bad cough so Hayley could take a seat.

Hayley stayed on her feet. "Where's Kitally?"

Tommy stood. "She was beat up last night. The neighbors heard a commotion. By the time the police got to her house, she was unconscious."

"So she's alive."

He nodded.

"So what's the deal?" she asked, relieved, but determined not to let on that she was worried about her friend. She wasn't a worrier. "What's wrong with her? Broken nail, messed-up hair? Because, shit, that would really piss her off."

Tommy exhaled. "Broken nose, messed-up face. At this point she's unrecognizable."

"She's going to live, though. So why are you all sitting here looking as if you're already mourning for her?"

Jessica looked at Hayley and said, "I'm here because I like Kitally, and I want to hear what the doctor has to say about her recovery process. They're still checking for internal bleeding. This wasn't your regular everyday street fight."

Hayley looked at Lizzy.

Lizzy stood. "I've been walking on eggshells around you for two years now. You rarely say two words to me. No 'thank you' or 'see you later' or even 'how ya doing, Lizzy?' You want to stop eating until your clothes fall off . . . stop talking until nobody remembers the sound of your voice? You want to piss off the last four friends you have left and spend the rest of your life in your own little private shithole? Well, good, have it your way." Lizzy pointed down the hallway. "Kitally is in surgery because you're so damned determined to get revenge. Some scumbag wanted to teach her a lesson so he could send *you* a very important message."

Hayley didn't say a word. Frustration clawed at her insides, making her want to kick something. How many times did she need to be reminded that she should have killed Brian when she had the chance?

"I've been here for most of the night," Lizzy went on, her face all angry lines. "The police called me after they found a stack of business cards she'd had made on her own dime. I was right there next to her when she was wheeled in. She told me that the two men who beat her up wanted to send Hayley Hansen a message: lay off or you're both dead."

Hayley stared at Lizzy, unblinking, not sure what to think about all the anger pouring out of her.

"My dad is dying of cancer on the fifth floor," Lizzy said, "and I have a few things to say to him, too."

They all watched Lizzy walk toward the elevators.

"I'm going to go," Jessica said. She looked at Tommy. "You have my number. Do you mind giving me a call once you hear something?"

"Not a problem."

Hayley watched the two of them hug. Apparently everyone had formed some sort of bizarre bond when she wasn't looking.

"Don't you have something you need to do?" Hayley asked Tommy after Jessica left.

"Nice try," Tommy said with a smirk. "Your badass attitude doesn't work on me. I'm not going anywhere."

"Music to my ears," she said before plunking down into one of the empty seats.

Tommy shook his head as he took a seat next to her. "Why are you trying so hard to push everyone away? I don't get it."

"I'm not *trying* to do anything."

"Then maybe you don't even realize what you're doing. You were never a warm, cuddly person, but you never used to be such a bitch either."

She said nothing in response.

"Kitally came to my housewarming party last night," Tommy said. "My friends really enjoyed her company. Nobody as much as me."

"Are you two hooking up?"

"Would you mind if we did?"

She shrugged, wondering why she'd bothered to ask the question. She felt a strong desire to tell him to fuck off, but she didn't know why, so she remained quiet. Words always caused problems for her.

CHAPTER 45

Cathy had flown to Portland, Oregon, yesterday and rented a car. She told her live-in ex-husband and her daughter that she was visiting a friend in Oregon, but no one else knew she'd left town. At the moment, she was sitting in the rental car across the street from a charming English Tudor with a brick front and a detached garage.

This was the house where Michelle and Emma lived. After Lizzy told her about the possibility of a half sister, she hadn't been able to think about anything else. Life had a way of tossing obstacles at people when they least expected it.

Hadn't she been tested enough? She didn't like surprises. She liked having a daily routine; it made her feel safe. She liked to wake up every morning, enjoy a nice cup of hot coffee, and move on with her day in the same way she'd moved through the day yesterday and the day before that. Some people, like Lizzy, seemed to think of change as being synonymous with adventure—with living, even. Good for them. Cathy hated change.

A car pulled into the driveway.

A friend who worked at the DMV back home had helped Cathy verify that Michelle still lived at this address. The database she used also confirmed that she had a five-year-old daughter named Emma. If Emma was five years old, she was probably in kindergarten, which meant she'd be getting out of school around noon. Cathy figured she could be a detective just like her sister. So far, she'd found the house and determined the correct ETA.

She watched two people get out of the car.

The resemblance between Michelle and Lizzy was so remarkable it took her breath away. As she watched Emma skip alongside her mother, she couldn't help but imagine Emma being the child Lizzy never had. Emma was a darling little girl with curly brown hair and a paper flower clipped to her hair.

As she stepped out of the car, Cathy inhaled a lungful of courage.

Lizzy walked into her father's hospital room. The television was on. He was awake and he glanced at her before returning his attention to the television. She walked to the side of his bed, leaned over, and kissed his forehead. He flinched. She didn't care.

"I know about Michelle and Emma," she said.

Nothing. No response to that.

She took a seat in the chair that was there for visitors. "So walk me through this. Because you've been leading a double life—and by the way, I'm stunned you've had enough energy for the second one, given the way you've sleepwalked through the one you've had with us."

He was looking at her now, at least.

"Anyway. Because you're leading a double life, you somehow blame me for everything bad that happened in your life? Seriously?" She sighed. "Still the sphinx, huh? Thanks for the eye contact, anyway. I used to try so hard to get you to look me in the eye. God, if you only knew how badly I wanted you to pick me up in your arms and tell me you loved me."

She had to laugh at that image. She sat there for a moment, tried to put it in order. "The best part of knowing about your other life is that it kind of makes a little sense. After Samuel Jones took me to his hideout, the media attention must have been suffocating for a man like you. Your every move suddenly under a microscope. I read the articles from that time. People thought you had something to do with my disappearance. That must have shot your supposed sainthood right to hell. Did your mistress wonder about you, too? I bet she did."

His lips moved and for less than a second she thought he might say something. He could talk. She knew that after seeing him the last time. But no, still not a word.

"Cathy wasn't perfect either," Lizzy told him. "She lied to you, too. Most teenagers lie to their parents about where they're going or not going at one point in their lives. But the difference is," Lizzy said, speaking her thoughts, "is that Cathy loved you unconditionally. She never cared whether or not you showered her with affection, did she? Just being there every once in a while was enough for her. Cathy used to get so excited when you walked through the door. Her words of adoration and love were never returned, but she didn't seem to mind. She loved you. She still does."

Why was I so stubborn? Why couldn't it be that easy for me?

His eyes, dry as the desert, remained fixed on her. For the first time in her adult life, she had his attention. Strangely, a feeling of calm washed over her as she realized she no longer cared. "I am sorry you didn't get to live the life you wanted. I truly am. I wish you could die knowing that you lived a good life and did the best you could. There's no going back now, though. Regardless of your never forgiving me for messing up your life, I forgive you for messing up mine."

He stared blankly ahead.

"OK, that's it." She came to her feet again, reached through the bed rails and took his hand in hers. "I've said what I came to say. I won't be coming to see you anymore. I tried and now I'm done." She leaned over the railing and kissed him on the cheek one last time, wishing things could have been different, but knowing they could never be. "Goodbye, Dad."

CHAPTER 46

Four days after Kitally had been admitted to the hospital, Hayley walked next to the nurse as she pushed Kitally in the wheelchair through the halls, down the elevator, and to her car. After easing Kitally into the passenger seat, she strapped her in. They had been driving for five minutes before Kitally attempted to say something.

"Your words are coming out garbled. Can you speak up?"

"Everything hurts," Kitally managed. "I don't feel good. I'm gonna barf."

"Well, hell, don't do it yet. Give me a minute." Hayley pulled over to the side of the road, jumped out, then ran around the front of her car. Another car honked and she flipped him the bird. She opened the passenger door not a moment too soon. Kitally leaned out and then there was barf everywhere. Thankfully not on Hayley's boots, since she'd jumped back in time. When Kitally was done heaving, Hayley handed her some tissues.

Most of Kitally's head was covered in bandages. Hayley could see just enough of her to see that one eye was still swollen shut. Her face was black and blue and swollen. It was like looking at a Picasso. All the right features were there—they just weren't aligned correctly.

"What do I look like?" she asked after Hayley climbed in behind the wheel.

"You look like shit, worse than shit. I wouldn't look in a mirror for a few weeks if I were you. You know, because you care about shit like that."

"Shit like what?"

"Like looks: fingernail polish, clothes, hair. You know . . . that kind of shit." Hayley merged back onto the main road, keeping her eyes focused ahead.

"You really don't care about any of that?"

Hayley ignored her.

"Maybe your friends are right. Maybe it's time for you to change things up and start tending to yourself. Maybe think about—"

"Stop right there. I've already been lectured by Lizzy and Tommy . . . I don't need anyone else telling me how to live my life."

"Where are we going?"

"My place," Hayley said.

"Who's going to help me with these bandages?"

"I am."

"And what about my painkillers?"

"I've got it all taken care of."

"I can't drive for another week."

"Not a problem."

"What if I need something?"

"Like what?"

"Who's going to wash my hair?"

"That would be me," Hayley said. "Do you have a problem with this setup?"

"I guess not."

"Good."

"What if those guys come back?"

"I'm counting on it."

"What are you going to do?"

"Me and you are going to spend the next few days, maybe weeks, getting ready for them."

"I don't think I'm ready to pick up my machete, though I do want it close by."

"You have one good eye. I need you to do some research and order a few things."

"What do you have in mind?"

"I'm going to get the guys who did this to you," Hayley said.

"I don't think you'll see them again unless you do something to provoke them."

"That's exactly what I plan to do. Brian is obviously watching us. When he realizes I'm determined to find him and have no plans to give up, believe me, he'll send someone else, and this time we'll be ready."

"I need a few days to recuperate."

"I need time, too," Hayley said. "I want to surprise Brian and his friends with something so explosive it will literally blow their minds."

"Sounds good," Kitally said as she reached for her water bottle, tilting it just enough so the water dripped into her mouth.

CHAPTER 47

Killing was addictive. Who knew?

As he waited for Madeline's hairdresser, Megan Vos, to return home after a long day of cutting and styling, Seth sat inside a small room, a basement of sorts that Megan used for storage. There was a heavy chair and a foldable table. There were boxes stacked and set against the wall that were labeled with things like "kitchen items" and "ski clothes." There were also high stacks of books and magazines. As he flipped through one magazine after another, he happened upon an article about the psychology of murderers. *Hello.* Interesting. It contained a list of the reasons someone might commit murder. Number-one reason: easily frustrated, limited impulse control. *Not true. I have full control. I know exactly what I'm doing.* Number two: frequently expresses anger. *Sure, yeah, maybe I'll give them that one.* Number three: resents authority, insubordinate. *Definitely.* Number four: a killer would never admit to it, but extreme pleasure is derived whenever they are able to express their irritation or fury. *Right again.*

He inwardly laughed at the ridiculous mind games he often played to keep himself occupied in times like this. One thing the article didn't mention was that becoming a predator of sorts, no matter the reasons, could be lonely at times. So much waiting. So much work, keeping his mind busy.

He lifted his head at the sound of her footsteps upstairs.

The wait was over. She was home.

He rubbed his fingers and had to stop himself from cracking his knuckles so she wouldn't hear him. It wasn't easy. His guess was that she didn't come downstairs very often. Boxes were stacked up against one wall. No washer or dryer or second freezer. She kept her suitcases down there, which was why he hadn't brought one of his own this time. This wasn't the first time he'd come to her house. He wanted to experiment with Megan. He had a lot of new toys he wanted to try out and his excitement threatened to ruin everything. He was eager to just run upstairs, stick her with the syringe and get started. He was considering doing just that when he heard another voice—a man's voice.

His jaw twitched. He needed to stay calm. *Think. Think. Think.*

Looking around the room, he tried to figure out how he could deal with two people in such a small space. He didn't like last-minute changes, but it didn't matter; he needed to figure this out. He had only one syringe. He looked through his bag, examined all the stuff he'd been gathering for weeks now: stun gun, hammer, Mace, knives, box cutter, ropes, and duct tape. He'd thought about bringing the blowtorch, but decided against it at the last minute. He put the syringe in the front pocket of his shirt, grabbed the hammer, and began to pace. This wasn't part of the plan. He should leave, but he knew he couldn't. He was too excited.

"This is Madeline's fault," he said as he walked up the stairs and opened the door, surprised to see that nobody was in the main room.

He looked around as he made his way to the kitchen. Nobody was there.

Music. Music sounded from another room. For Christ's sake, what was Megan doing? He headed that way, walked right into the bedroom, and didn't hesitate to bash the hammer into the guy's head. "Madeline's fault," he said over and over, oblivious of everything around him until he suddenly realized he needed to shut the hairdresser up before she alerted the whole fucking neighborhood.

There was blood all over the bedsheets. He grabbed the woman and choked her until she passed out. For a minute there, he thought he might have killed her, but then he put two fingers to her wrist and felt a pulse. He did the same for the man and felt nothing. He pushed the woman off the bed and made quick work of using the pillowcases to wrap the man's caved-in head. After wrapping the man's body in the sheets, he ran around the room collecting the guy's stuff—his clothes, wallet, shoes. He tossed it all in a heap on top of him before rolling him up in the bed cover.

More blood splatter on the headboard, a few spots on the mattress, but all in all it wouldn't be too difficult to clean up. He dragged the rolled-up sheets to the floor. *Thunk.* Thankfully the guy weighed well under two hundred pounds; he dragged him through the kitchen and into the garage. Megan's car was parked in the garage—all part of the plan—but he needed her keys so he could open the trunk.

Back in the house, he was looking around for her purse when he saw the hairdresser crawling across the floor to the front door. What the hell had he been thinking leaving her in the bedroom? Fucking idiot. Shit. Everything was turning to shit.

He reached her in time to grab a fistful of hair and yank her back into the house just as she opened the door. She tried to scream, but he covered her mouth and used a back kick to shut the door behind him.

She was clawing at him, her fingernails raking across his face and neck. She was strong and he had to use every bit of strength he had in him to keep her down. He reached for the syringe, but she slapped it out of his hand and it flew across the room.

They were both breathing hard.

He straddled her to keep her from going anywhere.

She was screaming again. Her long, sharp nails continued to rip into his chin, desperately reaching higher, trying to claw his eyes out. She was a fighter. She wasn't going down easy. He needed to forget about the damage she was doing to his face and shut her up. He rammed his knee into her stomach.

She gasped for breath.

He did it again, harder this time. "Don't fuck with me," he told her.

Her hand fell limp across her chest.

He took a moment to collect himself and that's when she went for his eyes.

The bitch had been playing dead.

Big mistake. He'd told her not to fuck with him and he'd meant it.

CHAPTER 48

Before Lizzy could ring the doorbell, Madeline's neighbor opened the door and invited her inside. James Whitton was the man who had passed out a flyer warning the neighborhood to be on the look-out for a silver Honda Civic. According to Madeline, he was a retired military-police officer and his wife, Teresa, was a retired teacher.

Mrs. Whitton offered her a seat on the couch in the living room and didn't waste time with small talk. These people were serious about keeping their neighborhood safe.

"Your neighbor Madeline Blair showed me the flyer you passed around, and I was interested in learning more about the car you saw. It says on the flyer that it was a silver Honda Civic, but every few years the look of that particular make and model changes, so I brought you some photos to look at." Lizzy laid six pictures across the coffee table. "Do any of these look like the car you saw?"

Mr. Whitton pointed to the 1990 model. "It looked just like that. One of the back windows was partly rolled down and there was water damage in the backseat. There was a lot of stuff back there, too—clothes, trash, empty cans of soda pop."

"Did you speak to the driver?"

"I certainly did. He was male, probably in his midforties to early fifties. He wore eyeglasses, too."

"Could you give me specifics? Color of hair, things like that?"

"He had a lot of gray and his hair was thinning. His hands were trembling. It was freezing cold outside but he was perspiring."

"Would you say his hair was dark brown or blond?"

"Light brown peppered with dull gray. No sideburns or facial hair to speak of. He had on a dark jacket and some strange-looking pants."

Lizzy lifted a questioning brow.

"You know . . . blue . . . those papery things that doctors wear."

"Scrubs," Lizzy offered.

"That's right. Why would a man in scrubs be sitting in his car for that long? Definitely odd behavior."

"So that's when James played a trick on the man."

Mr. Whitton nodded. "I asked him if he needed help with something. He appeared to give the question some thought before he told me his mother had passed away recently. He then gestured toward Dr. Blair's house and said he used to live there and was just going down memory lane or whatever."

"But James didn't believe him," his wife added, obviously proud of her husband for being extracautious.

"So what did you do?" Lizzy asked.

"Although we've only lived here for a few years, I pretended to know who used to live in Dr. Blair's house. I made up a name, I can't remember exactly—"

"I remember," Mrs. Whitton cut in. "You came right into the house after the man drove off and told me you asked him if he was one of the Johnson boys, to which he replied, yes, he was one of the Johnson boys."

Lizzy smiled at Mr. Whitton. "Very clever."

Mrs. Whitton agreed wholeheartedly. "James told the man to go ahead and take his time, figuring he could go inside and call the police," she went on, "but that's when the man said he needed to get home to his wife, who was probably worrying."

"He left before you could call the police?" Lizzy asked.

"He hightailed it out of here," Mr. Whitton said.

"Did you get his plate numbers?"

He shook his head. "That was my plan all along, but the back plate was missing. I would have taken a look at the front of the car if he hadn't taken off so fast."

Frustrated, Lizzy looked over her notes. She needed a name, a license plate, something that might tell her who was after Madeline. "Anything else?"

"I'd appreciate it if you told us what's going on. My wife saw the police gathered at Dr. Blair's house last week, but she was afraid to step out of the house. I thought I had some clout with the department, but the only thing they could tell me was that everything was under control and there was nothing to worry about."

"Look," Lizzy said, "I can't pretend to know what the police know. They have protocol on when to contact the public and I'm not privy to that information, but I can tell you that Madeline Blair has reason to believe she has a stalker." Lizzy truly didn't want to scare these people, but they were Madeline's neighbors and they might be her best hope of seeing something and reporting back. "This vehicle you saw could very well belong to the man who's been causing her a lot of grief."

"He hasn't physically harmed her in any way, I hope."

"He broke into her house, which is when you must have seen the police cars."

Mrs. Whitton gasped.

"I don't mean to scare you, but at least two of Madeline's friends have gone missing. As far as I'm concerned, this man you spoke to could be dangerous."

"Nobody came knocking on our door," Mr. Whitton said, clearly upset. "Are you saying the police know that her friends are missing and yet they haven't warned us?"

She nodded. "I've asked Detective Chase for twenty-four-hour surveillance in the area, but nothing has been done."

"Do these friends live close by?" Mrs. Whitton asked.

"I do know that one of the missing persons happens to live a few blocks from here."

Lizzy knew she was stirring up shit, but she needed all the help she could get. She had a feeling Detective Chase would be getting an earful as soon as she left.

CHAPTER 49

"Why are you doing this?"

"Because I have to."

"Please, let me go."

"I will," he said. "Give me a minute." He picked up the Taser he'd bought online, examined it, made sure the cartridge was loaded and then set it aside while he untied the ropes from her arms and legs. He'd brought Megan downstairs over an hour ago. The minute he untied her, she bolted for the door. He grabbed the Taser, pulled the trigger, and sent an electric charge through her body before she could get the door open. She went to the ground; her body twitched once or twice and that was it. She couldn't move. He dragged her back to the chair and tied her up again. By the time he was done, he was sweating.

It took a while, but she came back to life. "Where's Brent?" she asked.

He figured she must be in shock. Or maybe the volt of electricity had caused her to experience a bit of amnesia. Brent was in the trunk of her car. Hadn't she seen him drag him out of the bedroom? Maybe not. "He's gone. Maybe he went to get help."

She didn't look convinced. "What do you want with me? Take my money," she said, "my car, anything you want—just let me go, please."

"You all say the same thing. *Let me go. Please. I won't say a word.* Do you realize how that sounds?" He gave her a moment to answer. His hands rolled into fists. "It sounds like bullshit and I hate bullshit." He cracked his knuckles. "I'll tell you what I'm going to do. I just might let you go if you tell me everything you know about Dr. Madeline Blair."

"Madeline? This is about Madeline?"

He got a thrill out of seeing her surprise. It was like an explosion of colorful fireworks going off inside his head.

"Does Madeline know you?"

He smiled. "Better than most. I used to be a figment of her imagination, but that woman brought me to life."

"What do you want to know?" she asked.

There weren't a lot of things people wouldn't do to get out of a tight predicament, and Megan wasn't any different than most. "Tell me something Madeline might have told you in confidence, anything you think that not too many people would know about her."

"I don't understand," she said, her voice excessively squeaky. "Why do you have to tie me up to ask me these questions?"

Because you're my guinea pig, he thought but didn't say.

"Let me go and I'll tell you whatever you want to know."

He sighed as he walked to the desk and picked up the Taser. He brought it back to where she sat and held it to her temple. "Do you really want to find out what a jolt to the head at close range will feel like?"

"No. Please. I'm sorry. I'll tell you about Madeline. I promise."

She was crying now. *That's better.* He put the Taser aside. "Stop your sniveling and start talking."

Her legs were shaking now, her knees literally knocking together. "She's in her thirties. Um, she used to want to be a model.

I've been doing her hair for many years. We're in a book club, too." She dared to look at him. "Is that enough?"

"Not even close."

Between hiccuping sobs she said, "Madeline is athletic. She enjoys skiing at Heavenly."

"You can do better than that."

"I don't know. I can't think."

"Sure you can. Your life is depending on it. I want dirt, lady. I'm not letting you go until you tell me something juicy enough to ruin your friendship with Madeline."

Her bottom lip trembled. "She slept with her best friend two days before his wedding."

"Now we're talking. Please tell me the man's name was David Westlake."

Surprise lit up her watery eyes. "That's him."

"Does his wife know?"

"No."

"Give me the particulars . . . hurry . . . we're almost done here."

"David's wife didn't want Madeline at the wedding . . . is that what you mean?"

"You got it." He cracked all ten fingers.

"His wife was jealous of Madeline's friendship with David, so she laid down the law and told David that Madeline could not attend."

"I bet she was furious," he said.

"At first she was sad, but then the idea of not being at her best friend's wedding ate at her."

"I bet it did. Go on."

"Madeline went to see David." She gave her head a shake. "God, she'd be so upset if she knew I—"

He pressed the tip of the Taser to her temple and she jumped and screamed. When she'd quieted down, eyes rolling wildly up toward the Taser, he said, "Do you think I care how upset Madeline would be?"

"No!"

"I'll bet she told you it was her deepest, most shameful secret. I'll bet she made you swear on your life you wouldn't tell, didn't she?"

She nodded.

"Well, who do you think is the biggest threat right now—Madeline, or me?"

"You." Her lips trembled.

"Good call." He traced the tip of the Taser down the side of her face, then back to her temple. "You were saying Madeline went to see David . . ."

"She brought pictures and yearbooks from their past. They shared memories and they ended up in bed together."

"Madeline, Madeline, Madeline," he said over and over.

"Can I go now?"

He walked to the desk where he'd set up all his tools and picked up a scalpel. "If you think that little electric charge hurt, you might not want to find out what this baby can do. It has a zirconium nitride–coated edge to improve sharpness."

She struggled and cried out.

He set the scalpel down and picked up a recorder, then walked back to Megan. "When I hit this button right here and you see the little red light go on, I want you to say, 'Don't hurt me, Madeline. Why have you done this to me? Let me go.'" He let that settle in for a moment. "Got it?"

Between the sobbing and crying, she managed a nod.

He hit the button and held it close enough for Madeline to get the full effect when she heard the recording.

"Perfect."

"Oh, my God, please, can I go now?"

"Absolutely." He moved behind her chair and pretended to fiddle with the ropes.

"I won't tell a soul," she said, relief lining her voice.

He reached into his pocket, pulled out the syringe that contained a lethal dose of fentanyl, and just before he plunged the needle into her neck, he said, "I believe you."

CHAPTER 50

Three raps on her door prompted Hayley to look through the peephole before she slid open the new deadbolt she'd installed and let Tommy inside.

"Hey, there," he said as he walked past her and set a large box along with Kitally's leather bag on the floor next to the couch.

Hayley had just washed Kitally's hair without getting the bandages over her nose wet. There was a lot of dried blood and matted hair and the whole ordeal took about forty-five minutes. The bandages covering her broken nose started at the middle of her forehead and ended at the tip of her nose. As of yesterday, Hayley no longer needed to pack Kitally's nostrils with dampened gauze strips coated with antibiotics. That was good news. The bad news was that Kitally could talk at her normal capacity again.

"How's the face feeling?" Tommy asked Kitally.

"Like it's been run over by a truck." Kitally frowned. "I better not need to have my nose fixed. I liked my nose just the way it was."

"I'm just glad to see you looking human again. It looks like Hayley has been taking good care of you."

"Yeah, she's been pretty good," Kitally said. "I think she's getting used to me since it's been twenty-four hours since she asked me to stop talking."

The dog was curled up on the couch next to Kitally. Tommy scratched its head and then handed Kitally the keys to her house. "I waited until the house cleaner was finished, then I locked up your place. I don't think there was a vase or a picture frame that wasn't broken. According to the police, the contents of your purse were scattered across the garage floor, but your wallet is missing."

"Son of a bitch. That means I need to start calling credit card companies."

"Do the police have any leads?" Hayley asked from the kitchen.

Tommy shook his head. "There have been several burglaries in the area recently. It sounded to me as if they're writing this one off as a home robbery gone bad."

Hayley cleared the wooden chest of papers and set a bowl of chicken soup in front of Kitally.

"That smells good," Tommy said.

"There's plenty on the stove. Help yourself."

"I'm good. So," Tommy said as he looked from Hayley to Kitally, "what's the plan?"

"Plan?" Hayley asked.

"Well, apparently you two have spent a week passing out flyers offering a reward for anyone who knew where Brian might be. Kitally just got her ass kicked with a message telling you both to lay off or die. Looks like you found Brian. So now what?"

Kitally swallowed a spoonful of soup as she looked at Hayley. "Maybe we should tell him."

"Tell him what?" Tommy asked.

As Kitally repositioned herself on the couch, she winced in pain. "We could use his help, Hayley. If those guys show up again in the next few days, I'm not exactly ready to fight anyone."

Hayley crossed her arms, her gaze set on Tommy. "Why do you want to know about any of this? I thought your Karate Kid business was keeping you extra busy these days."

He raised both hands in the air. "I'm the boss. I have dependable people working for me. I can take as much time off as I need." He took Kitally's machete from the box he'd brought in and made a few quick, well-practiced moves: overhead, outside, and inside body cuts. He stepped into each strike, stopping the machete before the end of each swing.

"Nice," Kitally said.

He put the machete back in the box, then looked at Hayley. "I'm sure there's something I can do to help. Neither of you look like you're in any shape to defend yourself against Brian and his friends."

"I'm ready," Hayley told him.

"Bullshit." He positioned himself in the middle of the room. "I haven't seen you at UFC training in a while. Show me what you got."

Kitally sighed. "Don't be an idiot, Tommy. She'll kick your ass."

Hayley didn't want his help. Didn't need his help. But it was time to shut him up. She walked up to him and got into the same position she used to use when she and Tommy would visit schools in the area with Lizzy and teach kids self-defense.

Tommy struck first.

Hayley ducked.

He kicked.

She jumped.

And then *bam*, he had her on the floor and she wasn't sure how it had happened. They were on the carpet. She was on her side. His legs were interlocked with hers; one of his arms held her arm behind her back.

"Let me go."

"No."

"Let her go, Tommy," Kitally said, worry in her voice.

Hayley gritted her teeth and told him to get out.

"I'm not going anywhere."

His face was inches from hers. She tried to twist her arm out of his grip, but she already knew he had her right where he wanted her and he wasn't budging. That really pissed her off. Not only did Tommy train young kids at his karate place every day, he'd obviously been training hard at the UFC gym.

"If you really want to get Brian and his friends, you need to stop being so stubborn and actually prepare."

"What are you going to do, train me?"

"I thought you'd never ask."

Hayley growled.

Tommy leaned in close to Hayley's neck and sniffed. "You smell good. What are you wearing?"

"Chicken soup and soap."

"You two need to get a room," Kitally cut in.

"If you don't get off me right now," Hayley ground out, "there's no way I'm going to let you help us."

"Ah, that's more like it," he said as he let her go.

She was tempted to put him on his back, but it wasn't worth the energy it would take.

"You need to replace all of that pent-up anger of yours with grit."

Hayley was on her feet, rubbing her wrist. For some reason, she hadn't noticed until now that Tommy had grown in the last couple of years. Not only in height, but in bulk. He'd filled out all over. He was still on the lean side, but more defined. He was twenty-four and he'd finally lost his baby face.

"OK," Kitally said happily, "looks like we've got our own little Justice League."

Justice League? "Listen," Hayley said. "This is my fight. I never intended to drag anybody into this." If she had any sense at all, she thought, she'd pack up and head out alone.

"Take a good look at Kitally," Tommy said, "and tell me that other people aren't already involved in this." When nobody responded, he clapped his hands together. "Let's get started. The first thing we're going to do is whip the two of you back into shape."

Hayley rolled her eyes and went to the kitchen to wash the dishes in the sink.

"Come on," he said, "right now. We're going to the park."

"I just took a painkiller with my soup," Kitally said. "Today you're going to have to focus on Hayley."

"Come on, Hayley, let's go," Tommy said, already annoying the shit out of her. "When you can take me down like you used to, I'll leave you alone."

"Promise?"

"Cross my heart, hope to die."

CHAPTER 51

Lizzy parked a block away from Madeline's house and then walked past a news van and through more than a few angry people hanging out on Madeline's front lawn.

Reporter Stacey Whitmore from Channel 10 News stood near the steps leading to the front door. The moment she saw Lizzy, she gestured for her cameraman to get moving. In an instant, Lizzy found herself face-to-face with a giant lens and Stacey's microphone.

They exchanged knowing looks. They had worked together in the past, when Lizzy found herself in the middle of the Lovebird Killer debacle. Stacey had a knack for finding a story when there wasn't much to go on. Clearly the past few years had given her confidence. She appeared to be much more poised and self-assured, confidently directing her crew to keep filming. "We're talking to Sacramento PI Lizzy Gardner. Ms. Gardner, according to our sources, you've been working closely with Dr. Blair for a few weeks now. Perhaps you can shed some light on why people closest to Dr. Madeline Blair are disappearing."

"Madeline Blair is a killer!" a woman standing on the sidewalk shouted.

Lizzy had seen the commotion on TV even before Madeline called to let her know what was going on. Madeline's hairdresser, Megan Vos, had gone missing. Megan's friends and family wanted answers, especially after they'd caught wind that Megan wasn't the only person associated with Madeline Blair who had recently disappeared.

Megan's family went straight to the press. They wanted information about Madeline. Why hadn't the public been told what was going on? What was being done to find these people? Mostly they wanted to find their daughter.

"The police department handles all missing person cases. Since I am not involved with the police department, I don't have the answers you're looking for."

"Is the police department aware that four people connected to the popular radio host have disappeared recently?"

"Detective Chase is aware of the situation. You'll have to talk to him about specifics."

"Maybe you're not aware of the most recent disappearance, Megan Vos?" Stacey pressed, going so far as to follow Lizzy up the stairs until they both stood in front of Madeline's front door.

"I saw the news this morning just like everyone else," Lizzy said. "I don't know any more than you do."

"Investigators are at Megan's house as we speak," Stacey told her, obviously hoping to get a reaction, but getting none. "The family has confirmed that there are signs of a struggle, including blood splatter in the master bedroom."

"I don't know anything about it," Lizzy said, knocking on the door, thankful when Madeline let her inside.

Madeline shut and locked the door behind her.

Lizzy looked around the main room, then glanced into the kitchen. "Where's your bodyguard?"

"I've been fired from my job. The man did nothing but sit on my couch watching television and eating my food. I can't afford a bodyguard."

"You can't afford not to have one."

Madeline expelled a breath as she took a seat on the edge of the couch. "What am I going to do? The maniac is taking names right out of the address book he stole."

Lizzy's eyes widened. "What address book?"

Madeline looked at Lizzy as she tried to think. "I didn't tell you about it? I told Detective Chase about the book before you arrived the morning I was attacked."

"So your stalker has the names, addresses, and phone numbers of everyone you know?"

She nodded.

"Is there any connection between David, Chris, Amber, and Megan? Anything at all?"

"I'm in a book club with Amber and Megan. We meet once a month, although, of course, with everything that's been going on, I missed the last meeting."

"Who else is a part of the book club?"

"Oh, my God," Madeline said as it all sank in.

"Give me names, Madeline, now."

It wasn't until hours after Madeline and Lizzy had talked to every member of her book club and Lizzy had left her house that Madeline remembered Cindy St. Louis, the receptionist at work, had recently joined the club.

Staying calm, not wanting to panic her, Madeline called her cell phone. She paced the room and gulped down a breath or two. "Pick up your phone, Cindy."

"Hello."

"Cindy, thank goodness. I'm so glad I caught you at home. This is Madeline."

"Madeline," she said, her tone ridden with sympathy. "How are you?"

"I'm doing fine, Cindy."

"I am so sorry about everything that has happened. I know you didn't have anything to do with David's disappearance. I told the police that there was no way you could ever hurt a fly."

"Thank you, Cindy, but I really need you to listen to what I have to say."

"I can't thank you enough for sending me the book I need to read for our next book club meeting," Cindy went on. "That was so thoughtful of you."

Madeline had no idea what she was talking about. "What book?"

"*Obsessed*. I cheated and sort of skimmed through the book. It's really creepy and definitely not my favorite genre, but I'm going to read it, I promise."

"I don't know what's going on, Cindy, but I didn't send you—"

Madeline heard the doorbell. At first she thought it was her own doorbell, but then she realized someone was at Cindy's door.

"Can I call you back?" Cindy asked. "Someone's at the door and I'm expecting a package."

A feeling of dread washed over Madeline. It couldn't be him, could it? "Don't get the door," Madeline said, but Cindy had already hung up the phone.

CHAPTER 52

Brian wasn't sleeping well. Nearly every night since he'd recovered as much as he ever would from Hayley Hansen's mutilation of him and forced himself off of the painkillers that had allowed him to sleep, he would wake up in the middle of the night with visions of her hovering over him. Unable to move, he had no choice but to watch her prepare her knives. First, she pulled out what looked like a diamond-encrusted sharpening stone. Next, she poured a fair amount of mineral oil on the stone. He would ask her what she was doing, but she never said a word as she worked.

On this night, as on every other, she purposely took her time setting the blade at just the right angle before stroking the knife away from the stone in perfect sweeps. Before she could test the sharpness on his chest, he awoke in a cold sweat. Damn it. He'd never thought the little bitch had it in her. He'd fucked her up royally. He'd been so sure that killing her mother would destroy her, but ultimately it only seemed to have made her stronger. He'd known Hayley since she was a little girl. He raked his fingers through tangled hair and realized a part of him took pride in her determination to see this strange sort of relationship between the two of them through to the end. The girl was not going to give up. He shook his head.

Knowing it was pointless to try to get back to sleep, he unlocked the door and headed upstairs, where he found Merrick in bed with two broads. "Get up," he said. "We need to talk."

Merrick came out of his bedroom, half-dressed, and shut the door behind him. "What's going on?"

"I can't sleep. I want you to take care of Hayley and her friend."

"Seriously?" Merrick raked both hands through his hair. "I don't know if it's a good idea."

"I don't care what you think. I want them both dead."

"I don't know, Brian. It's risky. We've worked too hard to let that bitch ruin everything we've built."

Brian lit up a cigarette. "I can't keep the business running smoothly with this hanging over my head."

"Listen," Merrick said. "If we're going to do this, we need to be smart about it. Let me put one of our guys on watch for a few days, make sure she's not working with the feds."

"Sure. I'll give you the rest of the week to figure out what's going on. If Hayley and her friend are working on their own, I want them killed, though, do you understand? No more fucking around. This is the last message I'm going to send and this one is for *everybody* . . . fuck with me and you're dead. Plain and simple."

CHAPTER 53

With everything that was going on of late, doing something normal like making Rice Krispies treats set Lizzy at ease. She set a plate of the marshmallow goodies on the kitchen counter in front of her assistants and said, "Now that Kitally is on the mend, I thought we should get together and see where we're all at."

"These taste pretty good," Kitally said after she swallowed.

"What's with all the Rice Krispies treats?" Hayley asked. "Who are you going to bribe this time?"

"You know me too well," Lizzy said. "I made these for the nurses at Sutter . . . for taking such good care of my father."

"How's he doing?"

"He's hanging in there," she said, doing her best to ignore the pang she felt in her chest.

"How cool is this?" Kitally asked as she held up her cell for them to see.

"What is it?" Lizzy asked.

"It's a GPS tracking application. Anyone can download it and keep track of family and friends. For instance, I can see that my mom has just arrived at Nordstrom's in San Francisco and Dad must be working from home."

"Can anyone use that?" Lizzy asked.

"Absolutely. Here, give me your cell phone. I'll download the app and then you just have to accept my invite."

Lizzy handed Kitally her cell and after only a few moments Lizzy was able to accept. A few minutes later, Kitally showed her the red dot that placed them both at the same exact location.

Kitally gestured for Hayley to hand over her cell phone.

"Not going to happen," Hayley said. "I don't want everyone to know where I go and what I do. Nobody's business."

"Your loss," Kitally said as she grabbed the newspaper sitting on the counter in front of her. "I didn't realize Dr. Blair made front-page news." Kitally read the article, then set the newspaper aside. "Another friend of Madeline's went missing?"

"Two men and three women now. All three women are in a book club with Madeline."

"I'd hate to be a member of that book club," Kitally said.

"Madeline is letting the other members know that they need to be aware of their surroundings."

"What about the police? Are they doing anything about this?"

Lizzy sighed. "All eyes are on Madeline right now."

"What about Chris Porter?" Hayley asked.

"It doesn't look good," Lizzy said. "I found his ex-wife. She lives in the Bay Area. He was supposed to pick up his daughter last weekend, but he was a no-show and she hasn't heard from him."

"Madeline must be freaked out."

"I finally have a lead," Lizzy said. "Madeline's neighbor Mr. Whitton told me that the man sitting in his car for hours was wearing hospital scrubs."

"Ah," Hayley said. "So that's the real reason for the Rice Krispies treats."

"You're right. There's a nurse named Margery who likes to talk. I'm hoping a mouthful of marshmallow treat will get her going."

"It says in the paper that Madeline lost her job," Kitally said. "How is she holding up?"

"As well as can be expected. God knows she's made a lot of mistakes, but I believe she honestly never thought they would jeopardize the lives of her friends."

Lizzy took a seat. "So what about our own missing person case? What's up with Owen Santos?"

"Owen's wife is not even a little bit interested in locating her husband," Hayley said, "which we found odd, considering her financial situation. But then Kitally found something that might explain her reticence."

"What did you find?"

Kitally pulled a file from her purse and showed Lizzy the pictures of Abbi.

Lizzy frowned. "Where did you get these?"

"On a site where people are paid to post pictures of their kids. Ninety percent of the site's clients are parents. They get paid for every click."

"Is there any way to tell if both parents are involved?"

"Highly doubtful that Robin knows anything about it," Kitally said. "Everything I found—user name, et cetera—points to Owen Santos."

"So Robin Santos has not seen these."

"Not yet."

"Prior to finding the pictures," Kitally said, "we did get a chance to talk to Robin's brother and both of her daughters. We got mixed reviews about good ol' Dad."

"Meaning?"

"The older daughter is a cutter," Hayley said. "There's no love lost between her and her father, which is understandable under the circumstances."

"But the younger daughter misses him, or at least the way her family used to be," Kitally added. "Lara said that everyone was happy before her father left."

"What about Owen's friends and coworkers?"

"Nobody can imagine him even having one affair, much less being the kind of lothario his wife paints him as. If there's one consistent comment, it's that he was a homebody."

"He talks to fish," Kitally said.

Lizzy stared at her for a moment. "Say again?"

"Talks to fish," Kitally repeated. "According to Robin's brother, the guy was either on his computer or talking to his fish when he visited. Now we know what he was doing on the computer."

"I need to talk to Robin and show her these pictures," Lizzy said.

"If it's OK with you," Hayley told Lizzy, "I'd like to talk to a few more people before I hand over the file to you."

"That's fine," Lizzy said. "I have two new workers' comp cases." Lizzy handed two files to Kitally. "I figured you could do some surveillance while you're healing." Lizzy looked at Hayley. "If you could loan Kitally your camera, we'll need pictures."

"I have a camera I can use," Kitally told her.

"Great. Let's meet at the office next week. You can give me the Santos file then. If there are no new leads, I'll talk to Robin and her brother and determine where to go from there. No reason to search for a man who would exploit his own daughter. It makes me sick."

As soon as Hayley and Kitally got into the car after Lizzy walked them out, Hayley said, "We're going to pay Robin Santos another visit."

"Right now?"

Hayley nodded, pulling away from the curb.

"Why?"

"I just need to look around a bit. Robin Santos doesn't want to talk to us for a reason. I want to know why."

"I'll go next door and make chocolate cookies with the old lady while you talk to Robin Santos."

"Nope. You wanted this job and now you've got it. You're going to earn every bit of your nine dollars an hour."

"I thought Lizzy agreed to ten."

"Talk to Lizzy if you have a problem. Now listen closely," Hayley said as she merged onto the highway. "Robin isn't going to be happy to see us at her house, but I'll tell her it's important that we talk to her. Once we're inside, I'm going to say I need to use the restroom. That's your cue to start talking and keep her busy while I take a quick look around the back of the house."

"What are you looking for?"

"I'm not sure yet. Do you think you can keep the woman occupied?"

"I can do that."

"Great." After a quiet moment, Hayley said, "We're supposed to meet Tommy at his karate place today. Are you up for it?"

"This is my first day without painkillers."

"Maybe you should just watch and learn."

"And let you two have all the fun? No way."

Less than ten minutes later, they pulled up to the curb outside the Santos home. Hayley rang the doorbell. A few minutes later, the youngest daughter opened the door. "Hi, Lara. I don't know if you remember us. I'm Hayley and this is Kitally."

"I remember you," she said, looking at Kitally. "What happened to your face?"

"I fell down a hill."

"A hill with lots of rocks, looks like."

Kitally brushed her fingers over her swollen jaw. "Yeah, lots of big rocks."

"Is your mom home?" Hayley asked.

"No, but if you want to wait inside, you can. Mom should be home soon."

"Sure, that would be great."

Lara led them into the family room.

After making sure it was OK if she used the bathroom, Hayley gave Kitally a squinty-eyed look, letting her know it was time to start talking and keep Lara busy.

Kitally asked the girl about school and by the time Hayley was halfway down the hall, they were talking about fashion.

The first room on the right was the bathroom. The next room was the office. Bingo. Hayley looked through every drawer, skimmed quickly through a stack of bills on the desk. Everything was neatly organized. The bank statements showed about fifteen hundred dollars in the bank, which confirmed Robin's claims that she was out of money.

Hayley searched through another file cabinet, scanned the books on the bookshelf, looking for anything that might not belong. If the woman was hiding anything, she did a good job hiding her tracks.

Since she could still hear Kitally talking a mile a minute, Hayley moved to the master bedroom at the back of the house. She looked through dresser drawers and under the bed, but came up empty. A glance into the walk-in closet revealed the woman had a shoe fetish. Using the footstool to reach the shoeboxes on the top shelf, she began opening boxes, one at a time. She hit pay dirt on the eighth box: a checkbook and two statements. The account was opened two months ago and there was more than two hundred thousand dollars in it.

A car door sounded. She stopped and listened. Nothing. No sounds of the front door being opened and closed. Working fast, she used her cell phone to take a picture of the bank statement before sliding everything back into place.

Once that was done, she walked back into the family room and went directly to the sliding glass door leading to the backyard.

Kitally glanced her way, noticed Hayley wasn't finished, and quickly moved the conversation to boys. As Hayley slid the door closed behind her, she heard Lara giggle.

The koi pond was large and deep. Rocks of all sizes and shapes encircled the outer edge, along with green ferns and some sort of Japanese pine tree. The fish shimmered in the water in every combination of gold, black, orange, and yellow. They were fascinating to look at, but she didn't have time to admire the fish. As she walked around the pond, her gaze sweeping across the yard, she noticed a large section of grass that had been dug up for a rose garden.

At closer view, she noticed that the rosebushes had been hastily planted.

She sniffed the air, wincing at a sharp, foul smell. When she sniffed again, the smell was gone. Depending on where she stood, the smell eluded her, then returned.

Who planted roses immediately after their spouse went missing?

Kitally and Lara made their way outside.

"Looks like you guys have been busy planting a new garden out here," Hayley said to Lara.

"Mom's been working out here a lot lately. I think the flowers make her happy."

"You need to take a good *long* look at those koi," Hayley told Kitally. "They're mesmerizing."

Kitally took the hint and asked Lara to tell her the names of each fish while Hayley sneaked around to the side of the house and took a side door into the garage, where she made quick work of looking through drawers and cabinets. Her gaze settled on rakes and shovels hanging on the wall. She examined the shovel. Fresh dirt, just as she'd suspected.

"What are you doing in here?"

Hayley whipped around, surprised to see Robin Santos standing two feet away. Hayley stiffened. "We need to talk."

"I thought I made it clear I didn't want to talk. Get out before I call the police."

"Kitally and I have seen the pictures of your daughter, pictures that your husband sold online."

The woman took a shuddering breath.

"Is that why you killed him?" Hayley asked.

Her shoulders fell and she dropped back a step—if the workbench hadn't been there, she might have fallen over. She rubbed hard at her eyes with a thumb and forefinger. "He was raping my daughter," she said in almost a whisper. When she took her hand from her eyes, they were red and puffy. "For seventeen years I was married to that man, and I had no idea what was going on in my own house."

"When did it all start?"

A haunted look took over Mrs. Santos's features. Her lips twitched; her eyes became focused. "I'm not sure. Abbi won't talk about it, but I didn't find out until recently."

"How could that be?"

"Every so often, Owen would bring me a cup of tea before bedtime. On one particular night, I thought I saw him slip something into my cup. I poured the tea down the drain but I didn't tell him. That night I caught him in my daughter's room. He'd been drugging me on the nights he wanted to …" Her voice crackled with anger. She couldn't finish her sentence.

"Abbi never told you what was happening?"

"She was ashamed," Robin said. "She thought it was her fault."

"Does Abbi know you killed him?"

"No, of course not." Robin's hands were shaking. "I never planned to kill Owen. The night I found him in my daughter's room, I kicked him out of the house. I threatened to tell everyone he knew what he did if he didn't go far, far away. Instead of leaving town, though, Owen found a way to clean out our bank accounts. He came home while the girls were at school and said he wasn't going anywhere, said if I told anyone, he would swear I knew what was going on." Mrs. Santos inhaled a sharp breath as she looked Hayley in the eyes. "I had to protect my daughters."

"So you hit him over the head with the shovel when he went outside to take care of his fish?"

Robin nodded. "I hit him more than once. I had to protect Abbi. It was awful, but I had no choice." She held her head high, her hands rolled into fists as if to stop herself from breaking down and at the same time daring Hayley to defend the man.

"Nobody needs to know. Scrub the shovel until it shines and then get rid of the smell in the garden."

Robin's eyes narrowed as she listened closely.

"Agricultural lime should take care of the smell until decomposition has taken place. And I suggest you transfer the bank papers from the shoebox to a lockbox."

"You're not going to turn me in?"

"I know what it's like to be damaged by someone you trust. I only wish I'd had someone like you to take care of business."

Mrs. Santos sucked in a ragged breath. "What about everyone else?"

"The police are already convinced that Owen took the money and ran, so that leaves your brother. Once he drops the case, Lizzy Gardner will drop it, too."

"My brother will never stop looking."

"Maybe he will if you tell him the truth about what Owen was doing to Abbi."

Silence.

"He doesn't need to know what you did. Nobody does. Do you want me to tell your brother what we found on the Internet?"

"No," she said. "I'll tell Andrew what I need to—make him understand that we're better off without Owen."

"So what happened in there?" Kitally asked as they got in the car.

"I found evidence that Owen is in another country and won't be returning."

"I'm glad," Kitally said.

"Yeah, me, too. Is there any way you could hack into that website again and get rid of all the pictures of Abbi?"

"Already taken care of."

Hayley inwardly smiled. She was about to drive off when she saw the neighbor, Helen Smith, calling their names and waving an arm.

Kitally rolled down her window and took the bag of cookies Helen had for them.

"Any luck yet finding Owen?" the woman asked.

"I don't think you'll be seeing Owen Santos again," Kitally said. "It turns out he took the money and ran—left the country, in fact."

"How's Robin handling the news?"

"Robin is going to be fine," Hayley told her.

"I'm glad." Helen beamed at them. "You two girls are quite the pair, you know. With your wild fashion sense and flair for solving mysteries, I bet the two of you will make a big difference in many people's lives."

"That's the plan," Kitally said. "To make the world a safer place for everyone."

Hayley had no words.

"If you're ever in the mood to have a good chat while baking a mean batch of cookies, you both know where to find me."

"You'll definitely be seeing me again," Kitally told her. "Maybe you'll let me style your hair—you know, add a little color to your bangs."

Helen laughed. "It's probably time for a change. I just might take you up on that kind offer."

Kitally reached into her bag and handed the woman a card. "Here's my number if you ever need a private eye."

After they drove off, Hayley glanced at Kitally. "When did you have cards made?"

"I ordered them at the same time I got the cards for offering a reward for Brian's whereabouts. Speaking of which, have you gotten any calls on that burner yet?"

"A few. Nothing substantial."

"At this point it's just a waiting game, I guess."

She's got that right, Hayley thought. It was a waiting game. And she'd wait until the world ended if she had to. Tomorrow or ten years from now—it didn't matter. She would make him pay for what he did.

CHAPTER 54

Lizzy delivered the marshmallow treats to the nurses' station, glad to see Margery was one of the nurses on shift. "Good morning," Lizzy said. "I brought you all some treats for taking such good care of Dad."

"How sweet of you. I'll be sure and put these in the break room for everyone to enjoy."

"Great," Lizzy said as she eyed a picture of Margery dressed in purple at a basketball game. "Looks like you're a Kings fan."

"You betcha. I've had season tickets for years. I did my best to help smash the Guinness World Record for loudest crowd."

"That's terrific. Good for you. I haven't been to a game in years, but I'll never forget that shot Kevin Martin made to beat the Spurs."

Margery laughed. "That was in 2006. I used to love watching Bibby, especially during the 2002 playoffs. Gosh. I could go on and on, but I'll spare you." She eyed the plate of treats. "Do you want one?"

"No. Those are for you and the rest of the staff, but you go right ahead."

"Don't mind if I do," Margery said, plucking one of the treats from the plate. "Come on, have a seat here with me in the junk food nook." She ushered Lizzy around a partition to a round table littered with boxes of store-bought cookies and chips. When Lizzy raised her eyebrows at the display, Margery shrugged. "This is a very stressful job, let me tell you. Better than drinking or drugs, I always say."

Lizzy joined her at the table, and it was simple enough to lead Margery to the subject she had in mind: drinking to relieve stress became popping pills which became Lizzy asking if there were ever any problems with staff dipping into the hospital's pharmacy.

"Oh, I think any hospital has to be on guard against such things," Margery said. "Much too common."

"Oh, really?" Lizzy said. "Well, makes sense. So stressful, as you say. You make it seem like you've had some recent experience with the issue here."

"Do I?" Margery said around a bite of her second Rice Krispies treat.

"Or maybe I heard one of the other nurses mention it. Some problem with missing syringes of . . . what was it? Fentanyl and etorphine." She smiled. "Why I would remember *that* particular detail, I have no idea."

"Well, you certainly did remember correctly," Margery said with a twinkle in her eye. "Very impressive."

"Any idea who might be responsible?"

Margery looked both ways. "I hate to say it, but we all have our eyes on Tim Hughes." Margery made a zipping motion over her mouth. "It's all very confidential, so you didn't hear that from me."

"I understand," Lizzy said.

"Um, I shouldn't say any more than I already have, but you might be wise to stay away from him."

"Why is that?"

She lowered her voice. "He's a bit of a perv, if you know what I mean."

"How is it that he's still working here?"

"Most of the females on this floor have complained, but he's never touched anyone, so there's really not a lot we can do about it. He has a bad habit of staring at the female nurses." She shivered. "It's seriously creepy. Every once in a while he slips someone a note telling her how sexy she looks. He's been reprimanded, and his hours were cut, but evidently until he makes a move, our hands are tied."

Lizzy glanced around. "Is he here today?"

Margery shook her head. "Tim and another nurse share a shift. Tim works Mondays, Wednesdays, and Fridays. That's how we figured out he must be the one responsible for the missing syringes."

Lizzy thanked the woman before she headed out. Back in her car, she used her cell phone to log on to the Internet. The name and address for Tim Hughes popped right up in the second database she searched. He lived in Rancho Cordova. If there wasn't any traffic, she could be at his house in thirty minutes.

The house belonging to Tim Hughes turned out to be a faded-brown one-story that blended in with the oak trees surrounding it. The walkway was cracked and the front yard was covered with dead leaves. Lizzy sat in her car for a few minutes while she thought about what she would say if he answered the door. She decided to go with the truth.

After making sure her gun was loaded and strapped into her shoulder holster, she climbed out of her car and walked up Tim's driveway.

He answered the door right away, even held it open as if he had nothing to hide. The man wore jeans and a white button-down shirt. He stood at about five foot ten and had big ears and a pointy chin. "If you're selling something," he said, "I'm not interested."

"I'm not selling anything," Lizzy told him. "Dr. Madeline Blair hired me to investigate a problem she's having at her radio station."

His expression didn't change. No sign of recognition whatsoever. "I don't listen to the radio much. What sort of problem is this lady having?"

"Her friends are missing and I have reason to believe you might be able to help me locate them."

"Really?" He looked her over, slowly, starting at her ankles and working his gaze all the way up to her chest. "I'm in the middle of lunch right now," he said, "but if you want to come on in and rattle off a few names while I eat, I don't mind."

"Well, I hate to be a bother and interrupt your lunch," she answered, looking past him. No one else appeared to be inside.

"Inviting a pretty lady to join me for lunch isn't exactly what I would call a bother. It's more like a treat."

Lizzy forced a smile and stepped into his house. The place had a moldy, dank smell and she fought the urge to cover her nose. She gestured for him to go first. There was no way she was going to give him the chance to bash her over the head when she wasn't looking. He made a beeline to the kitchen table, where his sandwich and a tall glass of milk awaited him. He opened the refrigerator, pulled out a pitcher of juice, and poured her a glass. He set the glass on the table across from him and gestured for her to take a seat. "Can I get you anything?"

"No, thank you. I'll just stand right here while you finish up."

"I won't feel comfortable eating unless you take a seat." He gestured again to the seat across from him. "Come on. It's nice cold cranberry juice. After I eat my sandwich, I'll make us both a real drink and we can watch a movie together. This is my day off, after all."

"No, thank you," she said again. She flashed him the diamond ring on her left hand. "Not interested."

He approached her then, stepped close enough for her to feel his warm breath against the side of her face. "Are you sure about that?"

The beat of her heart kicked up a notch. "I'm sure." She took two steps backward.

"Not too many women I know would enter a man's house if she weren't interested."

She looked into his eyes. "Do you know Chris Porter?"

"Never heard of him," he said as he stepped closer again.

"What about David Westlake?"

"Doesn't ring any bells. Come on. Sit down. Have some juice."

"Ever heard of Amber Olinger?"

He shook his head. "Did anyone ever tell you what pretty green eyes you have?"

Lizzy had had enough. She reached her hand over her shoulder and pulled out her gun.

"Whoa, whoa, whoa," he said, both hands up, fingers splayed.

"Sit down and eat your goddamn lunch," she told him. "Now!"

He sat down, but didn't take a bite of his sandwich.

"Now tell me how you know Megan Vos," Lizzy said, "and make it quick because I'm feeling a little twitchy."

"I've never heard of any of those people. I don't know why you're here." His face reddened as he reached into his back pocket.

About to draw her gun, Lizzy relaxed when he pulled out his wallet, put it on the table and pushed it toward her. "Is this what you came for? Take it. Take whatever you want. I don't want any trouble."

"If you didn't want any trouble, why have you been stealing syringes from the hospital where you work?"

"Oh, God. Is that what this is about?" His head fell forward, his chin hitting his chest. A long moment passed before he gathered the courage to look at her again. "Are you with the DEA?"

Lizzy didn't know what to think of the man. She hadn't seen the slightest glimmer of recognition when she'd said the names of the missing people. But he definitely knew about the missing drugs.

"What did you do with the fentanyl and etorphine you stole from the hospital?"

"I don't know about any fentanyl or etorphine. The only drug Seth sold me was the Rohypnol."

"The date rape drug?" she asked.

"I never raped anyone."

"Oh, please. And bears don't shit in the woods. Maybe I should take a good look around this place."

He exhaled. "I swear on the Bible I never took any fentanyl or etorphine."

"OK, let's pretend you're telling the truth. You said a guy named Seth gave you the Rohypnol. Does Seth work at the hospital, too?"

"If you so much as mention that I'm the one who told you any of this, his wife will fire me on the spot."

"His wife?"

"Janelle Brown, head nurse at the hospital. Her husband Seth is off his rocker . . . some sort of skiing accident damaged his frontal lobe when he was a kid. None of us at the hospital understand why Janelle puts up with his odd behavior, but she does. Margery told me he didn't used to be so bad. Apparently Seth has gotten worse over the years. He used to be a male nurse like me, but the hospital had to let him go. Now he's nothing more than a volunteer."

"You mean like a candy striper?"

"Yes, that's exactly what I mean."

"Does he have access to all the places you have access to?"

"He sure does. He's not supposed to, but he's always helping Janelle set up the surgery room."

"Unbelievable."

"It happens all the time."

Today was errand day.

After calling in sick, Seth had delivered a letter to Debra Westlake's mailbox. The letter detailed everything he knew about her husband's affair with Madeline Blair. Debra Westlake would not be happy to discover that Madeline had destroyed her life both before and after her husband's disappearance.

His next stop had been paying Cindy St. Louis a visit. With a smile on her young face, Cindy opened the door. The receptionist recognized him, but couldn't recall where they had first met until he reminded her. Ten minutes later, he carried her dead body out in a duffel bag and shoved her into his trunk. Nobody stopped him. Nobody cared. He took her home and hid her body the best way possible under the circumstances. He would take her to the woods later, but first he needed to take care of Lizzy Gardner.

Now, Seth peered through the binoculars. There she was. Lizzy Gardner. Clear as day. Blonde. Petite. Fresh faced, little or no makeup. A natural beauty. He sucked in a breath. Pretty or no, the woman really was becoming a problem. Not only had she been hanging around the hospital asking too many questions, now she was visiting his coworkers.

She was up to no good and he didn't like it one bit.

Tim answered the door. The female nurses at Sutter always complained about Tim's roving eyes, especially the way he looked at their breasts when he spoke to them. But the private eye didn't seem to care if ol' Tim was a lecher or not—she just walked right inside.

He had followed Lizzy Gardner from Sacramento to Rancho Cordova. If he'd known where she was headed, he would have called Tim and told him not to answer his door.

In just a few hours, it had become very clear he was going to have to take care of Lizzy Gardner sooner rather than later. One thing was for sure: he wasn't going to let her out of his sight. He had everything he needed in the trunk of his car. He picked up his phone and decided to play a little Candy Crush while he waited.

CHAPTER 55

Hayley could feel somebody looking at her. Sure enough, Dog was sitting close by, staring her down. The vitamins the vet had told her to give him were actually working. His fur had grown in, covering the bald spots. She went to the kitchen. Dog followed her and then watched her prepare his meal.

"This is it—your last meal. Seriously." She turned the can over to show the dog that it was empty. "Don't worry, though; Kitally told me she found the perfect home for you. They have a big family. You'll like hanging out with a bunch of kids. They're not like Hudson, who just sits around and pets you. These kids like to run around outside and play tag all day long. You'll probably fall over dead from happiness within the first fifteen minutes."

The dog tilted his head.

I'm doing it. I'm talking to a dog. She placed the dog dish in front of him and then found herself watching him eat. Lizzy was a pain in the ass. She was good, Hayley had to admit. She'd done it again . . . found a way to get her to keep the dog, make the animal matter to her. Fuck that. She would show Lizzy. The dog had to go.

As she rinsed the can out in the sink, she saw a car pull up to the curb.

Unbelievable.

It was the same guy she'd seen driving the Chrysler LeBaron, the man they'd chased after. She watched him look around before he climbed out of his vehicle and shut the door.

He was here in broad daylight and he was coming her way. That could only mean one thing and it wasn't good.

She opened the cupboard next to the refrigerator, ran her hand over the top shelf until she felt her Glock and her Taser. She shoved the Taser in her back pocket and the gun in her waistband. Moving fast, she bent down and scooped up Dog. "Sorry, pooch. You'll have to eat later." She left everything else where it was. There wasn't time to do much else. She hustled out the door, locked it, then jogged down the stairs and ran to the other side of the building. With the dog clutched to her body, she stopped to listen to the man's footfalls as he trudged up the stairs. She heard him knock on the door.

The dog whimpered. She clamped a hand over Dog's nose. After a moment she peeked around the side of the garage and saw the man picking the lock. He then pulled out his gun and walked inside.

Fueled by adrenaline, Hayley looked around the parking lot, saw the Dumpster and ran that way.

It was less than ten minutes before she heard him returning to his car. She couldn't believe Brian would be stupid enough to send someone she would recognize. After all this time, he really was back? Did he think he could just kill her mother, hide out for a few years, and then come back to Sacramento like nothing had ever happened?

The door came open. Hayley was curled up tight in the backseat, hidden beneath some of the crap left in his car: an old sweatshirt, a pair of boots, a pile of fast-food wrappers. What was he doing? Had he seen her? Why wasn't he closing the door?

Afraid he might be looking over his seat at her, she tried not to breathe.

A minute later, she felt movement as he climbed the rest of the way inside and shut the door.

It was now or never. In one swift movement, she rose and put the barrel of the gun to the back of his head. "Turn the ignition on and drive into the garage over there."

He didn't say a word. He just did as she told him. Once they were inside the garage, she said, "Turn off the ignition and throw the keys out the window."

He looked in the rearview mirror, his gaze locking on hers. He dared to smile. "You're not going to shoot me," he said, his tone smug and all knowing.

"How did you know?" With her left hand, she got him with her Taser. The noise he made sounded like a whistle as his body convulsed. She gave him another jolt just to be sure before leaning over him and grabbing the keys.

Working fast, she climbed out of the car and shut the garage door. As she dragged him out of the car and toward the support beam in the middle of the garage, his head dropped hard against the floor. He was definitely going to feel that when he came to. She duct-taped his legs, arms and mouth so he wouldn't be able to scream for help.

The ringing of her cell phone stopped her. The sound was coming from his pants pocket. The asshole had taken her cell from the apartment. She emptied all of his pockets: two of her best pocketknives, her cell phone, and two of Kitally's Pop-Tarts, still wrapped. She grabbed an empty fast-food bag from the backseat of his car and put all of the items inside. She took his cell phone, too, then searched his car for weapons.

After using a combination of twine and rope to tie him to the beam, she locked and bolted the garage from the outside.

By the time Hayley climbed to the top of the Dumpster and looked inside, the dog had eaten half of the neighborhood's leftovers. He looked up at her, his tail thumping against some cardboard as he quickly swallowed a wrapper from an old Whopper. She jumped in and got him out before he could eat any more crap. "That's not good for you. You're going to be sick."

"What are you doing in there?"

Hayley looked over the edge. "Here, take the dog."

Kitally took the animal, but quickly put him on the ground. "He stinks. That's disgusting. Why didn't you tell me you didn't have enough money for food? I would have brought you something."

"I don't need food. It's a long story." Hayley climbed to the top of the bin, jumped to the ground. Dog followed her back to the apartment. So did Kitally. "Let's go inside," she said. "It's going to be a long night."

CHAPTER 56

Madeline was upstairs changing when she heard the doorbell. She prayed it was the police coming to tell her that they'd found Cindy or Megan—anyone. Cindy had already been missing for over twenty-four hours. Madeline's nerves were shot. But when she peeked out the window, it was Debra Westlake's car parked in front of her house. She grabbed a sweater and pulled it over her head before making her way downstairs.

The doorbell wouldn't stop buzzing.

She prayed Debra had news about David. Although it didn't make sense that she would come all this way to give her the news.

She looked through the peephole before opening the door.

Debra barged right in.

Madeline looked around outside before shutting the door and locking it.

Red in the face, Debra held a crumpled piece of paper in her trembling hands. She slammed the paper on the dining room table. "I want you to read this and then I want the truth."

Madeline read the letter aloud. " 'Dear Debra, we have never met but I think you should know the truth about Dr. Blair. She had an affair with your husband' "—she was committed to reading the thing aloud now, but her throat was constricting nearly shut—"'two days before you were married. In light of your husband's disappearance, I thought it was important that you know the whole truth. Sincerely, Concerned.'"

Debra was pacing the room with her hands jammed into the pockets of her thick parka—back and forth, head down. When she realized Madeline had finished reading, she stopped and looked at her. "Is it true? Did you sleep with David two days before our wedding?"

"Debra, it wasn't like that. We spent one night together long before you two ever met."

"It's written all over your face. You're lying."

"It's the truth."

"David would have told me if you two had slept together years before we met, but he never would have told me if it happened two days before we took our wedding vows."

Madeline couldn't believe this was happening. All this time had passed and nobody knew about their one night together. Nobody. "We had been drinking. We both regretted it the moment it was over. It never should have happened. We didn't want it to ruin our friendship, so we put it behind us, pretended it never happened."

Debra pulled out a gun and aimed it at Madeline's chest. "You are a terrible person. You know that, don't you?"

"What are you doing?"

Madeline's phone began to ring in the other room.

"Stay right where you are," Debra told her.

"Debra, whoever gave you that letter is the same person who's been trying to discredit me."

Debra groaned. "Oh, give me a break."

"You don't want to use that gun. What about your children?"

"Shut up and tell me what you did with David."

Madeline tried to stay calm as she tried to think. "I swear to you, Debra, I don't know where David is. I want to find him as badly as you do."

"Are you still in love with him?"

How had it come to this? "I was never in love with David. We're friends. That's all we've ever been."

"I truly don't think you understand what you've done, Madeline. All of these years, it's always been about you. *Madeline, Madeline, Madeline.* I'm so sick of hearing your name. You would do and say anything if it was to your benefit."

"That's not true. I've always thought of you and the girls as family."

Debra let out a short, caustic laugh. "I don't want to hear it. You've ruined my life and my children's lives. You deserve to die."

CHAPTER 57

Tommy, Hayley, and Kitally had been racking their brains for hours. According to his ID, the guy tied up in the garage below them went by the name of Frank Briggs.

Tommy was in the process of going through the contacts on Frank's cell phone, writing down names and numbers, anything that might lead them to Brian.

"I've searched his car," Hayley said. "There isn't one damn thing in there that will help us find Brian, but the strange thing is that I think I've met this guy before."

Tommy frowned. "Does the name mean anything to you?"

"No, that's the weird part. But he was one of Mom's drug connections, I'm sure of it."

"I can't find anything on Frank Briggs," Kitally said. "It's as if the guy doesn't exist."

"Shit," Hayley blurted. "His name isn't Frank." She paced the room. "I remember him now. His real name is Pete." She snapped her fingers. "Pete Lasko. Brian went to a lot of trouble to cover his tracks."

"I would too if I were wanted for murder," Tommy said.

"Whatever his name is," Kitally said, "I don't like having him beneath us. I feel like we're sitting ducks."

"I'm not letting him go until he tells me where Brian is," Hayley said. "If you have a better idea, I'm all ears."

"We could put a GPS tracker on his car and let him go," Tommy offered.

Hayley shook her head. "Too risky. There's no way I'm letting him go at this point."

"Let's think about this," Kitally said. "We need to know Brian's whereabouts, plain and simple. So I suggest we take turns interrogating the man. I'll go first since the asshole stole my Pop-Tarts."

"I'll go with you," Hayley said. "I'll stand outside the garage door and make sure nobody comes around. Don't remove the tape from his mouth unless you turn up the music. There's an old boom box inside the garage."

For the next few hours, the three of them took turns trying to wear the man down, but he wouldn't talk, even after listening to Kitally badger and threaten him with her machete for at least an hour straight.

Hayley went last. She would have shot the guy or given him the waterboard treatment if she thought it would mean getting a chance to see Brian face-to-face, but a gunshot would alert the neighbors and the last thing she needed was for the police to get involved.

Tommy looked up from his laptop when she walked through the door. "You think Frank/Pete came here to take you out?" he asked.

Hayley nodded. "I'm sure of it. As soon as I saw him pull up and climb out of his car, I knew he wasn't here to beat me up. For some reason, Brian decided sending a message wasn't enough . . . the ten-thousand-dollar reward must have scared him."

"If that's true, then I think we can assume Brian is going to be calling his boy sooner rather than later to see what happened."

"That makes sense," Hayley said. "So what do you have in mind?"

"When Brian calls, I can use information from a mobile infrastructure to track him down. We'll also be able to listen in on his voice-mail messages and calls."

"I don't care who he's talking to," Hayley said. "I just need his location."

"This is perfect," Kitally chimed in. "I don't know why we didn't think of it hours ago. There are a couple of ways we can handle this, but I suggest cell-tower triangulation."

"How long would that take?" Hayley asked.

"Not long if we had a connection with Verizon or AT&T," Tommy said.

Kitally smiled. "Ask and you shall receive. I've had access to both for years," she said. "We'll need to use the computer room at my parents' home in El Dorado Hills."

"It won't work," Tommy said, "unless we have access to MMC, MNC, and LAC codes, not to mention unique cell-tower ID."

"Not a problem."

"How close will you be able to track Brian?" Hayley asked, desperate to keep them on the *real* subject and away from technobabble.

"If Tommy is able to find the coordinates of the three closest towers, we can pin Brian's location down to what side of the room he's standing in."

"Unless he has a decent cell phone jammer," Tommy added.

It couldn't be that easy. "What if his phone is turned off?"

Kitally shrugged. "Doesn't matter. We can still track him."

"Won't he know he's being tracked?"

"Nope, his phone won't even ring. Even if he's on a call, there's less than a ten percent chance he would hear something odd."

"We could call his phone with a spoofed caller ID," Kitally added. "If he doesn't answer, we just enter his voice mail without a PIN—"

"How would you enter it without a PIN?"

"Just getting in to the point where it *asks* for the PIN is far enough."

"Right," Tommy chimed in. "It's all about fundamental vulnerabilities in the way mobile providers interoperate over the GSM infrastructure. There's a weakness in the cell phone network . . . it all has to do with how these companies connect. They literally reveal entire interfaces to one another, which leaves them exposed and open for attack."

"It's like attacking the Internet at router level," Kitally said.

Tommy agreed.

Hayley was beginning to get a headache, but as long as they could get Brian's exact location, she didn't care if they talked like this all night. "What do we need to make this happen?"

"We need to get to the computers in my father's data center."

"Won't your parents wonder what we're up to?" Tommy asked.

"Nah," Kitally said. "They'll be thrilled I have new friends. Wait until you see this room. We have HD data projectors, servers, scanners—the equipment is sweet."

Tommy looked at Hayley. "What do you think?"

"I think we need to make this happen before Brian discovers what we're up to."

"Once we find Brian's location," Kitally asked, "are we ready to go?"

"We have explosives, guns, and knives," Tommy said. "But what we don't have is manpower. Three of us, and who knows how many of them."

"Hopefully we'll be enough," Hayley said. "Let's do this."

CHAPTER 58

Lizzy rushed out of the elevator and walked at a good clip to the nurses' station. She needed to find Seth Brown, wanted to meet the man face-to-face and see what he had to say about taking the drugs. Maybe Tim Hughes had lied to her, but before she could call the police about either man, she needed to know exactly whom and what she was dealing with. She didn't have much on either man. There was no way Detective Chase would believe a word she said without solid proof.

Not one nurse was to be found in the nurses' area. She glanced in the three hospital rooms closest to the counter where the nurses could usually be found when they weren't with a patient. Nobody was there, so she went to the break room where she knew Margery liked to hang out. There she was, talking to another nurse.

Margery skittered over to the door and told Lizzy the break room was for hospital personnel only.

"That's fine, Margery, but I have a quick question and I figured you would be the one to ask."

"What is it, dear?"

"Do you know where I can find Seth Brown?"

"He called in sick today. His wife, Janelle, would know where he is, but she'll be in surgery for another hour at least."

"You wouldn't happen to know where they live, would you?"

"Oh, yes, indeed, but I couldn't give out private information like that. Maybe if you tell me what this is about, I can give Seth a call."

"No, that's OK," Lizzy said. "I'll come back later."

"If you're sure," Margery said. "Everyone's been enjoying the treats you dropped off."

"I'm glad." Before Lizzy left, she thought of something else and called out Margery's name before she returned to her seat.

Margery looked at her and waited.

"I realize this might sound like a strange question, but you wouldn't happen to know what kind of car Seth Brown drives, would you?"

Margery shook her head, but another nurse sitting at a different table nodded her head while she finished chewing. After she swallowed, she said, "He drives a Honda Civic. The only reason I know that is because he hung a picture of it on the corkboard." She pointed to the wall where Help Wanted signs and other random notes and pictures were pinned.

Lizzy walked that way. Sure enough, there was a picture of the same car Mr. Whitton had seen in his neighborhood. Also included on the piece of paper pinned to the corkboard were little paper tabs with Seth Brown's name and telephone number. "Mind if I take one of these?" Lizzy asked.

"Are you looking for a car?" Margery wanted to know, as though suddenly suspicious.

Lizzy ripped off one of the tabs. "It's not for me, but this might be the perfect car for my niece."

The other nurse smiled. "Seth will be thrilled. He just put that up yesterday."

"Kitally, this is Lizzy. Is Hayley around? She didn't answer her phone."

"She's around here somewhere. Is there something I can help you with?"

"That would be great. I need an address for Janelle and Seth Brown. For some reason, they're not coming up on my database."

"No problem. Just give me a minute."

Instead of taking the elevator, Lizzy walked up the stairway to the fifth level of the parking garage where she'd parked her car. She passed a couple on her way.

"Here it is," Kitally said. "The Browns live in Sacramento."

"Can you go ahead and text me their address?"

"Sure." After a short pause, she said, "Done."

Lizzy reached the top of the landing and looked around.

"Does this have to do with Madeline Blair's stalker?" Kitally asked.

"Yes, it does. I might have identified the man. I'll update you and Hayley later. I've gotta go."

"OK," Kitally said. "I'll talk to you later."

Lizzy thought about calling Detective Chase, but she didn't trust him. Her next thought was to call Jared, but he was out of town, so she decided to call Jared's old FBI friend Jimmy Martin. She told Jimmy everything she'd learned so far about Seth Brown. Although she didn't have any proof yet that he was Madeline's stalker and the person responsible for five missing persons, she felt the need to let someone in authority know what was going on.

She hung up the phone just as she reached the floor where she'd parked her car. Because she'd been in a hurry when she'd first arrived at the hospital, she couldn't remember where she parked.

She walked down a long row of parked cars, peering around the poorly lit, deserted garage. Then she inwardly scolded herself when she realized she could use her key fob to find her car. She held her key in front of her and pushed the unlock button. A beep sounded not far ahead of her—she was headed in the right direction.

The moment she wrapped her fingers around the door handle, she saw movement out of the corner of her eye.

But it was too late.

Something jabbed the back of her arm. She reached over her shoulder, yanked out what had stabbed her—a syringe—and tossed it away, already spinning and cocking one leg, but before she could kick her attacker, her leg buckled.

She held on to her car to keep from falling to the concrete. A woozy sensation enveloped her, causing her to stagger as her attacker came at her. With the last of her strength, she jammed the palm of her hand into his nose.

Blood spurted. He cursed.

It was no use. Both legs gave out. Her body felt weightless as he picked her up, her limbs numb as he carried her and dropped her into the trunk of a car. Before the lid of the trunk was slammed shut, she saw a glimpse of madness: unkempt hair, bulging eyes, and a smirk of satisfaction playing on his lips.

CHAPTER 59

Hayley and Tommy followed Kitally inside her parents' home.

The house was massive, all marble columns and stone floors. According to Kitally, if you stood in the backyard, you could see 270-degree views of Folsom Lake. Hayley half imagined she'd find a heliport out there.

Kitally's mom greeted them. She didn't look anything like Kitally. She was taller and big boned. The only features tying them together were the brown eyes and the wide smile.

People were talking in the other room.

After making quick introductions, Kitally got right to the point of their visit. "We need to use the computer room. We won't be too long."

"That's fine, dear. Come closer, though, so I can take a closer look at your face. The injuries are much worse than you let on. I think you need to give up skateboarding."

"Don't worry, I gave my skateboard to Tommy. He's better at it anyway."

Tommy shrugged.

"Are you and Dad entertaining tonight?" Kitally asked. "You look great, by the way."

"Thanks. We're just waiting for another couple before we head out for dinner and a show in San Francisco. Come say hello to everyone."

Kitally told Tommy and Hayley to stay where they were. She would be right back. Then she followed her mother into the living room.

There were four couples and right away Kitally recognized one of the ladies as the woman she'd seen with her dad—his mistress.

Her dad visibly stiffened, but the woman either had no idea Kitally knew about her and her dad or she just didn't care.

Her dad frowned. "I had no idea your injuries were so bad."

"It's pretty bad, I know," Kitally agreed. "My face looks as if a couple of guys followed me home and beat the crap out of me, doesn't it?"

"That's enough," her father warned.

"Are you going to introduce us to your friends?" her dad's mistress asked.

"No."

The woman smiled as if Kitally were merely playing with her. "What do you kids do for fun these days?"

Kitally wanted to tell her to fuck off and that it was none of her business. The fact that she referred to her as a kid was enough to make her want to drop-kick the woman and then put an elbow to her face. It made her crazy to think her father was entertaining this woman right under her mother's nose. She knew she should just let it go, ignore the woman and walk off, but she didn't have it in her. "We're going to use Dad's computer room and see if we can hack into a governmental GPS tracking system, but I don't think it's going to be easy."

Nervous laughter erupted.

Her father gave her mother a stern look, as if to say, *I told you not to introduce her to our guests.*

"Don't worry, Dad, we won't be staying long."

He let out a ponderous sigh. He knew if he pushed her, she would tell her mother right then and there that he was having an affair.

Kitally was about to walk off, but she couldn't do it. She couldn't leave without asking her dad's mistress a question. Kitally looked at the woman and said, "Where did you find that amazing dress? It's beautiful."

The woman put a slender hand to her chest to make sure Kitally was referring to her.

"Yes, you. Where did you get that dress?"

"I've had this old thing for years."

"Funny," Kitally said. "My father bought me the exact same dress." That was the truth. Her father had bought the dress for her before she'd gone to detention. When she came home, the dress was gone. "I wonder if you and Dad found the gown at the same store, because I was told it was a one of a kind."

Silence.

"Well, it's probably not the exact dress," Kitally fibbed. "The crystal beads on your dress don't pick up the light quite the same as mine. OK, well, it's been nice meeting all of you."

"Make yourselves at home," her mother said, oblivious as ever of everything going on around her.

"Will do," Kitally said as she walked off. Next time she saw her father alone, she would get an earful, but she didn't care. If her mother knew he was bringing his mistress to the house, flaunting her right under her nose, she would divorce him and take half his millions.

Kitally often thought about telling her mom, but she just couldn't do it. Her mother loved her father, flaws and all. Kitally wasn't going to be the one to tell her the truth and ruin her life.

When they walked into the computer room, Hayley didn't have to be a techno geek to be astounded by the room. It looked like mission control. There were ten screens and five laptops, all lined up in a perfect row.

Tommy was speechless.

Kitally smiled. "Pretty cool, huh? Dad is into all sorts of stuff, but he was once given a grant to build a high-performance computer system designed for scientific research and computing. This is a smaller model of what he built for a secret project he worked on years ago. This room has made it easy for me to hack into every broadband and telecommunications company in the country."

"Precision air-conditioning?" Tommy asked.

"Of course. And it can all be remotely controlled. Temperature, particle filtration, humidity, you name it."

"Cool. We could do anything in here. Intercept, decipher, analyze."

"Exactly," Kitally said. "It's more than a data center. I've been able to cryptanalyze and break ridiculously complex encryption systems."

"I'm surprised your dad allows you to come in here."

"We have a deal. I don't touch NSA, foreign military, and diplomatic secrets, legal documents, et cetera."

"Can we stop talking and get to work now?" Hayley wanted to know.

Hours later, Kitally looked around, bored out of her mind. Hayley had borrowed her car and told her she would be back soon. Giddy with all the equipment, Tommy had taken the reins. He didn't need any help. Kitally's parents and their guests had left for dinner and a show. She and Tommy were alone in the house. With nothing better to do, she checked out her GPS tracking application. Her parents were in San Francisco and Lizzy was on the highway headed east toward Reno.

Why was Lizzy headed toward Reno?

She waited another fifteen minutes before she walked back to where Tommy was sitting. "How's it going?"

"I've located the first two towers. Brian is in Placerville."

"That's only ten or fifteen miles from where we are right now."

"Exactly," Tommy said. "Is Hayley around?"

"No. I'm not sure where she went, but she said she would only be an hour at most."

"Let me know if you hear from her. How much longer before your parents return?"

"My guess is we have at least another two hours. I'll leave you alone for now. Let me know when you've found the last tower."

Tommy didn't answer. He was already back to work.

Since he didn't need her help, Kitally returned to the other side of the room and took a seat. The first thing she did was turn on her GPS application again to check Lizzy's location.

Hmm. Odd. She glanced at the clock on the wall, trying to figure out how long it had been since she'd given Lizzy the address she asked for.

Where is Lizzy going?

The GPS screen showed her moving in the opposite direction of where Kitally had told her to go. That didn't make sense. When Lizzy had called, she'd sounded excited, as if she were onto something big.

Kitally looked around the room, tapped her fingers, came to her feet, sat back down, and then finally broke down and dialed Lizzy's number.

No answer.

She called Hayley next, relieved when she answered. "Brian is in Placerville," she blurted.

"No kidding?"

"Tommy should have an address in another hour or so."

"Thanks. I gotta go."

They hung up before Kitally could ask her what to do about Lizzy.

Kitally tried Lizzy's number. No answer. She blew out a frustrated breath as she came to her feet, then walked back to where Tommy was sitting and hovered over his shoulder. He had three different screens on, all showing satellite imagery: maps, terrain, lots of trees and wooded area.

"Lizzy called a while ago to ask for an address. I think she knows the identity of Madeline Blair's stalker."

"Who is Madeline Blair?"

Kitally snorted. "Oh, forget it." She returned to her seat, where she resumed watching the little red dot on the GPS map. Lizzy was definitely headed east, away from Sacramento, which didn't make any sense.

Worry gnawed at her.

What if something happened to Lizzy after she hung up the phone?

Why wasn't she answering her phone? More importantly, why was she headed in the wrong direction?

She looked from the back of Tommy's head to the dot on her cell phone.

It would be a while before they could set into motion their plans to find Brian. She looked at the clock and watched the second hand go round and round.

She'd had enough. There was no way she could sit there and do nothing, knowing Lizzy could be in danger.

Without saying goodbye to Tommy, she grabbed her bag and headed out, figuring she would have to take one of her dad's cars since Hayley was driving hers.

CHAPTER 60

Wolf was not happy to see Hayley at his doorstep again. "You've got another fucking question to ask me?"

"No, I have information I think you might be interested in."

"I've done some research since we met, Hayley Hansen," Wolf said, "and I know you're pals with that Jessica chick, and my main man tells me she's an FBI wannabe. I don't want anything to do with you."

"What I have to tell you involves Brian Rosie. We need to talk in private."

After telling a couple of his watchdogs to stay put, Wolf ushered Hayley into a different room than the last time she was here. He shut the door and took a seat in a plush leather chair behind a mahogany desk. "I got Kiki back," he said, "and you got the name you asked for. That was it for you and me, far as I was concerned. This better be good."

"I know who's cutting into your turf," Hayley said. "Not only are they selling drugs on every street corner, they've been selling everything at a cheaper price than your foot soldiers."

"You thinking about getting into the drug business?"

"No."

"Then stay out of my business."

"Brian Rosie is very much my business. I've come here to tell you that before midnight tonight, I will know exactly where Brian is hanging out."

"Last I heard, he was in the Bahamas soaking up the sun."

"I just got word that he's hiding out somewhere in Placerville."

Wolf raised a brow.

"That's right. I came here to ask for your help, but the truth is, whether I have enough manpower or not, I'm going to find him and kill him. And it's going to happen tonight."

Wolf gave her a long, hard stare. "What you probably don't realize is that I have to think about the economic aspects. If I go after this guy and lose a couple of my boys in action, then I'm going to have a slowdown while I find replacements, not to mention the increased heat any kind of firefight brings down. I need to analyze the risk trade-offs."

Hayley didn't know a lot about the drug business, but she'd done some research and she knew just enough to hopefully make him think she knew more than she did. "Brian is hiring street-level boys," she said. "He's paying them less than minimum wage, but they don't care because they need jobs. He's already got three guys out there for every one of yours. At this rate, it won't be long until he's gotten more than a foothold on your turf."

He slammed a fist on his desk.

She didn't flinch.

"No shit," he said. "I know what's happening on my streets. What you don't seem to understand is that gang wars are costly. Not only in lives but in lost profits."

"I get it," Hayley said. "Violence keeps customers away and the last thing I want on my streets is more violence."

"These are your streets now?"

"You know what I mean," Hayley said. "Brian Rosie could move right in on your territory."

"What the fuck did that guy do to you?"

"What didn't he do would be an easier question to answer." Hayley exhaled, wondering how she was going to convince this guy to take a stand on such short notice. "I know Brian and his men are stationed somewhere in Placerville. Any moment now, I should have an exact location for you. If you give me a number where I can text you with the location, you'll know Brian's whereabouts in under two hours."

"How many men does he have guarding him?"

Hayley had no fucking idea, but she wasn't going to tell him that. "Close to a dozen."

"And you're going to go after him?"

"That's right."

Wolf got a good laugh before he said, "You're just looking to get yourself killed, aren't you?"

"I'm not afraid to die."

"It's more than that. You, girl, are afraid to live. It's written all over your face."

After a long bout of silence, she said, "There's one more factor you haven't yet taken into account."

He tilted his head as if he were enjoying himself now. "What's that?"

"If you send your men within thirty minutes of my texting you his location, your men will be on the offensive, prepared to fight. While Brian Rosie will have no idea what hit him."

For the first time since she'd entered his office, Wolf looked as if he might be considering his options.

"Brian has been expanding his organization, working with suppliers in other regions," she added, keeping the pressure on.

"Is that so?"

She nodded. "He's got twice as many people as you collecting dues and recruiting new men. It won't be long before he runs you out of town. If I've done my homework right, nearly one-third of your guys are imprisoned as we speak."

"That's enough. You've had your say."

She lifted her hands in surrender. "Thanks for your time." She prayed she'd been convincing enough because the truth was, as much as she hated to admit it, she needed the scumbag.

She heard him chuckling as she made her way to the front door and let herself out.

CHAPTER 61

Lizzy's head felt as if it were filled with bricks.

Pain shot through her right side. As the fog cleared from her brain, she realized she was being carried over a man's shoulders, hanging down his back with her arms dangling toward the ground and knocking into his legs with each step. She hung limp. Played dead. She could see the ground: dirt, mud, leaves. She wondered if her attacker realized she'd pulled the syringe out of her arm before it was emptied into her system.

The man grunted as he leaned forward and dropped her. She rolled into a deep pit. He planned to bury her alive.

She could hear him walking away. This was her chance. Tearing at the soft earth, she pulled herself upward, using what strength she had left to crawl out of the pit and make a run for it. She didn't know which way to go, but she weaved through the trees.

Leaves crunched behind her, and then she could hear his labored breathing.

She ran on through dense underbrush until she fell, then scrambled on hands and feet. Branches clawed through her skin and threatened to gouge her eyes out. She reached under her arm, hoping for a miracle, but of course her gun was gone.

Back on her feet, she twisted her way through thicket after thicket before breaking through into a clearing surrounded by mossy trees.

She stopped to listen.

Crickets and frogs chirping and croaking in the distance, and her own breathing.

She couldn't stay in one place. She needed to keep moving. The medication he'd shot into her system made her feel as if she was hallucinating.

Nausea swept over her as she took off running again.

It would be dark soon.

She could only pray she was moving toward the highway and not farther into the woods.

CHAPTER 62

Hayley knocked on the door to Kitally's parents' house. When nobody came, she opened the door and peeked inside. Everybody was gone. She called out Kitally's name as she made her way up the spiral staircase with iron railings. Everywhere she looked there was custom cabinetry and chandeliers dripping with sparkling crystals. She could easily get lost in a place like this, but somehow she managed to find the computer room. Tommy was right where she'd left him.

No sooner had she walked into the computer room than he jumped out of his chair and said, "Got it!"

"No kidding?"

"No kidding!" Tommy picked her up and twirled her about the room. Then he kissed her on the mouth before she could decide whether or not she wanted to be kissed. It was over almost as quickly as it began.

Pretending what just happened hadn't happened at all, she went to the computers and stared at all the images. There were dozens of still shots of a house in the woods surrounded by chain-link fencing. "Is this his location?"

Tommy sat back down. "This is it. Quite the setup. He's been hiding out in the woods for two years. This guy isn't fooling around." Tommy pointed to one of the screens. "You can see part of the wire fencing and a gate right here. And over here you can see more chain-link fencing topped with razor wire. At the time this picture was taken, he had four people securing the property." He pointed to a couple of the tiny, blurry figures on the screen. "This is a satellite shot from who knows when. It could have been taken two months ago or two days ago. I was able to get six cell phone signals in this one area, so we can easily assume that Brian has up to six men protecting the grounds at any given time."

Hayley scribbled the address on a piece of paper, then pulled her cell from her pocket and sent a text.

"What was that about?" Tommy asked.

"You were right about our needing manpower. I'm trying to round up some help. Let's get going."

Tommy looked around. "What about Kitally?"

"I don't know where she's at, but she left us a note saying she was taking one of her dad's cars. I tried calling, but my call went directly to her message box. She must be out of range."

"She did say something about Lizzy and a woman named Madeline."

"We'll have to do this without her," Hayley said. "Besides, she's still healing. It's better this way."

CHAPTER 63

Kitally pulled onto a dirt road. It was muddy from recent rains and there was no way she was going to get very far in her dad's Ferrari. She pulled over, shut off the engine, grabbed her phone and her bag, and headed off. At speeds close to a hundred mph, it had taken her more than thirty minutes to arrive.

Glad she had opted to wear boots instead of heels today, she followed the GPS tracker, which told her she didn't have far to go. The signal was strong enough that she knew Lizzy couldn't be too far ahead. She had called Lizzy's phone dozens of times, to no avail. All movement on the tracker had stopped a while ago. Lizzy had arrived at her destination, wherever the hell that was.

What was going on?

Kitally couldn't think of one good reason Lizzy would come to the woods . . . especially alone.

Unease crept up her spine as she followed the tire marks. If Lizzy was following someone, why wouldn't she have called or at least answered her phone? Worry quickened Kitally's pace. She started to run. It wasn't long before she found a Nissan parked to the side of a dirt road. The trunk was open. The GPS signal led her right to Lizzy's purse inside the trunk.

Someone had Lizzy.

Kitally walked around the area, peering into the trees. All she saw were shadows as the tree branches moved and danced with every breeze. Frogs croaked in the distance. Dead leaves covered the ground and that's when she realized she could make out footprints in the beaten-down leaves. There were footprints . . .

The trail led her to a muddied pit. Another area ten feet away looked as if it had been covered up recently. There was a strange smell in the air. Definitely funky.

Once again, Kitally examined the ground for any sign that might give her a clue about which way they had gone. It didn't take her too long to find tracks. But it was getting darker by the minute, and she didn't know how much longer she would be able to see where she was going.

Kitally put her phone in her back pocket and then pulled out her machete. Leaving everything else behind, she took off through the trees and brush.

CHAPTER 64

After talking Debra Westlake down, convincing her to put her gun away and go home, Madeline realized it was time to leave town. She would go to San Francisco and stay with her brother for a while, lie low and decide what to do next. She no longer had a job. Her reputation had been severely damaged. Until the police found Chris Porter and David Westlake, all eyes would be focused on her.

She went upstairs and checked phone messages. Two missed calls from Lizzy, who was hopeful she had found their man. Sitting on the edge of the bed, she prayed it was true. She reached into her purse and pulled out the driver's license she'd found on her passenger seat two days ago: it belonged to Megan Vos. This man, whoever he was, had killed Chris Porter, David Westlake, Amber Olinger, Megan, and maybe even Cindy. He was doing his best to point all evidence her way. He was getting away with murder. She wanted to take the ID to Detective Chase, but she was afraid he would lock her up for good. The media still came around every once in a while. They stood on her front lawn and waited for her to make an appearance.

She looked around her. Her actions truly had caused all of this craziness. What had she done? Tears flooded forth. She cried for her friends, for all the lies she'd told, for the person she'd become.

After a while, she went to the bathroom and washed her face.

When she returned to the bedroom, every sound, every creak caused her to jump. Making quick work of packing, she tossed in a few changes of outfits and her toiletries and headed downstairs. Before she could make it to the door, there was a knock.

Taking quiet steps, she left her suitcase at the bottom of the stairs and tiptoed toward the door so she could look through the peephole. Her body relaxed the moment she recognized the nurse from the hospital, the odd, intense one with the streak of white hair. The woman was alone.

Madeline opened the door.

"Hello, Dr. Blair. I don't know if you remember me—I'm Janelle, head nurse from the hospital. Is this a bad time?"

Madeline noticed her stethoscope hanging around her neck. She wore a white lab coat over her blue scrubs. "I do remember you, but I am in a bit of a hurry."

"It's standard procedure that we check up on our patients, you know, a follow-up on all assault cases. I don't live too far from here, so I thought I would drop by, get your blood pressure and check your heart. After that I can sign off on these papers and wrap this up."

The last thing Madeline wanted to do right now was spend time taking her vitals. "Maybe some other time. I'm going to visit my brother and he's expecting me."

Janelle held up her little black bag. "It will only take a moment of your time. If we don't take care of this now, the rape crisis center will badger you until they get this taken care of."

"It will only take a minute?"

"I promise," the woman said as she stepped inside and shut the door behind her.

Flustered, Madeline pulled the strap of her purse off her shoulder and set it next to the bag she'd packed at the bottom of the stairs. "Where should we do this?"

"Why don't you just take a seat right there at the dining room table?"

Madeline turned one of the dining room chairs outward away from the table so that the nurse could examine her.

She watched the woman set her black bag on the table, open it, and then slide on a pair of latex gloves. After Madeline took a seat, the nurse asked Madeline to raise her arm and pull up her sleeve so she could take her blood pressure. A moment passed before the woman said, "One twenty over eighty. Looks good. Have you been feeling any anxiety?"

"Definitely," Madeline said. "It's been a very stressful time."

The nurse unhooked her stethoscope from around her neck. "It's going to feel a little cold. Do you mind unbuttoning the top buttons of your sweater?"

Madeline sighed. She did mind, but she wanted to get this over with. "There," she said, holding open her sweater. "I really don't know why this is necessary." Perspiration covered her brow. The stress was getting to her.

The nurse placed the cold metal disc on Madeline's chest and listened. "Breathe in. Good. Now breathe out. Perfect. Almost done."

Thank God.

Behind her, Madeline heard the nurse shuffling through her bag.

Wondering what was taking so long, she looked over her shoulder and saw the nurse writing down some numbers.

Madeline's heart raced as she closed her eyes and tried to stay calm. She needed to get out of this house, out of this town. She'd made so many mistakes in her life, but she was ready to make amends and set things straight. Debra had been right when she told her she was self-absorbed. Madeline couldn't remember the last time she'd spent any quality time with her sister or brother.

She couldn't even remember the last time she'd called her parents, who lived only thirty minutes away. It was time to reach out to her friends and family. Going to San Francisco and staying with her brother for a while would do her a world of good.

"This is for you, Seth."

Madeline wondered what the nurse was talking about. But then she felt a sharp sting. She reached her hand over her shoulder, felt something sticking out of her neck and yanked it out.

An empty syringe.

She looked up from the syringe to the nurse, watched her quietly pack up her things.

"We're all done here," the nurse said as she moved to stand in front of Madeline.

Madeline's hands felt numb. She wanted to ask her about the syringe, but she couldn't find her voice. The needle dropped to the floor.

The woman, still wearing gloves, picked it up and dropped it into her bag. "You should feel a tingling sensation in your limbs. And then your tongue will start to feel thick. In a few moments, you might find it difficult to swallow, but don't worry, you won't feel any pain. It'll be like you just fell asleep. The only difference being that you'll never wake up."

Madeline reached out and grabbed a fistful of the woman's suit jacket. The nurse wasn't worried. She didn't budge. She just stood there watching and waiting until Madeline crumpled to the floor.

CHAPTER 65

Hayley stopped the car and turned off the engine and the head-lights. It had been a long day. She looked at Tommy. "You don't have to do this."

"Funny," he said. "I was going to tell you the same thing."

"But I do have to do this and you know it."

"If we call the police, they'll put him behind bars."

"For how long? Criminals are being let out of jails across the country as we speak. You don't need to come with me, Tommy. Take the fucking car and go. I never asked for your help. And just so we're square and you know where my head's at—there will be no parole for Brian Rosie."

"You're going to be judge, jury, and executioner, is that it?"

"Yes, that's right. That's how it's going down."

Hayley climbed out of the car. A sharp intake of breath was followed by goose bumps. The air was crisp, filled with the scent of pine. They were in Placerville, in the Sierra Nevada foothills. The car was well hidden within a thicket of underwood and small trees.

She sucked in a lungful of fresh air. Tonight was the night . . . a long time in coming.

She opened the trunk and began to strap on her load-bearing suspenders. The harness had a magazine pouch on one side and a holster on the other. After adjustments were made, she slipped on a lightweight chest rig with three front pouches and began the process of loading up on ammunition.

She didn't know if she would live to see another day, but her mind was set on what needed to be done. She was focused. She'd been waiting for this day for a very long time. Although she had hoped Wolf would show up, since they could use some help, it would be too risky to hold off for another twenty-four hours. Brian could find another hideout by then.

Tommy climbed out and began strapping knives to his legs. After outfitting himself with a lightweight bulletproof vest, he clamped a nightstick to his waistband.

They both had gloves, footwear, and headgear—all lightweight, all black. They each had a Taser holster connected to a detachable belt loop.

"This isn't about revenge," Hayley said, breaking the silence as she worked. "I'm not trying to change the past."

He said nothing, just kept putting on gear.

"This isn't about restoring dignity and pride," she went on as she filled a front pouch.

Tommy had spent time earlier preparing his gear. He was ready to go. He shut the car door, then made his way around to where she stood. "Who are you trying to convince?"

She yanked her straps tight.

"You can stop with the self-righteous bullshit," he told her. "It doesn't become you."

She grunted.

"I'm not going in there for you," he said. "I'm doing this for me, OK?"

"OK," she said. She shut the door. "Let's do this."

But he was already three feet ahead, blending into the night.

CHAPTER 66

Kitally wanted to shout out to Lizzy, but if Lizzy was in a safe hiding place, it wouldn't do any good to alert whoever had her. She had no choice but to make some noise as she moved through the brush, using the machete to chop her way through branches and scrub brush. Her face was numb from the cold as she continued on. The snap of a branch when she paused alerted her to the fact that somebody was close by. She stayed frozen and listened.

Somebody was running.

Was it Lizzy?

Following the sounds of crunching leaves, Kitally broke through the dense scrub and into a clearing. As she ran, hoping she was going in the right direction, pain shot through her leg where she'd been kicked a few weeks ago. No wonder Jessica had quit working for Lizzy. Kitally liked excitement and adventure more than most, but this was ridiculous.

Again, the loud snap of a branch caused Kitally to stop and listen.

The footfalls and crunching of leaves sounded as if more than one person was running through the woods. What was going on? *Damn it, Lizzy, where are you?*

She took off again, ran as fast as she could in the direction of the snapping twigs and crunching leaves. She ran so fast she didn't see the dark shadow step out from behind a tree. She rammed into a solid chest. Her machete flew from her hands and she hit the ground hard enough to knock the air from her lungs.

Before she could get to her feet, a man hovered over her, a knife in his hand.

He lunged. She rolled to her right, stabbed the heel of her boot into his side.

He grunted, then pulled the knife from the dirt and came at her again. With gravity on her side, Kitally rolled down a muddied slope and then jumped to her feet and quickly scoured the grounds for her machete.

Knuckles cracked and popped—an eerie sound coming out of the dark forest. As if he had all the time in the world, he began to walk down the hill after her. About to take off again, she stopped when she heard Lizzy's voice.

"Leave her alone, asshole!"

His knife was pointed straight ahead, the blade glimmering in the night. He didn't bother turning around or even looking over his shoulder.

"Why did you kill all of those people?" Lizzy asked, her legs wobbling as she stumbled after the crazy man.

Lizzy was obviously trying to distract the man, but it wasn't working. It was also easy to see that Lizzy had been drugged.

"Run! Get out of here," Kitally shouted.

"You know the answer to your question," the man answered Lizzy as he continued down the slope toward Kitally. "Madeline needed to be punished for betraying her listeners," he said. "You can't save her now."

Kitally didn't know what to do. She had nothing. Or did she? She pulled out her cell phone from her back pocket and pushed the alarm application. Sirens sounded.

He didn't care, didn't even flinch. As she watched, his face distorted into a mask of rage and then he flew at her.

Kitally had no time to run, but as she readied to strike, she saw Lizzy careen down the slope toward the man like a banshee from hell, leaping on his back like a lioness going for the kill, screaming as she clawed at his face.

He staggered but kept his feet and hacked at Lizzy's left arm with his knife.

Kitally drove a high kick into his groin, crumpling him for an instant before he recovered enough to curse and twirl in circles, throwing Lizzy off his back and onto the ground.

Kitally kept on him. She threw an elbow into his ribs followed by a snap kick to his side. She didn't let up: a kick to his leg, a slap to his face, lunge and punch, all while ducking and sidestepping his mad swipes with the knife.

Finally he threw himself at Kitally and took her to the ground with him.

Kitally raked her nails across his face and then twisted, ate dirt as she struggled to pull herself out from under his substantial weight. Her hand fell on a branch and she grabbed it and whirled and clubbed him on the head with it. He cried out as Kitally vaulted to her feet again, adrenaline soaring.

The man was back on his feet, too. Shit. This guy was making up in crazy whatever he lacked in fighting skills.

Swinging the branch back and forth before her, Kitally took a small step backward for every step he took forward. Behind the maniac, she saw Lizzy stagger to her feet, the machete clutched tightly in her right hand. Eyes wide, Kitally watched Lizzy take careful steps his way, then wind up and, using both arms now, stiff and strong, swing the machete in a perfect arc through the night air, slicing the man's head off with one powerful, sweeping blow.

He didn't crumple to the ground. Instead, his headless torso remained rigid, arms to his side as he toppled to the earth at Kitally's feet.

The head rolled down the hill past her. She heard a continuous *thump, thump, thump*, like a ball bouncing off the soft layer of leaves and then harder ground before the head finally rolled to a stop somewhere in the dark.

Silence.

Kitally stood there for a moment, taking it all in. A light breeze hit her face, turning the perspiration to ice. She looked at Lizzy and said, "Holy shit. That was fucking awesome."

Lizzy sank to the ground.

"Come on," Kitally said, taking the machete out of Lizzy's hands and leaving it on the ground so she could help her to her feet. "Let's get out of here."

CHAPTER 67

Detective Chase pulled up to the curb in front of Seth and Janelle Brown's house. Neither of these people had records; they were upstanding citizens. They paid their taxes and didn't break the law. Together, Seth and Janelle Brown had spent years organizing blood drives in their community.

And yet here he was. One call from Lizzy Gardner and her friends from the FBI were all over his ass to check out the home belonging to Seth Brown.

If he had his way, he would be at Lizzy Gardner's home, going through her things, seeing what the nosy private eye might be hiding, what sort of illegal deeds she was performing in order to obtain information. Because there was no way she could have found the person responsible for all the recent disappearing acts.

More frustrating was the fact that evidence against Madeline Blair continued to grow. Yesterday he'd received a recording of a woman's voice pleading with Madeline to stop, begging for her life to be spared. He'd passed the evidence on to Sergeant Hollister, but had yet to receive permission to play the tape for the families of Amber Olinger and Megan Vos to see if they recognized the voice.

Madeline Blair was toying with him, he was sure of it. And Lizzy Gardner was assisting her, helping her get away with murder.

He knocked on the front door. Waited. No answer.

He peered into the front window. Couch, lounge chair, coffee table, television. Nothing out of place. Nothing happening in there. He hitched up his pants that his wife had never gotten around to hemming for him. With a grunt, he headed to the side of the house. He reached over the side gate and unlatched the metal fastener before pushing the gate open. It creaked. He plugged his nose as he passed by two garbage canisters. The Browns must have had fish recently. Nothing beat the foul odor of dead fish.

He'd been told to be careful, that Seth Brown could be armed and dangerous, but he saw no reason to pull out his gun. He scraped the heel of his boot across the dying lawn in the backyard to get something sticky off his shoe. There was a small shed in the far corner of the backyard. He really didn't understand why Jimmy had been so insistent about him checking the place out. Jimmy had said he'd do it himself if he was in the area. But he wasn't, so that left Detective Chase to be gofer boy. He should have sent one of his rookies at the station. They loved this kind of shit.

He looked through the window on the side of the shed. There were shelves lined with old paint cans, maybe some paint thinner, gardening tools. Three bags of fertilizer were stacked on the ground next to a push mower. If it weren't for the powerful smell, worse than the dead fish odor he'd already gotten a good whiff of, he would have left already. But that smell bothered him. He opened the door. The powerful stench forced him to take a step back. It smelled like excrement and rotted eggs.

Using a hand to cover his nose, he peeked his head inside and used his other hand to hold his Maglite and take a look around. There was a dead rat on the floor. That had to be the source of the smell. Ready to head back to his car, he spotted droplets of red paint on the floor. Still using his Maglite, he stepped inside the shed and followed the trail to a plastic bin. It took some muscle, but he popped the lid open, wanting to make his search official. Nobody would be able to say he hadn't been thorough.

Not quite sure what he was seeing, he leaned in closer and moved his Maglite around until the beam of light fell squarely on a human mouth, open, as if frozen in terror. Confused, wondering if it was a Halloween mask, he moved the Maglite higher until the beam of light revealed a nose and two eyes—wide-open eyes—looking up at him, screaming for help.

Stumbling backward, unable to comprehend what he was seeing, he tripped over a rake and dropped his light. He knocked a paint can or two off a shelf before he was able to get out of the shed. He fell to his knees and lost his lunch right before his beeper sounded, one beep after another. *What the fuck was going on around here?*

CHAPTER 68

Lizzy's arm was wrapped up. She would need stitches later, but for now the tape and gauze would do the trick.

The woods were abuzz with a coroner's van and police vehicles with their flickering strobe lights. Yellow police tape was being tied from tree to tree. A truck backed into the area, filling the woods with its high-pitched beeps before it finally came to a stop. A thin metal structure grew straight up out of the back of the truck until the metal bar forming its roof beam drew even with the trees. At the top of the structure were two massive floodlights that illuminated the area, giving eyes to dozens of technicians and uniformed officers.

Each technician was assigned a designated area. They didn't waste any time getting to work. They knew the drill, each man working diligently to collect evidence in plastic containers and bags that would be taken to a secure place, where the evidence would be removed and allowed to air-dry before the moisture could cause any growth of microorganisms.

Farther back in the woods, crime-scene technicians wearing boots and overalls were preparing to dig up what looked like recently dug graves. Most of the action, though, was over the hill and beyond, where Seth Brown's body lay among the dead leaves, his head somewhere north of that.

It was freezing. Kitally was huddled beneath a scratchy wool blanket while she and Lizzy waited for the detective on the site to finish questioning them. He kept getting called away, though, and they had both turned down his offer to sit inside the police vehicle.

"What are the chances of that machete being returned to its rightful owner?" Kitally asked Lizzy.

"It might take a while, but I'll give your chances of being reunited at fifty-fifty."

"Not bad odds."

Lizzy had to force a smile, since she felt thoroughly conflicted by what had happened in the woods. Yes, she'd been justified in taking the life of a man who was trying to kill them, but she had never killed a man until tonight. She held up her hands. "No shakes. No quaking at the knees. My breathing is steady. Not normal."

"I can't imagine that killing someone would feel good," Kitally said, being the perceptive young woman she was, "but don't forget that the man drugged you and was trying to kill you. It was self-defense."

They both grew quiet as they watched a body bag being carried over the hill toward one of the vans.

"I don't know about you," Kitally went on, "but I feel pretty good to be alive right now. I saw the look in that man's eyes. I've never seen anything like it. He was possessed."

After a few quiet moments between them, Lizzy asked, "How did you know to come?"

"I was bored. I had nothing better to do than track your whereabouts and that's when I noticed you were headed in the opposite direction of where I told you to go. It didn't make sense.

When you didn't answer your phone, I knew something was wrong."

"You went with your gut," Lizzy said.

"Exactly. I've always trusted my instincts."

Lizzy wondered why it had taken her so long to give Kitally a chance. She was a remarkable young woman. As the detective approached them, someone called out, "Detective, we've got a body. Male."

"What kind of shape is he in?"

"Bashed-in skull. Not a pretty sight."

"Another one over here," a different voice called out from behind a copse of trees. "Female. Victim was stabbed multiple times. The front of the skull has been crushed."

Lizzy knew they might find two more bodies before the night was up, maybe more; she didn't know much about Seth Brown.

"You're shivering," Kitally said, holding open her blanket.

Lizzy stepped closer and huddled beneath the blanket with her.

"Case closed, Boss?"

"Yeah, case closed."

CHAPTER 69

Just as they had seen on the computer screen earlier, perimeter fencing had been installed around the boundary of the property. Once they got through, there would be another fence around the main building. The outer fence was definitely higher than they'd thought, though. The fence was ten-foot-high chain link, the kind of fencing you would see around a tennis court, except the top of this particular fence was lined with razor wire.

"At least it's not electric," Tommy said before he knelt down and used heavy-duty wire cutters to cut through the chain link. He held up a section and waited for Hayley to crawl through before he did the same.

If she looked straight up, she could see the sky blanketed with stars. The only sounds, other than the crunching leaves beneath their boots, were the occasional hoot of an owl and a trickling stream in the distance. When they got to an area that had been cleared of trees, they had to tread carefully over rotted tree stumps and dead branches.

Moving at a slow but steady pace, Hayley followed Tommy, absorbing the weight of her body in her knees, staying low to the ground, crouching under low-hanging branches as she moved along, concentrating on the terrain and her environment. Eyes focused on the ground, she watched for anything that might make too much noise: crackly sticks and brush.

They both saw movement ahead and stopped, neither she nor Tommy so much as flinching as a figure walked past no less than twenty feet away from the copse of trees concealing them. As planned on the ride to the mountains, Tommy headed after the man. It wasn't long before she heard a *thunk*.

She headed that way and found Tommy fast at work, covering the guy's mouth with duct tape. The man was out cold. Hayley helped drag the body to a tree. While Tommy secured him, Hayley kept an eye out for anyone else who might be patrolling the area.

Tommy took the two-way radio clipped to the guy's belt along with his cell phone before they headed off again. Another twenty feet in, they heard voices.

Hidden behind a grouping of trees, Hayley saw three figures on the other side of the chain-link fence. One of them was leaning against an SUV; the other two stood nearby, sharing a smoke. At the sound of grunting, she looked over and saw Tommy and another man rolling around in the dirt just a few yards away from her, legs and arms flailing.

Shit. Staying low, she pulled out her stun gun and ran to where they wrestled in the dirt. Almost dragged into the scuffle, she jumped back and out of the way.

Grunts and moans echoed off the trees. They were being too loud.

After Tommy got the guy in a choke hold, keeping the guy from shouting for help, Hayley saw the other guy's fingers wrapped around his radio, his thumb trying to find the switch.

It was now or never. Hayley moved in and pumped the guy with an electric charge. His body twitched.

Tommy pushed the guy off him and held up his hands. "You could have shocked me."

"Nope. Not how it works. Taser is designed to go from one point to another—I'll explain later." They made quick work of fastening the man to a tree in the same fashion they had handled the other guy. When that was done, Tommy took hold of Hayley's shoulders and said in a whisper, "I'm going to go in and take out those three. Keep your eye out for more stragglers."

"Oh, no, you don't," she said in a low voice. "You're not taking those guys out on your own. That would be a suicide mission. You stay here and watch my back. I'll do it."

"I know you want to get Brian," Tommy said. "I want you to get Brian, too, but you'll be dead before you ever get to the guy."

"But you won't be? This is my problem . . . my mission, not yours."

"Look, you're going to blow this thing. I've got this. Let me go in and do my thing. Then you get in there and take care of Brian."

She didn't like it one bit. "We need to be patient and wait until we know if there are any other men patrolling the area."

He shook his head. "It's too risky to wait any longer. Once Brian, or whoever is inside the compound, catches on that they've got two men not responding to their calls, they'll be scouring the grounds and you'll never get inside that building."

Hayley exhaled.

"I know you're perfectly capable of taking all three of those guys on your own, but I've got this."

She watched him walk off. What choice did she have? She needed to get in that building. Moments later, she held her breath as Tommy cut into the second fence and crawled through. This fence was also chain link but without the razor wire.

This was ridiculous.

What was she doing standing there watching him? Three armed men against one. She never should have let him go off alone. As she stood tall, she saw Tommy, his back against the backside of the building as he sneaked closer to the three men. His gun was drawn. No tree covering. It was a suicide mission. That's when she saw the unaccounted-for figure sneaking up from behind Tommy. She wanted to shout to him, but that would only serve to alert the other three men.

Once again, Tommy was rolling around on the ground, fighting. It felt like forever before one of them stood up. The man started shouting to the other guys. *Shit.* She saw Tommy struggle to get to his feet.

"Run," she said under her breath.

The other three men were headed their way, everyone shouting at once.

A shot rang out and then another. Tommy fell to the ground.

No. Hayley stared in disbelief. Fury swept over her in one giant wave, snapping her out of her stupor. She reached over her shoulder for her gun, ready to charge in, when a hand clamped over her mouth and dragged her back into the wooded area. She bit at the hand, twisted and kicked, tried to get away.

"Fuck. Knock it off," her captor said. "We're here to take care of Rosie, same as you."

She stopped fighting long enough to see that there were five guys hovering over her. They were dressed in camouflage pants and dark shirts. She recognized two of them as part of Wolf's entourage. "Is Wolf here?"

The guy in front of the pack shook his head and asked her to fill them in on what all the gunfire was about. It rankled to know that these guys weren't much better than Brian, but she needed their help. She needed monsters to fight a monster. In fact, she never should have allowed Tommy to get involved. It had been a selfish move on her part.

But these guys? These guys were expendable.

Without wasting another second, she told them how many of Brian's men she'd seen. She also told them about Tommy, described what he looked like and told them he'd been shot and needed help.

They would take out the men outside, while she planned to head inside the building.

She led the pack, crouching low and making little noise as she moved along, showing them the way.

CHAPTER 70

Jessica opened the door, surprised to see Magnus, a DEA special agent, standing on the other side.

She frowned. Two years ago, she'd fallen for the guy. Fallen hard. And then he'd been called away to work on a case in El Salvador. She'd called and e-mailed but it wasn't long before she could tell she was cramping his style, so she'd stopped. And hadn't heard from him since.

He was wearing gray corduroys and a black sweater. His hair was dark and much longer than the last time she saw him. His jaw was unshaven. The fact that he looked sexy as hell unnerved her. "It's been a while," she said.

"Too long. You look great."

"What's going on?"

He raised a questioning brow.

"Why are you here, Magnus?"

"Ah," he said. "You're angry with me."

She crossed her arms. "Why would I be angry?"

"Can I come inside? Just for a moment?"

She let him in, watched him look around her apartment for a moment before she realized she was acting childishly. Magnus wasn't the first guy who had disappeared after she'd made her feelings for him clear, and he wouldn't be the last. She followed after him and offered him something to drink, decided to show him she was a big girl now: confident, secure, all grown-up.

When he turned around, she was right there next to him. He reached out and took hold of her waist, pulled her close so that they were chest to chest.

He smelled amazing—just like she remembered—but she pushed him away. "You can't just come in here and start cuddling me as if there's something going on between us. I haven't heard from you in almost a year."

"Three hundred and ten days, sixteen hours. But who's counting?"

Nice touch.

"We screwed up," he announced.

"*We* didn't screw up. *You* screwed up."

He rubbed his jaw. "We should have made rules before we parted ways."

"Rules?"

"Relationship rules," he explained. "One call or e-mail every week, rain or shine."

"I tried that," she said. "It didn't work."

"You're right. I suck at long-distance relationships. Maybe we can try to work on a short-distance relationship."

"Your timing sucks, Magnus. I was accepted into the academy. I'm moving to Virginia in a few weeks, right after Lizzy Gardner's wedding."

"I know."

"You know what?"

"I know you got into the academy. I'll be your instructor. Or at least one of your instructors."

She plunked a hand on her hip. "Are you serious?"

"I knew it was fate the moment I saw your name on the list."

"Fate?" She shook her head in disbelief. "You believe in fate?"

He lifted his palms up. "What else could it be?"

She laughed. "You're a jerk."

"I know." He stepped closer.

"You could have called before you came."

"You might not have opened the door."

"True."

He reached for her again.

Her cell phone rang. She turned away and picked up the call. It was Kiki, Wolf's girlfriend. Jessica had visited her in jail and given her her number, told her she would get her out of jail if Wolf cooperated. The girl was talking fast. Something big was going down, Kiki told her, and she figured she owed Jessica a favor for getting her out of jail, which Jessica had had nothing to do with, but whatever.

Jessica told Magnus she'd just be a minute. Then she went to her bedroom and shut the door. "Slow down," she told Kiki.

"A chick named Hayley came to see Wolf. She's intent on taking down a guy named Brian Rosie."

"How did you know I knew Hayley?"

"Wolf said something about the two of you being friends. She's your friend, isn't she? Because if she isn't, there's no reason for me to be telling you any of this."

"She's my friend. You did good."

"So if I tell you the rest, we're even, right? You got me out of jail and I help you help your friend."

"That's right," Jessica said, wishing the girl would just spit it out already.

"It seems your friend wanted Wolf and his guys to help her take out Rosie."

"Did Wolf agree to help?"

"No. I don't think so."

"Did they say anything about where Rosie is?"

"Placerville. That's all I know."

"Why would Wolf care about Brian Rosie?" Jessica knew why, but she wanted to see how much Kiki was willing to tell her.

"I'd rather not say. I'm just letting you know that if you want to help your friend, you might want to find out where she's going so you can call the cops on Brian Rosie."

Now they were getting somewhere. Kiki obviously thought she was helping Wolf by calling her, figuring Jessica would hunt down Brian Rosie and that would take care of all of Wolf's problems.

Jessica had no problem calling the police. But first she needed to know where they could find Brian Rosie. "Where is Hayley now?"

"She left a little while ago. Someone's coming. I need to go."

Jessica's heartbeat kicked up a notch. She needed to find Hayley and talk her out of doing anything crazy. She also needed an address so she could let the feds do what they did best.

She gathered her coat and her purse, then ran into the other room. Ironic, she thought, that there was a DEA agent standing right in front of her, but she didn't have time to explain everything to him. If she didn't find Hayley, it would all be worthless information anyway.

"You're leaving?"

"Sorry, gotta go," she told Magnus. "Lock up when you leave, will you?"

CHAPTER 71

Hayley led Wolf's men to the area of the fence where Tommy had gone through. Single file, they made their way to the other side. Hayley watched Wolf's guys cut away from her to the left, toward the side of the building where Brian's men had taken Tommy.

Hayley wanted to check on Tommy, but there was no way to get to him. She had no choice but to trust Wolf's thugs to take Brian's men out. She watched them disappear around the corner. Within seconds, she heard gunfire rip through the night.

She had to work fast.

Following the outline of the building, she located a back door. She'd figured it would be locked, but she hadn't counted on the door being made of galvanized steel. She removed her backpack and pulled out the explosive device that Kitally had made from materials she'd accumulated from the Bay Area demolition company her father co-owned. Hoping it would be powerful enough to get the door open, she pressed the claylike body of the explosive under the gap in the door, then set the detonator and wires just as Kitally had shown her. Then she unraveled the wire, ran back into the woods and crouched down behind the trunk of a tree, and hit the remote.

Seconds felt like hours.

Boom!

The door flew open, bounced off the outside wall. Pieces of metal framing crashed to the ground. The main block of steel dangled from one bottom hinge.

Hayley was on her feet, gun drawn, ready to fire as she moved in. Finding the stairwell inside the door quiet, she moved to the top of the landing.

Another door. *Shit.*

Pissed off and revved up, she pulled out a semiautomatic and pulled the trigger four times before the lock busted through and the door opened. Gun aimed straight ahead, she headed inside.

A television was on. Two empty glasses on the table in front of a black leather couch. Johnny Cash was displayed on the sixty-inch screen. Dressed in black, he played the "Folsom Prison Blues."

She could go right or left. She went left. Taking quiet steps around the room, she checked closets and looked behind furniture as she went.

A picture on the wall reflected movement in the kitchen where she was headed. Someone was waiting.

The figure moved.

She dove to the floor, somersaulting across the floor.

Gunfire exploded around her. The glass table shattered next to her; chunks of wall blew up around her as she ran in the other direction and threw herself through the first door she came to. It was a bedroom: a dresser, bed, and a nightstand. No windows. She ripped open her front pouch, pulled out a smoke grenade, released the lever and tossed it in the other room.

Within minutes, the gunfire stopped.

She pulled a gas mask from her pouch and fitted it to her face just as she heard coughing in the other room.

Not wanting to give the shooter time to regain control, she crawled toward him beneath the thick fog of smoke until she could see his legs. As he hacked and coughed, she Tasered him in the calf muscle. He dropped, writhing, to the floor.

As the smoke began to clear, she saw a slight figure on the other side of him go for his gun. Hayley lunged for it, too, ramming her elbow into her opponent's jaw as they fought over it, the blow hard enough for her to gain control of the weapon and draw a bead on the figure's chest. It was a woman. Hayley told her to lie on the floor, face down. Instead, the woman ran past her and exited through the back door.

Most of the smoke had cleared. Hayley made quick work of cuffing the guy with his hands behind his back. She didn't recognize him. It definitely wasn't Brian. She checked his pockets for an ID. Merrick Waldron. The name meant nothing to her.

She dropped his wallet, left him there and headed for the stairs leading to the top floor.

There were three rooms. Two were empty. The door to the other was locked. It took two bullets to get it open.

Gun raised, she dropped to a knee and ducked her head into the doorway once, twice, and again. It was an office. No sign of anyone in the room, though the mahogany desk or the corners out of sight could conceal someone.

She took a breath, gathering herself. Another exchange of gunfire sounded outside, and she thought about Tommy, although she knew there was nothing she could do for him at the moment.

The office proved empty. A wall of security screens revealed Wolf's men fighting it out with Brian's thugs.

There was a closed closet door across from her.

She padded over to it and ripped it open, ready to fire. Nobody was inside.

There was only one place left—the bathroom. She tried the knob. Locked. "Don't be shy, Brian. You knew this day was coming."

No answer.

"Don't make me blow this door open. I'm counting to three. One, two—"

The door came open.

There he was.

Brian Rosie in the flesh. He wore a silk robe. His arms were raised. He was, impossibly, unarmed. It was like a dream for Hayley, seeing him standing there, absolutely at her mercy.

Snap out of it. This was Brian Rosie. He looked the same. He hadn't changed a bit. He wasn't unarmed. Or maybe another shooter hid behind the bathroom door.

It wouldn't matter. His mistake was thinking she'd hesitate to finish him.

Arms locked before her, she raised the gun and drew a bead on the center of his forehead. She'd show him more mercy than he showed her mother.

"Don't do it, Hayley!"

What the fuck? Hayley chanced a glance behind her at the familiar sound of Jessica's voice before snapping back around and resecuring her aim on Brian's forehead. "Are you pointing that gun at me?" she demanded.

"Drop the gun, Hayley." She wasn't denying it. Jessica *was* drawing down on her. "I'm not letting you spend the rest of your life in jail for killing this piece of shit. It's not going to happen."

"You're fucking kidding me, right?" Jessica would have to pry the gun from Hayley's cold, dead hands if she wanted it bad enough. She'd come too far to let it end like this.

"I mean it, Hayley. Put your gun down and step away."

What had been a dream had become some sort of bizarre nightmare. Knowing Jessica had both of them covered, Hayley lowered her weapon and turned toward Jessica, ready to tear her a new one.

"Watch out!"

Hayley spun around in time to see Brian had gone for the gun holstered beneath his robe. Before he could tear it free, Jessica put two bullets into his chest. He staggered back into the bathroom, then went over hard, his head smacking against the tile floor.

Hayley walked over to him, then knelt down and felt for a pulse.

He was dead.

It was over. She turned toward Jessica. "You bitch."

Jessica's face puckered. "What did you say?"

"You fucking bitch." Hayley marched up to Jessica and put a finger on her chest. "Who do you think you are?"

Jessica slapped her hand away and then slid her gun into its holster. "I just killed a man. Could you give me a minute?"

"No. I won't. Do you know how long I've waited for this day?"

"What were you going to do, Hayley? Shoot the man while he stood there with raised hands? You didn't even know if he had a gun."

Hayley stabbed her finger at her own head. "Use some logic for once in your life, Jessica. Of course he had a gun."

Sirens sounded in the distance.

A caustic laugh came out of Jessica's mouth. "Your goal was accomplished. Maybe not by your hand, but who cares?"

"I care."

"I'll probably get written up, if that makes you feel better."

Hayley said nothing, consumed with trying to swallow her anger. It wouldn't stay down.

Jessica just stood there.

Police used a bullhorn to announce their arrival, telling everyone to come out with both hands raised in the air where they could see them.

Without another word spoken, Jessica turned and walked out of the room.

After watching her leave, Hayley walked back to where Brian lay in a growing pool of blood.

She couldn't take her eyes off him. Her heart beat against her rib cage. Brian was dead, but she didn't feel any different. Evil swirled around her, a supernatural force, alive and thriving. The coppery, metallic taste in her mouth was still there. As she watched a continuous flow of blood turn his robe red, she realized Brian's death wasn't enough. It hadn't solved anything.

The realization caused her to stiffen with resolve.

She would fight . . . not her inner demons, but every piece-of-shit rapist dirtbag walking the earth.

Until her dying breath, she would fight.

CHAPTER 72

"Mom, look at Hayley. She's all dressed up."

Hayley watched Hudson run toward her as she and Dog came down her steps, the kid's attention already transferred entirely to the mutt. Hudson threw himself to his knees and Dog bounded over to him to bathe his face with his slobbery tongue as he hugged him and laughed.

Becca came out of the house carrying a large cardboard box that she loaded into the trunk of her car parked right outside the door. She took a moment to look at Hayley and see what all the fuss was about. "Well, would you look at that? Is the pope visiting and I'm the last to hear about it?"

"Just a wedding." Hayley gestured toward the car, already filled to the brim with boxes and crates. "What's going on?"

Becca planted both hands on her hips. "We're moving in with my sister and her kids for a while. She has a farm in Ojai. I think it's time Hudson and I had a change of scenery."

"Sounds like the perfect setting for a dog named Dog."

Hudson grinned, his big eyes praying for a miracle.

"I thought someone else was taking him," Becca said.

Hayley shook her head. "Dog didn't like the kids pulling on his ears and on what little bit of tail he has left, so I told them I changed my mind."

She gave Hudson the leash, and he knew what to do. He followed Dog to a little patch of grass.

"Are you sure you want to part ways with him?" Becca asked.

"Yeah, he's more of a nuisance than anything else."

Becca grabbed paper and pen from the car and scribbled something down. "Here's our address if you ever want to visit Dog. And just so you know, I plan to get a job and pay you back every penny I owe you."

"No need," Hayley said. "Put it toward dog food."

"I'm selling the house, but until then, the apartment is yours."

"I think it's time for me to make a few changes, too."

Becca looked around, her face pinched as if there was more she wanted to say but couldn't find the words.

"Take care of them, will you?" Hayley asked.

Becca nodded, her eyes glistening.

CHAPTER 73

Lizzy was in her car, heading for home. This was her wedding day and a beautiful day it was. The December sun was out, shedding its wintry light on her little part of the world. She felt dizzy with happiness, a sentiment that boggled the mind, considering she'd never thought the day would come when she would feel this way.

Lizzy was almost home when her sister called. She hit the answer button on her console and said hello.

"We're all here at the church," Cathy said. "Are you on your way?"

"I had to run to the store to pick up the gift I ordered for Jared. I'll be home in a few minutes to grab my dress and then I'll be on my way."

Cathy sighed. "Sure, don't let your own wedding rush you."

"I'll get there. My makeup's all done."

"Has been since you got out of bed this morning."

Unfazed by her sister's teasing, she laughed. "This is true."

Another sigh from Cathy. Lizzy hoped she wasn't about to get all emotional—mainly because she wasn't sure of her own ability to stave off tears if Cathy started. Everything about the day so far had felt surreal.

"OK, Cath," Lizzy said. "Just a few more blocks. I'm hanging up before—"

"Lizzy, I realize this isn't a good time to tell you this, but I wanted you to know that I flew to Oregon and met our half sister, Michelle."

Lizzy didn't know what to say.

"She's a lovely person. Her daughter, Emma, is adorable. They can't wait to meet you."

All right, even more surreal. Lizzy's throat had closed up tight.

"Are you still there, Lizzy?"

"I'm here."

"Are you crying? You are, aren't you? I'm sorry. I should have waited."

"No, no. I'm glad you told me. These are happy tears."

"I'm sorry, Lizzy. Sorry for all the pain and suffering you've endured . . . sorry for not being there for you when you needed a shoulder to cry on. And I'm proud of you, too. I couldn't have asked for a better sister. I love you."

"I love you, too," Lizzy said, trying to keep it together but losing the battle. Thank God she was home. She pulled in the garage and shut off the engine before she looked at her face in the rearview mirror. "Great. Now I *do* need to do my makeup. My nose is red and my eyes are puffy. I look horrible."

Cathy laughed. "Grab your dress and get to the church. All of your girls are here. We'll fix you up."

"Thanks."

They hung up. Lizzy wiped her eyes and took a deep breath. She glanced at the watch she'd had engraved for Jared. She'd also made a book of memories the two of them had shared over the years and had it professionally bound in leather.

She shook her head at how ridiculous it was that she'd made Jared spend the night in a hotel last night, since it was bad luck to see the bride before the wedding ceremony. Then she saw the time. She needed to get moving.

Leaving the gifts in the car, she climbed out and hurried inside to get her things.

As she walked through the home where she and Jared had lived for the past two years, she breathed in the life they had built together and felt content as she made her way upstairs to the master bedroom. She went to the bed and wrapped her arms around Jared's pillow, breathing in his scent and smiling at this unfamiliar mushy side of herself.

There it was again . . . that crazy, intangible thing called happiness flowing through her veins.

She opened the door to the walk-in closet and grabbed her dress. She walked into the bathroom next to get her makeup and accessories needed for her big day.

A noise sounded downstairs. She stood still. Listened.

Nothing.

Three weeks ago, Madeline had been murdered in her home. Although there were no witnesses and no evidence found, Seth Brown was assumed to be the culprit. His last victim before attempting to add Lizzy and Kitally to the list. His wife, Janelle Brown, had been questioned and investigated, but there was no proof that she'd had any knowledge of her husband's activities, so she'd been sent home. She'd struck Lizzy as a strange woman—that shock of white hair, those angry eyes—but still, her heart went out to her. What could it possibly be like to live alone in the house you'd unknowingly shared with a madman? All that sadness turned loose on the world by one damaged man. Lizzy was saddened above all to think she hadn't been able to save Madeline, but she was thankful she'd at least been able to prove that Madeline had had nothing to do with her friends' demises.

Lizzy looked into the mirror. "No more jumping at every sound," she told herself. "It's over. It's all over. Today you're going to marry the man of your dreams. When you walk up that aisle, your only care is making sure Jared knows how much you love him." After her speech, despite her determination not to freak out at every noise, she walked out of the bedroom, leaned over the railing and looked around.

Nobody was there.

Sending Jared away for the night had been a mistake. She missed him.

Back in the bedroom, she made a pile on the bed of the things she would need. She glanced at the clock on the nightstand and realized she was barely going to make it in time. Grabbing her cell phone, she called Jared.

Her heart drummed against her chest as she took a seat on the chair in the corner of the room and waited for him to pick up.

As Jared walked from the parking lot to the church, he looked at his phone to see if he'd missed any calls. He wanted to call Lizzy, but he was pretty sure that was against the wedding-day rules. No sooner had the thought gone through his mind than his phone began to ring.

"You called," he said, sounding surprised.

Lizzy laughed. "Why wouldn't I?"

"You made me spend the night in a hotel last night. I thought we weren't supposed to talk to one another."

"It's bad luck if we see each other before the ceremony," she told him, "not if we talk to each other."

"Do you really believe all of that malarkey?"

"Not one bit," she said. "Biggest mistake I ever made. I feel like we've been apart a lifetime."

"I feel the same." He peered through the glass door leading into the church, but decided to stay outside while he finished talking to Lizzy. "Looks like your bridesmaids are all ready to go. Are you on your way?"

"How do they look? Did Hayley wear her dress?"

He took another look. "They all look amazing. Everyone is in blue, just as you wanted. I've never seen Hayley in a dress. She looks great."

"I'm so happy, Jared."

"I'm glad."

"It's the weirdest thing," Lizzy told him. "For the past few months, I just wanted the two of us to go to the courtroom and get married. I didn't want flowers and cakes and friends and family, but I was wrong. I can't wait to walk down the aisle and say my vows. I love you so much."

"I love you, too, Lizzy."

"I'm sorry I'm running so late. There was something I had to get, but I'm home now. I'll be there in fifteen minutes."

"Good to know. I didn't see your car in the parking lot and I was afraid you might leave me standing at the altar, looking like a fool."

"Never. I've waited a lifetime for this day. I'll see you soon."

After they hung up, Jared took a moment to look around him and take it all in. It was December, five days before Christmas, but the sky was blue and there wasn't a rain cloud in sight. He thought about everything he and Lizzy had gone through to get to this point. Their journey had been a winding road of craziness and mishaps, but they'd made it. Lizzy always talked as if she was the one who needed him, but it was the other way around. Always had been. There was nobody else in this world for him but Lizzy.

He turned back to the doors and pushed his way through the early arrivals. Heather rushed up to him, gave him a long squeeze and then wiped a tear from her eye and straightened his tie.

"I still think you should have gone with the tuxedo," she said, "but I guess I'll have to wait for my own knight in shining armor to come along before I can walk up the aisle with a handsome man in a tux."

"The flowers look great," he said, looking at the pews, feeling awkward, since Heather had given off not-so-subtle hints that she was into him the last time they were together. "I hope you sent me the invoice."

"Nah, the flowers are on me. I had a lot of fun helping you."

"That's too generous. I can't accept."

She shrugged him off, but he figured he'd settle the matter later. Jared looked over Heather's shoulder and smiled at Hayley, Kitally, and Jessica. He held up a finger, letting them know he would just be a minute.

"This is horrible of me to say—even worse that I'm going to tell you this on your wedding day—but I've had a mad crush on you for a while now."

He said nothing.

"I was hoping there might be something there, but you never wavered. Not once."

"You know there's only one girl for me. I've waited a long time for this day. Nothing could ever stop me from loving Lizzy Gardner."

She blushed and looked away.

"No reason to be embarrassed. I want you to know that I appreciate your friendship. You deserve to be happy, Heather. If that means finding the right man, then it will happen for you. Not when you're looking, though. It never happens when you're looking."

"Lizzy is a lucky girl," she said before motioning toward the organist. "I better make sure Mrs. Peters knows where to go."

After Heather walked off, he made his way to the front of the church, where Lizzy's sister, niece, and the other bridesmaids were gathered.

"I don't know if you remember me, but I'm Kitally." She offered him a hand to shake, but Jared chuckled and gave her a bear hug instead.

"Of course I remember you. I haven't had a chance to thank you for helping Lizzy out. You did good work. You're a hero."

"Lizzy did all of the hard work. I just provided her with the right tools to get the job done."

He couldn't argue with that, but neither could he promote carrying a machete around, so he merely nodded.

Cathy hugged him next, and then her daughter, Brittany, followed by Jessica and Hayley.

"You girls look terrific. Thanks for being here."

"Where's the bride?" Jessica asked. "I brought the hairpins she asked for." She looked at her watch. "We don't have much time to get her dressed. Another few minutes and most of the guests will be here."

"You know Lizzy," Jared said. "She likes to keep everyone on their toes."

"I talked to her," Cathy said. "She's grabbing her dress and heading over here as we speak."

Jared's heart began to race. Seeing the people gathering in the pews, being there at the church, he realized he was getting nervous. "How's Tommy doing?" he asked Hayley, hoping to stop his nerves from getting the best of him.

"They took two bullets from his left arm. He'll need some rehab, but his doctor said he should be released in the next few days. He's bummed he can't be here."

"I'm glad he's doing so well."

"Look who's here," Jared said to Jessica, nodding to Magnus, who'd just walked through the doors at the other end of the room. "I didn't realize you two were still an item."

Jessica blushed. "We're not. He recently finished a job in El Salvador and since he's back in town, Lizzy told me to go ahead and invite him today. I hope you don't mind."

"Not at all."

"Come on," Cathy said to the group. "Lizzy is going to come through the back door of the dressing room. It's this way."

"I'm going to say hello to Magnus and then I'll be right there," Jessica told her.

Jared watched them all walk away. It made him happy to see everyone together and doing well. Jessica, he noticed, had been all smiles when she'd headed off toward Magnus. But suddenly she looked over her shoulder at him, her smile replaced by a look of fear before she turned back the other way again.

Following her gaze, he saw a woman he didn't recognize. She wore a white lab coat. Polka-dotted sneakers peaked out from beneath blue scrub pants. *A nurse?* Her hair was disheveled and there was a frazzled look about her. She turned and that's when he saw the gun in her hand.

Without hesitation, she started shooting into the crowd, pulling the trigger again and again.

Jared saw Magnus throw himself on top of Jessica, pushing her to the ground, his back violently arching as if he'd taken a bullet to the back.

The shooter aimed and fired, aimed and fired.

People were screaming, falling to the ground, hiding wherever they could.

Heather was draped over the seat of the organ, her dress covered in blood. The organist was slumped over the black and white keys.

Jimmy Martin, good friend and FBI agent, crouched low between the pews, protecting his wife as he used his cell phone to call for help.

The chaos was all around him. Everything felt as if it was happening in slow motion. Jared looked to his left, where he'd seen the bridesmaids moments ago. They weren't anywhere in the room. *Thank God.*

Kitally was crawling on all fours. He wasn't sure if she'd been shot.

Bullets were still being fired when he spotted Hayley moving up the side aisle. Why hadn't she stayed with the others? Unlike the panicked guests, she appeared steadfast and calm. She marched forward along the wall, then turned and headed straight for the woman with the gun. There was anger in Hayley's expression, power in every step she took.

Get out of there, Hayley. Now was not the time to be a hero. She needed to run, get out of harm's way.

Somebody yelled Jared's name at the exact moment he took a bullet to his arm and then another to his chest. A searing pain shot through every part of his body at once. "Hayley," he shouted. "Get down!"

He took a step forward, but that's all he could manage. He needed to get everyone out of the way, needed to stop Hayley from getting herself killed.

Another bullet ripped through his thigh. A fierce heat rushed through him.

He looked at the nurse with the gun. A shock of white hair, a crazed look in her eyes.

Numb. He felt numb. He hardly felt the next two bullets. His arm. His chest.

He willed his legs to move, wanted to take the shooter out, but all he could do was stand there and watch.

The shooter was focused on the frenzy in front of her, making it easy for Hayley to strike her from behind and knock the weapon from her hand. As Hayley grabbed the gun from the floor, the woman reached into the pocket of her lab coat and pulled out another weapon, aiming it at him.

Jared realized then that he was the shooter's target, the one she'd come for. But why?

Before the nurse could fire, Hayley thrust the barrel of the revolver to the shooter's temple and pulled the trigger.

Blood sprayed across the neatly lined bouquets of fresh white roses.

The continuous sound of gunfire was replaced with cries for help, moaning and sobbing. That's all Jared heard as he slunk to the ground.

Silence enveloped him. Unable to keep his eyes open, the only thing he saw in his mind's eye was Lizzy.

She looked beautiful.

He'd waited so long for this day and it was finally here.

He was by far the luckiest man in the world.